THE
BROKEN
PLACES

OTHER BOOKS BY MIA SHERIDAN

Bad Mother

All the Little Raindrops

THE BROKEN PLACES

A NOVEL

MIA SHERIDAN

Published by Montlake, Seattle

www.apub.com

Amazon, the Amazon logo, and Montlake are trademarks of Amazon.com, Inc., or its affiliates.

ISBN-13: 9781662523052 (paperback)
ISBN-13: 9781662523069 (digital)

Cover design by Caroline Teagle Johnson
Cover image: © Javier Díez / Stocksy; © jamie grill atlas / Stocksy; © Flavio Coelho / Getty

Printed in the United States of America

To the city by the bay where I left my heart

CHAPTER ONE

"Cherish"
Episode from podcast *The Fringe*
Host of podcast, Jamal Whitaker

"Hello, welcome to *The Fringe*. Thanks for being here, Cherish. Very pretty name."

"Thanks. It's my real name, not just my street name. That's what my mom named me, Cherish Joy."

The interviewer, Jamal, sitting in a chair across from Cherish, smiles. He's a dark-skinned man with a shaved head who appears to be somewhere between forty and fifty. "Can you tell us a little about yourself?"

The young prostitute with the pale, sallow skin, wearing a pink crop top and jean shorts that barely hit the crease at the top of her thighs, brings her thin legs underneath her on the blue velvet sofa. "Who's us? You and the mouse in your pocket?"

"For now, just me and my cameraman, Franco, but the show has three and a half million subscribers."

Cherish repositions herself, sticks her hands between her knees, and then removes them almost as quickly. It's difficult to tell whether she's nervous or on something. "I was just jokin'. One of my stepdads used to use that line about the mouse. Can't remember which one, and I never really knew what it meant anyway. It seemed stupid, but here I am repeating it."

"How many of them were there?"

"Mice or stepdads?" She lets out a throaty laugh that fades almost immediately. "Sorry. I make dumb jokes when I'm nervous."

Jamal smiles kindly. "Don't be nervous. If, at the end of this conversation, you decide you don't want this interview aired, you have my word no one will ever see it."

She gives a jerky nod. "Anyway, yeah, there were a lot of stepdads. My mom only actually married two of them, or maybe three, but she made me call the rest of them dad, too, so that's what I did, and I guess that's also why they blend together."

"Did you grow up here in San Francisco?"

"Yeah. Over in the Mission."

"So, it sounds like your mom had a lot of men in her life while you were growing up. Other than that, what was your childhood like?"

Cherish plays with a long string on the edge of her shorts for a second and then shifts again. "Pretty shitty. I hated school and got in trouble a lot. My mom did drugs, so we never had much food in the house. She tricked, too, when there was no man in the house, and she'd bring me with her sometimes."

"Bring you with her?" Jamal's eyebrows rise, but his voice remains calm and almost unaffected in a way that makes it obvious he's used to hearing stories like Cherish's. "For what reason?"

Cherish shrugs, and she seems to zone out for a moment before sitting up straighter. "Sometimes I just watched, or I waited in the bathroom. Sometimes I went next."

"Went next?"

"Yeah, you know, the trick paid to have sex with me too."

"When did this start?"

"I don't know. Maybe six."

"Six years old?"

"Mm-hmm."

"What do you remember thinking about that?"

"It sucked. I didn't like it."

"Why do you think your mom let that happen? Even arranged it?"

Cherish's shoulder jerks, and she wraps her arms around herself as though suddenly cold. "She'd do anything for money, so she could buy her drugs."

"And do you take drugs? Now?"

"Yeah. Well, I'm tryin' to get clean. But you know . . ."

"What's your drug of choice?"

"Heroin."

"Okay. And why do you think you followed in your mom's footsteps as far as the prostitution?"

Cherish shrugs. "I mean, I need money. What other way do I have, you know?"

"How far did you get in school, Cherish?"

She looks away for a moment as she twists a piece of her lank brown hair. "Ninth grade, I think? Maybe tenth? I can't remember. I was flunking out anyway, didn't matter, so I just stopped going." Her eyes meet his. "I never got good grades. When I was in elementary school, I used to try to hump the boys in my class. Freaked the teacher out."

"Did the school address it?"

She zones out again, then meets Jamal's eyes. "Address it? With who? With my mom?" She looks away. "I got sent to the principal's office a lot. But he was gettin' some too."

"The principal was molesting you?"

"I guess. But I was okay with that. He had this big bowl of candy on his desk, and he'd let me take as much as I wanted afterward. It wasn't so bad. But anyway, I never got taken away from my mom or nothin', so

I guess the teachers didn't call anyone but him."

Jamal remains quiet for a moment. "Has anything bad ever happened to you while working the streets?"

Cherish pauses, her eyes moving upward for a moment. "Sure. Yeah. I've got beat up a few times. Once real bad, spent some time in the hospital. And you know, I've been stiffed out of the money after servicing a trick."

"The streets can be rough."

Cherish nods, tucking her hands between her knees. "Yeah, they can. You gotta be careful. Especially if you don't have no one taking care of you."

"So you don't have a pimp, then? You work on your own?"

"I did have a man, but he got shot three months ago. Killed. So now I'm on my own."

"Killed? I'm sorry. That's awful."

She bobs her head, removes her hands from between her knees, and begins picking at a sore on her thigh. "Yeah. He was one of my sons' fathers, so . . . you know, that was hard."

"How many kids do you have?"

The first flutter of what might be despair moves across her expression before she sighs. "Two. I got two boys. They got taken by the system, though." She looks away, zoning again.

"I'm sorry." Jamal gives her a moment. "How old are you now, Cherish?"

"I'm twenty."

"Twenty years old. You've been through a lot for someone so young."

"Yeah." Cherish laughs again, that same hollow sound. "Too much."

"Do you have any aspirations, Cherish?"

"Aspirations? Like goals?"

"Yeah."

Her eyes slide to the side again. "I'd like to get my kids back." She picks at that wound again. "But I don't know. I'm just tryin' to survive, you know? Just tryin' to stay alive."

CHAPTER TWO

The recently closed Surfside Motel was within walking distance of the homes featured in *Mrs. Doubtfire* and *Full House*. Unfortunately, the people inside room 212 wouldn't be engaging in any tourist activities in the near future—or anything else, for that matter. One DOA was lying prone on the floor, only her legs visible, the two others supine on the bed.

She smelled blood, and also the evidence that the victims' bowels had emptied in death. "Hi, Sullivan," she said to the first-responding officer standing in the outdoor hallway to her left.

"Hi yourself, Lennon."

Lennon took a moment to glance around at what she could see of the motel room through the open door. Stained, dusty curtains, peeling striped wallpaper, and a myriad of brownish-yellow water stains on the ceiling.

A few furniture items remained: one bedside table, mostly blocked by the bodies; a writing desk; a black, unplugged minifridge with its door wide open; and the headboard and stripped mattresses, now featuring a large dark bloodstain on the side facing her.

She removed a pair of booties from her pocket that she'd taken from the kit in her trunk and started pulling them over her shoes, stalling as she mentally prepared herself to enter the room. "Just you here so far, huh?" she asked Sullivan.

"Yup. Except for them." He nodded his head back toward the room.

Them. The dead.

Damn. She snapped the bootie over her loafer and set her foot on the ground. She would never purposely drag her feet when a call came in for a triple homicide, but she didn't particularly like being the only one in the room with the recently deceased victims of a brutal killing. It was the very worst part of her job.

"Sucky wake-up call, huh?" Sullivan asked.

"It's not my favorite way to start the day," she said as she took out a pair of gloves from her pocket. "But I was already up and on a jog." She'd been running the path along the beach when the call had come in. She'd gone home, taken a quick shower, changed, and driven there. All that, and the sun was barely up. And no one else had arrived, other than the officers she'd passed on her way through the parking lot, who were stretching crime scene tape across a second set of stairs.

"It's not safe for a woman to be jogging alone in this city. Not anymore," Sullivan offered.

"I'm painfully aware of the crime rate, Sullivan. I'm good, I promise."

He gave a short grunt. "I hope so, because we can't afford to lose any more inspectors."

She glanced at him and then away as she stretched one glove over her hand. Sullivan was a good guy. He'd already been an officer for over a decade when she'd started at the SFPD, and while she'd worked to move up the ranks to homicide inspector, Sullivan was content to remain a beat officer. She respected that, and in his position, experience mattered a great deal. So did numbers, and he was right: they couldn't afford to lose any more staff of any rank.

"Who was it that called this in?"

"An anonymous call. I wouldn't be surprised if it was a homeless person looking for a place to sleep who came upon this. I'd bet anything it'll come back to a temporary burner phone someone stole from Walgreens."

She snapped on the second glove and then glanced down at the doorknob. It was hanging partway off the door, but whether that was because someone had kicked at it or just because this whole place was old and rickety and falling apart at the seams, she couldn't tell. Lennon leaned inside a little more. There was a door near the back that she assumed was the bathroom. "You clear it?"

"Yeah. All clear."

"This one looks similar to the others?" she asked.

"At first glance? Yeah."

"How far out are the criminalists?"

Sullivan glanced at his watch. "Ten minutes, give or take. I heard on the radio that there was a mass shooting in Bayview right before this was called in, so a few probably headed there first."

Lennon gave a succinct nod and stepped inside the room. During normal hours, it was more common that she arrived after the forensic team was already working on the scene, stepping into the hustle and bustle of coworkers collecting evidence and tagging items. As if murder kept to "normal hours."

She walked past the open closet near the door, one lone wire hanger dangling on the broken rod, and approached the bed. The scent of death and bodily fluids was far stronger inside the room. A minor wave of nausea came over her, and she took a moment to breathe through it. Beyond the unpleasant sensory experience, and even with the door open, the room felt stuffy, and eerily—*unnaturally*—still. It made the hairs on the nape of her neck stand up.

The skirt of the woman on the floor at the end of the bed had ridden up and was showing half her backside. It almost felt like Lennon's presence here was inappropriate, that she should look away and give these people the dignity they hadn't received in their final moments.

But her job was not to deliver dignity to the dead. Her job was to deliver justice. And to do so, she had to look and to probe and to consider these bodies from every angle. She had to try her best to ignore that they'd once been people with their own busy lives and consider them as simply victims. *Part of the scene.* At least initially, on first sighting.

She squatted down and leaned to the side to better see the woman on the floor. Her light-brown hair was matted with blood, and Lennon used one gloved finger to lift some of it off her face and hold it aside. Lennon drew back slightly when she saw the expression on the woman's face—eyes wide and mouth open as if frozen in a never-ending scream. There were tear tracks through the heavy makeup on her pale skin. *God.* Sadness dropped over Lennon like an invisible net, and she did her best not to get tangled in it. It helped no one. *What living nightmare would cause an expression like that?* She looked away for a moment. She hated this. She really did. Nine years on the force, and she was still so damn affected.

Breathe out. Assess. Do your damn job. She looked back at the dead woman. *Young.* Late teens or early twenties.

"Sores that indicate drug use," she said aloud, breaking the quiet of the room, a verbal clinical assessment calming the nerves and the unwanted emotion that always transpired when standing amid a crime scene. The smell of urine was stronger near the body. "Victim urinated either in death or in fear." She'd wait for the criminalists to arrive to turn the young woman over fully and determine cause of death. But whatever it was, it'd been very bloody. Lennon's stomach churned. The pool from the woman's injuries had spread several inches beyond her body. Lennon used her gloved index finger to touch the pool. It was dry and cracked around the edges with a gelatinous center. It appeared this woman, at least, had been here for several hours.

Lennon's gaze moved downward to where the woman was clutching something, the item mostly underneath her, arm still wrapped around it. *Is that . . . ?* Lennon gently lifted the woman's stiff arm. Yes, just as she'd thought. It was a teddy bear, its beady eyes staring at her. She lowered the woman's arm again and covered the black, soulless eyes of the stuffed animal. "That's creepy as hell," she murmured.

She stood and walked around to the other side of the bed before leaning over to get a look at the man and the other female victim. The woman appeared older, perhaps in her fifties, and she estimated the man to be in his late twenties, his arms heavily tattooed.

At least these two didn't have expressions frozen in horror, though they also didn't appear to be sleeping, the way some DOAs did. Their faces were contorted, as if in pain, and this woman, too, had tear tracks through her makeup. And because of their positions, the cause of death was clear. They'd been stabbed, the blood pool indicative of the same timeline as the woman on the floor.

Lennon stood straight, glancing around the room, her gaze lingering on the array of sex toys on the bedside table that had been blocked by the bodies while she'd been standing in the doorway. *Okay, that's different.* A purple dildo, a studded dog collar, a few butt plugs. *Huh.* So whatever this had turned into, it'd started out as a sexcapade—whether purchased or otherwise—in an abandoned motel? Pretty seedy all around. But honestly? This job ensured she was well acquainted with *seedy.*

She looked around at the other surfaces. There didn't appear to be a weapon anywhere, unless it was still in the younger woman lying on the floor. There were, she noticed, items on the desk near the window. This was the similarity Sullivan had been referring to when Lennon had asked if it appeared to be connected to two other recent murders involving homeless victims. She leaned closer. There were the same pale-purple tablets with a "BB" imprint left at two other scenes, which had turned out to be homemade hallucinogens. Not that *homemade* meant there wasn't a lab involved, but it had been determined they were not an FDA-approved pharmaceutical product. Hallucinogens had been an oddity at the other scenes, and they seemed especially unusual amid sex toys. In fact, other than these recent cases, Lennon couldn't remember ever seeing psychedelics at a murder scene. *Weird.*

Then again, she'd never seen a purple dildo either.

She turned back toward the bodies, considering the scene as a whole, and then removed her phone and took photos of each of the victims.

Her gaze moved back to the numerous stab wounds on the man's body. The older woman's held almost as many. Had they turned a weapon on each other? Or had someone else been here? "What happened to you?" she asked out loud, almost expecting her ex-partner to chime in with a comment of some kind. God, it was times like these that she missed Tommy the most. She missed the level of comfort with each other they'd come by over the last five years they'd been partnered up, both speaking aloud at scenes and bouncing initial observances off each other so nothing got overlooked. She missed Tommy's ability to stay so even keeled at the most macabre of murder scenes. He'd provided an emotional buffer for her and sometimes a gallows humor that helped her separate herself from the victims so she could view the situation more objectively. She'd relied on him, and she knew that made her weak, and possibly not cut out for a job like this. But dammit, she'd been fine until he'd left.

Lennon turned when she heard feet ascending the outdoor steps, a woman's voice greeting Sullivan. *Thank God.* For the moment, she'd had all she could take.

Teresa Wong came through the door, and Lennon felt a small release of tension as Teresa set down the black case in her hand. "Hi, Lennon."

"Teresa. Hi. Is it just you?"

Teresa had been a criminalist with the SFPD about the same amount of time Lennon had been an officer, and they'd worked together often over the years. Teresa was excellent at her job, extremely fastidious and very professional. She also had an easygoing nature that put everyone on the scene at ease, even if the scene was one that naturally inspired upset, or even horror, in the most seasoned officers and inspectors.

"Just me for now," Teresa answered as she started suiting up. "Did you hear about the shooting?"

"Yeah, unfortunately. How many victims?"

"About twenty injured, and two dead, including a five-year-old."

Lennon cringed.

"It looks gang related," Teresa went on, "but you never know."

"A five-year-old. What the hell is going on in this city?"

"The lunatics are running the asylum. Anyway, the other criminalists are headed to that scene, so you've got me."

"I've got the best. Thanks, Teresa."

Teresa nodded toward the room. "Same Benjamin Buttons?"

Lennon managed a smile as she remembered the conversation about what the "BB" might stand for when they'd first come across it. "Yeah, they're on the desk. I'm going to check outside while you do your thing. I'll be back shortly."

Teresa was already moving toward the woman on the floor and opening her bag.

Sullivan yawned as Lennon stepped outside. She peered down into the parking lot: her car, the two police vehicles, and now Teresa's were the only ones there. "I'm going to walk around the grounds and see if I spot anything," she said. "Maybe there's a car out back that brought the victims here."

Sullivan nodded. "A couple more uniforms are on their way to relieve me, so if I'm not here when you get back, it was nice to see you, Gray."

"You, too, Sullivan. Take care."

Lennon pulled in big breaths of dwindling morning fog as she descended the steps. The sun had fully risen, the yellowy light making the abandoned motel look all the more dilapidated and somehow unreal, like the wavery image from an old-fashioned film. This place appeared to have been built in the fifties and featured a pristine view of the bay. It was likely once used by tourists and businessmen who wanted to be central to a myriad of San Francisco attractions. Eventually they'd tear this place down, and all the stories of trips and perhaps honeymoons and weekend rendezvous would be carried away in an industrial-size garbage bin.

She made a slow walk around the parking lot, keeping her eyes peeled for anything out of place, but also allowing her heart rate to return to normal and her stomach to settle. She needed to regroup and get hold of her nervous system for a few minutes before she could begin attempting to analyze what might have happened in that upstairs room.

Thankfully she'd known better than to eat anything before answering this call. Once her equilibrium was mostly back to normal, she headed toward the motel and then took a few minutes to walk along the bottom corridor, peering into the rooms that had curtains open and trying a few door handles and finding them all locked.

She walked around the front office, noting a sign in the window that said LOT FOR SALE and had a phone number listed. She took a photo of it and continued around the corner just as she heard a car pulling into the lot behind her. The uniforms were here to relieve Sullivan.

The space behind the motel was a weedy plot of nothing. It wasn't even strewn with garbage, which told her that this motel, in general, probably wasn't well used by vagrants, at least not yet. Even so, she took a few minutes to wander around, looking for anything on the ground that might tell her a person or people had been there, but didn't find a thing. The crunch of the gravel beneath her feet further served to calm her nerves. *Good, that's good. You've got this.* And now that she'd had a moment to process the initial shock and horror of the scene, she could go back and at least pretend to be the professional she was supposed to be.

Lennon turned and ran solidly into a hard wall of man, then let out a surprised squeak. She jerked back, and hands gripped her elbows, steadying her. "Shit, sorry," she breathed.

His grip tightened as though she might still topple over. "Whoa. Are you okay?"

"I'm fine." She shook her arms, and his hands dropped before she stepped away. The stranger peering down at her was tall and good looking and had these *eyes* that took her aback as much as had her head smacking into his broad shoulder. *Bedroom eyes.* The thought took her further off balance because she couldn't remember ever once using that phrase, but also because he was looking at her like he was trying to read her mind, and she certainly didn't want him to be privy to her first impression.

And there went her equilibrium, right out the door.

"Sir, this is a crime scene. I'm going to have to ask you to leave immediately." Her tone was a tad harsh, but he'd surprised her. She hadn't expected a civilian to interrupt her brief respite from death's gruesomeness.

"I know it's a crime scene," he said. He looked off behind her at the weedy lot, his gaze flickering around and then back to her in a way that made her think he knew she'd been basically hiding. "Are you Inspector Lennon Gray?"

Hearing him use her name caused a small jerk of her head. "Yes. Who are you?"

His heavy gaze met hers, slight breeze rustling his dark wavy hair. "I'm Agent Ambrose Mars. I'm with the FBI, and I'm your new partner."

CHAPTER THREE

New partner? FBI? She hadn't been told the feds were getting involved in these cases. "When did this get decided? And why?"

He'd unclipped the badge he had hanging on his pocket and now held it up to her as though she were a suspect who'd demanded identification. "Just yesterday. You were off. Which, ah, you probably know." He gave her a fleeting boyish smile. "Anyway, Lieutenant Byrd called thirty minutes ago and informed me about this call. I didn't expect there to be another scene this soon."

"No, neither did I."

"Same pills? Same victim description?" He looked over his shoulder to the second floor, where police activity was increasing, and then turned back to her.

"Yes," she said. "Was the bureau sent all available details regarding the two previous cases?"

"Yeah. I looked over the basics but haven't had a chance to read them in depth."

"Okay. Come on," Lennon said, moving around him and heading for the stairs. Whoever this Ambrose Mars was, he was temporary as far as she was personally concerned. She'd speak to Lieutenant Byrd the minute she got back to the station and shake the guy. She'd been told she was going to get paired up with someone else as soon as possible, but she'd expected it would be one of the other inspectors she already felt comfortable with. She had no desire whatsoever to work with some stranger over others she already *knew* had her back, and was annoyed she hadn't received a heads-up. As if she needed one more thing to make her feel less than competent. But regardless, if the FBI had sent him here and he was going to work this particular case, he'd need to see the scene before anything else. And maybe Teresa had some information by now too.

He followed her to the room, where two officers were now standing guard, greeted each of them, taking a moment to pull on booties and gloves, and then stepped inside, where Teresa was just setting her camera back on top of her case. She'd lifted the woman slightly, and Lennon could now clearly see the stab wounds on her chest and torso too. Her heart clenched. That look on her face. *Jesus.* What had she experienced in her final moments? No one should die violently, but clearly, her death hadn't been quick. She'd cried. She'd screamed. She'd suffered.

"All three were stabbed, just like the others," Teresa said. She looked up, her gaze hanging on Ambrose for a moment.

"Does it look like they did this to each other?" Lennon asked.

"It's hard to say without an examination of the wounds, but I can't imagine how it would work for three people to stab each other to death. Wouldn't there be someone left standing?"

"Unless his or her injuries were so severe, they just lay down next to the others and died once it was all over."

Teresa appeared to consider that for a moment and then shrugged. "Anyway, again, no murder weapons present. Whatever was used might have been stolen from the first two scenes, but all three? Also, with three people, you'd definitely need more than one weapon." Her eyes moved back to Ambrose, who was looking around the room, a small frown hanging on his lips.

"Teresa Wong, this is Agent Ambrose Mars. He just got here yesterday." She hadn't even asked where he'd arrived from, but all that could wait. And didn't matter to her anyway.

"Hi, Agent." Teresa used her gloved wrist to push her glasses up her nose. "Welcome to the jungle."

He gave her a small smile that held some confusion, as though he wasn't sure if she was being sarcastic or not, and then walked over to the desk where the unknown pills had been left. His spine seemed to straighten in some minute way as he stared down at them. "Do you recognize those?" Lennon asked.

He startled slightly and looked back at her as though he'd forgotten she was there. "Only from the two previous case files. These substances appear to be the same as what was found at the other scenes, yes?"

"Yes. That lavender color is unique. The lab will confirm but they're most likely the same, which means they're hallucinogens."

Ambrose walked toward where Teresa was on the floor, taking samples from under the woman's fingernails. "Defensive wounds?" he asked.

Teresa held up the woman's uninjured palms. "Not on her, but the man has some."

She'd cried and screamed and suffered, but she hadn't fought back? Maybe she'd been too out of it to defend herself.

"So if there was an unknown perpetrator, the women were drugged and didn't fight back, but the man wasn't? Or became lucid at some point, at least enough to fight back," Lennon surmised. Ambrose didn't react to her statement, still looking around the room, seeming both thoughtful and troubled. She didn't require his input, however; the toxicology report would confirm or deny her guess.

One of the police officers guarding the door laughed at something the other one said, and Ambrose's chin rose quickly, his eyes hanging on the two men. *What's with this guy?* The dude was different. And quiet. And for whatever reason, he did not strike her as an FBI agent, even though that's what he'd said he was and he had the badge to prove it.

She wasn't usually judgmental, but he made her feel unbalanced, and she decided she definitely didn't want to work with him. No maybes about it. She'd fix this when she got back to the station. He could do his bureaucratic thing, but Lennon didn't need to hold his hand while he did it. In Lennon's world, she'd learned to trust her first impressions. She was analytical to a fault, which was one of the qualities that served her well as an inspector, but she had no desire to dig deeper and unpack this dude.

Teresa had turned the woman on the floor slightly, and the eyes of the teddy bear beneath her peeked out. "What do you think is with the stuffed animals?" she asked. "Creepy, right?"

"Yeah, and different than the first two scenes."

"There are more toys in the bathroom," Teresa said.

Lennon glanced at the mostly closed door. "Seriously?" She walked to the bathroom and pushed the door open. Inside was a row of plastic toys on the edge of the bathtub. A chill rolled down Lennon's spine. She'd stepped into the aftermath of plenty of murders, but there was something about toys amid a brutal crime scene that was very disturbing.

Especially one that also had overt sexual overtones.

When she turned around, Agent Mars was behind her. She hadn't even heard him approach. "What are you thinking?" he asked, his eyes stuck to the children's figurines lined up on the bathtub. Two princesses, a light-green bear . . . a unicorn with a rainbow mane. *Girls' toys.* "About this scene in particular."

"I don't know," she said. "Just looking at this scene unconnected to the others?" She chewed at her lip. "A role-play, maybe?"

"Role-play?"

She turned toward him fully, and he backed up immediately, a step, and then two. The distance he put between them was excessive. She'd brushed her teeth and showered after her run, so she didn't think it was that. "Well, sex toys," she said, gesturing to the bedside table, "and kids toys? The two absolutely do not go together. So. Say the guy"—she pointed back toward the dead man on the bed—"has a thing for kids and hires a couple of prostitutes to role-play his kiddie sexual fantasy, right? That's how they end up here at this abandoned motel. And then a fourth party shows up and stabs them to death."

He seemed to think about that. "What would be the motive?"

"Maybe the dude"—she inclined her head back toward the male's body—"didn't keep his fantasy strictly to role-play. Maybe someone who knew that offered him free drugs and then came here where he knew he'd be, and killed all three of them."

The agent's brow dipped, and he looked around again. "Someone came to this hotel while he was in the middle of . . ." He waved his hand toward the purple dildo. From this angle, with the light shining on it, Lennon could see that it had glitter either on it or in it. "To avenge something he'd done to a kid?"

"Just spitballing." It was Tommy's word, and he'd used it regularly.

He watched her closely, obviously assessing, and it made her uncomfortable, so she looked away. And again, she missed the hell out of her partner. They were in the habit of throwing out every possibility at a scene, no matter how far fetched. It helped her. The constant dialogue. The mental removal from the physical location. Ambrose obviously didn't work that way.

"Or," he said, surprising her so that she turned back to him, "there was another partner, the drug-fueled orgy they all agreed to partake in went sideways, and the killer stabbed all the partiers." His expression was strangely hopeful, and she got the feeling he'd thrown out the idea—which was an actual possibility—as a way to work with her rather than against her.

"Why?" she asked.

He blinked, those bedroom eyes widening and then drooping again. "Why what?"

"Why did the fourth mystery partner, if there was one, stab the other orgy members?"

He looked at the man lying on the bed, his gaze then moving to Teresa, who was putting the teddy bear into an evidence bag. "This kind of scene? Who knows. Could be anything. Might be nothing. Drugs don't exactly make people logical." His eyes met hers, something passing over his expression that she didn't catch in time to name. The guy was taciturn, and it made her trust him even less.

She crossed her arms and chewed at her lip. Reticent or not, he wasn't wrong about drugs making people illogical and impulsive. She'd seen people killed over a baggie of weed or a side-eye. The idea of motive could be dialed way back when drugs and mental issues were involved. On the streets, you might be killed over nothing at all. A personal scenario going on in an individual's mind and nowhere else.

Hell, someone might have taken one turn too many with the purple, glittery plastic phallus.

Whatever was going on, she still couldn't figure out where the cocktail of hallucinogens came in. Lennon heard at least a few voices just outside the room, and a moment later, two more criminalists came through the door.

Her muscles relaxed slightly. Lennon's job was done here. Now it was time for the tech team to gather and catalog and arrange for these bodies to be sent to the medical examiner. She greeted the criminalists and then stepped outside the room. She heard Agent Mars introducing himself to them but didn't wait for him to join her before heading toward the stairs.

As far as she was concerned, her very brief partnership was now over.

CHAPTER FOUR

The next morning, Lennon made it her first priority to go straight to Lieutenant Byrd's office. "You stuck me with a *fed* without even consulting me?" she said as she sat down in one of the chairs in front of his desk.

"Dial it down, Gray. The call came down from the chief's office, so you'll have to take it up with him when he gets back into town. But if it really is a serial killer we're dealing with, we're going to have to manage this properly. Hell, even if it's only a new toxic street drug that just hit the market, we'll need some assistance. Agent Mars worked in a field office outside the city and is transferring here to San Francisco. He's never worked this kind of case, so he might need some guidance."

Lennon felt a buzz of both agitation and anxiety. Lieutenant Byrd set his coffee aside and opened a file sitting on his desk in front of him. "You want me to train him?" Lennon asked. She was in no way interested—or qualified, for that matter—to train anyone. Half the time, she was busy managing *herself.* "He's not just a fed, he's a *rookie?*"

Lieutenant Byrd's dark gaze met hers. "I don't know his exact background, just that he's an agent. Apparently, he's thorough and good at his job, and has a real way with the down-and-out. But he's never worked in a city. He hasn't seen crime like we see here. Get him acclimated. Help him collect the answers the FBI wants and send him on his way."

He has a real way with the down-and-out. What did that mean? "Criminals or victims?" she asked suspiciously.

Lieutenant Byrd stared at her for a moment, obviously rewinding the conversation to determine what she was asking about. "Both."

Both. What did that say? No wonder she hadn't known how to read him. But at least if he'd worked with victims of any kind, he wasn't *only* a paper pusher. "Anyway, I thought you were putting me with Penny." Lennon resisted a grimace. She sounded like a brat. She was sitting there with her arms crossed and her lip jutted out, too, like a brat. She unlatched her arms and put her palms on her thighs. Why did the thought of partnering with an FBI agent rankle her so much anyway? Why did those dark, sleepy eyes make her feel . . . unsteady? *Like running away.* She hadn't been consulted when her last lieutenant had placed her with Tommy five years before, either, and that had ended up being the best thing that could have happened to her, both professionally and personally. Tommy was like the older brother she'd never had, and his wife was like a sister.

But she'd liked Tommy right off the bat. She'd gotten a good feeling about him, and they'd clicked immediately.

They were a natural team.

"Penny's transferring," Lieutenant Byrd said.

"What?" Penny hadn't said a word about leaving. Not that they were close friends, but they'd worked together for years. "Transferring where?"

"Sacramento. There was an opening, and she applied. I wrote her a letter of recommendation. It happened quickly. I think she needed a change of scenery."

A change of scenery. Apparently, everyone around here needed a change of scenery. "Who else is leaving?"

"Today? No one. But if your point is that everyone is leaving the SFPD, then Agent Mars is one of the only ones arriving. Let's all be grateful. We could use the help." He picked up his cell phone, pressed some buttons; then she heard a ding on her phone in her pocket. "I forwarded you the agent's number, in case you didn't get it from him yesterday."

"Humph."

"Is there anything else?" Lieutenant Byrd's voice broke Lennon from her thoughts, and she looked up to see her boss leafing through the papers he'd removed from the file. Lennon sighed. She was obviously being dismissed.

"No, nothing else," she said, standing.

"Good."

She exited Lieutenant Byrd's office and went back to her desk, dropping down into her chair.

"I heard you've been partnered up with a fed," Adella Haffey said from her nearby desk. "Lucky you. Is he hot at least? One of those young bucks who's eager to bust down doors?"

Lennon rolled her eyes. Whether Agent Ambrose Mars was eager about anything, she had no idea, but he wasn't exactly a "young buck." She'd estimate him to be midthirties. Lennon smiled but turned away from Adella, who was looking at her expectantly. With all the tragedy they dealt with constantly, one would think police officers could rise above turning the precinct into a middle school dance, but experience told her they couldn't. Or chose not to. There was constant internal drama. She glanced over at Tommy's empty chair for a moment and then took out her phone, ignoring the text from Lieutenant Byrd that she knew was Mars's contact information and dialing a different number.

Just when Lennon thought Tommy's wife Sam's voicemail was going to pick up, she answered, sounding slightly breathless. "Hey, Lennon."

"Hey. You sound like you just ran a marathon."

She let out a breathy laugh. "I might as well have. I left my phone upstairs and had to hustle my pregnant butt to get it. You called at a good time, though, because my two little wild men just got picked up for school. Thank heavens for carpool."

"I won't keep you long. You should take the opportunity to rest."

"No rest for me. I'm in full nesting mode. How's work?"

"Fine. Another day, another shooting, another stabbing." She cringed as soon as the words left her mouth. She didn't want to bother Sam with death and destruction right now when she should be focusing on life and new beginnings. "Anyway, sorry, you don't need to know about the crime rate in San Francisco when the point was to get away from all that. How's Tommy?"

"I want to hear about the crime rate in San Francisco because that's part of your life and I worry about you. Tommy's fine. He hasn't given out so much as a speeding ticket in the two weeks we've been here. He's bored, but we're both sleeping great, and my stomach doesn't drop every time an unknown number shows on my phone while he's on duty."

"You deserve that, Sam. You need it. It's not healthy expecting constant doom all the time." Tommy and Sam were expecting their third child, a big motivator for why Tommy had left the SFPD when the climate in the city had simply become too much for them. Tommy had transferred to a small town across the bay. It had been the right move . . . *necessary*. And she got it—more than anyone—but she still missed the hell out of him.

"No, it's not a healthy way to live," Sam agreed. "And Tommy's new department is hiring. You should think about applying." *But if your point is that everyone is leaving the SFPD, then Agent Mars is one of the only ones arriving. Let's all be grateful.*

The thing was, she *wanted* to transfer to a smaller department where the crime rate wasn't dialed up to eleven, day in and day out. She wanted to be able to take a full breath during her shift; she wanted to close her eyes and sleep all the way through the night. But she couldn't. She *couldn't* because doing so would feel like giving up in a way she would not allow. "I'll take it under consideration," she told Sam.

"Okay, good. How's it riding with Penny so far?"

"Penny's packing for Sacramento."

Sam groaned. "God, how many is that who've left so far this year? They'll be promoting someone new then, right?"

"If someone applies. In the meantime, I was partnered up with an FBI agent from a field office outside the city."

"A fed? Why?"

"They're interested in this slew of new cases involving a homemade drug. I'm not sure why."

"Oh. Well, how do you feel about that?"

"I don't know. I mean, I'm not thrilled about any stranger tagging along after me. And I'm not sure about him. He's hard to read."

"Well, if anyone can figure him out, it's you."

Lennon let out a small grunt. But this was why she'd called Sam. She'd needed to hear a familiar, friendly voice, someone who knew how her brain worked. *Someone who knows me well.* "His position is temporary, so there'd be no point. Anyway, what are your plans for tomorrow? I hope someone is cooking that Thanksgiving turkey for you this year?"

"I *am* the Thanksgiving turkey this year." Sam let out a groan that melted into a laugh.

"Stop. You do not resemble the shape of a turkey. A cute sweet potato, maybe. But not a turkey."

Sam laughed. "Thanks. I'll take it. But no, Tommy's parents are hosting this year." As Sam described a side dish she was making, Lennon's gaze moved to the window of the station, where she could see a slip of gray sky. She had a brief out-of-body feeling, as though she should be the one talking about carpools and nesting and side dishes, and instead she'd woken up from a strange dream and found herself living someone else's life. "You're going to your folks' house, I'm assuming?" Sam asked, bringing her back to the metal desk in the police department, where she'd drifted from for just a moment.

"Yeah."

"Tell them we said hi. And hey, I'm sure it's going to be just fine with this temporary agent."

"It will. Call me with any baby updates."

Lennon heard the smile in Sam's voice when she said, "You're one of the first on our list."

~

The diner near the precinct, where Mars told her he was when she texted him, had several empty tables, the breakfast crowd dwindling now that it was midmorning. Lennon spotted him immediately. She supposed he was hard to miss. Tall and dark, with broad shoulders and that come-hither stare. She pressed her lips together, disturbed by the fact that she kept thinking of Mars's visible attributes. *Highly inappropriate, Gray.* As it turned out, she was as much of a middle schooler as the rest of them.

She also couldn't help noticing the way the server's gaze hung on him as she passed by the table he was sitting at. Apparently, she wasn't the only woman who noticed his physical appeal. Which, strangely, made her feel much better. Mars didn't seem to notice the server's heated glance, however, his attention focused solely on his plate of food as he carefully speared a piece of cantaloupe from the fruit cup next to his eggs.

She slid into the chair across from him, and he looked up. "You're not very observant for an agent of the law," she said.

He tilted his head and considered her.

"You didn't even notice me come in the door until I was right in front of you."

He slid the piece of fruit in his mouth and chewed for a moment, appearing to intensely consider what he was eating as though he might deem it unsatisfactory and spit it out. "I didn't think I needed to be on high alert sitting in this diner eating my breakfast. And I did notice you."

"So you say," she mumbled. She had a feeling he was telling the truth, however. He'd noticed her enter. He just hadn't reacted.

"Are you always on high alert?"

She sighed. "Not always, but probably too often. A hazard of the job." And the fact that her nervous system was apparently hyperactive. The server stopped by and held up the coffee carafe in her hand in question. Lennon nodded and scooted her mug across the table so the server could more easily fill it. "Thanks," she said as the young woman moved away.

"Well. Now that we're going to be working together, do you have any questions for me?" she asked.

"What's your opinion on mandarin oranges in a fruit cup?"

She ripped open a tiny cup of creamer and poured it into her coffee. "Generally speaking, mandarin oranges can work with the right combination of fruit. Unfortunately, there are far too many crimes committed on the fruit salad scene. Syrupy canned fruit isn't the worst offense."

His lip twitched, his eyes squinting slightly. "Crimes?"

She nodded.

"Such as?" He leaned in minutely, as if highly interested in this conversation and also surprised that she'd unhesitatingly engaged in banter. But while her inspector persona didn't necessarily come naturally, this did.

She shrugged one shoulder. "Some flavors and textures obviously don't go together, but that seems to be lost on some. It's a simple art, but it does require at least some amount of thought and planning. This summer, my parents had a grill-out, and one of their neighbors brought a lackluster concoction of cantaloupe and seeded grapes, and as if that wasn't bad enough, they put sliced bananas on the top. It sat in the sun, and the bananas all turned brown and mushy. If it were me, I'd think long and hard about whether that neighbor should ever be invited back to any potluck event."

His mouth tipped, and she had this little shiver in her stomach that strangely felt like panic. "I see."

"Of course, my parents aren't nearly as judgmental as I am. My mom could find something delightful about bad bananas. She probably plucked them off the top and made banana bread out of them. It's hard to believe we're related sometimes." Her heart warmed even as she poked fun at her mom to this virtual stranger. She wasn't exaggerating about her mother. The woman probably *had* made banana bread, but not only that, she'd likely delivered the loaf to the soup kitchen and served it by hand to hungry children. Because that was her mom.

She took a big sip of her coffee and then cringed as she swallowed, the drink too hot for such a large mouthful. "Sorry, I'm rambling. And I can be opinionated."

"That's a good thing," he said, spearing a sausage link and bringing the whole thing to his mouth. "You know who you are. Not everyone is as lucky."

She thought about that. Did she know who she was? She supposed she did. She just didn't necessarily like it all the time. Her life choices didn't seem to align with her personality, and that made her feel . . . lost, when she'd chosen the career she had for the exact opposite purpose—to feel found. But the man was looking at her in that assessing way again, and so she waved her hand slightly, as much to brush off the sinking feeling in her stomach as to distract him. "Well, I'm not sure luck has much to do with it. My parents spoiled me rotten." That was also a lie, and now she was really on a roll. Her parents loved and adored her, but she'd always had tough rules. They *had* taught her to be sure of herself, however, and comfortable in her own skin, so she supposed it was because of them that she wasn't afraid to express herself. At least when it came to matters of fruit salad.

The server approached their table again and asked if Lennon wanted to place an order, shooting another not-so-furtive glance at Ambrose. "No," Lennon said. "Just coffee."

"You already ate?" Ambrose asked when the server departed.

Lennon nodded. "I'm an early riser."

His eyes hung on her for a moment, and she resisted fidgeting under his heavy stare. She could see his wheels turning as he considered her, and though he remained still, he almost reminded her of the way her parents' dog, Freddie, tipped his head back and forth when she said a whole string of words he recognized but was working out the context. She doubted the agent would appreciate being compared to a dog, however, so she didn't mention it to him.

Again, though, the guy was different, and she wasn't sure if it was good different or not-so-good different. Whatever he was, he was trying very hard to size her up, and she had this feeling he was getting at least some of it right.

Apparently done assessing her, he picked up his orange juice and took a long drink, draining it and setting it back down. She noticed a white scar on the top of his hand, right in the middle.

"So, Agent Mars, tell me about you. Lieutenant Byrd said you worked at a field office? Where exactly?"

His eyes remained on his plate. "Pleasant Hill. And call me Ambrose."

She lifted her chin. "Are you from Pleasant Hill?"

He lifted his fork again and resumed picking through the cup of fruit. "No. San Francisco, born and raised. But I moved out of the city ten years ago to take a job as a correctional officer. I did that for a couple of years, and then applied to the FBI. When I graduated, I wanted to come back to the Bay Area, and so I put in a request and was sent to the field office in Pleasant Hill. I've been there for several years now."

That was a lot of back-and-forth, but two things stood out to Lennon. One, he was a local, too, and for some odd reason, even though there were almost a million residents in San Francisco, she was surprised she'd never come across him. Which made no sense at all. So she moved that aside, on to the second thing that had caught her attention. "You started your career as a correctional officer?"

"Yeah."

Her respect notched up, even if she didn't necessarily want it to. There weren't too many more pressure-filled jobs than that, where you had to be on constant alert. She'd only been somewhat convinced he'd noticed her enter the diner before, but she was certain of it now. You had to be observant—to say the least—if you wanted to survive in that environment. "That had to have been rough."

Ambrose shrugged and tilted his head. She waited for him to provide more details, but in the end, he simply put a strawberry in his mouth and looked into the distance as he chewed. Ambrose set his fork down. "So, since you're here, asking questions, you obviously weren't successful in shaking me."

She almost felt embarrassed. Almost. He'd obviously sensed her initial dislike or . . . suspicion? It wasn't like he'd actually done anything wrong. But if he hadn't just reminded her about the weird vibes he put off, she might have blushed. Instead, she shrugged. "No. I was unsuccessful in shaking you. I guess I'm stuck with you. For now."

Ambrose smiled, but there was no cockiness in it. No gloating, or even annoyance that she obviously was far from overjoyed to have been partnered up with him. There was almost an understanding in it, like he didn't blame her for trying to get rid of him.

Which in itself was odd. Most people sought to make a good first impression. They wanted to be liked, or at least welcomed. Most people would take offense at being dumped right off the bat—or at minimum the attempt.

Maybe he was only here to make a report about the unknown drug found at three murder scenes and the possibility of a serial killer in San Francisco. Beyond that, it was anyone's guess at the moment if Ambrose could even—professionally speaking—handle the mean streets of the city. Some days she barely could, and she carried this vague assumption that she'd put her guilt aside and transfer somewhere else sooner or later. Somewhere with less crime and more emotional stability. Bored, like Tommy, but able to sleep at night without reliving visions of the constant depravity city cops were confronted with. And that wouldn't really be giving up, would it? She'd still be doing the job, even if she was only doing accident reports and responding to minor thefts?

Ambrose signaled the waitress for the check. "Since you're stuck with me for now," he said, "should we go see what the medical examiner has to say about the three latest victims?"

CHAPTER FIVE

"Jett"
Episode from podcast *The Fringe*
Host of podcast, Jamal Whitaker

"Hello, welcome to *The Fringe*. Jett."

The young man nods and takes a drag of his half-smoked cigarette before leaning forward and putting it out in the ashtray on the coffee table in front of him. "Yeah. Jett or J.D. Some people call me J.D." His gaze darts around. "We don't gotta give last names here, right?"

"No, of course not. Did you grow up in San Francisco, Jett?"

"Nah." Jett shifts. His obvious lack of health—sallow skin marked with sores, severely underweight—makes his features look droopy and gives him an almost cartoonish expression of sadness. Even so, it's obvious he'd be a good-looking guy if he wasn't so haggard. "I grew up in Kentucky."

Jamal tilts his head. "Kentucky. That's quite a ways from here. How'd you end up in San Francisco?"

Jett shifts again, bending his leg so his ankle rests on his opposite knee. "Hopped a bus, man. I didn't know where it was going. Rode it until I ran out of money."

"That's pretty brave."

Jett laughs, but then the laugh dies quickly, and his expression morphs into confusion, as though he knows the statement was a joke but doesn't understand it. He runs a hand through his greasy, overly long white-blond hair, and then his hand flutters in the air for a moment as if he's not sure what to do with it. "You got another smoke?"

Jamal nods to someone off camera, and when Jett is shown again, he has a lit cigarette in his hand, and a portion of it has been smoked. Obviously, the scene has been edited to move forward slightly.

"Why'd you leave Kentucky, Jett?"

"Because there wasn't shit to do there."

"So, boredom?"

Jett shrugs. "Boredom. Disgust. I was sick of that shithole."

"So home wasn't great."

"Wasn't great." Jett lets out a sound that's sort of a laugh but mostly a snort as his face twists. "You might say that."

"Can you tell me about it?"

"Home? Shit, man, I don't even know what that means. *Home* was a backwoods slice of hell. I got out of there the minute I could."

"Did you have both your mom and dad at home?"

Jett takes a drag of the cigarette and then snuffs it out even though—again—it's only half-smoked. He shakes his head as the smoke fills the air in front of him. "I was raised by my grandparents."

"Mom's or dad's parents?"

"Mom's."

"Where were your mom and dad?"

"My mom took off when I was a baby and then died of an overdose when I was . . . I don't even remember when. Maybe ten or twelve? I never knew my dad."

"I'm sorry to hear that. What were your grandparents like?"

Jett lowers his leg and puts both feet on the floor and then bounces his knees, a jerky, uncoordinated movement. "My grandma was mostly a shell. My grandpa was the devil himself."

"There was some abuse?"

"Some abuse." Jett makes that strangled chuffing sound again. "Yeah, there was some abuse."

"Physical or sexual?"

Jett's eyes shift, and his knees bounce again before he reaches for the cigarette, seems to remember he's already stubbed it out, and drops his hand. He sits back on the couch. "Physical. He beat the shit out of me whenever he felt like it, which was just about every day of the week. He beat my grandma, and if we weren't enough, he'd find a dog to beat too."

"I'm sorry. That's awful."

Jett's gaze meets Jamal's, and he looks vaguely confused. "So, yeah, I got out of there as soon as I could."

"And you ended up here. How far did you make it in school?"

"I graduated high school."

Jamal looks slightly surprised. "You did? That's great."

"Yeah, I liked school. It was a place to get away, you know? Get away from home."

"Did you have friends?"

Jett shrugs. "People I got high with."

Jamal nods as Jett fidgets. "What's your drug, Jett?"

"Meth. Heroine. Whatever." The knees start up again.

"So both stimulants and opioids. Do you prefer one?"

"Depends." Jett doesn't elaborate.

"Any diagnoses?"

Jett pauses. "Yeah, uh, schizophrenia, anxiety, depression, can't really remember them all. Long names."

"Do you take prescription medication along with the street drugs?"

"Sometimes. When I remember to make it over to the free clinic."

"When you remember. And how do you pay for the street drugs?"

Jett glances off camera and then back at Jamal. "Illegal shit."

"Have you been arrested?"

Jett brings his hands to his knees and stills them. "Nah, haven't caught a case yet. No arrest record so far. Lucky me." He laughs at that, but again, the laugh dies quickly.

CHAPTER SIX

Ambrose had never been inside a medical examiner's office before. Right off the bat, he hated the smell of the place, and he also hated the cold. He had to admire people who spent all day with the dead in a frigid, stark room that smelled like formaldehyde and decay in an effort to bring those souls justice. Or at least answers.

Or maybe they deserved some amount of general skepticism, considering they could tolerate a work environment like this without going mad.

Whatever the case, many of the people who ended up here had families who'd do far less for them than the doctors at this lab. A tragedy that the first time some of these individuals were taken care of was after they'd ceased breathing.

"Just as suspected," said the medical examiner, Clyde Gates, whom he'd met a few minutes ago and insisted Ambrose call him Clyde. "The homemade hallucinogens are the same as the ones found at the previous scenes. A mixture of ecstasy, dextromethorphan, psilocybin, and food coloring. However, these ones have the fun addition of a light LSD coating."

Jesus. When he'd seen the "BB" on the top of the purple pills, he'd guessed at the concoction, but hearing it confirmed made his stomach roll. The additional LSD coating was unexpected, though, and he'd need to inquire about that. "And it was found in these victims' systems too?" he asked.

Clyde nodded. "In high doses. They'd popped more than one. These people were certainly in la-la land. And this one"—he pulled the sheet back to reveal the young woman who'd been on the floor of the vacant motel the last time Ambrose had seen her—"was pregnant."

Across from him, Lennon's eyes flared subtly. "How far along?"

"About twelve weeks."

"Long enough to know she was pregnant if she was at all in touch with her body," Lennon murmured.

He had a feeling this woman on the slab in front of him was not even remotely "in touch" with her body. Thankfully, however, her face had been cleaned, eyes shut, and mouth closed. That awful scream he'd last seen on her face was now an expression of peaceful slumber. His gaze moved to the dead woman's arm, where there were clear track marks at the crease, and then farther down where there was a line of pale red scars, each about the same width and length. "She was a cutter," he noted.

"Most definitely. She has scars on her thighs, too, some years old, others more recent."

"That one always gets me," Lennon murmured. "Why hurt yourself more than you're already hurting?"

"The pain is better than the numb," Ambrose said. "Pain reminds you you're alive." Lennon's eyes met his, and even in this cold, sad room, standing over the body of a young woman who'd suffered in—very likely—more ways than just one, or even two or three, he was struck by the inspector's beauty. She was intriguing to him, too, and he'd have liked time to figure her out but knew that wasn't going to be possible.

She looked away from him, back to Clyde. "The thing that keeps bothering me about this scene in particular is that I've never heard of hallucinogens being part of an orgy. I'd think that would make things . . . very bizarre."

"Some people like bizarre," Clyde said.

True enough. But the case already disturbed Ambrose, and this only added to it. The light-purple hallucinogens with the "BB" imprint . . .

the teddy bear and the children's toys. "No, you're right," he said to Lennon. "Hallucinogens are typically used for a mental or spiritual experience, not a physical one."

"Right. Exactly," she agreed.

"These people appeared to be drug users, however," Ambrose said. "They might not have been very discerning if given free product."

Lennon's brow knitted. "Could you tell if she'd had sex?" she asked Clyde after a moment. "Willing or otherwise?"

"I'm going to get the second female up on the table this afternoon, but there was no semen in—or on—this one. As far as I can tell, she didn't have sex recently."

"And the shower didn't appear to have been used," Ambrose said, recalling the report they'd received that morning from the criminalists who'd worked the scene and sent the samples they'd gathered to the lab for testing. The water had still been on at the property, but the shower had been dry, and there weren't any towels available to mop up the residual water.

"And no condom or fresh semen found either," Lennon murmured. "So maybe it hadn't gotten sexual yet."

"The footage from the bank up the street showed all three of them headed in the direction of the motel at midnight, though," Ambrose said, referring to the footage they'd received early that morning. "You estimated time of death to be about three a.m.?" he asked Clyde.

"Give or take an hour," Clyde answered.

"Three hours would be a long time to sit around and chat," he said. "So if they weren't having sex, what were they doing for all that time?"

Lennon chewed at her lip for a second. "Yeah. It doesn't fit." She paused again. "What can you tell us about the wounds?"

"Well, the male has some defensive wounds on his hands, but they're very light and shallow, practically scratches. Which aren't congruent with the wounds on his chest, and especially the one to his heart that ultimately killed him. Those ones are deep slashes. Considerable strength was used for those."

"And conviction," Ambrose said. Whoever had stabbed him with enough strength to penetrate his heart muscle had gone all in. Literally.

"Yes," the doctor agreed. "No hesitancy whatsoever. And from a visual aspect, there doesn't appear to be blood spatter on either of the female victims—blood, yes, which I suspect is only their own. But there most certainly would have been spatter had they stabbed him with the force necessary to cause the weapon to go through his chest wall and into his heart."

"Which means neither of the women killed him. So in this case, at least, there was a fourth person present who walked away from the scene," Lennon said.

"I'll have more definitive answers shortly, but yes, I strongly suspect so."

"Which leads me to wonder if there was another person at the first two murders as well."

"Evidence confirmed those people stabbed each other, though, correct?" Ambrose asked.

"Yes. But some of the wounds were deeper and more . . . purposeful?" She looked at Clyde for confirmation, and he gave her a nod. "Because of the hallucinogens, it was difficult to say whether the wounds held different levels of vigor, for lack of a better description, because of multiple knife wielders or because of the drugs."

"That makes sense. People tripping on hallucinogens can morph quickly between emotions, reactions, et cetera," Ambrose said.

"Right. But now—"

"Now it's looking highly likely there's a killer who probably walked away from each scene."

Lennon nodded slowly before looking at Clyde. "The more superficial wounds—what's your take there? That the killer was just warming up with the ones the male victim fended off?"

"Could be. Or the killer didn't expect him to fight back, and the fact that he did made the person holding the knife angry enough to go for gusto."

"Or if the women did partake in some violence, perhaps he was angry that they weren't stabbing with enough force to do any harm. The victims at the other scenes became very violent with each other. But maybe these ones didn't. Maybe that made the killer mad, but also meant he had to take over the job if their death was his goal," Ambrose said.

"Okay, yes," Lennon said, and Ambrose swore that even though he didn't know this woman at all, he could see the wheels turning behind her eyes. She definitely had layers, but one thing was clear—she was also deeply intelligent. "That's a possibility too. And further, if this killer who was there walked away, does that mean he set it up?"

"I think he would have had to," Ambrose said, and that specific more than any other caused him great distress.

"Anything else?" Lennon asked Clyde, who had been watching them volley comments back and forth.

"Well," Clyde said, lifting the woman's hand and showing them her dirty fingernails. "Cursory glances at all three of them tell me they were likely living on the street, just like the other victims. Heavy drug use for all three at some point—though, again, I only detected the hallucinogens in their blood."

"That's a little odd, too, isn't it?" Ambrose said. "All three of them were clean except for the drugs found at the scene. Was that true of the four other victims?"

"It was," Lennon said. "It is odd, actually, that they'd all gotten clean for at least some amount of time before arriving at the scene of their death."

The scene of their death. That description made a shiver dance over his skin because it was another nod to a preplanned event. "Few show up willingly to the scene of their death," he said, meeting Lennon's eyes.

"No, not many," she said.

"So they probably didn't."

"Agreed. These people likely showed up expecting something very different than what it turned out to be."

"I do have something that might offer a lead," Clyde said, turning and reaching for something on the table behind him. He held up a plastic bag with a pair of folded jeans inside. "The man was wearing these."

"Please tell me you found an ID in an inside pocket," Lennon said. They both knew there hadn't been one in an obvious spot, as the criminalists had carefully searched them all. ID'ing the victims had proved difficult, as was often the case with those considered transient. Locating records, if they existed, wasn't easy, especially since these folks often came from all over the country. The fact that arrests for drug offenses—which would have put them in the system—were way down only upped the challenge.

"Unfortunately, no. But this might help." Clyde folded the bag slightly so that the tag at the back of the jeans was showing. Ambrose and Lennon leaned in, and he caught a whiff of her perfume. He was amazed that anything could remain light and fresh in this particular room, and the brief pull of her air was a too-short but welcome reprieve.

"Does that say . . ." A line formed between her brows as she obviously strained to make out the black ink on the white tag.

"Gilbert House," Clyde said. "I googled it, and it's a shelter for homeless men in the Tenderloin."

"You could have led with that, kind sir," Lennon said with a cock of her brow.

Clyde chuckled. "Yes, but I have so few breathing visitors. I wanted to make sure you stayed for longer than a minute."

Clyde brought the sheet back over the woman. "I'll call you this afternoon if I find anything else that might help immediately. Otherwise, the report will be sent over as soon as possible."

"Thanks, Clyde."

Ambrose walked with Lennon out to her city-issued vehicle and got in the passenger side. He pulled his seat belt over his chest and then looked at Lennon, who was now just sitting there, moving her fingers distractedly on the steering wheel as she stared out the window. She stretched and tapped as though playing on an invisible set of piano keys. "What are you thinking about?" he asked her.

"I was thinking about the items we found at the first two scenes. I'll have to look back at the list because I don't remember it all. Mostly, it was stuff the victims carried around in their backpacks or bags . . . extra clothing, a blanket, a hairbrush, et cetera." She paused. "But at the first scene, there was a belt lying near the man."

"Were there other things strewn around, or just that?"

"Just that, which is why I remember it. The other things were cataloged from the bags lying nearby. No identifying information, but it all seemed like stuff a homeless individual would carry with them."

"But the belt had been removed."

"Yes. And it was right near the man's body, just like the teddy bear at the most recent crime scene."

Ambrose thought about that. "Are you thinking those specific items are clues? Or . . . messages?"

She played a few inaudible notes on the steering wheel again. "Maybe. Or maybe the belt is a prop like the teddy bear, also used as part of a role-play."

"What sort of role-play would involve a belt?" Although he had his own ideas, ideas that were making him more and more uncomfortable by the moment. In fact, a feeling of mild dread was beginning to drift nearer. He wanted to know what the inspector thought, however. She was familiar with murder scenes, while he was not. Not only that, but he had his preformed suspicions, and he didn't want those to get in the way of clear sight.

"Well," she said. "There's the obvious bondage angle. S and M? Fifty shades of fucked up?"

He huffed out a small chuckle. "A singular belt is a pretty skimpy prop collection for a domination scenario."

"Red rooms of pain are expensive. Our victims weren't exactly rolling in dough." She frowned as she ran her tongue over her teeth. "But yeah, one belt doesn't tell us a lot. It might be a role-play, and it might just have fallen out of one of their bags."

"Or one of them could have removed it to use as a weapon."

"Maybe, but there was no blood or tissue found on it."

He looked away out the passenger-side window as he pictured the photographs he'd seen of the two people who'd died bloody deaths in the abandoned building, thinking about what exactly might have happened there. Lennon had proposed that the belt might have been a prop because she'd made a guess that the toys at the other scene were used that way. But . . . "We have no direct evidence the teddy bear was part of a role-play, so this line of thinking might be moot."

"No, I know. I'm just thinking aloud." She turned toward him. "It helps me sort through things. Does it bother you?" There was no sarcasm in her voice. She seemed to be posing an honest question, and so he took a moment to think about it.

He usually worked alone, so it'd never been an issue. But for Inspector Lennon Gray? It wouldn't be a sacrifice. "It's not my usual style, but I can adjust."

She let out a small breathy laugh, and in the bright daylight of the car, he could see the faded freckles scattered across her nose. The glow caught the golden hazel of her eyes and brought out the pale ring of green. Her eyes were like the clearing he'd once stood in in the redwood forest, gazing up at those impossibly massive trees as sunlight seeped between the gaps in their feathery branches. He'd closed his eyes and felt connected to some greater whole even while he'd never been more aware of his own smallness. There had been something . . . wonderful about that feeling. A letting-go. An acceptance. An understanding that was beyond him and yet was more real than anything he'd ever experienced before that moment. And for whatever reason, he felt some small remnant of that feeling now, though he couldn't begin to explain it, couldn't imagine how that moment and this one were remotely similar. "I appreciate that, Mars," she said. "There might be hope for this partnership yet."

He smiled. He couldn't even remember what she was responding to, his mind had drifted so far away. But regardless of why, he liked what she'd said. And despite his deep uneasiness about this case, he hoped that was true, because he enjoyed being around this woman who was a confusing mix of traits that he hadn't yet managed to make sense of. Typically, that bothered him. He liked categorizing things, identifying and naming them. He found comfort and satisfaction in both the process and the result. But in Lennon's case, he didn't mind being in somewhat uncharted territory. *Interesting. What is it about you that makes me comfortable with a lack of boundaries?*

Lennon turned over the ignition and looked in the rearview mirror as she began backing out. "I have a meeting with the lieutenant in an hour, and then I need to look through the other footage from nearby businesses. Unfortunately, several in that area closed in the last few years, so we're limited. But an alert just came in that some more was delivered. I'll call the Gilbert House this afternoon and make sure they're open tomorrow, and we'll meet up in the morning?"

"Yeah, sure. That sounds good," he said. "I need to bring myself up to date on the details of the other scenes. Hopefully in the morning we can get at least one ID."

CHAPTER SEVEN

It'd been several months since Lennon had reason to be in the Tenderloin neighborhood. It seemed that even in that short time, the stark squalor and human misery on Hyde Street, onto which she and Ambrose had just turned, had increased significantly.

It was Thanksgiving Day, and apparently none of these people had anywhere to go. Or maybe it was early enough that they hadn't made their way over to one of the churches serving meals.

She had called the Gilbert House the day before and wasn't surprised when she was told they'd be staffed this morning. Places like that didn't get a day off. The homeless problem didn't go away on holidays. Neither did crime.

She'd been forced to park several blocks away, and as they began walking toward the Leavenworth address, she saw Ambrose glancing around, the expression on his face slightly stunned. "When was the last time you were in the city?" she asked.

He glanced over at her. "It's been years."

She stepped around some trash. "Compared to the suburbs, this must look like a dystopian hellscape."

He gave a gravelly laugh. "You could say that. Things are bad here."

Yes, things were bad here, even if, geographically speaking, the TL was prime real estate, smack-dab in the middle of one of the most expensive cities in the world. *San Francisco's purgatory.* Lennon was a local, but even she didn't know all the historical reasons why gentrification had failed here. But it most certainly had.

"What'd you do in Pleasant Hill anyway?" she asked. She knew it was unwise to become distracted on a street such as this one, but a small sliver of distraction, frankly, was also necessary.

He turned his head toward her, and despite the hollow look in his eyes, his pace didn't slow. His body language told her he was more surprised by the state of this place than scared by the inhabitants, and that made her feel more at ease with him. She might be able to count on him not to run and hide if they faced a physical threat. For now, however, the only threat was being waged on their olfactory lobes.

"We did a lot of everything. My interest area was missing persons, but there aren't a lot of cases there, so when we learned they couldn't spare any agents here in San Francisco and were contacting local field offices regarding this case, I volunteered for the chance to get some experience related to violent crime."

He'd said it smoothly, but Lennon had this odd feeling that he'd rehearsed his answer. Was there something more to this case that the FBI knew but weren't sharing with them? "Why exactly was the FBI called in on this case, though? I mean, I get that the idea of a serial killer always alerts the feds, but we aren't even certain that's the case yet. It seems . . . early for you—or any agent—to be here working this case."

Ambrose stepped around a pile of vomit on the sidewalk. "I think they might be concerned about a new street drug taking hold. A few years ago, a drug that's a mix of fentanyl and a horse tranquilizer called xylazine started becoming more widely used. It began as a small problem, but it's since blown up. I don't think the government wants to be caught on the wrong side of something like that again."

"Is that the zombie drug?"

"Tranq. You've heard of it?"

"Yeah." She'd personally seen the effects, too, namely the rotting wounds that often led to amputation. And she'd heard of a case in Oakland where a man literally ate part of his friend's face while under the influence. And it didn't respond to Narcan, which was a whole other problem. "So it's not so much the serial killer possibility but the worry that the homemade drug found at the scene is a mix of hallucinogens that causes people to become homicidal?"

"Possibly. Either way, it's best to get ahead of the situation. These things can easily become political. They affect the state of health care and a hundred other bureaucracies. At the moment, it's not known if the drug was cooked up in someone's basement, an illegal lab, or if it came across the border."

Ah. Political. Well now it all made sense. The feds were involved because the government was afraid this might come back to bite them in the ass and raise questions about certain policies they preferred not to have questioned. And so they'd sent Ambrose Mars to keep them informed.

She thought about the conversation with Clyde regarding hallucinogens being a mental experience more than a physical one. "From what I know, hallucinogens typically bring about euphoria, not violent tendencies."

"But in the right combo, and with the right triggers, maybe it's more likely to bring out violent tendencies than other mixes of drugs," he said.

She cocked her head to the side. "True, I guess. I've heard of people having bad trips. Maybe it caused one of those. You know, the people given that drug thought the other person was a giant spider or something, and attacked accordingly? I'm halfway tempted to volunteer to take it just so we know what we're dealing with."

He gave her an uneasy look.

"I'm kidding," she said. "I didn't even smoke weed in college."

"I've never heard of such a unicorn."

"That's me. Unicorn extraordinaire, at your service."

He gave her a boyish smile that somehow seemed completely out of place in this gritty landscape. She had this strange instinct to tell him to put that away, as though the vestiges of innocence behind that expression might suddenly and violently become corrupted on this filthy street. What? Did she imagine the stale air itself was toxic to sweetness?

And is that the impression you get of Agent Ambrose Mars? Sweetness? Sort of, though of a different kind than she'd ever been acquainted with before. And perhaps that was the oddity that had set her off balance upon first meeting him. He was this distractingly attractive man who'd likely seen more wickedness than most based on his job, and yet there was something almost . . . guileless about him. Unusual.

They walked in silence for a few minutes, Lennon taking in the graffiti that was splashed over every available surface of the empty stores and old buildings that served as a backdrop to the line of tents where the homeless lived. She brought her hand to her nose, inhaling the fragrance of her hand lotion in a vain attempt to block out the intense smell of urine and feces.

"God, that makes my eyes sting," he said, his voice muffled by his own hand.

"It's not a natural way to live."

"These people are ill," he said. "Twisted by drugs and who knows what else."

He wasn't wrong. It was terrible. And truthfully? Even though it was her job to help society, to wade through the ache and the ugliness, to *show up* anywhere—*anywhere*—there was a victim, she wanted to turn away from this. She wanted to leave, get in her car, and drive anywhere other than here. She wanted to pretend it didn't exist, because even she felt helpless to help these people. And God but that was a depressing feeling.

She stepped over and around the trash that littered the sidewalk, glancing into the gutters that were filled with needle after needle, some capped, most not.

Lennon's head swam. It wasn't just the stench of piss and vomit that filled the air. It was something else, something deeper and more cloying, a hormonal fear sweat that seemed to hang suspended underneath the more identifiable odors of human waste. A noise she couldn't even identify came from one of the tents, and she picked up her pace, not wanting to know what was going on in that small nylon capsule that smelled like death.

This type of scene always struck her with a singular thought: *My God. These are humans living like this.* And how had this city—or any city, for that matter—ended up in a place where this was even halfway normal?

They turned onto the street where the Gilbert House stood. An old woman was cackling to herself on the corner as she walked in circles, flailing her arms. Others, obviously strung out, shuffled past the woman, paying her little mind, one man's pants hanging so far down his hips it was a wonder they weren't falling off. There was a man curled up near the wall of a building, his mouth hanging open, the pipe that had put him in that state still perched on his bottom lip.

They walked on, passing two liquor stores, one at each end of a block, a strip club featuring a performer called "Lil' Baby Girl," a vape shop, and other businesses that had metal roll-down, garage-type doors signaling they were currently closed.

"Hey, mama, what's a fine thing like you doin' down here?" a man said, stepping out from a doorway, blocking their path and causing Lennon to startle and take a quick step to the side. He came closer, and she smelled his scent—weed and human stink. His eyes were bloodshot, and he had open sores on his cheeks.

"My man," Ambrose said, holding up his hand. "You're cool." He reached in his pocket and took out some bills and handed them to the man. "Go get yourself something to eat, okay?"

The man's eyes lit up before he grabbed the bills from Ambrose's hand. "Bless you. Thank you, my brother." Then he turned and veered away, off to spend those few dollars on whatever vice was calling out his name. As long as it wasn't her, she didn't care what it was.

She let out a breath and continued walking. "Lieutenant Byrd said you have a way with people. Is doling out cash your secret?"

"Not always, but it's generally the quickest method."

"I'm sure." She stopped in front of what was obviously once a single-family home but now served as a shelter for men affected by homelessness. The sign that told them they were at the right place was obviously hand painted and featured a rainbow and a peace sign and a number of bluebirds, wings spread. There was something sad about it, and Lennon looked away.

A heavy metal security gate covered the front door, and Lennon pressed the bell, glancing over her shoulder as though the man who'd looked like a zombie might be hot on her trail. And though she saw a few obvious junkies shuffling along the sidewalk, none of them seemed interested in Ambrose and her. None of them seemed interested in much of anything other than putting one shaky step in front of the other.

"Hello?" a voice came over the intercom next to the gate.

Lennon leaned in. "Inspector Lennon Gray and Agent Ambrose Mars here. I called yesterday and spoke with Ellen? She said someone would be available to answer a few questions."

There was a pause, and then the woman who'd greeted them said, "Hold on, please. I'll be right out." Less than ten seconds later, the inner door swung open, and an older woman with short black curls stepped onto the porch. Both Ambrose and Lennon held up their respective badges, and the woman unlocked the gate, granting them entry.

They closed the security gate behind them and followed the woman inside the house. It smelled wonderful: literally a breath of fresh air. Lennon assumed that wherever the kitchen was, it was bustling with people cooking up a feast for the men who lived here. They stepped into a large foyer with a set of steps in front of them. A man was just disappearing around the bend in the stairs, and a few other men sat in a room to the right, where there were tables holding older-looking computers, and bookshelves on the far wall.

"Ellen left a note," the woman told them. "I'm Myrna Watts. I'm the director of the house. Is this something that requires privacy? We only have one office here, and staff are currently using it, but I can ask them to step outside."

"This is fine," Lennon said. "We won't take much of your time."

Ms. Watts nodded. She didn't look alarmed or concerned by their visit, and Lennon wondered if perhaps the police came by somewhat often to inquire about one of their boarders.

She opened her phone and quickly located the photo of the man who'd been wearing the pants with *Gilbert House* written on the tag. It was a close-up taken at the morgue, and the deceased now appeared to be sleeping. Lennon turned it toward Ms. Watts. "Do you recognize this man?"

Ms. Watts lifted the glasses hung on a chain around her neck and took Lennon's phone to better see the photo. As the woman studied the image, Lennon's eyes moved to a bulletin board near the door. There were flyers and notices and one brightly colored invitation to the Heroes for Homelessness Annual Rays of Hope Award Dinner, featuring DJ Fair Play. Was there anyone who didn't fundraise off the homeless population? Where did the money go? And who exactly deserved an award when the problem was so out of control? Where were the heroes they spoke of? "Oh, dear," Myrna said, pulling Lennon's attention back to her. "That's Cruz. He's stayed here off and on for the last couple of years. He preferred the streets, unfortunately." She sighed, her shoulders lifting and falling. "He's dead, right? I'm not surprised, but . . ." She looked back and forth between them. "If you're here, his death must have been connected to a crime."

"Yes, Ms. Watts. We believe he was murdered."

Ms. Watts shook her head. "I'm not surprised. I'm actually shocked he lasted as long as he did. He'd been brought back from the dead so many times, he was sometimes called Tony Narcan."

"Tony?"

"That's his first name. Sorry, most of us around here referred to him as Cruz. But that was actually his last name. Anthony Cruz. How did you connect him to this place?"

Lennon felt the first zing of hope that they'd pulled a thread that might unravel more leads. "He was wearing a pair of jeans that had the Gilbert House on the tag."

Ms. Watts gave Lennon a small, sad smile. "Ah, I see. Yes, we give all the men a clean outfit and a bag of toiletries when they get accepted here."

"Are there conditions to staying here?" Ambrose asked.

Ms. Watts nodded. "They must commit to staying for ninety days, during which time they're clean and sober." She gestured toward the large room to their right, where a couple of tired-looking men sat staring at computer screens and two more sat near the bookshelves, one snoozing and the other reading a magazine. "We help them create a résumé and then job hunt. We have a room full of professional attire upstairs that they're free to borrow from for interviews."

"You said Mr. Cruz stayed here a few times. Did he complete his ninety days?"

"Mr. Cruz never even completed *nine* days." She sighed again. "We really shouldn't have kept taking him back, but . . . that man had a gentle soul. And honestly? It seemed like he *wanted* to get clean, it really did. He never could quite find the strength to follow through." She frowned. "I do remember him talking about a miracle treatment the last time I saw him." She gave a wistful smile. "I'd heard talk like that before in reference to addiction. There's always some new pill that's going to fix them, you know? Take away all their cravings. If a fix like that existed, I'd put it in the water myself."

Miracle treatment. Unfortunately, she'd heard people talk like that too. And the pharmaceutical industry was all too happy to go along with that false idea. A substance to fix an addiction to a substance and then another one after that. And on and on.

"Do you have any idea where he tended to hang out?" Ambrose asked.

Ms. Watts puckered her lips to the side as she thought. "I'm not sure. But if anyone would know, it's Darius Finchem. His father used to run the youth outreach program over on Golden Gate, but Darius took over about five years ago."

Ambrose looked up. "Youth outreach?"

"Mm-hmm. I know it's surprising, but Cruz was only twenty, even though he looked quite a bit older. Drugs and lack of medical care will do that to you. Anyway, maybe twenty isn't even a youth by definition, and Cruz was too old for the center. But Darius has his father's heart, and the man can't turn anyone away. And he knows everything that goes on in the Tenderloin, and most everyone who lives on the streets has taken advantage of one of the programs there. He used to deliver meals, but that stopped because of some permit issue or another."

Lennon was tempted to roll her eyes. "Figures," she muttered. Of *course* bureaucrats had deemed it necessary that folks pay a fee and fill out a stack of paperwork before feeding hungry people.

Lennon quickly scrolled through the other victim photos she had in her phone, asking Ms. Watts if she recognized them too. But the woman shook her head sadly. "I wish I could help with those ones as well."

"We appreciate what you have given us," Lennon said. It was more than they'd arrived with. "Thank you."

"You're welcome. Tell Darius that Myrna said hi when you see him. There are only so many of us who still live and work here and haven't given up on the TL yet."

~

Lennon made the executive decision that they'd drive over to the youth center rather than walk, especially since she wasn't sure it would be open. They went the opposite way around the block to her car this time, to avoid the worst section of Hyde Street. Agent Mars might call her a coward, but she could only handle so much squalor and suffering in one day. She had to hand it to the people who worked in neighborhoods like this one, trying to make things better, day after day—and likely seeing little, if any, improvement, whether that be in individuals or the area itself.

The youth center was a small square building sandwiched between two other small square buildings. They found a parking space just across the street and jaywalked when the light down the block turned red and traffic stopped. The door stood wide open, and Beethoven's Fifth Piano Concerto could be heard from inside. The classical music seemed out of place, and Lennon glanced over at Ambrose and was surprised to see a smile on his lips, as though he'd expected to hear Beethoven pouring forth from a youth center in a drug- and crime-infested neighborhood.

Inside, young men and women were sitting on sofas and easy chairs, feet kicked up as they chatted, one man dramatically playing "air piano" as two people near him laughed. One of the women spotted them, and the others, obviously noting their friend's expression, turned to see whom she was staring at suspiciously.

A man who'd been sitting on the couch with his back to them stood and turned the music down. "Hi. What can I do for you?"

"Are you Darius Finchem?" she asked.

"Guilty as charged." The man smiled warmly, his teeth white and straight, long hair in dreads and gathered at the back of his neck.

"Yo, Darius, the cops are here to take you in? What'd you do?" one of the young men called, at which the rest of them laughed and snickered.

Darius walked over to Lennon and Ambrose and shook each of their hands in turn. "Officers. Or wait, detectives, right?"

"*Inspector* is the title the SFPD uses in place of detective, but yes. What gave us away?" Lennon asked. But she smiled after she said it. The atmosphere in here was anything but hostile.

"You stick out like a sore thumb. But that's okay. We're welcoming of everyone at the youth center." The high-pitched squeal of brakes sounded right outside the door, and Lennon looked over her shoulder to see a bus pulling up out front. Darius leaned around Ambrose and addressed the young people lounging around. "Bus is here," he said.

"Go ahead and start lining up outside." The men and women all got up and headed to the door, shooting Lennon and Ambrose looks that were only slightly curious as they passed.

"Field trip?" Ambrose asked. Darius moved aside as a couple more teens who had been somewhere in the back of the building headed out the door.

"Yeah," Darius said, looking at Ambrose and cocking his head. "Mount Tam. We're going on a hike, and then we're heading over to Glide Memorial Church for dinner."

"A hike?" Lennon was honestly surprised to hear that, but pleasantly so. "That's great. Mount Tam is beautiful." Lennon had hiked Mount Tamalpais several times with her brother. Amazing trails. Beautiful views. And less than an hour outside the city.

Darius smiled. "My dad always said that nature heals the soul." He paused, glancing at the line of young people boarding the bus. "Most of these kids are wounded in some way or another, so we take as many field trips as possible. Last week we went to the beach. If nothing else, it exposes them to something other than these streets."

Ambrose looked away, squinting in a manner that made Lennon think he was holding back some emotion or another. "Your father sounds like a wise man. When did he retire?"

"Just last year. Cancer. But he's doing well, taking advantage of all that nature he loves so much. Anyway, hey, what can I do for you? I gotta . . ." He gestured toward the bus, only a few kids still left to board.

"Yes, sorry," Lennon said, pulling out her phone. "Myrna Watts over at the Gilbert House sent us to you. She says hi, by the way. We're trying to identify a couple of people who were, sadly, part of a crime scene. At least one of them frequented this area."

She held her phone up to Darius, and he frowned at the photo of Anthony Cruz. "Cruz," he said. "Yeah. He's dead?"

"Yes, I'm sorry to say. Is there anything you can tell us about him?"

Darius thought about that. "Me and Pops help serve food at Glide on the regular, and Cruz used to stop by for a meal. But I haven't seen him in months. Damn, he was a nice dude. What a shame."

Lennon ran her finger over her screen to the next photo of the older woman, and then the other victims found at the earlier scenes. Darius glanced up at the bus and raised a finger to indicate to the driver he'd just be a minute. Then he studied the photos. After a few moments he shook his head. "I've never seen them."

Lennon swiped to the final picture, the young woman who'd been clutching the teddy bear, even in death. "Aw, shit. Yeah, I know her. She's a prostitute who works over on Geary." He met Lennon's eyes. "Or worked. She's dead too?"

Lennon nodded even as a small jolt of victory buzzed inside. Another ID. "What's her name?"

"Cherish. I don't know her last name or even if that name is real. But it's what she went by. The women over on Geary will have more information, but you'll have to pay for it." His gaze moved upward for a minute. "She might have done gigs over at this basement club called the Cellar. Real sleazy. You can get whatever you want in the back rooms—and I mean whatever you want—but of course, that's not advertised. You gotta know someone. Several of the girls supplement their income there, but a lot of them consider it too much. And if you know these girls, that's saying something. The cops used to make busts, but they gave that up."

A kid slid open one of the bus windows and leaned out. "Hey, Dar, you coming or what?"

He waved at the guy. "Hey, I gotta go," he said. "But give me a call here at the center if you need anything else."

"Thanks, Darius. You've been very helpful."

With a nod, he walked quickly to the waiting bus, jogging up the short set of steps as Lennon turned to Ambrose. "Anthony Cruz and Cherish," she said to him.

"It's a good start," he said. "Are you up for a walk along Geary?"

She glanced at her watch. "It's only three p.m. Do you think the working girls are out?" And on Thanksgiving? Wouldn't most of the johns be at home with their families, eating turkey and pumpkin pie?

He shrugged. "Maybe one or two. Let's go find out."

They crossed the street and turned toward the car, parked halfway down the block. "The club he mentioned, the Cellar. That sounds like a real nightmare." To Lennon, it sounded like an entire horror movie could take place in a joint like that. Meanwhile, others thought of it as their workplace. She resisted a shudder and tried her best not to see the face of the dead—*pregnant*—woman she'd just learned was named Cherish. Lennon wondered if she had even been of legal drinking age.

She wasn't surprised the cops had stopped making busts there, however—just like the prostitutes that walked the streets, you could arrest people engaging in consensual sex work, but they'd just be out in an hour or two and right back at it. It'd likely be decriminalized soon anyway, and cops knew it. No one was willing to put their neck on the line in any sense for something that wasn't treated as a crime by the courts anymore. What was the point?

They got in the car, and both reached for their seat belts. Lennon glanced at Ambrose. "He said you can get whatever you want in the back rooms. Do I even want to consider what that means?" she asked.

"You know you don't."

She conceded what he'd said with a nod before clicking her belt into place and then turning toward him. "Answer me this. If there are places like the Cellar, why would people need to break in to an abandoned motel without electricity? Why not just go in some back room set up for anything-goes trysts?"

He gave a small shrug. "Looking for even more privacy, an assurance that no one would interrupt?"

Or hear screams and respond. Only . . . in a place such as the Cellar, wouldn't screams be expected?

She let out a small grunt of agreement as she pictured the three dead bodies from the last crime scene, blood puddled around them.

"What's weird is that both Myrna Watts and Darius Finchem remarked on what a sweet guy Anthony Cruz was, despite his obvious problems. Doesn't seem like the way a guy who was looking to fulfill a pedo fantasy would be described." *A gentle soul.* Wasn't that what Myrna had called him?

"You don't always know people," Ambrose said. "Drugs warp people, and predators hide in plain sight."

"I guess. But those two don't seem like people who would be easily fooled. How could you be, working in a neighborhood like this?"

"You're also assuming it was the male in the scenario fulfilling the pedo fantasy. Maybe it was one of the women."

Lennon chewed on the inside of her cheek. *Sadly true.* She'd been thinking statistically, but making assumptions like that was a mistake in a murder investigation. "Any thoughts on the so-called miracle treatment Anthony Cruz mentioned to Myrna Watts?"

Ambrose shrugged. "Like she said, those looking for lifelines will grab for anything. The government funds a drug trial involving human subjects, people like Anthony Cruz are the first ones they go to."

"Those who need money and have a sketchy sense of body sovereignty?"

He nodded, his expression morose. "Yeah. Or it could have been hope based on nothing. Who knows what he was referring to." Ambrose gave her one last troubled look before he turned toward the window so she could no longer see his face.

CHAPTER EIGHT

Seventeen Years Ago
Patient Number 0022

Jett reached into his pocket and pulled out the pack of cigarettes, attempting to tap one into his hand before realizing the pack was empty. "Mother *fuck*."

Some dude had dropped the almost-full pack last night coming out of a bar, and Jett had been just a few steps behind him. He'd scooped it up, and the guy had been none the wiser.

A lucky son of a bitch. That was him.

Something rose in his chest that might have been laughter, except that most times, he had a hard time telling a laugh from a scream. He swallowed whatever it was down, not trusting his body to know the difference.

He'd seen an old homeless woman shrieking with laughter at a bus stop a few months before. People around her had looked terrified, giving her a wide berth as they walked by on the sidewalk. After a few minutes, her laughter had morphed into sobs and then wails, even though a smile still stretched across her cracked lips. Jett had watched her, feeling nothing except a vague understanding.

Eventually the woman had fallen asleep—or into a drug-induced stupor—and slunk to the ground in a heap. Jett had searched her pockets and come away with three crumpled dollars and some change. It wasn't enough to buy any dope, so he'd taken it to the McDonald's up the block. All the money would buy him was a hash brown that he wolfed down in two bites before opening the paper pack and licking the grease off the inside.

But now he had fifty bucks in his pocket from sitting on a velvet sofa and answering questions about his shitty life.

Physical or sexual?

Jett tripped on the curb, almost falling but catching himself. Something hot and acidic shot through his limbs, making them feel both energized and singed. He shuddered and stuck both hands in his pockets and then removed them almost as quickly. Maybe he'd call that interviewer dude and tell him he'd changed his mind. He didn't want that interview aired. But in any case, he'd answered the guy's questions and gotten paid for it. He needed some smack, and he had the money to buy it. A few droplets of relief cooled the inner burn. He could practically taste the illegal mix of chemicals that he'd snort or shoot the minute he had them in hand.

"Hey, Jett."

He turned to see a prostitute named Dawn, wearing a silver sequined dress that barely covered her crotch, wobbling toward him on her ridiculously high heels. "Wanna party?"

"No." He had no interest in what Dawn was offering, and he didn't have time for her bullshit either. He'd smoked with her a couple of times, and she'd gone on and on about how she got left some money from a relative and then had it stolen from her. She never stopped talking about that. She was like a broken record that just kept replaying the same fucked-up song over and over. It was boring as shit and gave him a headache.

What he wanted to tell her was that it didn't matter that someone had stolen her money. If that someone hadn't, she would have lost it anyway. People like them didn't know how to keep good things. That money never had a chance in hell of saving her or changing her life or whatever she imagined it might have done. People like them squandered anything of value. Knowing didn't help him change it, and he couldn't have even expressed those thoughts in words. But he knew it was true. He fucking did. And yet he still wanted. Still craved. And maybe if he'd have ever had anything of value and lost it, he'd be talking about it constantly too.

Jett picked up his speed, easily ditching Dawn, and turned the corner, onto the street where he knew he could score. A car backfired, and Jett startled, blood pressure spiking as he almost tripped again. A little boy in a faded red T-shirt appeared from behind a dumpster at the entrance to an alley. Jett sucked in a breath and jerked to a stop. *Oh no. Oh no.* The kid's eyes were glued to him, expression somber, as he walked toward the street where cars were whizzing by. Their eyes held, and Jett stood frozen, his muscles seized up. *No!* "No," Jett whispered, but he wasn't sure if he'd said the word or not. *No, no, no!* His nerves vibrated and then burst into flames. He yelped, and a woman walking by him on the street jumped aside and then hurried on.

The boy was almost at the curb, about to step into moving traffic. *No, please.* Jett flung himself forward and ran into the street, arms outstretched as a car swerved, brakes screeching, as Jett barely avoided being hit.

The world grew unbearably bright so that Jett could hardly see. His nerves flamed, scorching the underside of his skin, and he raised his arm to shield his eyes.

The little boy was walking toward him, too, and even from the distance and through the overwhelming brightness, Jett could see the tear rolling down his cheek and the purple marks around his neck.

A car came barreling forward, and Jett screamed as it hit the little boy, rolling him under its wheel and flipping the kid upside down like a rag doll. He landed on the street. Jett's scream continued as he went down next to the kid, attempting to pick him up as more brakes screeched and two cars collided next to him in a cacophony of intense impact and scraping metal.

"What the hell? What are you doing? Holy shit!" A man's voice. "Are you fucking crazy?"

Jett trembled so violently his teeth chattered, clutching the little boy's body. But then there was a hand on his arm, pulling him up. He reeled and stumbled, trying desperately to get his bearings as he held on to the boy. "The boy, the boy," he repeated, his voice a dusty whisper.

"What boy? There's no boy, you goddamned nut."

Jett gasped, squeezing tighter, realizing he was hugging only air. His arms dropped, an avalanche of ice joining the raging fire inside and yet somehow not extinguishing it. He froze and he burned. He was a frigid inferno. He needed rescuing, but there was no one to rescue him from himself. The world dimmed, sound rushing into the void around him.

"Call the police," someone said. "He's high. He's on something."

Jett gasped, stumbling back, looking around. So many eyes. There was no boy. He'd made him up, just like the doctor told him. But he wasn't on something. That was the problem. *Take your meds, take your meds, take your meds.* Or the voices come back. The boy comes back.

But it was Sunday, so the free clinic was closed anyway. And even if it wasn't, he didn't want medication that made his face, hands, and feet jerk and move constantly, so that he felt like jumping off a bridge to make it stop. At least the dope he acquired on the street made him drift away. It stopped his pain, didn't make it worse.

But he'd go to the clinic when the smack was gone. He would. He would. Because despite the side effects of the medication, he didn't want to see the boy. It bent his brain. It hurt so fucking bad.

The people were all staring at him. He took another step back. He wouldn't let them put him in jail. He knew what happened there, and he'd die before he'd be locked up. At least on the street he could curl up and hide. He could sleep behind the rusted, junked car next to the abandoned strip mall, or under the ivy growing along the chain-link fence near the old motel used mostly by prostitutes and their tricks. The one where he sometimes heard screams from the girls that no one answered, including him.

"Get your fucking hands off of me," he growled to the man whose hand gripped his upper arm. Whatever was in his voice made the man step back. Behind him, another man was helping a woman out of her car. She looked dazed as she scooted past her deflating airbag.

Jett glanced back once to ensure the little boy wasn't actually there, lying in a puddle of blood on the street as people stepped over him. But the asphalt was clear except for some broken pieces of headlight, not a drop of blood in sight.

Help, he heard, the voice young and weak. He shook his head, moving it rapidly from side to side, searching. There was no boy, but yet he'd heard him. He was somewhere. Somewhere.

He's inside your head, Jett. You have to take your medicine. You have to remember.

Dawn was standing on the sidewalk, swaying slightly in her spiked heels, her thumb in her mouth.

A siren grew louder in the distance, and the sound propelled Jett forward, out of the street and back onto the curb.

"Hey, you can't just leave," the man who'd held his arm said. "You caused this. This is your fault. Get back here!"

But Jett didn't listen. Jett ran, clutching the cash in his pocket, the money that would buy him at least a few minutes of peace.

CHAPTER NINE

Ambrose added a packet of sugar to the paper cup of coffee and took a sip, relaxing his shoulders as the hot liquid slid down his throat. The case files for the crime they'd been at two days before, including the two similar cases involving the dead men and woman who'd once lived on the streets, were sitting in the center of his desk. He didn't want to appear too eager to read them. He set them aside as he put his cup down in front of him and took a seat.

He and Lennon had driven over to Geary Boulevard after leaving the youth drop-in center. But there had only been a couple of bedraggled prostitutes, and they'd both snatched up the money Lennon had offered, looked at the photo of the woman named Cherish, shook their heads, and turned away. Maybe he'd go back later on his own, once the night-life started and the line of cars with men looking for a quick-and-dirty hookup started forming.

If nothing panned out there, he'd head over to the Cellar, where women let others use them to play their perverted games. The TL was a fantasyland for sickos looking to take advantage of those dissociated from their bodies. What easy victims they were. The same could be said of many other neighborhoods throughout the country. And the world too. He'd been all over at this point, and perverts came in all colors and creeds.

He pulled the case files toward him, flipped open the top one, and began reading through the evidence. Twenty minutes later, he had a more detailed picture of the first two crime scenes.

At the first scene, three months before, hallucinogens had been found in the abandoned building, next to the bodies of a man and a woman who were almost certainly homeless. Those two had gone at each other with their fists and fingernails, and at first glance, it appeared that the bloody scene was simply a case of a bad drug trip that had caused them to claw each other's faces and then stab each other to death. And though there had been plenty of blood on both victims' hands, no murder weapons had been found. Originally, it was surmised that perhaps another individual had come along and stolen the murder weapon or weapons. But it was strange that the drugs hadn't also been stolen.

Then again, Ambrose thought, if the person who came upon a scene like that had any wits about them, they'd want no part of a substance that made you behave the way those two had.

The second case, a month ago, was similar to the first. Two homeless men had been found in a clearing in a park, the weird concoction of hallucinogens on the ground next to their bloody bodies. The medical examiner had determined they'd likely used a knife, or knives, on each other. But again, no weapons were found.

In both cases, no IDs had been made. Four people who had once frequented the streets in one neighborhood or another had disappeared, and no one had even noticed.

A heaviness pressed on his chest. The crimes described in the case files in front of him and the one he'd been at two days before had happened in three different neighborhoods, miles apart. And yet, the case had still come back to the TL. He wasn't completely surprised. Something inside had known, hadn't it? That's why he was here. But he was even more unsettled than he'd been before. He—*they*—had to figure out what was going on. And if it was related to what he thought it was, they'd need to take care of it in whatever way necessary.

But he had a few leads, and he had the case files, so he'd acquired what he'd come here for. He could leave now, or he could stay and potentially collect even more. Because he had a strong feeling that whatever was going on had just gotten started.

Lennon came back into the room, where their desks sat next to each other, holding her own cup of coffee and sipping it as she walked slowly toward him.

She stopped to chat with a woman police inspector, bending forward slightly as she laughed. He didn't like lying to her. He didn't like lying in general, but especially to her. She acted sort of tough, but there was something vulnerable about her, something that told him maybe she'd been hurt. It was in the way she'd gazed at the people they'd passed, who were obviously suffering, on the streets of San Francisco. She was empathetic. She cared about others. Then again, maybe that didn't have anything to do with something from her past. Maybe some people just came by that naturally.

Every once in a while, he still questioned his own assumptions, questioned what was innate under natural circumstances and what had to be learned in most. *Practice knowing,* a wise man had once told him. *Everything you need to know is inside of you,* he'd said, tapping Ambrose's chest as though all life's knowledge, his path, from beginning to end, were written on scrolls contained between his ribs. Or at least that's what Ambrose liked to picture. It was all there, just inside, pressed against the underside of his skin. *It's just been covered up for a long time. So it will take practice. But it's a worthwhile effort. Practice knowing.*

And so he did. And one of those scrolls had told him that the crimes being committed here had everything to do with people he loved. Those imagined scrolls told him before he arrived that someone knew things they shouldn't know, and now he had the evidence to back it up.

"Hey, Mars," he heard from behind him and turned around. Lieutenant Byrd stood there, jacket on, briefcase in hand, obviously on his way out of the station. "I haven't received your paperwork yet."

Shit. His time here was ticking, and fast. "Really? Okay, I'll call over and see what the holdup is."

Byrd gave a nod and then raised his hand at the rest of the people working nearby and disappeared around the corner. Ambrose let out a long breath.

Lennon sat down in her chair as two officers came in, one stopping in front of the desk of the same female inspector Lennon had just been talking to. The other officer took a seat at an empty desk and bent his neck one way and then another.

"What's up with you, Brymer?" Lennon asked.

"Sore as hell. I've been directing traffic for six hours. A woman jumped off the Golden Gate Bridge this morning." He resumed stretching for a moment. "Shit. Who wakes up and decides to jump off a fuckin' bridge?" He ran his hand over his buzz cut. "I'll tell you who. Someone fucked in the head. You agree with that, Mars?"

Ambrose's eyes moved slowly to Brymer. The guy was hoping to rile him or annoy him or test him or whatever he was doing, for some reason that Ambrose wasn't even going to try to figure out. Maybe the guy was bored. Maybe he was annoyed that he'd had to do a job he thought beneath him because someone had decided to end their life on his watch. "Fucked in the head seems like as good a diagnosis as any," Ambrose said.

Brymer huffed out a laugh, assuming incorrectly that Ambrose agreed with him. "It's gotta be attention, right? To wanna go that way? You can't just off yourself in your bathroom, you gotta jam up traffic for hours, make a spectacle. A big, grand exit where a dozen people have a ringside seat."

Ambrose glanced at Lennon to see her staring at Brymer. "Yeah, attention whores are the worst, aren't they, Brymer?"

"Sure are," Brymer said, either ignoring her sarcasm or missing it completely. "Gotta make everyone else suffer for your issues."

"Shut up, dude," the other cop snapped. The name on his name tag said **C. Kennedy.** "Those people are suffering. My take? It's not about attention so much as certainty. You down a buncha pills or, hell, even cut your wrists and it might not work. Someone could find you, pump your stomach, bandage you up. But jumping off a bridge? You're guaranteed to die, and quick."

"Not true." Several heads turned toward Ambrose, including Lennon's. "Thirty-five people have survived that particular jump," he said, his gaze meeting Lennon's. "In 2000, there was a nineteen-year-old kid who attempted to commit suicide there." He leaned back in his chair. "The second he went over that rail, he realized he'd made a horrible mistake." Ambrose paused, looking at each of them in turn. "He hit the water headfirst at seventy-five miles per hour, four seconds later, shattering three sections of his vertebrae. He was alive, but he couldn't move his legs. And in those four seconds, as he'd plunged toward the water, he'd realized he wanted to live."

Lennon stared, lips parted as though she was semimesmerized. He liked that look on her face. Soft. It was soft. She'd lowered her guard completely, and all it had taken was a story. *She cares. Her empathy is so obvious.* And he liked that about her. It was rare. "What happened then?" she asked softly.

"He felt a bump beneath him," Ambrose said. He bounced on his chair as though something were headbutting him from the seat, and Lennon gave a minuscule start. "Something was in the water."

"Holy shit, a shark," he heard Kennedy say.

Ambrose shook his head. "No. At first that's what he thought, too, but it wasn't a shark. It was a sea lion, and that sea lion bumped him again, and then again. It kept him afloat—kept him alive—by bumping him repeatedly so he didn't go under, until a rescue boat showed up."

Lennon tipped her head, her eyes still holding a vague sense of wonder. "Is that a true story?"

"Yeah."

"Where'd you hear it?"

Ambrose shrugged. "I don't remember. But it stayed with me. It reminds me that some things can't be explained."

Her eyes hung on his. "And you like that? For a man whose job it is to find answers, that's somewhat surprising."

"I think it's important to be able to determine when answers are necessary and when they're not."

She appeared to think about that for a moment. "Anyway, it's a good story."

He gave her a half tilt of his lips. "In the end, all we have are stories."

She chewed on the inside of her cheek as she regarded him. "Tough ending on that bridge today," she said after a moment.

"Yes," he agreed, looking over at Brymer, who yawned and stood up. "It was."

"Well," Brymer said, "if story time is over, I'm gonna get back to work. See ya."

The cops left the room, and Ambrose turned in his chair and pulled the case files toward him. He needed to find a moment when he could make copies of everything, so if he had to leave in a hurry, he'd have what the cops had. Those files were why he was here. The cops didn't know to look for certain things. He did. The specifics about the pills. The swollen eyes. The silent screams.

"You're a good storyteller," Lennon said. He looked up to see her smiling at him.

"Thanks."

Their gazes caught for a beat longer than he would have allowed his eyes to remain held to someone else's, and he felt a small internal hiccup of concern. He was attracted to her, this homicide inspector who didn't strike him as a cop of any rank. He'd told himself he wasn't interested in romantic or even sexual relationships—simpler that way, fewer entanglements—but apparently his biology hadn't quite gotten the memo. But it didn't matter if he found her attractive. Nothing could happen between them. He broke eye contact and opened the files on his desk. From his peripheral vision, he saw her begin shuffling through her paperwork, too, the moment between them over.

And suddenly he wasn't so concerned about the fact that his time here at this department was limited. Suddenly it seemed crucial that it end as soon as possible.

A woman he hadn't met yet leaned in the wide door. "The assistant chief is making a stop here in about thirty," she said. "I hear it's just a morale boost—and a nod to all you poor saps who have to work Thanksgiving."

She saluted and turned as someone called out, "Is she even bringing us a turkey?"

"Why? Your mother won't save you some meat?" the woman called back.

"There's a sick joke in there somewhere," one of the cops said. "But I'm too innocent to figure it out."

Thanksgiving. He'd forgotten it was a holiday. Not only because they'd been working this morning and afternoon but because the places they'd visited had been open too. Now all the references to dinner made more sense. The fact that he'd forgotten made him feel sort of pitiful. He had zero plans. Not that any of his friends in town even knew he was here—he hadn't contacted any of them yet. His family? They never cared. So what did it matter? It was just another day. He didn't need a specific date to remember what he was thankful for.

Anyone from the chief's office stopping by might be a problem, though. "I'm gonna get out of here," he told Lennon, standing and putting on his jacket.

Her head came up. "Oh. Yeah. Of course. Me, too, actually. My parents are expecting me." She tilted her head. "Are you staying with your family while you're apartment hunting?"

"No, a hotel," he answered.

"Ugh, apartment hunting. Good luck with that," the woman inspector whose name he couldn't remember said as she took a seat at her desk to his left. "The housing market here is a shit show. You're better off commuting." While Lennon was looking away, he slipped the files into his briefcase.

"She's not wrong," Lennon said with a sigh. "Where are you looking?"

"I don't know yet." He gave her a close-lipped smile. "Happy Thanksgiving, Lennon."

She didn't smile back. Instead her expression was mildly worried. "Happy Thanksgiving, Ambrose."

~

"Dammit." What the hell was going on with all the Ubers? He'd been around the corner from the station for thirty minutes now, trying to get a ride, and still none had come available. Did people like turkey that much?

He'd watched the assistant chief's car, followed by several other city vehicles, drive by about five minutes before and heard them stop in front of the station. He'd expected to be long gone by now.

A raindrop hit his cheek, and he looked up at the cloudy sky, a few more splashing over his cheeks before they began to fall in earnest. *Great.* He brought his briefcase close to his body, and shielded his phone as he looked back down at his app. Still nothing.

Ambrose stepped backward into a doorway on the side of the building so he could search Google for a cab company, which he should have done fifteen minutes ago. The rainfall increased, splashing up from the sidewalk and hitting his khakis. A car slowed and then came to a stop at the curb in front of where he stood, and the passenger-side window rolled down. Lennon leaned over the seat, peering out at him. "Are you okay?"

"Yeah," he called. "I'm fine. Just . . . no Ubers. I'm gonna call a cab. I'm good, really. Have a nice holiday."

She nodded, sitting straight as the passenger-side window rolled up. She pulled away from the curb, and Ambrose watched as her brake lights went on and she reversed back to where she'd just been. She got out of her car, an umbrella blossoming over her as she splashed through the puddles to where he stood. She looked sort of hesitant and a little shy as she said, "You said you were from here, so I assumed your family still lives in the city? But you're not staying with them, so maybe—"

"My family and I are . . . estranged, so . . ."

"I'm sorry."

He shrugged. "Sometimes it's for the best."

She gave a single nod. "Do you have plans for dinner, Ambrose?"

He felt embarrassed and was tempted to lie to her, but he'd already told her too many lies, and he didn't like it. And so he answered truthfully. "I was going to stop and get a pizza and bring it to my hotel room."

"That sounds very sad."

He laughed, but it quickly turned into a sigh. It did sound sad, but he'd experienced things much sadder than that, and so it didn't bother him as much as it might have bothered her or anyone else who'd never spent a holiday alone. As for him? It was far from the first, and it wouldn't be the last.

She glanced up the street and then back at him, and he had this weird feeling of déjà vu, standing on this rainy street with this woman, half under a doorway, the umbrella she was holding creating this strange feeling of intimacy that felt both electric and dreamlike. After a moment she blurted out, "Would you like to join me? At my parents' house?" She held up her hand. "Before you answer, I have to warn you: my family, they're a whole situation. You'd have to prepare yourself. My mom was a flower child in the seventies, and she never quite moved on. She'll definitely find a reason to foist some herbal concoction on you. And my dad, well there's this comet or something or another tonight, and so he'll be nerding out with his microscope."

"Telescope."

"Telescope. Right. Yes. Well, there you go. He'll consider you far more of an asset than me."

She seemed to be breathing at an increased rate, and he wasn't sure if it was because of the number of words she'd just spoken. But the idea that she also might be nervous and feel that same dreamy electricity he did was what propelled him to say, "Yes. Thanks. I'd love to join you for dinner. But . . . I don't have anything to bring."

"It's okay. I already dropped off a couple of pies a few days ago, and my mom has plenty of food. Trust me, they'll be thrilled by another guest. They used to live on a commune. For them, it'll be like the good ol' days."

He laughed as they turned and ducked through the rain to her car.

CHAPTER TEN

The man wearing the hoodie walked around a handful of orange-capped needles, fisting his hands in his pockets as he made his way past the tents.

Disgusting animals.

Worse than animals. Even animals knew better than to shit where they ate. Instead, San Francisco now had a "poop map," where all the many locations of human waste had been reported. *Foul.*

Why should anyone have to put up with that?

Why were clean, decent people made to live among human filth?

They were taking over the city, using it as a public restroom. Making it stink, spreading disease, causing stores to close their doors and relocate to places where poop maps didn't exist. And who could blame them? Hollowing out once-vibrant neighborhoods and replacing tourists with rats and tents and sewage.

And as if their revolting existence weren't enough, they were also criminals who would put a knife in your neck for the twenty-dollar shoes you had on your feet if given the chance.

Who knew that better than he did?

A bolt of pure rage boiled his blood.

Completely irredeemable.

How many treatment centers were there? How many do-gooders? How many handouts and freebies? How many government programs? The geniuses who ran the city had even deemed it "kindness" to supply addicts all the needles they could ever want, for fuck's sake. What a sick joke. And when the druggies ran out of free needles, the clinics would gladly give them more so they could shoot their drugs into their veins and leave the disease-ridden evidence lying on the sidewalk for school-children to step over. Or get poked by.

He would have supported supplying free needles if it ensured more overdoses. But no. When the fuckers overdosed, they were given Narcan or naloxone and revived just so they could suck more money out of honorable citizens, whether through taxes or theft.

Even the police had given up. You might be mugged right in front of a precinct, and the cops would just stand around, watching. Even if one or two of them wanted to do something, their hands were tied by laws and do-nothing DAs and citizens salivating to pull out their cell phone and catch them manhandling a mental.

Leeches. But at least leeches had a purpose. These people had no purpose. They did nothing worthwhile. They caused only harm. Only sickness.

And they fucked like rabbits, popping out one kid after another, all of them showing up drug addicted and damaged. Yet another drain on society, the cycle repeating with each new worthless generation.

Parasites. Yes, that's what they were. They did nothing except feed off others. Infecting and depleting. They had to be dealt with, or they'd consume society. No one was willing to do what really needed to be done—a mass extermination—even though, deep down, most knew everyone would be better off. They just didn't want to say it out loud, because then they'd be labeled *intolerant.*

The diseased perverts didn't *just* need to die, though; they needed to be punished for the harm they'd already caused. They needed to be gone, yes. But they shouldn't get off scot-free.

He'd pretended to be a user a few times and "shared" his goods—what had really been a lethal dose of fentanyl—with a couple of obvious addicts and watched them die. The ingredients necessary to make the deadly concoction had been far simpler to obtain than he'd thought they would be. He could easily make more. But that hadn't been satisfying, because the addicts had just peacefully drifted off to sleep. No pain, none of the suffering they deserved. Still, he'd killed a few others. An overdose here, an overdose there. A few knifings, too, which he'd found he enjoyed far more. Just street crimes where no one blinked an eye. There were pages and pages of unnamed victims on police websites. If you wanted, you could scroll for hours.

Sometimes he'd stay and watch the ambulance arrive to cart away the bodies of those he'd killed. And no one had been any the wiser that their death was more than a simple overdose or a gang retaliation. The police were probably happy to have one fewer criminal on the streets. But other than that? Mostly unsatisfying. And once their body had been removed, another one was quickly sprawled in the space they'd vacated.

But then he'd come up with an idea, and he'd *known* how he could make them suffer—and suffer in the most nightmarish way they could imagine. Because after all, it was their nightmares he was after. And now he knew precisely how to make those come to life.

The sun was lowering, and soon the sickos would all crawl from their hidey-holes to suck and fuck and terrorize the community. But not all of them, not for long. He was taking care of that. One by two, by three and four.

He kicked aside a pile of needles and watched them fly, whistling as he passed the last grungy tent on the block and turned the corner.

CHAPTER ELEVEN

Ambrose took a deep breath as he watched Lennon twist the knob and open the door of her family home. "Mom?" she called. "Your door is unlocked again." Her expression was perturbed as they both entered the foyer, and she began taking off her jacket. Ambrose followed her lead, hanging his coat beside hers on the coatrack just inside the door. It'd stopped raining as they drove here, and the heat in Lennon's car had ensured they were dry enough that they weren't dripping all over the floor. "Mom?" she called again, shutting the door and engaging the lock.

As with many homes in San Francisco, they had climbed a high set of steps to make it from the street to the front door, and there was another set in front of them that led from the small foyer up into the house. He followed Lennon upstairs, and as they reached the upper landing, an older woman in an apron came bustling down the hall. "Hello, sweetheart. Oh, hello. Ambrose. A strong name, and now I see it's for a strong man. Welcome to our home. Happy Thanksgiving!"

"Hello, Mrs. Gray. Thank you for having me."

"Oh, we're thrilled to have you! And please call me Natalie."

"Happy Thanksgiving. Mom, your door was unlocked," Lennon said. She still looked at least a little distressed, and Ambrose sensed whatever was going on with her insistence on locking the door might not be about a door at all.

"Oh, was it? Oh dear. Sorry, honey. I told your father to be more careful about that, but you know how he is. His mind is always on a hundred different things. Follow me. I have drinks waiting in here."

"Mom, you've gotta remind him. This neighborhood is safe, but you never know."

"You're right, sweetheart, of course. Believe me, I can't even watch the news anymore or I'll be so worried about you." They entered a large open kitchen with a deck off the back that overlooked a tiny fenced-in yard featuring rows of raised planting boxes. Lights glowed throughout the space, and even in the brief glance Ambrose gave it, he saw the myriad of pinwheels and tall in-ground bird feeders and other garden decor placed in the corners of the boxes.

The kitchen itself wasn't fancy, but it was warm and inviting, with tall oak cabinetry and a stove that looked like it was original to the Victorian house. "But," Mrs. Gray said, "it's wonderful what you both do for a living. I feel better and worse about it, because so many out there *need* you, and there you are." She brought her hands together. "Saint Ambrose, the Bishop of Milan. He donated all of his land and gave his money to the poor. And because of it, he was widely beloved and had more political power than the emperor," she stated.

"You looked up my name?" Ambrose asked, feeling charmed by the gesture—and the fact that she must have done it in the last twenty minutes, since Lennon called from the car and told her she was bringing a coworker to dinner at the last minute.

"Please have a seat," she said. "I did look up your name."

"Mom, really, you're something," Lennon said. Her cheeks had taken on a slight tinge of pink, but her eyes were warm, and she seemed more relaxed than he'd seen her thus far. Though that might not be surprising considering he'd mostly seen her standing at murder scenes and in rooms of hardened cops. Softness, playfulness even . . . those traits seemed to come far easier to her than the stoic detachment she'd attempted—somewhat unconvincingly—amid crime and death. He had this feeling she considered it a weakness. But to Ambrose, it made her even more attractive than he'd found her to be before she'd even said a word.

"Thank you, sweetheart," Lennon's mother said. "Names are very important. They're our first story."

"Ah. See, Ambrose. You have something in common. Ambrose likes stories too." Lennon smiled at him, and his stomach dipped, then rose. He felt slightly shy as he smiled back at her. Her head tipped minutely as her gaze hung on him, and then she looked away.

"A widely beloved bishop who served his people well," he repeated. Even he had never thought to look up his own name. Come to think of it, he had no idea where it'd come from. "Those are big shoes to fill."

"Indeed they are." Mrs. Gray smiled. "Your mother must have had big dreams for you."

Doubtful. But he hardly wanted to discuss the mother who'd been absent most of his life. "Where does *Lennon* come from?" he asked.

Mrs. Gray turned, bringing her hands together and pulling in a breath, as though she was about to share her favorite story of all. "I named her after John Lennon, one of the great peacemakers of our time. So see, together you're the peacemaker and the emperor."

"Sorry," Lennon mouthed to him, rolling her eyes. But Ambrose couldn't help smiling. He was enthralled by this family, and he'd only met two members so far.

"Anyway, I've made a batch of sangria, and it's quite lovely, if I do say so myself. I used the singular orange from my orange tree, so does that make it extra special?" She laughed. "I think so. I'll call this batch 'Lonely Orange.' It has a ring to it."

"'*Only* Orange' would be better," Lennon said.

"Oh, you're right. I do love a good alliteration. Can I make you a glass of Only Orange, Ambrose?"

"Uh, thank you, Mrs. Gray, but I don't drink."

"Oh! Well that's lovely too. Water? I would have made some fresh-squeezed orange juice but, well, the one orange and all."

Ambrose smiled. "I'll take a water. Thank you."

"Where's Dad?" Lennon asked as she gestured to a chair on the other side of the large well-worn wood table. Ambrose sat down, and Lennon took a seat across from him.

Mrs. Gray set a glass of water in front of him, a thin slice of lemon on the rim. His eyes held on that lemon wedge, and his heart gave a knock for some unknown reason. No, he did know the reason. Not counting food servers, no one in his life had ever put a lemon wedge on his glass of water. And it . . . touched him. Silly, maybe, but there it was. "Your dad's fixing something on the telescope in the garage," Lennon's mom said. "He'll be up in a few minutes."

The sound of the front door opening and closing could be heard from downstairs, and then the clomping of feet as a male voice called out, "Hello? Anyone home?"

"In here," Lennon called. She stood as a young man who looked a little like Lennon but had darker coloring entered the room. Ambrose assumed it was her brother.

"Hey, squirt."

Lennon's cheeks flushed, and she pushed at him when he rubbed his knuckle on her hair. "Are you kidding me?" she hissed. "Peter, this is my *work* colleague, Ambrose Mars, from the Federal Bureau of Investigation," she said, enunciating the words. She looked at Ambrose and gave him a tight smile and then muttered under her breath, "I knew this was a bad idea."

Peter, who had just handed his mother a bottle of wine and was now taking a beer from the fridge, stood straight and raised the bottle to Ambrose. "No shit? Man, do you want a—"

"Ambrose doesn't drink," Mrs. Gray said, turning from the sink with a colander of vegetables in her hand that she placed on the opposite counter. "Another lemon, dear? I do have plenty of those. And they flush toxins."

"Why would you assume Ambrose needs to flush toxins?" Peter asked. "He doesn't even drink."

"In this world? Everyone needs to flush toxins," Mrs. Gray said.

"Speak for yourself." Peter plopped into the chair at the head of the table. "So, the FBI's really getting a bad rap these days, huh?" Peter took a swig of his beer. "Rightly so, in my opinion. Nothing personal. The rot is at the top."

"Peter!" Mrs. Gray said. "Stop causing controversy at the dinner table."

"You love controversy at the dinner table," he said. "And it's not a dinner table at the moment. But in any case, you've always said mild-mannered conversations never get at the heart of a topic."

She grinned. "It is true. But Ambrose might need to be broken in slowly."

"It's okay," Ambrose said. "I don't take it personally. The public should be able to trust institutions. Eventually most of them end up in service to themselves. It's just the nature of the beast."

"Damn, I actually might like this guy," Peter said. "And agreed. So what should be done about that?"

"Outside checks and balances."

"What if the checks and balances are captured by the institutions they're supposed to be keeping accountable?"

Ambrose took a sip of his water. "Then you have to burn the whole system down and start again."

Peter laughed. "Now I definitely know I like this guy."

Ambrose smiled. "What do you do, Peter?"

"I assess the security posture of companies. Which basically means I monitor network vulnerabilities and gaps in security controls."

"Which *basically* means he's a supernerd," Lennon offered, giving her brother a grin that held far more pride than the mocking Ambrose thought she'd shot for and missed by a country mile.

"Everyone makes fun of us supernerds until they need us," Peter said. "And trust me, if you're doing anything worthwhile, that day always comes."

They heard feet ascending a set of steps somewhere, and then a man walked through a door at the back of the kitchen that Ambrose had thought might be to a pantry but must be to the steps to the garage. A pug-dog scampered in with him, beelining for Ambrose.

"We're going to have to take turns with the telescope," Lennon's dad was saying. "I can't get the other one to work. Oh! Lennon, you're here. Peter. And this must be Ambrose, the FBI agent. Happy Thanksgiving. Thanks for joining us."

"Happy Thanksgiving, sir. Thank you for having me."

The dog started barking, trotting under the table, where he latched on to the side of Ambrose's leg and began humping it with gusto.

"Hi, Dad—"

"Freddie, Jesus," Peter said, tilting his head as he watched Ambrose trying to unlatch the dog. "Mom, your horny dog is humping the guest's leg again."

"Oh dear. Freddie! No!"

Everyone started scrambling around the table, Lennon's chair grating over the floor as she practically jumped to her feet. Mrs. Gray bent and wrapped her hands around Freddie's midsection and began pulling, Mr. Gray leaning under her and unwrapping the dog's front legs. Freddie was barking and humping, and everyone was yelling at it, and Ambrose was trying hard to hold back the hilarity that threatened. Because it felt like just moments ago, he'd been standing in the rain trying unsuccessfully to get an Uber, and now he was in the middle of this unfamiliar kitchen, the entire family shouting and trying to pull their dog off his leg. It was . . . surreal.

Mr. Gray finally managed to remove the dog, and he turned with it and headed toward the doors to the deck. "It's just his instinct," Mrs. Gray said. "You must smell good." She leaned forward. "Oh, you do smell good."

"Mom! Oh my God," Lennon said, sinking back down into her chair and putting her face in her hands. "I'm so sorry."

"What?" Mrs. Gray asked as she returned to the stove. "That's a compliment. You don't want to smell good?" Mr. Gray came back in after delivering Freddie down into the backyard to do his thing on whatever inanimate object he might find. "Honey," Mrs. Gray said. "Come help me take the Tofurky out of the oven."

Lennon looked up at him. "You didn't think it could get worse, did you?"

But Ambrose only grinned.

~

The Tofurky turned out to be even worse than he'd thought it would be, but the sides were some of the best food he'd ever had. He watched the family interact with each other, and he could feel the affection in the room. These people not only loved each other; they genuinely enjoyed one another as well. He allowed himself to bask in it, even if it wasn't his. It was how the world should be. It was what everyone should have. And though he had no real right to be here, he was glad he was, because it was a reminder of why he did the work he did. This was the point.

After he and Lennon helped clear the table and Mrs. Gray booted them out of the kitchen, Lennon led him out to the deck, where the sky was already dark. "I hope you don't mind staying another half an hour," she said. "My dad will be heartbroken if we don't watch his comet."

"I don't mind."

The rain had stopped, but this deck space had a fabric covering over it and so only the edge still held some evidence of the rain. He heard the other three Grays still inside having a robust debate about something and glanced at Lennon. "Bitcoin," she explained with a roll of her eyes. He chuckled, and they both sat down on deck chairs situated near the back of the house.

"There's a piano in the living room," he said. "Who plays?"

"Oh. Me. I mean, I used to, but it's been years. I've probably forgotten how to by now. They should get rid of it. It's just collecting dust."

Ambrose wasn't the least bit surprised by the fact that she'd once played piano proficiently enough that her family had bought one. He also knew she hadn't forgotten, but it confirmed for him that she didn't realize she still played when she was deep in thought. So why had she convinced herself she no longer knew notes that were obviously muscle memory? He kept trying to form a picture of Lennon and then learned something else that threw off his assumptions.

She was a puzzle. But a good one, one he could tell by the outline he was going to like. But the vital parts remained mysterious. He kept wanting to go back and add pieces.

They'd put their jackets on to come out here, but the night was cold, and he crossed his arms against the chill. Lennon leaned over and opened the lid to a deck box and removed a couple of blankets and tossed one his way. She brought her legs up under her and wrapped the blanket around her, and he placed his over his lap. The wind chimes from the garden below tinkled in the slight breeze, and something pleasant met his nose from a nearby pot. "It's peaceful out here," he said. "And something smells good."

"Rosemary," she said, nodding to the potted plants. "And sage. My mom will burn some over you to drive out negative energy, if you want her to."

He chuckled. "Negative energy? What is that exactly?"

She appeared to think about the question. "I don't know. I was never given a definition."

"Well, it doesn't sound good, so I'm glad your mom has a remedy."

She let out a breathy laugh. "Me too." The wind chimes rang softly again. "But yes, this is a peaceful spot. I used to come out here in the mornings before high school and drink my coffee." Something passed over her face that he couldn't read in the dim light of the deck. Another one of those puzzle pieces that didn't yet fit anywhere. "Of course, the world in general was more peaceful then. Ignorance is bliss and all that."

He smiled. "It's important for people who do jobs like ours to seek out moments of peace." It was a sort of remedy, too, against getting sucked into the whirl of wickedness they confronted on a regular basis.

Her eyes held on him a moment before she let out an agreeable hum. "Those are hard to find." She regarded him for a moment longer. "What was the last truly peaceful moment you can think of?" she asked.

She seemed to be hanging on his answer, and so he took a moment to really think about that. Then he blew a small gust of air, his breath appearing in front of him in a ring of white vapor. "About a year ago, on a cold morning in South America," he said, "I watched a songbird's breath whirl and rise in front of him as he sang. It was the most beautiful thing I ever saw." He'd not only heard the melody being sung by that bird; he'd seen it, too, dancing through the air and then dissipating along with the notes. In his house, religion had been drummed into him from birth, used to shame and punish, but he'd never once felt the grace of God until that moment in an Argentine dawn. And when he doubted the underlying goodness of the universe—which was more often than he wished it were—he brought that ephemeral yet deeply poignant moment to mind.

Lennon had leaned her head back on the chair and was watching him, her expression soft. "South America," she murmured. "Why were you there?"

He looked away. *Damn.* He kept telling these stories that set him up to lie to her, and he regretted it. He had to lie often in his line of work, and he usually did it with ease, because he knew well the end justified the means. But with Lennon . . . well, he didn't like furthering falsehoods. Especially sitting on her family's deck after being welcomed for dinner in their home. It made him feel low. "Just traveling," he said.

"Where else have you been?"

"All over. I like to travel when I have time. What about you?"

"Me?" She played with the edge of her blanket. "I've never been out of the country." He detected an almost imperceptible cringe. "But someday . . . I'd like to see the pyramids." She smiled, and their eyes met, and he allowed his gaze to linger on her expression, dreamy and soft, so different from the pinched way she sometimes held her face at work. She'd opened her mouth to say something, when the sliding glass door opened, bringing Ambrose from his reverie.

They both looked up as her dad came through the doors, a telescope under one arm and a bowl of popcorn in his hand. "We should be able to see the comet any minute," he said. "You two check if you can see anything while I get the drinks." He set the bowl of popcorn down and handed the telescope to Lennon.

Lennon smiled over at Ambrose and then got up and extended her hand. He grasped it, and she pulled him up. "Let's see if this comet has anything at all on that songbird," she said.

She set the telescope on the wide deck railing and then leaned forward, squinting through the lens. "I don't see a comet, but the stars look pretty fantastic through this," she murmured. "Check it out."

Ambrose did, squinting like she'd done and gazing through the eyepiece. The sky opened up in front of him, the stars glittery and plentiful, and for a brief moment, he felt like he was floating among them. "Wow," he said, turning his head slightly to look at her. She was so close, and again, their eyes held. It was slightly awkward, but he also didn't want it to end.

"You do smell good," she said, giving him a teasing smile.

He laughed, and they both stood straight. Ambrose tipped his head and looked up at the stars he'd just been up close and personal with, thinking how much wonder there was in the world. How much beauty and how much cruelty.

When he looked over at Lennon, she was gazing up at the night sky too. "I can't see the stars very well from my apartment," she said. "But I have a pretty decent view of the city. Sometimes I sit out there and think about how beautiful it looks from far away, all sparkly and still. And then I remember what's actually happening in those little pockets of darkness."

Little pockets of darkness. She looked at him, and he nodded. She was right, and he'd been thinking about that darkness too. But he'd also been thinking about the pockets of hope, and tonight was one. It had been such a simple, beautiful night surrounded by the chatter and laughter of a close-knit family. He'd had so few of those, and though it wasn't his to keep, he knew he'd hold the memory close forever, the same way he did that cold January morning in a country where he'd gone to hunt down a predator.

Later, after he'd said goodbye to Mr. and Mrs. Gray and Peter, Lennon drove him to the hotel where he'd told her he was staying and pulled up in front. "Thanks for tonight," he said.

She smiled. "My family, they're a special case."

"They are. In a good way. I . . . had a really good time. Surprisingly."

She tilted her head. "You didn't expect to have a good time?"

"Not that good a time."

She laughed softly. "Okay. Well then, my utter humiliation was worth it."

He glanced out the window, up at the building next to them, and then back at her. "You're lucky." He wondered if she knew just how fortunate she was and thought she probably did. They were characters, but the love in that room was so bright, it'd practically blinded him.

"They're good for some comic relief anyway. Kind of a little break from murder and mayhem."

"A break is good. It keeps you sane."

"It does."

He paused, and there was a short moment of awkwardness before he said goodbye one last time and got out of her car. He watched as she waved and drove away, waiting until her car disappeared out of sight. And then Ambrose turned away from the hotel that he'd lied to Lennon about staying at and began walking in the opposite direction.

CHAPTER TWELVE

Seventeen Years Ago
Patient Number 0022

"Hi, I'm Dr. Sweeton. Please, have a seat. Can I get you something to drink?"

"Vodka," Jett murmured.

Dr. Sweeton smiled. "I'm afraid the strongest I have to offer is diet soda."

Jett let out a short snort. "Water then." He ran his hands over his thighs toward his knees, and then reversed course. The jean fabric felt rough on his palms. Painful. The doctor took a bottle of water from a minifridge near the window and brought it back to Jett. He wasn't thirsty, but it gave him something to do with his hands. Or maybe he was thirsty. Sometimes it was hard to tell. Sometimes all his physical needs ran together, creating a vast open hole of what he could only call hunger that he had no idea how to feed. But sometimes that same feeling came when he'd eaten and had water and was warm enough and gotten at least a few hours of sleep and even had some dope, and so he wondered if the need was something other than physical. Didn't matter. He could barely fulfill the demands of his body, much less needs far more vague.

Jett unscrewed the cap and took a long drink. The doctor observed him, but not in the way most doctors did—lips thinned, impatient expression, gaze constantly darting to the clock on the wall. The ones Jett had seen were used to dealing with junkies. Dr. Sweeton opened his chart and glanced over it. "You're on quite a few prescription medications," he noted. He closed the folder and set it aside. "But you're self-medicating, too, yes?"

Jett hesitated, but there was no disapproving tone in the doctor's voice. And Jett knew it was obvious he was a user anyway, so who cared? "Yeah."

The doctor leaned forward. "Tell me about the schizophrenia. What are your symptoms?"

Jett blew out a breath, capped the water, and set it aside. He wanted a smoke, but there was a NO SMOKING sign in the lobby of this building and right inside the door of the doctor's office too. He glanced at it and then away. "Hallucinations."

"Auditory or visual?"

He pictured the little boy, heard his voice and the way a strange bleating sound started up every time he saw him. "Both."

"Is there something specific you see, or does it vary?"

He picked up the water again, took a sip, dropped the cap, and set the open bottle aside. "I see a kid. A boy. He . . . he torments me. He runs into traffic or off buildings. He hides. But I feel him there all the time. I know he's not real, but it's like, he is. When I see him, I doubt myself and think he's real, and I have to save him or . . ." His breath came fast, heart clamoring.

"Or what?"

Jett ran his hand over his thighs again. "Or . . . I don't know. But something bad will happen. If I have to watch him die, something bad will happen."

The doctor sat back. "And other doctors have diagnosed you with schizophrenia based on that."

"Yeah. Uh-huh. What else? I'm not always trippin' when I see the kid. I've been totally sober."

"Does the prescription medication help?"

Jett shrugged. "I'm not great about taking it. It makes me jumpy and shit." He scratched the back of his neck. "Like I'm not already jumpy enough, you know?"

"Yes, Jett. I do know. I do."

And for whatever reason, Jett believed the guy, when he rarely believed people with letters behind their name. In his experience, they were the biggest liars. The most skillful con artists, when Jett had known a shitload of con artists in his life. And no doctor had ever helped him, either, on purpose or by accident. He'd never even gotten the feeling they really wanted to. Jett knew drug pushers. He relied on them. And those guys—those doctors—were some of the best. Even if, mostly, he didn't want the shit they were pushing.

"Thank you for coming to see me, Jett. It was nice meeting you at the clinic last week."

Jett scratched the back of his neck again, and then his elbow. Once the money he'd gotten from doing that interview was long gone, he'd spent three days suffering before deciding to walk over to the clinic for the prescription meds he was supposed to take. He'd met Dr. Sweeton, and the doctor had asked if he wanted to make some extra cash. Jett always wanted to make extra cash.

"You said you had some tests to run and that I'd get paid for them." He'd made money in similar ways before. He'd donated plasma, at least when he was clean enough that they'd take it. He'd done a questionnaire at the free clinic about needle usage. If they wanted to see how many holes were in his brain from drugs, or something like that, then why not let them? As long as he got cash, he'd be anyone's guinea pig. His body meant nothing to him. In fact, most of the time he wanted the hell *out* of it and hated living under his skin.

"Yes," the doctor said, "but the tests come with some strings attached. And a few questions. Nothing tricky, nothing dishonest. I promise to always be completely up front."

Completely up front. Jett had never known anyone to be completely up front. Everyone had an agenda, even if they didn't always know it.

It eventually came out, though, and usually sooner than later. "What kind of doctor are you?"

Dr. Sweeton smiled. "The talking kind."

"Talking doesn't mean shit. It never helped me before."

"I don't imagine it did. Talking can't help when your brain's all in knots."

Jett let out a strangled laugh. He'd never heard a description like that before, but that's exactly what his brain felt like. Like it was tied up in knots, and when he tried to untangle them, he just got confused and frustrated and it fucking *hurt*, and so ultimately he gave up. "That doesn't sound very doctor-ish."

The man smiled again. "I suppose I'm not always very doctor-ish in the traditional sense. But I've found that certain maladies require what some might consider extreme remedies."

His heart gave a knock. "Certain maladies?" What did that mean?

"Wouldn't you say you're sick?"

"I mean, yeah, because I'm a user."

"That's a symptom. It's not your illness."

"Okay, yeah, true. I've got mental shit going on, but there's no cure for that."

"I don't believe that's true, Jett."

He stared at the man, a feeling of . . . something opening inside him. Something small and fragile that he instinctively wanted to turn away from even before he'd fully identified it. "What type of extreme remedies are you talking about?" he asked. There had to be a hook here. Was this guy some wacko who was going to stick a needle through his eyeball and poke at his brain? *Do you care? Maybe it'd be a welcome escape.* And suddenly he craved it. He craved a needle piercing his brain so badly he briefly considered doing it himself and tucked it away as a possibility for later.

"I won't do anything you don't agree to," the doctor said. "There's quite a bit of testing involved, and some talking, but it's also a drug trial."

"A drug trial? What kind of drugs?"

"Hallucinogens mostly."

Jett was surprised by that. "Like magic mushrooms and shit?"

"There is some psilocybin usage," the doctor said. "All of that would be disclosed to you. You would have to agree to any and all of it. But that part would come second. First we'd need to make sure you're a good candidate for this treatment."

Jett ran his palms over his jeans again, the contact once more bringing him pain, but a pain he craved in some odd way. "Sure, okay, what the fuck. Sign me up."

The doctor smiled; it started slowly and then widened. "Wonderful, Jett. Wonderful."

CHAPTER THIRTEEN

Lennon's feet pounded on the wet sand, the dawn a bare gray slip on the horizon. For whatever reason, she'd hardly gotten a wink of sleep, tossing and turning all night until she finally decided to just get up and start the day, even though it was still dark outside. Her phone, tucked into the pocket at the back of her leggings, started buzzing, and she retrieved it as she came to a slow stop.

She glanced at the name on the screen before answering. "Lieutenant." Déjà vu descended, or the disturbing thought that she had found herself in her own version of *Groundhog Day*. Only one where a serial killer was on the loose and she'd have to hunt him into perpetuity.

"Gray, we have a situation over on Ellis Street. It seems like a straightforward overdose, but there's some product with a purplish tint at the scene. How soon can you be there?"

Her eyes moved to the parking lot beyond the sand where her car was parked. Déjà vu indeed. Only last time she'd experienced almost this exact same scenario, she'd gone home and showered and changed, not out of professionalism but because she'd been hoping someone else would arrive before her at what sounded like a gory triple homicide. If she went home now and changed and showered, it'd take her over an hour to get there. "I'm on my way. Give me thirty," she said.

"Great. Thanks, Gray. Keep me updated."

She jogged up the short set of steps that led to the lot, removed her things from the trunk, pulled a hoodie on, and got in her car.

It took her twenty-seven minutes to drive from the beach to the Tenderloin. Lieutenant Byrd had texted her the exact address as she'd driven, and when she pulled up, there were already a couple of patrol cars double-parked at the corner, lights turning. The sun was just beginning to rise, but it was a foggy morning, and so the streetlights offered the only real illumination. She clipped her badge on her leggings and strapped her small holster on, covering it with her hoodie.

She didn't recognize the officers standing at the corner in front of the short wall that separated the sidewalk from the stairs that led down to a Muni station, and so she introduced herself when she approached. The two young men both gave her an odd look because of her attire but identified themselves as Boddie and Meads. "What's the situation?" she asked.

"The owner of the corner store right there"—he pointed next to him—"called in two dead bodies in a tent just up the street." He pointed to the small grouping of three tents situated about fifty feet down the one-way street that they had blocked off with their car. "We looked in the yellow one on the end, and sure enough: one male, white, one male, black, both deceased. And there are pills scattered around, and something purple in a baggie. We didn't touch anything, just called it in."

Shit. "Okay, thanks. What about the other two tents?" She nodded to the two sitting to the right of the yellow one.

"Unoccupied as of now. Just a bunch of junk in both. And they smell like shit."

She couldn't hold back the ick face. "The store owner, he's inside?" she asked, nodding over to the store.

"Yeah. A Mr. Allen Cheng. He's the only one there."

Lennon nodded, turning toward the corner store with signs and ads covering the two front windows. She walked the short distance and pulled the door open. There was an older man at the register, and when

Lennon entered, he stood, rounding the counter. "Are you with the police?" he asked in a heavy Chinese accent.

"Yes. Hi. Mr. Cheng? I'm Inspector Gray. I'm going to go check out the tent but wanted to stop by here first and get a little more information."

"Yes, okay. Good."

"You discovered the two men this morning?"

"Yes. I open the store every morning at four thirty. If the sandwiches pass the expiration date, I bring them around to whoever is awake. I don't feel right, tossing food when there are hungry people right outside my door. It's not right. So I get a ticket, so okay."

"No one's going to ticket you, Mr. Cheng." People like him were few and far between. The people living hand to mouth in this community were lucky to receive his kindness. "So you went to the tents up the block? To see if anyone inside wanted some food?"

"No. There was a man sleeping on a bench near the tent. No shoes. No coat. I set one of the sandwiches next to him so he would find it when he woke up. That's when I saw the blood."

Dammit. So there was blood. The lieutenant hadn't mentioned blood. A small cramp knotted in her lower stomach.

"So I thought maybe someone is hurt," Mr. Cheng went on, "needs medical care. I used my phone flashlight and pushed the flap aside. It was partway open already. And I see the two . . . dead. I can tell they're dead. Still. One had his eyes open." He gave a small shiver. "Drugs on the ground. It's always drugs."

"Okay, Mr. Cheng. Thank you for calling us. Will you be here for a little bit in case I have any more questions?"

"Yes, I will be here."

Lennon thanked him and left the store, taking gloves from her pocket. She started to head down the block toward the tents, and one of the officers called out, "Do you want one of us to come with you?" She did. She really did. In fact, she didn't want to check inside that tent at all. Not now, not in the dark, but also not in the light. She wanted to stand behind one of those officers as he checked, and it made her feel pitiful and unworthy of the badge she carried. She should have gone home and changed after she got the call, not only to stall but because right now she felt about as capable as Workout Barbie walking toward a double homicide, and she was dressed the part.

"No, it's okay," she said to the officer. "I'll check it out and be right back." She pulled the gloves on slowly as she made the walk. The people who'd placed their tents in the spot they had up ahead had likely done it because there wasn't a streetlight too close by. They wouldn't be kept awake by a bright light shining in their makeshift home, and if they were engaging in activities that they'd rather not advertise, then that worked in their favor too.

A car backfired up the street. In the quiet of the morning, it startled Lennon, and she gave a small jump. *Great.* Just what she needed to feel even more on edge.

She walked slowly toward the small grouping of tents, past the first and second, where she saw vague shadows moving on the nylon fabric. The morning was still dim, and the streetlight the officers were standing under, along with their flashing lights, were swallowed up by the fog, and so it gave the impression that the shifting light might be coming from apparitions inside. She'd been told they were unoccupied, but even so, a shiver went down her spine and the tiny hairs on her arms stood up.

The bench where Mr. Cheng had said a man was sleeping, was now empty. She stepped over a pile of vomit mixed with blood right next to the tent. That must be what Mr. Cheng was referring to and why the cops hadn't mentioned it. Rather than alert them to a homicide, it lent further evidence to an overdose.

The officers who'd looked inside the yellow tent hadn't propped the flap, and so the opening was closed now. She removed her phone and turned on the flashlight before she stepped up to the tent, turning her head slightly and bracing as she used her thumb and index finger to grasp the very edge of the flap and gingerly pull it aside. A sound of disgust moved up her throat, and the officers were far enough away that she allowed it to escape, holding her breath against the smell that hit her in the face, a combination of the dirty bodies that had been living in this small fabric space for a long while mixed with putrid bodily fluids that had obviously been marinating for at least several hours.

Breathe, just breathe.

One man was on his side, eyes open like Mr. Cheng had said, mouth ajar, a trail of bloody vomit leading from his lips and pooled in another gelatinous, lumpy mess on the floor of the tent. The other man was on the opposite side, turned away so that Lennon couldn't see his face.

Her eyes moved over the piles of clothing and what looked like a stack of government forms, brochures, and other paperwork. She caught the VA logo on a piece of paper peeking out from the bottom and assumed one of the deceased was a military veteran, as so many homeless were. It was one of the statistics she hated the most. They'd sacrificed so much for their country and then been—literally, in some cases—kicked to the curb. There were shoes and liquor bottles and a mostly eaten loaf of bread, and just like the officers had told her, there were pills scattered here and there.

And there it was: a baggie with a purple substance inside, the edge just tucked under the leg of the dead man with his back to her.

She leaned inside the tent, reaching for it, her fingers clasping the edge and beginning to pull it from under the man's jean-clad calf, when he very suddenly turned. Lennon sucked in a breath of horror and jerked away. The unexpected movement, when she was already leaning over, caused her to lose her balance, and she plunged inside the tent, twisting away from the man she'd believed to be nothing more than a corpse even as he began to sit up and reach for her, eyes wild.

She barely heard the bus roar by down the street as she screamed, but only for a moment, as the man grabbed her before she could use her hands to brace her fall.

It all happened so *fast*.

His hands came around her throat, cutting off her scream as she tried desperately to reach her gun in the holster at her hip even while kicking and punching and fighting the man who had a death grip on her neck. The man was yelling something, his putrid breath in Lennon's face, eyes bugged out. But Lennon couldn't make out his words over the bus's air suspension releasing as it stopped out on the street, just beyond where she was currently fighting for her life.

Adrenaline shot through her system, her inner alarm bells clashing and clanging. Her eyes felt like they were popping from their sockets as her lungs emptied, her vision going both bright and hazy. Her attacker let go with one hand, and she was able to draw in a trickle of air before he punched her in the face, once and then again, her head jerking backward against the hand still wrapped around her neck.

And then suddenly there was a hand on her back, and she was being hauled away from the man. But he didn't let go, and so both of them came flying out of the tent, the man landing on Lennon on the sidewalk. The last bit of oxygen in her lungs puffed from her lips in a tiny bubble of air, and the world blinked out for a brief moment before light and sound once again flooded her senses.

She sucked in a giant breath, shaking and rolling away from the man who she realized was no longer on her, no longer crushing her neck in his palms. She heard someone grunting and the smack of fists on flesh, and she turned and pulled herself up, crab walking back and then leaping up and going for her gun.

Ambrose was straddling the man, who was still trying to fight, his arms and legs flailing as Ambrose punched him repeatedly in the face. Lennon removed her gun and aimed it at the man on the ground. "Stop fighting give up you're under arrest." God, what was she saying? Her voice was shaking so badly that her words were all strung together and barely intelligible.

Feet pounded on the sidewalk, and the two officers who'd been standing on the corner skidded to a stop, pointing their guns at the man just as he went limp.

Ambrose sat back, his shoulders rising and falling as he, too, caught his breath. He got off the man in one fluid movement, coming to his feet as the two officers moved in, cuffing the homeless man who once again appeared to be deceased but almost certainly was not.

"Are you okay?" Ambrose asked, his gaze moving over her body, down to her tennis-shoe-clad feet and back up again. "Lennon? Let's go sit down. You're shaking like a leaf."

He put his hand on her wrist, and her gaze went there, the gun in her hands moving all over the place. He was right. She was shaking like a leaf. And if she'd have tried to shoot the man, she'd almost certainly have missed. Instead of attempting to reholster it, she allowed Ambrose to take it from her gently, and then she turned, taking the few steps to a concrete planter nearby that held a tree that was only branches, and sank down onto the edge.

The officers had turned the man over, and one of them was speaking into his radio. But Lennon couldn't even begin to make sense of the words. The inside of her head sounded like she was in the eye of a raging storm.

Warm hands spread over her knees, and she looked down to see Ambrose squatted in front of her. "You're all right," he said. "You're going to start shaking very badly now. You might feel dizzy. You're fine. It's normal, and it will pass."

She gave a jerky nod. It was all she could do. Sirens were drawing closer; in a minute the cavalry would be here. "H-how are y-you here?" she asked, trying to move her locked jaw as best as she could and barely succeeding.

"The lieutenant called me after he called you. I'm so sorry I got here after you did." He looked to the side, and she saw the muscle in his jaw tighten. It wasn't his fault, though. It was hers. Not only because she'd raced straight here with something to prove to herself but because she should have waited for backup, or had one of the officers walk with her down the block and stand guard as she checked out the scene. She hadn't, though, because again, she was trying to force herself to employ mind over matter. And look what had happened.

She might have been killed this morning by a homeless junkie she'd thought was dead. He'd been so high he'd had superhuman strength. Three more seconds and she'd have died in a foul-smelling nylon tent on the street as a bus driving by covered her screams.

Or maybe she wouldn't have died—not quickly anyway. Visions swarmed her mind, coming to her in bursts of horror. The officers looking around and seeing her gone, assuming she'd headed to some nearby store to question someone else, maybe, as they watched the bus trundle by the spot where they were standing? But instead, she'd be inside that small capsule with a drug-fueled monster. Something similar had happened the year before—a morning jogger had been attacked and dragged into a homeless encampment. She'd been raped and brutalized. And though Lennon hadn't worked that case, sometimes she had nightmares about it anyway.

A moan sounded in the air, and she realized it was her, and so she clamped her lips shut and closed her eyes. Her skin felt hot and clammy, and her right eye was throbbing. Why was her eye throbbing so badly?

"Lennon." His voice was soothing, and she realized her hands were covering his on her knees. The contact of his hands was keeping her from spiraling completely, and so she'd placed her palms on his knuckles to ensure he didn't take them away.

"Come on," he said, his voice so gentle it made her want to cry. "You need to be checked out."

She looked up to see that an ambulance had arrived, and she shook her head. She didn't want an ambulance or a hospital. She didn't want strangers looking at her and knowing how weak she was. "Not just for your eye," he said, sliding his hands out from under hers but then grasping them. "There might have been fentanyl in that tent or on that man. I'm going to get checked out too." He pulled her up, and she was relieved to find that she could stand, and even walk. And so she did, allowing Ambrose to lead her to the ambulance.

CHAPTER FOURTEEN

Into the forest I go, to lose my
mind and find my soul.
—John Muir

Seventeen Years Ago
Patient Number 0022

Thud, thud, thud, woosh, thud, woosh. Confusing sounds, bright, squeeze. Piercing cry, fear rising as his body was constricted, tight, tight, tight. Then flail. "I'm so glad you're here. Look at you. Perfect. Wonderful."

He heard the sounds, the voice, but he couldn't make sense of the words, only the hushing, soft sound. The lessening fear. *Thud, thud, thud.* Softer now. And then warm, tight but not too tight. Good.

He slept, and in his dream, hands reached for him, grabbing. Tearing. Scared. He cried. Alone. No one. Cold. Empty. His stomach knotted.

"Shh." The voice again. Then sweetness. Warm. The empty feeling abated, but the warm stayed. He moved back, forth, back, forth. *Thud, thud, thud.* The voice became song, and he floated. No dreams this time. No tearing, just warm.

Emptiness again. Fear. Then filled. Warm. Sweet. Good.

Thirsty. Drink. The song again. The one that meant back, forth, back, forth. Warm. Good. *Thud, thud, thud.*

Am I the song? Am I the thud? Am I the cold or the warm?

It didn't matter. He didn't care. He floated, and it was good. "There's that smile. What a beautiful smile for a beautiful boy."

Am I the smile? Am I the boy?

He became aware of something other than the empty and the warm and the cold, but he didn't know what to call it. Soft, pressing. Tickle. Fuzzy. It touched him. It caressed him. He was . . . *him*. He had a body. He was inside a body with parts that could feel things. He *was* the boy. Happy. Good. Beautiful.

"What a good boy. A perfect boy. I'm so glad you're here. You're safe."

The warm and the sweet and the full were *safe*. He drifted. He slept.

The cold came but was quickly replaced by warm. The empty widened but was soon made full. *Back, forth, back, forth.* The song rose and fell. *Thud, thud, thud.* Words whispered. Good. Beautiful. Safe.

He was the boy. The beautiful boy. The voice was happy. It sang him songs and hummed and hushed. The voice was good. The place was good. He was good. He was safe.

There was something outside the good, but he couldn't make sense of what it was. And it was okay because the singing voice was always close. Sometimes he felt the bad come closer, but then the voice hushed and shushed, and the bad went away, replaced by the *thud, thud, thud.* Both anchored him to the good and the safe.

Back. Forth. Back. Forth.

Thud. Thud. Thud.

He felt his skin and wiggled his toes. He felt his eyes move and became aware of light outside his lids. He didn't want to come out of his body. It was safe inside. Warm and full and good.

"There you are, sweetness," the voice said. "Are you going to open your eyes and say hi? I've been waiting for you."

Waiting. The voice was waiting. The voice wanted him to open his eyes.

Fear. Light. Space so big. Too big.

"Okay, that's okay. You take your time. There's no rush. You take all the time you need."

Time. No rush. Safe.

Back. Forth. Back. Forth.

Thud. Thud. Thud.

Cold. Warm. Empty. Full.

The voice again. Singing. So sweet. He wanted to see the voice. The voice was good. The voice took away the cold and the empty. The voice made him safe.

He raised his lids, the light seeping in. He knew the light because he'd known the dark. The space around him brightened, and the voice became a face. Smiling. "Hello. There you are, sweetness. I'm happy to see you." The voice was a she. She was happy to see him. Her smile grew bigger, and her eyes crinkled. He could feel himself smiling back. The woman laughed. "A smile too! My goodness, what a beautiful smile."

He wanted to see her smile some more. He wanted to smile more, too, because she thought his smile was good. But he was so tired, his lids heavy, and so he closed his eyes. And again, he slept.

Back. Forth. Back. Forth.

Thud. Thud. Thud.

CHAPTER FIFTEEN

A knock sounded on the door just as Lennon was tying the robe around her waist. She considered ignoring it, but what if her mom had decided hearing her voice over the phone wasn't good enough—even though Lennon had downplayed her injuries—and headed over with a dose of herbs and tinctures that would wipe away both her bruises and her memory? She'd gladly swallow it down, every drop. She knew she was one of the lucky cops, as she hadn't had any serious injuries since she joined the force. That streak had ended with the painful punch to her face.

She shuffled to the door and looked through the peephole, her heart stuttering when she saw Ambrose's face filling the small oval. She was both surprised to see him and also not, and before she could even consider it, she found herself unlocking her door and pulling it open.

He stood there, his hair still slightly wet from what must have been a recent shower, because she'd been home since right before noon, and there hadn't been a drop of rain all day. "Hi," he said. His gaze went to her eye that was now just red and slightly swollen but would likely be black and blue in the next few days. "How's the eye?"

"A little blurry, but otherwise okay. The boss is insisting I take the next few days off."

"Good." He was holding a bowl with foil over the top, and she had a momentary flash of all those neighbors and friends who'd shown up at her parents' door so many years ago carrying a casserole or a potato salad or a Bundt cake meant to feed their hearts as much as their bellies. She pushed those old memories away and stepped back so he could enter.

"I talked to Lieutenant Byrd. He says he spoke to you already and that you seemed okay, but . . . well, I thought I'd check for myself, because I missed you at the hospital. And I brought you this." He presented the bowl, and Lennon looked down at it for several beats before taking it from his hands.

"What is it?"

"A fruit salad." Her gaze held on the shiny foil cover. *Oh.* He'd brought her a fruit salad. It made her smile and oddly want to cry.

"Brave," she said. "After my fruit salad tirade."

"No guts, no glory."

She pressed her lips together, stifling a bigger smile, and she was honestly shocked that she could smile at all today. It had been over twelve hours since the attack, and she still felt shaky. "Come on," she said. "I was just going to make some tea, and I'll check this situation out."

Ambrose followed her to her kitchen, which was just a few steps past the small entryway, and she set the bowl on the table, carefully peeling the foil back so she could assess this fruit salad that he'd made. "Plenty of berries," she said. "Watermelon—a good choice. And, oh"— she met his eyes, her heart squeezing—"you cut it into stars."

"I thought that might score me a few extra points."

She nodded, a jerky movement. It did. It did do that. She couldn't help picturing him with that look of concentration on his face he wore so often, this enigmatic man who fought off attackers and told stories so well, leaning over a cutting board full of watermelon slices and carefully pressing a star cutter into the fruit, or perhaps even doing it by hand because how would he have a star cutter in a hotel room? In any case, he'd done it for her. To make her smile. And truly, she couldn't remember the last time anyone had done something nicer for her. "Mint," she said, and even she heard the emotion in her voice. "That's a nice touch too." Her throat felt full, and she swallowed, refusing to be brought to tears by some star-shaped melon and a few sprigs of mint. "It's good. I'd invite you back to my potluck, Ambrose Mars."

He squinted one eye, looking as if he was struggling with something humorous.

"Don't do it," she said. "I set you up for some form of a 'that's what she said' joke, but I know you can resist. I have faith in you."

He laughed, and she grinned, and God, she'd been beaten and terrorized and made to feel so low today, and here she was laughing over fruit salad in her kitchen with this strange, confusing man. It felt as though her mother *had* arrived with that elixir that would erase her memory. Rather, Ambrose had shown up and, with laughter and fruit, had done the very next best thing. Distracted her. From the smell of the attacker's breath on her face. From the pain of his hands around her neck. From the terrifying feeling that she was going to die.

"I wasn't sure how you felt about fruit dip, so I decided to avoid any potential pitfalls," he said, his eyes dancing.

"That was wise." She nodded slowly. "There are several."

"I figured." He tilted his head. "Cool Whip?"

She pretended to shudder. "Whipped marshmallow is the true villain of that story."

He grinned, and she did too. And for several heavy moments, they simply stared at each other, and Lennon felt lifted even further from her body—a blessed relief, considering the circumstances. But she also felt that same flutter of fear she'd sensed since the get-go with this man, and she was pretty sure what it was about, but she was too exhausted and emotionally fragile to ponder it right that moment. Especially with him staring at her with those sleepy eyes that made her think of crawling beneath the sheets at all hours of the day.

"How are you, Lennon?"

She sighed and sank down into a chair at the table. "Sore, but otherwise all accounted for."

"Emotionally?"

She shrugged and let out a short laugh. "Well, a case could be made for the fact that I wasn't exactly of sound mind before today anyway, so . . ."

A ghost of a smile flitted across his full lips before he went serious. "The two officers who checked the men in the tent before you did feel awful. But as many drugs as the man who attacked you was on, he might have actually been pretty damn close to dead when they took vitals. Something sparked his attack, and then he promptly died again on the way to the hospital. This time for good. Paramedics couldn't revive him."

She felt an internal sinking, and though the man had terrorized her, she felt sorry for him. That wasn't a nice way to die. "I should have waited for backup. I will next time I'm in a situation like that."

He assessed her for a moment, his expression inscrutable. "The purple drug in the baggie wasn't the same as at the previous scenes. It was something called purple heroin. Have you heard of it?"

She wrinkled her brow. "Maybe."

"It's mostly been found on the East Coast so far. This might be one of the first West Coast cases. It comes from China in pill form, but most dealers crush it up with heroin so they can sell smaller doses."

She rubbed at her brow. "What's in it besides heroin?"

"Brorphine, which is a synthetic opioid without a medicinal purpose, and carfentanil, which is an elephant tranquilizer a hundred times more potent than fentanyl."

An *elephant* tranquilizer. *Christ almighty.*

"Why purple?" she asked.

"No one really knows so far. Maybe just a marketing feature."

She blew out a breath. "My God. The things people will put in their bodies," she murmured. It did make her consider what had happened to her a little differently, however. The man who'd attacked her had not only been mostly dead but very literally out of his mind. Who even knew what kind of human he was when his body wasn't pumped full of opioids and large-animal tranquilizers. It wasn't that she'd taken the attack personally . . . exactly. But, well, maybe in some small, irrational way she had, and knowing what she now knew clarified for her that he'd have attacked a fly with as much vigor if it had landed on his arm. It didn't make it less traumatic, but it did put it in a clearer light. "He was possessed," she murmured.

"That's a decent way to put it," he said after a moment.

She looked up to see him watching her. "You were going to make tea," he said. "Stay there and let me do it for you." Without waiting for her okay, he picked the kettle up off the stove and brought it to the sink and began filling it.

She reached into the bowl of fruit and plucked out a star-shaped piece of watermelon and placed it in her mouth. It was firm and sweet and perfect. "You picked out a good watermelon," she told him. "Not always an easy feat."

He glanced up at her as he turned on the burner, the flame sparking to life, and then placed the kettle over the fire. "I bought three," he said. "I figured at least one would be good. Mushy watermelon would have ruined my recipe." He smiled, and she stared at him for a moment. And then she did cry, her face contorting as hot tears spilled from her eyes and rolled down her cheeks.

With a look of alarm, Ambrose approached her, leaning over and turning her chair so that she was facing him. He didn't ask her why she was crying; he simply gathered her in his arms and held her as she wept. "I didn't realize the thought of mushy watermelon would upset you so much," he said. She laughed. He was kind, and funny, and his sweetness was what had made her cry, what had made her feel safe enough to be vulnerable in his presence.

And God, but she hadn't cried in a long, long time, especially not in front of anyone. *Especially* not someone she barely knew. "Why aren't you married, Ambrose Mars?" she murmured when her tears had ceased. "Do you know how many women would scoop up any man who made watermelon stars?"

He removed his arms and stepped back, and she suddenly missed his closeness, the clean, masculine scent of him right against her nose. *I want to know you,* she thought, and the realization brought a buzz of fear, yes, but it also made hope glitter inside.

He smiled in that quizzical way of his and paused as if her question might have a double meaning or was more complicated than it seemed. "Marriage isn't in the cards for me."

She swiped at the lingering wetness on her cheeks. *Marriage isn't in the cards.* Well, that was an odd thing to say. "Have you sworn an oath to an ancient brotherhood?"

He lifted the kettle off the burner and placed it back on another. "No. I'm just . . . not great in relationships. I like my life the way it is."

She stood, stepping to the cabinet where she kept her mugs and handing him two before opening the second cupboard, which contained the tea bags and the honey. "Okay. That's fair, I guess. There's nothing wrong with being a confirmed bachelor."

"I'm glad you approve." Coming from someone else, the words might have sounded snarky. But Ambrose gave her a teasing tilt of his lips, and his eyes squinted when he did so, and honestly, it made her stomach flutter. He placed a tea bag in each mug and then handed one to her. They both took a moment to add a couple of teaspoons of honey, and then he followed her into the living room, where she curled up in a corner of the couch.

Her phone rang, and she reached for it on the coffee table, about to silence it until she saw it was the number of the station. "I should take this," she said. "One second." She answered and heard Adella's voice on the other end say her name.

"Hi, Adella."

"How are you? I was just calling to check in."

"Thanks. I'm fine. A little bruised." It was kind of Adella to reach out, especially since they weren't overly close at work. Maybe this was her way of letting Lennon know that even despite that fact, she had her back.

"Arnica gel. It will clear the bruise up in half the time."

She smiled. "I'll Instacart some tomorrow. Thanks for the tip."

"I could drop some off to you on the way home. Half an hour or so?"

"Thanks, but Agent Mars is here, and as soon as he leaves, I'm heading to bed."

"Oh." She paused as if Agent Mars being there had taken her by surprise. And maybe it had. Maybe she shouldn't have said it, but her guard was down at the moment and she'd simply told the truth. "Okay, no problem. Anyway, we were all worried when we heard what happened. Heal up quick, okay? Let me know if you need anything."

"Thanks for calling, Adella."

She hung up and glanced at Ambrose sitting on the other end of the couch as he took a tentative sip of the steaming tea. He set it down and looked over at her before picking up their conversation. "What about you, Lennon? Have you ever been married?"

She took a sip of tea, too, and then set it down on a coaster on the side table next to her. "Me? No. Single and satisfied. But . . . I'm not opposed to marriage if the right man comes along." And her mom and dad definitely weren't opposed. Even if they weren't pushy about it, she saw the flare of hope in their eyes every time she mentioned going on a date. And she knew it was solely because happiness had been ripped away from her and they wanted nothing more than for her to find it again. Because they loved her. Because they didn't want her story to end in heartbreak. "I was engaged once," she said. She immediately pressed her lips together, almost shocked by the admission. She hadn't meant to say it, and certainly wasn't in the habit of disclosing that fact to anyone, much less the hard-to-read FBI agent she'd so recently met.

When she looked over at Ambrose, she found him playing idly with the tag at the end of the tea bag and studying her. "What happened?"

Their eyes held, and something she had no idea how to describe moved between them. "I . . . he died," she finally said.

"I'm sorry."

She gave her head a small shake and was tempted to administer a few hard taps to her cheek, as though she'd temporarily gone into a fugue state and needed to be physically jolted out of it. She picked up her tea and took another sip just to stall. Once she'd placed it back down, she said, "It's . . . thank you. It was a long time ago." *Thirteen years and three months and only yesterday.* "And we were young."

"Things that happen when we're young have the most impact on our lives."

She looked away. She had to. There was something in those eyes of his that she didn't want to look into. She'd seen it before in the gazes of the victims she'd met. Hurt. And it embarrassed her because he was hurting for her and he didn't need to. She didn't want it. It was too much. She'd felt like a victim today. She still did, and she didn't want to be reminded of another time when she'd felt like a victim too. "You're full of wisdom, aren't you?"

He gave her a small tilt of his lips, but his eyes remained serious. There had been sarcasm in her tone, and she'd said it to push back against the uncomfortable feelings he brought out in her. It wasn't like her to do that, and it made her feel bad. "I'm sorry. No, you're right. It was hard. It changed me. But, well, time heals all wounds, as they say." She barely held back a cringe. She hated that saying, and it wasn't even true. In fact, it couldn't be further from the truth. Time buffed away the raw edges, yes, but underneath those edges were layers of what-ifs and what-could-have-beens, and they were as rough as sandpaper. If you rubbed against them too hard and too often, you would make yourself raw. You would bleed.

"How long ago did he die?" Ambrose asked.

"Thirteen years ago." She sighed, still surprised by her own candor. "He was my high school boyfriend. He proposed to me the summer after we graduated. We were going to get married after college." The whole future had stretched out before them, and when he died, that future had died along with him. She'd been adrift, with no idea where to go from there, the path that had once been so clear suddenly covered in dense fog. As dense as that which could swallow the entire city so that, from certain vantage points, you couldn't see it at all. Entire buildings. Entire lives. Gone. Lost in the mist. "I was going to be a teacher," she told him. "I hadn't even decided exactly what kind. I wanted to teach kids to read, but I also wanted to teach art history, or maybe music." She'd pictured it, her classroom, the way she'd decorate it in bright colors, the little faces that would gaze up at her with awe as she filled their minds with words and art and beauty. Not the most exciting of dreams, perhaps. But just the thought of it had warmed her heart and made her purpose feel so clear. "I'd completed a year toward my teaching degree. Tanner was majoring in criminal justice. The teacher and the inspector. What a beautifully simple life. And then . . . then it all blew up."

"You switched majors?"

She nodded. "It seemed right at the time. I can't even remember why it felt so right." Maybe it'd just been something to *do* when, in every other way, she'd felt so utterly helpless. *Devastated.*

"You did what he never got a chance to do." He tilted his head, seeming thoughtful, a little sad.

"I did. I tried to fill his void." It seemed so stupid now. So ill-conceived and irrational. She'd set herself up for a mighty fall. But at the time, she'd clung to it. The empty place where he'd once been had felt like a deep, dark pit that she was desperate to fill. And somewhere inside, it'd seemed like her *duty* to a world that had been suddenly deprived of his impact. Deprived at least in part because of *her.* It'd seemed like maybe it would serve to heal her heart in some way too. What had she imagined? That she could *become* him, in some sense? No. Instead, all it had done was make it obvious that no one could replace Tanner as a force of good in the world. Least of all her. Instead of filling his void, she'd made a mockery of what he'd intended to do. She turned her gaze to Ambrose. "I'm scared more often than not. Sick. Distraught. I care far too much to be useful." *Why am I telling him all this?*

"I'm not sure that's possible, Lennon."

"It is. It is possible because it makes me shit at my job. I relate. I spin stories in my head about what they felt. I picture them dressing in the clothes I find them in, not having any idea it's going to be the last outfit they ever wear. I hate the blood and the gore. I keep vomit bags in my car just in case, and I've used them more often than I want to admit."

"Your empathy isn't a bad thing. And it probably means you see things others don't. It can be a strength. But it hurts you."

His voice was so even, and he didn't sound judgmental, only understanding. And God, she appreciated it, but it also made her want to cry again. As if she didn't already look pathetic enough as it was. As if he would have shown up here tonight if he knew she was going to sob all over him. She let out a long, shaky breath, meaning to stop. But the words just kept coming. "I didn't love being a cop. I never said that to anyone. I thought being an inspector would mean I'd sit at a desk and pore through files and it'd be better. Easier. God, Tanner must be laughing down at me. He'd find it funny, he really would. I tried to take over his life, and I suck at it." Would he, though? Would he think that? Or was it her judging herself too harshly? Because Tanner had always been far more forgiving of her faults than she was, and it was one of the many reasons she'd felt so valued by him. And she didn't want to lose another part of him by misremembering that.

A small smile drifted over Ambrose's lips. "You don't suck at it," he said.

"Okay, I don't suck at it. But . . ." She sighed. "I don't know. I'm tired and I had a hard day. I'll be okay tomorrow."

"There are other jobs at the department that are more desk jobs than the one you're doing," he said. "Have you thought about applying for one of them?"

"Yes . . . maybe." She had thought about it, but then she'd felt like a phony. How could she lead others to do a job when she couldn't do it herself? No, the better option was to transfer to a department where she'd be less exposed to horrific crime scenes and stories that ripped her heart out. But she still hadn't quite worked up the courage or . . . whatever it was she needed to work up to not feel like a quitter. As if in doing so, she'd be letting go of the last piece of Tanner she'd managed to preserve.

Ambrose scooted a little closer, and he reached out and tentatively took her hand. "Lennon, you also have to realize that what happened to you today . . . no one would have handled that well, not even the most hardened cop."

"I know. You're right."

"Maybe you're a little too hard on yourself sometimes," he said. "Maybe it's more abnormal and worrisome not to be affected by other people's blood and suffering."

"There must be a happy medium, though, right?"

He smiled again. "Unfortunately, not every circumstance features a happy medium. Sometimes there are only extremes. Your job—our job—just doesn't make that easy to deal with."

She conceded his point with a nod. He was right. Perhaps it shouldn't be her goal to nonchalantly stroll through a room where people had died violent deaths. Perhaps she should stop beating herself up for her natural reactions. But she also had to do her job. In any case, talking like this with him was soothing her and helping her put her emotions into context. It was helping her let go of some of the pent-up stress. This was what she'd missed about having a partner, though she didn't at all feel toward him how she'd felt toward Tommy and still did—sisterly. But Ambrose was kind and understanding and he was making her feel safe, and she couldn't remember the last time she'd felt this way.

But it wasn't just that. She'd felt simmering attraction to this man since she first laid eyes on him, but she'd desperately tried to hold that back. His supportive words, his touch—the way he was looking at *her*—was crumbling her resistance. And once it started crumbling, it crumbled fast.

When she gripped his hand back, his eyes moved to their fingers, laced together. She saw his nostrils flare very slightly, and a muscle jumped in the corner of his eye. She became very aware of him, too, the air between them charging. Electricity sparked in her stomach, but it wasn't at all unpleasant—not like the buzz of anxiety she was so used to feeling. Ambrose Mars made her feel alive, energized, but in a way she loved and hadn't felt in so, so long. She leaned over, and she brought her mouth to his. He froze, obviously surprised, and she moved closer, bringing his hand inside her robe and covering her breast with it. She pressed her palm over the top of his, and he moaned, seeming to break out of the momentary shock he'd been in, using his other hand on the back of her neck to tilt her head so he could kiss her in earnest.

Without breaking their kiss, she climbed on top, straddling him, her blood heating when she felt the hard evidence of his arousal between her thighs. God, he tasted good, and he felt good too. Sleek and solid. Their kiss deepened, and he made that sexy sound of desperation in the back of his throat again. It sounded raw and primal, and it drove her higher, her pulse pumping blood to her core, nipples tingling. *Life.* This was life. Not death. The opposite of the thing she was trying to shrug off from today, to deny, to turn away from.

He flipped her off him, onto her back on the couch, and she bounced slightly and laughed. And then he was over her, claiming her mouth again, pressing his groin into her and grinding slightly. "Is this okay?" he asked, holding his weight off her. And that's when she realized that he'd thought about the fact that he was putting her in the same position she'd been in today when she was victimized, and he didn't want her to be reminded of it in any way. But she hadn't thought about that, and the realization brought a surge of relief.

"It's better than okay," she said. She'd needed this. She hadn't real-ized how much. She pulled him back toward her so he was once again pressing right where she needed him. Tingles of pleasure radiated from the place where he pressed, and she gasped and broke from his mouth, tipping her head back so he could kiss her throat.

He brought his mouth to her skin, dragging his warm lips down her bruised neck, feathering them over her wounded skin and then kissing the hollow at the base of her throat as he ground into her again.

Everything drifted away, and she realized what a weight she'd felt hanging over her—not just today, but for such a long time. She suddenly felt unencumbered. *Free.*

Kissing him like this on her couch reminded her of those teenage make-out sessions, but ten times better. All lips and tongues and still-clothed pressing bodies, hormones rushing crazily. She felt dizzy with lust. She'd forgotten the *joy* there was to be found in sex, the way it made everything brighter and hotter. She'd needed this. God, she'd needed this.

But she also needed more. And she wasn't a teenager anymore. There were no limits, no boundaries. She was a fully grown woman, and she could have sex with this man on her couch if she wanted to. It'd been years since she'd been with a man. Years! It made her want to laugh.

She wrapped her legs around his circling hips, tilting upward as her robe fell open, and she felt the cool air of the room on her naked breasts. Ambrose exhaled against her skin, lifting his head as he met her eyes. *Oh.* She blinked, momentarily stunned by his beauty: not only his face and his features, but the way those bedroom eyes looked when they were filled with lust. There was something else there, too, however. A vulnerability. A tentative joy that she'd never once seen on any man's face, ever. She felt inexplicably awed by it, even as she couldn't explain why or how or even who. Was it she who'd put that look in his eyes?

He exhaled, leaning back, his gaze moving from her face down to her breasts. She was glad to let him look, wanting a few moments to study him, too, to soak in that expression in his eyes that made her feel both honored and confused and slightly overwhelmed.

"Lennon . . . ," he began, his voice gravelly. She shivered as though the word—her name on his lips—had come to life somehow and scraped across her skin. Her nipples pebbled, and his eyes flared. "Maybe we . . . are you sure?" he asked. "Do you want this?"

This. Him. *Them.* "Is this against your brotherhood oath too?" she asked, to infuse some lightness into the moment. Because he'd paused, and now she was questioning it, too, despite the fact that her body ached for him. *This.* It suddenly seemed filled with far more gravity than she understood. And maybe he did; maybe that was the look in his eyes that she didn't comprehend. But he laughed softly at her question, bringing his eyes to hers. "No. I just don't want you to regret doing something in a moment of . . . well, after today."

"I want this, Ambrose. I want you." His gaze held to hers, and he must have seen her certainty—and perhaps her need—because he brought his lips back to hers, and then the next thing she knew, she was in his arms and he was carrying her through the living room and down the very short hallway to her bedroom.

He placed her down gently on the bed, pushing her robe aside, his gaze roaming over her naked skin. The look on his face . . . he seemed *awestruck*, and it made the shyness she'd momentarily felt at being naked in front of him melt away. "You are so beautiful, Lennon," he said.

She smiled, holding out her hand to him. He kicked his shoes off and then quickly removed his clothes before climbing into bed with her.

They kissed again, and their kisses were both languorous and filled with urgency. She relished his taste, his scent, the way his hard, honed body felt above hers, and the velvety roughness of his skin. She allowed herself to get lost in him, and it felt so good, so *necessary*. It was beautiful, he was beautiful, and the way he looked at her made her feel so beautiful too. His expression looked like she'd imagine on a person gazing at the Grand Canyon, or the first snowfall. Mesmerized. Entranced. Appreciative. His hand trembled slightly as it moved over her skin, exploring her, and reexamining the places that made her gasp or moan.

His hand lingered between her thighs, and she thought she might scream with frustration before he parted her with his fingers, and she gasped with pleasure, leaning her head back into the pillow as he stroked and teased, nearly driving her to the edge. "Condom?" he gritted. "Please tell me you have a condom?"

A what? She could barely think through the fog of lust. *A condom.* No, she didn't. Wait—yes, she did! "The closet," she said, as though she'd just remembered the buried treasure amid her clothing. With the raise of his brow, he climbed out of bed, and she was treated to the view of his muscular back as he opened the door and looked inside.

"Shelf to your left," she said.

He reached in, and when he turned her way, he was holding the ridiculous visor with condoms hanging from it that had been passed around at the bar from woman to woman during a coworker's bachelorette shindig. She'd forced herself to go to that and left the moment she could, still wearing that stupid hat that was now actually the most beautiful, wonderful creation she'd ever seen.

Ambrose tore one of the condoms off, climbed back into bed, and slid the protection on as his mouth returned to hers, her hormones taking up the same dance again as though the music had only briefly paused but the desire to revel had not. She almost laughed at the silly nature of her thoughts and that dumb hat that had saved the moment, just all of it. Of him. And how much she'd needed this brief vacation from reality and also from herself.

His mouth came to her breast, his tongue lapping at her nipple before he gave one long suck, causing a lightning rod of arousal to shoot between her legs, her hips bucking toward his hand. "Please," she said, the word ripped from her throat. She needed him inside her or she'd lose her mind. Her skin felt charged, her nerve endings vibrating with the need for release.

Their eyes met as he lined himself up at her entrance and then surged inside, his lids closing as his lips parted, expression contorting in bliss. *Oh God. Oh my God.* And then his hips began to move.

She watched him as he thrust inside her, his dark lashes lying in a crescent beneath his eyes. They were thick and fringed, and there was something beautifully boyish about them that was so contradictory to the muscular breadth of his shoulders beneath her palms and the masculine scent of his skin. And of course, the way his body was moving over her, and inside her, a steady pace that was nudging her higher with every quickened press. He'd been a study in contrasts to her since the moment they'd met, but one thing she could not deny was her attraction to him or this thrilling feeling of watching his reaction to her. Watching the way he was trying so mightily to hold on to control, and almost managing but not quite.

She had a flash of the way he'd gazed up at her as he knelt before her after the attack, hands warm on her thighs, and then of the way he'd looked when he described the songbird in South America. Both those expressions were flitting over his features now—concern, peace, focus, but with the addition of naked desire. God, he was so expressive when he wanted to be. Or maybe when he couldn't help himself. And those eyes, those sleepy, sexy eyes that nearly sent her spinning.

He gave a twist of his hips that sent a shock wave of pleasure to her toes, and she gasped, wrapping her legs around him and tilting her hips so he could go even deeper. "Lennon," he whispered, a plea of his own. And she didn't want this to end but could feel the pinpricks of pleasure dancing between her legs and tightening her belly.

It only took three more strokes before she came, shattering apart and then slowly coming back together, blinking up at him as he increased his pace, finally shattering, too, as he groaned and panted and pressed his face into her neck, rocking slowly and then stilling with a pleasure-filled sigh.

They spent long minutes just breathing together, as she ran her fingernails over his back and he feathered his lips along her shoulder. When he leaned back to look at her, he appeared just a little bit drunk, and she breathed out a short laugh. He kissed her lips and then rolled to the side, gathering her in his arms, her cheek pressed against his warm skin.

She didn't remember falling asleep, but the next time she woke, a slip of gray was showing around the blind. She extricated herself from Ambrose's arms and scooted to the other side of the bed, grabbing her discarded robe as she stood.

She used the bathroom, and when she came back out into the bedroom, Ambrose was sitting on the side of the bed, fully dressed, his features shadowy in the low light of dawn. "I should go," he said softly. He looked up at her, and she detected the uncertainty in his expression, and perhaps just a bit of regret. He stood, running his hand through his tousled hair as she fumbled to pull her robe all the way closed to her neck, disappointment and a drip of embarrassment making her feel slow and gawky. She wasn't sure what to say, didn't know if she should ask him to stay. He'd obviously wanted to be with her—she knew she hadn't imagined his response. But she'd also begged him at a certain point.

"Okay," she said. What else could she say? And whether he'd responded to her or not, he'd only come over here to make sure she was okay and that she wasn't alone. She felt slightly rejected, and a little embarrassed, but she was also still exhausted. And however this had ended, he *had* made her feel better. Talking had helped. The rush of lust had helped, too, and so had the orgasm. Her muscles felt lax, her emotions settled. She'd slept like a rock in his arms for several hours, and she knew she'd have no problem going back to sleep. And truthfully, he was probably right to leave now rather than stay longer. What happened had shaken her, and she hadn't had much time at all to process it. She needed to sleep as long as her body told her to, and she needed to find her own equilibrium.

He paused, his heavy gaze moving over her face, cataloging. He gave a succinct nod.

God, this was awkward. And yet, she still couldn't bring herself to regret it. She was halfway back to sleep already, and she wanted nothing more than to fall back into bed.

She walked him to the door, and when he got there, he turned back around quickly, opened his mouth to say something, closed it, and then leaned forward and kissed her softly on her mouth. It looked like he was having an internal argument with himself, but finally he said, "Get some more sleep, Lennon. Goodbye." And then he turned and walked away, and she closed the door behind him, confused about why his goodbye had sounded permanent.

CHAPTER SIXTEEN

The elevator came to a bumpy halt as it stopped on the third floor of the hotel Ambrose was currently staying in. He stepped out, adjusting the grocery bags in his hands and heading down the long carpeted hallway toward his room, around a corner and down another short hall. He'd asked for something as far from the elevator as possible, though, and they'd certainly honored his request.

His mind was filled with Lennon, with the way she'd felt beneath him the night before, the memory of her quiet moans, the echoes of which still made heat flare through his veins. It wasn't only attraction he felt for her—if he hadn't known that before, he knew it now. He could fall for her so easily. He probably already had.

The way he'd felt when he'd realized she was being attacked by the man in the tent dispelled any notion that what he felt for her was the same concern he'd feel for anyone else being victimized in front of him. No, what he'd felt when he'd come upon the sight of Lennon fighting for her life was a primal response, the depth of which he hadn't even known he possessed.

He switched the bags from one hand to the other. He'd reacted in rage at the man hurting Lennon, but he'd pulled back before going too far. In a way it was a test that he'd have never confronted if not for this particular circumstance. And he'd passed. He'd been angry—rageful, even—and terrified, too, that she was injured beyond repair. And yes, he'd expressed that using violence because it'd been the only choice. But he'd remained in control of his mind and his body, pulling back when he'd overcome the threat. And he hadn't hesitated in responding, not even for a fraction of a second. A gust of cool relief was still blowing through him, along with the concern for Lennon and all the other feelings she stirred in him. He'd wanted to stay in that bed of hers, Lennon wrapped in his arms, more than anything he could remember wanting in a very long time. But it wasn't right for so many reasons, and so he'd gone.

A shadow moved, and Ambrose halted, his pulse jumping as he reached for his gun. The shadow stepped from the turn in the hallway, becoming a man. Ambrose let out a slow hiss of breath, dropping his hand from the holster at his waist. "For the love of Christ, Finch. I might have shot you."

The man grinned as he approached. "You can't kill me, Ambrose. Don't you know I've got nine lives?"

Ambrose grinned back and then pulled Finch into a hug as they both laughed. "Yeah, I know, but I don't want to take any of your last remaining ones. You've got a fight on your hands, and we're all counting on you to win it."

At the mention of his current fight, Finch removed the beanie he was wearing and ran a hand over what had once been a close-cropped Afro and was now a shiny bald head. "This cancer might take my hair, brother, but it won't take me."

Ambrose smiled, and he felt the relief of Finch's optimism, a necessary ingredient if he was going to win. "Come on in," he said, using the key card to open the door. The room smelled stale, the lingering scent of a time when smoking was allowed still ingrained in the walls and the furniture. This place definitely wasn't anything fancy, but it wasn't the worst place he'd ever stayed, either, not by a long shot. Ambrose set the grocery bags down on the desk and closed the curtains. "I met your son the other day. He seems like a good guy."

Finch pulled out the desk chair, flipped it around, and sat down backward. "He told me. I mean, he told me a cop and an FBI agent stopped by the center. I got this address from Doc. And Darius is a good guy. The kid has my fire and his mother's heart. He's a work of art, man, he really is. A human Da Vinci. I could stare at that dude all day." He laughed. "Is that weird? Eh, wait until you have kids, you'll get it."

Ambrose smiled but shook his head. "No kids for me."

"You might change your mind."

He wouldn't. Not on that. "Anyway, I wouldn't expect anything less than a human work of art, with a dad like you."

Finch ran his hand over his head again. "Thankfully the kid was so young when I got clean. If not . . ."

"Hey, no reason for regrets, Finch. You cleaned up, and you raised a great kid. That alternate life is somewhere twisting in the mist, unattached to you."

Finch smiled. "You always did have a way with words. All that reading. Twisting in the mist. Yeah, you're right, I know. It's easy to get lost in the what-ifs sometimes, you know? Sitting in that chair every week while they pump chemicals into my body gives me all kinds of time to consider an alternate life, the one I was heading toward." He paused for a minute. "Mostly, I like thinking about it. It makes me proud that I changed paths. But other times, it gives me the damn chills, you know? That kid . . . that kid would have been an entirely different person if I hadn't gotten my shit together."

"A lot of people would be entirely different people if not for you."

"Nah. I only helped a few people on the final steps of their journey."

"Bullshit."

Finch laughed and then squinted one eye. "You still box?"

"Hell yes, I still box." Ambrose ducked his head and did a few jabs into the air. "Do you wanna go a few rounds for old times' sake? Think you can take me?"

Finch laughed. "Probably not. You look cut. Good for you."

His expression became serious again, and Ambrose could tell he was still peering down that fog-filled road less traveled. And Ambrose understood, because he did that sometimes too. "Hey, Finch, those what-ifs, that other life that got cut short—it's the point of all this."

"I know, man. I know." He met Ambrose's eyes. "The project, it has to go on. It can't stop. All the work . . . all the lives. We've gotta protect it."

"That's what I'm doing. I'm taking a big risk. And it can't last much longer unless I wanna end up behind bars. I wouldn't do well in prison, Finch."

"Yeah, I know. What have you discovered so far?"

Ambrose took the six-pack of water bottles he'd bought out of the grocery bag, tore one off, and held it up to Finch in offer. Finch shook his head, and Ambrose opened the cap and took a swig as he thought back to the information he'd acquired from the police files on the two previous crime scenes. "The pills are almost identical to Doc's product. Same imprint. The concoction is the same in both ingredients and strength, with the singular addition of an LSD coating."

"LSD?"

"Yeah. Out of a therapeutic setting, these ones would send anyone for a loop, and likely not a good one."

"The shape is the same?"

Ambrose nodded. "Same shape, same color, and like I said, identical imprint."

"That can't be a coincidence."

"No, I don't believe so either."

"What does the addition of the LSD mean?"

"I don't know. Maybe a mistake. Maybe something to make it stronger, or more likely to achieve some sort of something."

"Maybe a message?"

"What kind of message?"

"That this person knows about the project and is adding his own twist?"

Ambrose thought about that for a moment. "Could be." A sign that this person wasn't simply stealing or recreating product but adding to it somehow. "Another thing that strikes me as a message is the scattering of pills left at each scene. Even if you purchased a drug like that on the street, you'd most likely buy one for each person joining you."

"Like ecstasy or acid," Finch said.

"Yeah. This isn't the type of drug to support a habit. It's a party favor."

"For a fucked-up party."

"Well, yes. But still. The fact that there are several left behind tells me the person leaving them very much wants us to see the pills themselves, and not just the ingredients that show up in an autopsy."

"Agreed." Finch blew out a breath. "What else are you thinking?"

Ambrose took another long drink of water. "I think someone is doing a bad mock-up of the project." It'd been his worry going into this, and the reason he'd taken the risk he had. The existence of the pills hadn't yet been released to the media, but Doc knew someone in the SFPD who had leaked the information to him after he'd recognized the pills—or thought he had—in the evidence room. Ambrose had been contacted, and he'd come to San Francisco to infiltrate the SFPD. He just needed to get his hands on the case files and make some copies, nothing more, nothing less. But not more than twelve hours after he'd arrived, he'd been called to a murder scene. The opportunity to set foot inside one that held the similarities he'd been looking for was a stroke of luck. The fact that it'd made him even more certain that the similarities were purposeful worried the hell out of him. Feeling immediately drawn to the inspector working the case had come completely out of left field.

Life. It sure could be strange.

"A bad mock-up of the project," Finch repeated. "There must be other similarities, then."

"The victims, for one. Homeless. Strung out. The police have only ID'd one and are still gathering information on him, but I'd bet anything that as soon as they ID more, they'll find that several have been diagnosed with PTSD." He paused. Or maybe they hadn't. Maybe it'd been missed and buried under a whole slew of other diagnoses that were the side effects of that one. "There's evidence that some purposeful regression occurred," he told Finch.

Finch's forehead crunched into folds of wrinkles. "What evidence was there of that?"

"Children's toys and also sex toys."

Finch seemed to think about that. "Some people get off on that stuff. Or they think they do. But . . . yeah, in the midst of the purple pills with a 'BB' imprint, it looks like something we need to figure out." He pinched the sides of his bottom lip. "Who the fuck would be doing this, Ambrose?"

"The only thing I can figure is that it's a member. Or a member who talked to someone who didn't agree with the project."

"That's never happened in almost twenty years. You know how we all feel about the project. Who would risk it?"

"People are people, Finch. They mess up. They trust the wrong person."

Finch still looked unconvinced, though, and still deeply troubled. "They'd have told us," he said. "They'd have let us know they made a mistake so we'd be prepared."

"Maybe they don't even know."

"We all know at this point. We all know there's a situation."

"I don't know what to say. I can only tell you what I know so far. Doc is formulating an antidote to the drug. Apparently there's a compound that blocks receptors involved in the uptake of hallucinogens. The science is all way over my head. Doc thinks he's close but needs time."

"What good will an antidote do if we don't know who to give it to until after the fact?" *After the fact*, of course, meaning they were dead and wearing a gruesome scream.

"That's the other problem." Ambrose reached for the folder of photos that had been included in the case files. "I need you to take these to Doc and see if he recognizes them. Some of those photos are pretty hard to look at."

Finch took the folder but didn't open it. "I'll take them to Doc tomorrow." He blew out a breath. "Anything else?"

"The man they identified told someone he'd found a miracle treatment for his drug addiction."

"That could mean anything. Man, some people refer to methadone that way."

"Yeah, I know."

Finch moved his tongue over his teeth for a moment. "Do the police have any theories?"

Ambrose took another sip of the water, capped it, and set it down. "Lennon . . . Inspector Gray theorized about a role-play at the most recent crime scene."

"A role-play is pretty on target with regression therapy."

"Yeah," he said. "She sees a lot. She was leery of me at first, but she wasn't sure why."

"And now?"

"Now she trusts me more." And that made him happy, but it also brought him more than a twinge of guilt. Because her instincts were right, and he'd slipped past her defenses anyway.

Finch narrowed his eyes, one side of his lips curling as he watched Ambrose. "Oh damn. You like her." He laughed. "Well, shit. This complicates an already complicated matter, doesn't it?"

"Finch . . ."

"You can't BS a BSer, man. Didn't I teach you that?" He grinned, and Ambrose paused but then laughed, tipping his chin as he conceded the point. He never had been able to lie to Finch, and more than that, he didn't want to. Finch was his hero, his mentor, and the best example of an honorable man that he'd ever known. He'd wanted to be seen by him when he was young, and he wanted to be seen by him now.

He leaned back and blew out a breath. "It's the damnedest thing. I get lost in her," he admitted. "For someone like me . . . you know. She makes me forget." And last night had been like nothing he'd experienced before. Even after she'd fallen asleep, he'd lain there with her in his arms for hours, just living completely in the moment. He was so damn *happy*, he wanted to sing. Or dance or do something so completely out of character that only *that* would convey the way he felt changed by her touch. Her taste. Being connected to her so intimately. Just *her*.

And yet he couldn't. He couldn't act on his happiness, his desire to see her, to touch her again, to get lost in her in ways he'd only scratched the surface of—or so he imagined.

Finch watched him for a moment as his thoughts flitted through his mind. "Does she make you forget?" he asked. "Or does she make it not matter?"

Leave it to Finch to strike right at the heart of it. It was a good question, and Ambrose took a moment to ponder it, a well of hope widening as he did so. He'd never thought it possible that his past wouldn't matter—and he didn't necessarily mean as far as others. He had people in his life who accepted him for who he was and what he'd done. Hell, he had a whole community of those people on speed dial if he needed them. What shocked the hell out of him was spending time—any amount of time—with a woman who made *him* believe, even for minutes at a time, that who he'd been just didn't matter. And for those small gaps of time, he felt the melting of all his past selves into one solid person, and he was only the Ambrose of present, the one he'd fought so hard to become. But thinking about it now? It awed him and humbled him and made him wish for things he'd sworn off long ago.

And she'd achieved that, the inspector who tried so hard to be unaffected by the suffering of others and twisted herself in knots because she never could get there and believed she should. "Maybe both," he finally answered.

"Does she know about your connection to the case?" Finch asked. "Does she know about Jett?"

"No. I haven't told her a word about that."

"Well tell me what she's like," Finch said. "This Lennon Gray."

This Lennon Gray. Named for a peacemaker. Her name even sounded like something he could fall into.

He sighed, and he let himself talk about her even though he shouldn't, because it just felt so damn good. "She's smart," he told Finch. "But she's even more intuitive. She doesn't like her job much, though. She doubts herself." *She's beautiful.* But he didn't say that. It felt personal. If Finch ever met her—which was unlikely—he'd see that for himself. Ambrose liked her shape and her skin and her hair. He was drawn to her features and her expressions. But even so, all those things felt like the least of what she was. "She's been hurt, but it didn't make her jaded. And she comes from this great family." He thought back to the evening he'd spent with the Grays, how it'd felt both surreal and like the truest thing he'd ever experienced. It knocked him for a loop. People *lived* that way, whole lives surrounded by love and laughter. He'd known it, of course, and he even considered himself to have that now. He had support, he had a large group of people who would give him the shirt off their back, and he'd do the same. But they were family by way of a circumstance that had brought them together later in life. None of them had had that as children or teens; none of them had been guided through the confusing time of early adulthood. Not even close. "Yeah," he said. "They're great and so is she."

"Family," Finch said. "You've got that, too, you know."

"I know. Yeah, I do." And he'd made it far beyond any self-pity he might have stepped toward in his younger years. He hadn't had a support system when he was a kid, but he did now. And damn, but he appreciated it.

"So what's the plan?"

"Inspector Gray's out for at least a few more days," he said. "I didn't make an appearance at the station either," he added. "But my informant there assures me everything's cool. I'm playing it by ear." What he was really doing was playing it by ear with another element thrown in that hadn't been a factor when he'd arrived here. He'd hated saying goodbye to Lennon earlier and wondered if she'd picked up on the solemnity of his farewell, his fear that the goodbye was final. Was there a way he could arrange things so that he didn't have to part ways permanently with Lennon Gray? Because it was the last thing he wanted to do.

Finch stood. "I better take off. I just couldn't resist stopping by to see you, man. Keep me updated. And hey, we have a session in two weeks. Can you be there? At least at the end?"

"Yeah, I can be there."

Ambrose walked Finch to the door, where he gave him one more hug. "Stay safe." And with that, Finch was gone.

CHAPTER SEVENTEEN

The best way out is always
through.
—Robert Frost

Seventeen Years Ago
Patient Number 0022

"There you go, take a step. You can do it. I won't let you fall."

Jett blinked. He was in a forest. He didn't know how he'd gotten there. He didn't know when or where or how or why. He took in a big breath. The air felt cooler, and several somethings met his nose. Pine. Dirt. Wet leaves.

Fear. He made a sound in his throat, pulling back.

"You're fine. I'm here. I won't let you fall," she repeated. "This place is safe. Those smells are safe. I'm here to keep you safe. Do you feel my hand in yours?"

Breathe. In. Out. In. Out. Just like the back and the forth, it soothed him and calmed his fear.

In the distance, he heard the *thud, thud, thud.* Very soft. A drumbeat. His breath came easier.

"Step forward," she instructed. "Put your feet on the dirt."

He took a step, the scratchy solid beneath his feet becoming softer ground. Earth. He looked down, bare toes coming into focus. They were his toes. He wiggled them in the dirt.

"That's it. You are you, and your feet are anchored to the ground." He felt her squeeze his hand. That was an anchor too. "Do you feel your feet touching the earth? What does that feel like?"

He didn't know. He wasn't sure. It didn't feel bad, especially not with her hand gripping his, keeping him safe. He wiggled his toes again and took a step. He was movement and skin on ground. He was separate but also not. He was him. He wiggled his fingers and heard her mouth turn into a smile. He felt warm on his face and turned it toward the source. The sun. He felt sunshine and breeze and dirt beneath his feet. He was inside his body, but he was also outside, feeling the world around him. He could touch it and smell it and feel it on his skin.

And he could see it.

The space in front of him widened beyond the spot where he stood. And then he saw the water, a narrow stream that splashed by, a small rocky shore along the edge. A fish jumped into the air and then plunged back into the water, and he could feel its slippery, scaly skin in his palm. He could feel it wriggling and flailing, and he didn't know how or why, but he could.

He took a step and then another. The woman walked with him, never letting go of his hand. He placed his foot on the sandy pebbles, feeling the bumpy texture on his sole. Other senses opened, and the flash of a blossom unfolding its petals blinked inside his mind. He heard the water now, bubbling and splashing, and he smelled it too. Fresh. Sweet. Good.

He stretched his leg and dipped his toe in. It was wet and cold, and it cascaded over his skin. It made him laugh. The woman laughed, too, and he heard her feet crunch on the rocks next to him. He turned his head to look at her, to see the smile on her face. Her skin looked both soft and papery, and a halo of red curls surrounded her face. Her teeth were big and white, and wrinkles fanned out around her eyes like sunrays. She was the back and the forth and the hand holding his and the *thud, thud, thud.* She was good. "Wonderful, isn't it?"

He nodded. There was something in his throat. "What's your name?" he asked.

"Mama Maisie," she said, her smile brightening.

Mama. The word scared him, but he didn't know why. "Or how about just Maisie?" she asked. The *thud, thud, thud* in the background grew louder, and his lungs filled with air.

He nodded again. *Maisie.* The voice and the song and the back and the forth were a woman named Maisie. And she held his hand in hers.

"What should I call you?" she asked.

His head swam. He had a name. Someone had given him a name. A woman. She'd smiled when she'd said it. "Jett," he answered.

"Jett," Maisie repeated. "Okay, Jett. And now, sweetness," she said, giving his hand another squeeze as he took his foot from the water and placed it back on the bumpy pebbles. "It's time to choose a guide."

"A guide?" He heard his voice. It sounded cracked and unused. He had to push it from his chest.

"Mm. An animal, maybe a bird? Your guide will stay with you even when I'm not here. Your guide will never ever leave you, no matter what."

Fear. He squeezed her hand tighter. "But I want you. I don't want you to go."

"Not yet. And I won't ever be far. But I can't come with you where you need to go. Only your guide can. What should that be?"

A guide? He didn't understand. Where did he need to go? He wanted to stay here, under the sunshine, feeling his skin and his toes and his hand in Maisie's. Safe. Warm. He wanted to use his voice, to test different words and different sounds. To feel it rush over his tongue and whisper between his lips.

"You can do it," Maisie said. "I know you can. Focus. Close your eyes and call your guide."

He did as she said, closing his eyes. But he didn't know what to focus on, didn't know who or what to call.

"There it is!" Maisie said. "Open your eyes. There it is." She sounded happy.

He opened his eyes and saw what she was looking at. A white dove spread its wings and flew from the branches of a tall tree, gliding nearer. He blinked in wonder and raised his arm, and it landed on his wrist. "A dove?" he whispered. A dove with snowy feathers and glossy black eyes.

"A dove, yes," Maisie agreed, her voice soft and sweet. "Beautiful. Doves signify peace. Did you know that?"

Peace. Yes. He'd wished for peace in a time and space he couldn't now recall. Somewhere different. "Peace," he repeated softly. Then the dove spread its wings again and soared into the sky, gliding above the trees.

"Follow it, sweetness. *Go.*"

CHAPTER EIGHTEEN

The call that four more bodies had been found came in just after 5:00 p.m. the next day as Ambrose was leaving for the ring. He'd tossed his equipment aside and pulled on his dress pants, button-down shirt, and tie. Then he'd taken a minute, just one, to sit there with the situation in front of him. Lennon was off, and so he'd likely be at the scene alone, at least for a few minutes. This was a good opportunity, one he hadn't thought would present itself. And he had to look at the bigger picture, because lives were involved, ones he felt responsible for.

He glanced at his phone, and for a moment he thought about giving in and calling her. Fuck, he'd practically had to sit on his hands all day not to pick up the phone just to hear her voice. But he'd already made a complicated situation even messier, and so he gathered his resolve and reached for his jacket, wallet, and keys before heading for the door.

Thankfully, an Uber was available immediately, and he was at the crime scene in less than twenty minutes. The abandoned building at Pier 70, located a few miles from downtown San Francisco, looked industrial and was likely once used for ship manufacturing. It had obviously been vacant for many years, however, and was now in a state of advanced deterioration.

Chain-link fences encircled the area, and NO TRESPASSING signs were posted everywhere. Clearly someone had disregarded those warnings. The officer at the door greeted him when he arrived, and Ambrose flashed his badge at the young woman. He felt mildly guilty. In his early years, it'd been somewhat surprising how easily a badge and the right name could get you through a guarded door. But he was used to it now. "Agent Mars. Lieutenant Byrd sent me."

The woman stepped aside, and he gave her a nod, ducking under the crime scene tape. He smelled the death even before his brain had fully parsed the situation in front of him. Bodies. Bloody. Mangled.

"We meet again," the crime scene tech he thought he remembered as Teresa said, from where she was kneeling next to one of the bodies to his left.

Dammit. He'd hoped he'd be the only one here. "Teresa, right?"

"Yes. Agent Mars."

"Ambrose. Have you been here long?"

"Fifteen minutes or so. Just enough time to take stock of the scene."

"What's the preliminary cause of death?" he asked.

"These people got violent. They were all stabbed and beaten. It was a melee, Agent. There's blunt-force trauma and deep lacerations, and the woman near the door back there was practically decapitated." Teresa pointed to the bloody footprints leading from the center of the room to where the woman now lay. "It looks like she managed to hold her head on as she staggered to the corner and died."

He grimaced. "Drugs?"

"Yup. The same Benjamin Buttons are on the windowsill over there." *Benjamin Buttons.* For a moment, he was confused. *Ah, "BB."* They'd nicknamed it because they had no idea what it stood for.

She pointed to the dusty window to his right, and as he walked over to it, he moved past a dead man on the floor wearing the same eternal scream that he'd seen on the face of the woman identified as Cherish. Jesus, that was hard to look at. Because it spoke of the suffering that man had experienced as he took his very final breath. But the term *eternal scream* naturally made him wonder if they'd landed in the afterlife unable to shake the horror of their death. For this man, and perhaps the others, there hadn't even been an instant of peace as the air drained from his lungs and his heart slowed to a stop. It disturbed him greatly, because this was the third face at similar scenes that had looked just like that. Two might have been a coincidence, but three meant some devil had figured out how to repeat the terror that occurred for these people just before they died. That face was not natural. That was the face you only saw in the mirror when you woke from the worst nightmare of your life, screaming and sweating and prying invisible hands from around your neck.

He had an idea of how it might have been achieved, but it was too demented to consider just now, especially with the scent of fear and human decay heavy in the air.

The pills were scattered on the dusty windowsill, same shape, same imprint—only these ones were a pale blue instead of lavender. What did that indicate? That something had been changed? Or achieved?

Teresa came up behind him. "Same 'BB' imprint. But a different color, so maybe they're from a different batch? Tests will confirm. I already took photos, but be careful about disturbing them because I haven't done more than that."

He gave her a distracted nod. Teresa turned, going back over to the body she'd been working on, collecting samples and evidence and whatever else she was putting in bags using tweezers. He needed some of those pills. And it was unfortunate that the windowsill was so dusty, because there was no way to take some without making it obvious. Not to mention she'd taken photographs of the number of pills. But he was here for a reason, and he had to do what must be done. It didn't mean he liked it. It meant he had his priorities in line.

He leaned over, pretending to peer at the pills, and brushed several off the ledge into his palm and then turned, walking to the body in the far corner and pocketing them as he moved.

He walked from one bludgeoned, bloodied body to another, his gaze moving over the wounds and specifics that he could see, taking stock.

He cataloged all the items he could see and came to the same conclusion he was sure Teresa would—they'd used any available items as weapons. A *massacre* had occurred here.

The first two scenes had featured two bodies, the third three, and now this one was four. Things were escalating, the pile of bodies growing. And there was some dreadful point here that he thought he was beginning to understand.

"Could you tell if all the murder weapons are accounted for?" he asked Teresa.

She looked up from the woman on the floor. "From an initial glance, it appears that all the weapons are accounted for and that they used items just lying around," she said, gesturing over to a piece of twisted metal on the floor by the wall. From this angle, Ambrose could see the blood on the sharp, rusted edge. "I haven't confirmed yet, but stick around."

Ambrose gave her a thin smile. That wouldn't be possible. And he trusted this woman's initial assessment. She seemed competent and observant, and she'd been doing this job for a long time.

He noticed some disturbed dust on the floor near the corner, where there were a few toppled crates. The marks next to them appeared to be shoe imprints, if the person had worn shoes with completely flat soles. *Or booties over his footwear.* He looked up to see a wooden beam stretching to the opposite wall. "Teresa, did you see this?" he asked, glancing back at her.

She looked up, her gaze going to the floor where he was pointing. "Imprints?"

"Yes, but it looks like these ones belong to someone wearing booties. The details of the soles are completely missing."

She frowned and then leaned so that she could see the soles of the shoes on the feet of the victim she was next to. Then she glanced over at the other bodies. "I'll check their shoes, but if the dust is recently disturbed, those might belong to an unknown subject. Maybe the one who anonymously called this in? I'll make sure to take some samples."

He nodded distractedly. Had the person who'd given these victims the pills used the crates to climb up and place something on the beam? A recording device, perhaps? One he came back to retrieve before calling this in? Was he watching it now? Replaying the carnage? The *aftermath* of this was awful enough. To see it live? And to enjoy it? He couldn't begin to imagine how sick you'd have to be. "I'm going to go look outside and see if I spot anything," he said to Teresa, who was once again deeply immersed in her work.

"Okay. See you soon," she murmured.

His stomach knotted, and regret was a strong acid burning the lining of his gut. Given all the emotions he felt, standing in a room with four people who'd died horrifying deaths, he felt like he might lose his lunch. He took a few deep breaths, managing to contain the nausea. He wished he had another choice than what he was about to do. He really did.

Lennon. What was she doing right now? It was after dinnertime. He pictured her cozied up on her couch, a blanket over her lap, and the picture his mind conjured made his heart squeeze with longing. The department wouldn't figure out what he'd done for a couple of hours. She'd probably be greeted by the news in the morning. And then she'd hate him.

As Ambrose stepped through the door, a couple of marked cars were pulling up, and two other criminalists were just ducking beneath the tape. He greeted them with a nod and then walked past, going around the corner and then taking up a slow jog as he moved away. He'd call an Uber once he'd gone a few miles. His "job" at the SFPD had come to an end.

CHAPTER NINETEEN

The sun had barely finished rising when Lennon drove through the cemetery gates. She parked and walked slowly toward the familiar grave, resting her hand on top of the stone when she stopped in front of it. It was cold beneath her palm, not just from the chill of the night but also because Tanner's family had chosen a beautiful spot beneath a large oak that kept it mostly in shade.

Lennon threw down the blanket she kept in her trunk and knelt on the dewy grass and ran her hand over his name. "Hi, Tanner. I'm sorry it's been so long." She reached out and plucked a dead leaf off the fall flowers planted in front of his grave. Unlike her, Tanner's mother came here regularly and made sure the plantings were fresh and his stone was free of dirt and moss. She continued to care for him in the only way she was able, and Lennon hoped it helped her, even if only a little.

"I haven't checked in on your parents in too long either." What had it been? Three months now? Four? In the thirteen years since Tanner had died, Lennon had never gone that long without contacting them, and now it almost felt like she'd have to explain herself if she called. So she'd kept putting it off. Because really? She didn't have an explanation. She'd just been busy living and working. And she'd thought about them, but she hadn't reached out. She hadn't even called to wish them a happy Thanksgiving. A lump formed in her chest, and she felt a flailing inside. Maybe being too busy was only an excuse. Maybe she'd wanted to put some distance between them. Maybe she was *ready*, and so instead of addressing it, she'd told herself she'd just forgotten.

"I don't want to let them go," she told Tanner as though he'd been keeping up with her inner thoughts, her inner struggling, "because it feels like letting another part of you go too." She let out a shaky sigh. "But sometimes I wonder if it keeps us all stuck, in a way. Sometimes I wonder if that ringing of the phone each month is just a reminder of the pain, and maybe, in a way, they dread it."

Or maybe I do.

Maybe those calls had started feeling like an anchor to the pain and she'd wanted to unmoor herself and create some distance. She wanted to know what that shore looked like from a different vantage point. Maybe if she drifted for a little while, the sunrise would come into view.

She shifted so she was sitting on her hip and brought her legs to the side. "Work has been intense though, Tan. You'd laugh so hard if you saw me walking around crime scenes and standing over dead bodies in the ME's office. Remember that time I almost passed out when you sliced your foot on a piece of glass at the beach?" She let out a huffy laugh. "I've changed a lot since high school. I wonder how you would have changed. I miss you, you know that?" The rawness of grief had faded, but sometimes, even more now than when she'd begun healing, she'd feel a wave of it. It felt like losing him all over again when she considered who he'd be now. Because she—they—hadn't only lost Tanner when he was nineteen; they'd lost him at every age he'd never be. And so in some sense, the loss never stopped. In many ways, it deepened over time.

She'd never forgotten the way the lights buzzed that night. A dying bulb, an electricity short; she had no idea what had caused it. But she did remember the loud buzz and the tremble of light and dark that had washed over his face the last time she saw him alive. And even now, when the sadness overcame her, in the background she heard that never-ending electrical buzz.

God, they'd have been married for almost a decade now, if their plans had become reality. They'd probably have a couple of kids. They'd have gone on that honeymoon to Tahiti. She'd have used the passport that, instead, had expired in the back of her sock drawer. That version of herself felt so far away suddenly, a dream within a dream, a movie she couldn't remember the name of. A song she still knew the melody for but could no longer sing the words.

The thought made her picture the songbird Ambrose had spoken of, the one that had appeared so vibrantly in her mind, the notes of a misty song trailing from its beak as it welcomed the dawn. The image had been so beautiful, and she'd only been told the story. What must that have been like in person?

Her finger paused over the last letter of Tanner's name as Lennon realized she'd been thinking about Ambrose while sitting in front of Tanner's grave. Ambrose, who hadn't even called her since they'd slept together. Ambrose, whom she couldn't seem to stop thinking about.

What are you doing here, Lennon?

"Anyway," she said quickly, moving her mind from that question. "I've been partnered up with an FBI agent. And . . . I don't know how to describe him. It's like he's jaded and innocent and gruff and soft. He walks around crime scenes and fights drug-fueled psychos, but then he also tells stories about songbirds and blushes when my mom says he smells good. I'm not sure what to make of him. You know how I am. I like straightforward. I like black and white. I'm not good with shades of gray." For whatever reason, she pictured Ambrose Mars eating that fruit cup, examining each piece of fruit as though it was a tiny marvel. And then she saw him telling the story about the man who'd been saved by the sea lion, his soft voice enthralling an entire room. The way his unusual eyes had hung on her and the way she'd felt held captive. *In the end, stories are all we have.*

"He's hard to describe," she murmured. "But I trust him—professionally, anyway. He proved that he has my back when things go south. I'm going to make sure he's not put in that position again. I'm going to be much more careful. I promise, Tan." She brought her hand to the bruised eye that she'd pretty successfully—she thought—managed to cover with makeup. "This won't happen again . . ." She trailed off. As if she needed to reassure Tanner of her safety.

"What I really came here to say is that I miss you. I don't want you to think that I don't. No matter what. I . . . if I don't come here as much it's not because I've forgotten. I never forget. I carry you with me, and I always will."

She didn't know what else to say to him, so instead she just sat there, watching the sun rise higher in the sky and picturing his face, forever young and beautiful.

~

"Good morning," she said to Adella as she took off her coat and hung it on the back of her chair. Adella gave her a nervous glance, her gaze going over Lennon's head right before she heard Lieutenant Byrd's voice behind her.

"Gray, can I see you in my office?"

"Sure," she murmured. What the hell was going on? She looked back at Adella, but she had already turned back to her computer screen.

Lennon followed Lieutenant Byrd to his office and closed the door behind her. "What's up?" she asked.

"Do you know who he is?"

Lennon sat down slowly on the chair in front of the lieutenant's desk. "Do I know who who is?"

"Ambrose Mars."

She gave her head a small shake. "You told me he's an FBI agent here to work the 'BB' pill case with me."

"Well, he's not. He's not an FBI agent, and apparently that's not his real name either. Ambrose Mars doesn't exist."

The internal alarm bells started slowly at first and then swelled into a clanging symphony. "I'm sorry, *what*?"

"He walked away from another scene yesterday and took a handful of evidence with him. When I called the field office in Pleasant Hill, where he supposedly came from, I discovered there's no one there by that name."

She felt dizzy and like she might puke. What the fuck was going on? There had been another scene yesterday? Why hadn't anyone called her?

"He doesn't fucking exist," the lieutenant practically spat out.

Doesn't exist. But he most certainly did exist. He'd been in her apartment. He'd been in her parents' home. He'd kissed her naked breasts, for Christ's sake. *He was inside my body.* God, she felt like she might be hyperventilating. He'd been lying to her? Posing as an FBI agent? She pressed her fingers to her temples, as if trying to stop her brain from misinterpreting the words the lieutenant was saying to her.

"This is a catastrophe," Lieutenant Byrd said. "Someone infiltrated the SFPD, stole three case files and crime scene evidence, and then up and disappeared."

"How, though?" she asked, her voice a mere croak. "I thought the call came down from the chief's office. They . . . sent him here." Someone called. They'd said he was good with the down-and-out. And he was. He'd seemed empathetic. He'd seemed . . .

"The call came from the right number, so there's either someone working with him internally or they managed to get hold of technology to make it look like the right number. It's being investigated with the utmost fervor." He paused. "They're looking at you, too, Lennon."

"*Me?*" she asked, the outrage that was beginning to spark inside her clear in her voice. He'd lied to her. He'd *used* her.

"He was at your house a few nights ago. After hours."

What? How did the lieutenant know that, if it wasn't him who'd given Ambrose her address like she'd assumed? Then she remembered the call. The bruise cream.

Adella. She'd ratted her out and made it look like Lennon was part of some scam the fake agent was running? She felt like tearing someone's eyes out and collapsing in tears. "He came over, supposedly to check on me after my attack." *He brought me watermelon stars and held me in his arms.* Those sparks ignited into flames, anger burning away the tears that had threatened to fall moments ago.

"Well, regardless, Internal is taking this extremely seriously. They want you at their offices right away. And Lennon, I'm sorry, but you'll need to turn in your gun and badge."

CHAPTER TWENTY

Your pain is the breaking of
the shell that encloses your
understanding.
—Kahlil Gibran

Seventeen Years Ago
Patient Number 0022

The sun grew dim, the warmth abated, but still Jett walked, following that elegant bird as it dipped and rose, its head turning now and again to make sure he wasn't lost.

Don't be afraid, it told him, speaking in some way he didn't know how to explain, delivering messages straight into his head.

The scent of pine increased, and then something else met his nose, mixed with the smells of the earth and the air. Animals.

Sheep. Pigs. Goats.

He moaned and gripped his head as acid fear rained down, penetrating his skin and melting his bones.

Feathers. He felt feathers on his cheek, ruffling over his neck, and he gasped, turning slightly to see the dove sitting on his shoulder. The dove let out a cooing sound, tilting her head and rubbing it on Jett's jaw. *Back. Forth. Back. Forth. Thud, thud, thud.* His hammering heart slowed; air filled his hollow lungs.

Feel your feet on the ground. Feel the air on your skin. Feel the beating of your heart within your chest.

The dove flapped her wings, and he felt the press of her feet as she pushed off his shoulder and flew into the air, swooping and soaring. Free.

Come with me.

I don't want to.

But you must. If you want to be free like me, you must. Your story is here, and we're going to find it. Together.

I don't want to find it. It's not a good story.

Even bad stories must be told. Especially those.

Why?

Because once it's over, a story is only something with a beginning and a middle and also an end. You'll see it as a whole, and there will be no need to live it anymore.

But he wasn't living it, was he? How could he be, when the memories of it only came in punching flashes of red light and shrieking pain? Jett watched his dove fly for a moment, flapping and gliding, soaring, above and away. The forest around him dimmed, and he knew the beginning of his story was up ahead, the one he didn't know but couldn't forget. He had no desire to find it, but he also didn't want his dove—his guide—to leave him behind.

A child darted from behind a tree, startling him so that he leaped back. The little boy was laughing, and his laughter both echoed sharply and was somehow muffled, as if two separate times had collided right in front of him. The boy was here, and he was there, or maybe the other way around. The boy didn't turn his head, so Jett couldn't see his face before he disappeared behind a different tree on the opposite side of the path.

Follow.

I don't want to.

Follow.

Jett lifted his foot. It felt like it was stuck in quicksand. But he put it in front of him and then lifted the other, moving forward into that dark wood where the little boy had run.

The animal smells came again. But still he clomped forward, his guide never flying out of sight, only dipping and rising and soaring so that he could keep his eyes on her as she led the way.

A farm. He'd come from a farm, and though he'd vowed never to return, he was returning there now. A feeling rose inside him, a prickly mass that was flavored with salt and acid. It tasted like his tears and his pain, and it felt like a boulder that might crush his inner organs into a bloody, soupy mess.

When he wept, he felt her feathers on his cheek. *Back, forth, back, forth.* And he felt his feet on the ground and the beating of his heart. And then he continued on because there was nowhere else to go.

The house came into sight first, a two-story farmhouse with peeling white paint and a dilapidated porch, sitting in front of a mournful mountain that rose into the sky. He saw the old tractor sitting in the field, its seat empty. The pewter sky yawned wide, stirring up the wind that blew the tall grass so that it bent sideways and stayed that way.

Where is he?

Where is who?

My grandfather.

I don't know.

Where are you?

Where am I?

The boy darted out from behind the tractor, running through the field. Running toward the small shed at the back of the property that throbbed with darkness and despair.

I'm there. I'm inside that shed.

Show me.

Jett didn't want to show his guide what was in that shed, but his feet moved anyway, the soft, gentle rustling of his dove's wings luring him along.

Again, his legs felt leaden, his steps so heavy each one made his muscles ache. A goat ran up to the fence on his right, sticking its small nose through the rails. Grief trembled. Fear. Sorrow. He recognized that goat. It was the one his grandfather had butchered because he'd stupidly shown a fondness for it. *I'm sorry. I'm so sorry.*

The goat made a sound and then turned and ran away, leaping and twisting, the way happy goats do.

Suddenly, the field was behind him, and he stood at the door to the small building, staring at the rough grain of the wood. The moan of the wind melded with his own, and despite his fear, despite the sick roiling of his guts, he reached for the door and pushed. It squeaked on its rusted hinges, opening slowly, the light trickling in to join that which filtered through the one dusty window covered in cobwebs.

His eyes tracked slowly over the contents of the shed, moving from the space beside the door toward the back. A three-wheeled wagon, a pile of scrap wood, four broken pots, one with faded yellow daisies on it. He wondered who'd chosen that pot when it was new, sitting on a store shelf. *My grandmother?* Did she think it pretty? Did it make her smile? Did she know what that pot would come to see when it was a broken heap of shards on a dirt floor in an old shed?

That wind again, moaning, shaking the drafty walls of the shed so that Jett wondered if it might blow over. It should. It had no right to stand.

His dove was on his shoulder again, caressing his cheek with her wing, cooing and humming, her voice so sweet. He raised his eyes from those broken pots and looked into the dim corner at the back.

There I am. I'm alone.

Snowflakes hit his cheeks, and he didn't know when it had started snowing, but he was shaking from the cold.

He was there, and he was here, both in that dark corner curled into a ball and standing at the door.

There you are. But you're not alone.

He gasped, his teeth chattering. "I'm not alone now, but I was . . . then. He put me here. He left me in the cold."

Why did he put you here alone? his guide asked.

To punish me. He walked toward the child, curled up on a burlap sack against the back wall. He stood over him, looking down. He felt his tremors, and his misery. His deep shame. He felt his utter aloneness. *To make me suffer.*

What does he need?

A blanket. Some food.

Let's get him some, and then you can tell me more.

Where do I get a blanket or some food? I'm helpless.

You're no such thing. And you have me. Just ask and I'll provide.

She was gone for a blink, and by the time Jett went down on his knees next to the small child that was him, his dove was back with a blanket and a warm piece of buttered toast.

He covered the little boy with the warm blanket, and the child's eyes fluttered open. He stared at Jett, who held the toast to his mouth and coaxed him to eat.

Tell me what he suffers, his dove said. *Tell me what he feels.*

So Jett told his guide about the frost and the hurt and the loneliness and the hunger. He told her about the door that clattered open to show the staggering man outlined by the moon. He felt hot wax dripping down his cheeks, because he was melting into the earth, dissolving like the candle his grandmother burned in the window of the house where he wasn't allowed. And yet he wasn't dissolving, because he felt the child who was him in his arms and the whisper-soft feathers of his dove just under his chin. *Back, forth, back, forth.* He smelled the cold and the pine and the dirt and the grease, but he also smelled the toasted bread slathered with creamy butter, and he tasted it on his tongue as he fed it to the child in his arms.

You're protecting him now, do you see that? Do you see how he looks at you? His rescuer. How do you feel about the child in your arms?

Jett looked down at the little boy. He saw the dirty tear tracks on his small face. He knew his pain and his fear. He felt the places in his body where he hurt, even the shameful ones. He knew his hopes, the ones he kept so small because thinking about them caused an agony deeper than his physical aches to rise up inside him so suddenly that he felt strangled by the pain. He knew nothing else to do but to rock the boy. And so he did. *Back, forth, back, forth.*

What else does he need, other than the blanket and the food? his guide asked.

Crystal tears shimmered on the boy's dark lashes, and Jett felt a light begin to glow in his heart that was both his and the boy's. It shocked him. He'd never felt it before, but now he did, and there was no question of what it was. *Love.* It came alive. It melded and mixed, a shimmering rainbow, the colors bright and sparkling, creating yet other colors that blossomed and burst and beat. *Thud, thud, thud.* The growing mix of twinkling colors pulsated in the air around him, enveloping him in the warmth, and he felt it, on his skin and in his soul. *Love. He needs love.*

Well, good, because you're loving him. He heard the smile in his guide's voice that wasn't a voice. *Hold him closer. Hold him tight.*

And Jett did, until there was only one of them sitting in that cold, dim shed.

Is there any reason to stay here?

His arms lowered. It was only him there, and a ray of sun had found its way through the single grimy window. Jett turned his face toward it and felt its warmth. The space brightened so intensely that Jett had to close his eyes from the glare.

No, there's nothing here now. I'm ready to go.

CHAPTER
TWENTY-ONE

Lennon turned onto Geary and walked with what she hoped looked like purpose toward the few girls who strolled the block waiting for a john to make an offer. It'd been three days since she'd found out that *Ambrose Mars*, or whatever his name was, was a lying fraud who belonged in prison, and had her gun and badge taken by Internal as they began their investigation. At first, she'd holed up in her apartment in stunned silence, trying to make sense of what had happened. Then she'd gotten angry and broken a few dishes on her tile floor. But when that had failed to satisfy, she'd decided the only way she'd find peace, or justice, was if she went looking for it herself.

She'd been duped and deceived, and at this point, she had to assume that even the intimate moments they'd spent together had been part of some greater plan to infiltrate the department, or steal evidence, or whatever he'd ultimately been there to do. And it enraged her, but it also ate at her pride, and if she was going to be honest with herself, she had to admit that it hurt her too.

Ambrose was the first man she'd really connected to since Tanner. And though she felt stupid for being conned, she also felt guilty because in some sense, it felt like she'd betrayed Tanner by giving even a small portion of her heart—the heart she'd promised to *him*—to a lying criminal.

I'm just . . . not great in relationships. What was that? A way to give her an out before he used her? An out she hadn't taken?

What was his point, though? Why had he taken a risk like that? If he was apprehended, he'd serve prison time.

God, she felt stupid. Stupid and gullible and pathetic. And she was driving herself crazy with questions that had no answers. *And* she suddenly had all this time on her hands. She could sit around and stew and beat herself up over the situation. Or she could do something about it.

She didn't currently have police powers, and so she'd have to be creative—and smart—but decided that a personal investigation wasn't going to hurt anyone. And if Mars had impersonated an agent to find out more about the "BB" pill case, then maybe he knew something she didn't. Maybe this was bigger to someone than even the police understood. She was certain other inspectors had taken on the case since she'd been removed and sent home, but that meant the whole investigation was behind, as they'd have to read through the case, reexamine evidence, interview people who'd already been interviewed and try to get up to speed. All while juggling the cases they were already in the middle of.

But she'd collected some leads before getting attacked in that tent, and dammit, she was going to throw caution to the wind and follow them. The people she intended to interview didn't want anything to do with the police, a double-edged sword that meant they might not talk to her. But they were also very unlikely to report her, should they be suspicious. Maybe the leads wouldn't go anywhere. Or maybe once she was reinstated, she'd already have a leg up. Either way, it seemed worth it to try. And who knew, maybe she'd run into the criminal known as Ambrose Mars, because if he'd been interested enough in the "BB" pill case to infiltrate the police department, he likely still was. Which meant that he, too, would be searching for more answers toward whatever end he had in mind.

As soon as the sun had begun its descent, she'd headed to the TL, hoping it was late enough that there'd be at least a little traffic but early enough that the women would have a few minutes to speak with her.

That was, if they were willing at all.

First, though, she'd stopped in at the bar called the Cellar that Darius Finchem had mentioned, a dank underground establishment that would likely fail a firesafety inspection. It was creepy, but she'd gone early enough in the evening that there was still light spilling in through the entrance, and there were barely any customers.

Because you're chickenshit. And fine, she didn't really want to be there when the party, such as it was, was in full swing, though she would come back if she struck out on Geary. And, no surprise, the lone bartender hadn't given her any information about supposed women who worked the back rooms. In fact, he'd outright denied knowing anything about that at all. So here she was on Geary now, hoping for a bigger break than she'd achieved at the Cellar.

There was a woman wearing a skimpy black dress, eating an apple and mumbling to herself on a bench, and though she was dressed like a prostitute, Lennon decided she'd leave her to her mumbling. Instead, she approached a woman in a pair of tight red shorts who leaned back against a light pole, smoking a cigarette. But when she attempted to speak with her, the woman raised her hand, showing Lennon her long spiked fingernails, and said, "Take off, pig. I'm not doin' nothin' your boyfriend isn't happy to pay me for." Well, at least Lennon wouldn't have to flash an empty badge holder and hope no one noticed. People living here clocked her in a moment. Fine. That made things easier, in light of her current circumstances.

"I just have a few questions," Lennon called after her.

But the woman raised her hand and shot her the bird, and then yelled, "Fuck you!" in case Lennon hadn't taken the gesture to heart.

She sighed. Tommy had always had better luck getting information from the working girls. They'd proposition him first, but when he politely declined in that charming way of his, they still seemed sort of eager to please him anyway, in whatever way they could. Her? Not so much. "What the fuck are you lookin' at?" asked another girl Lennon had started to approach. Lennon gave her a thin smile and turned the other way.

After a few more unsuccessful attempts, she decided that this was getting her nowhere and turned to leave. Wallowing in her misery at home wasn't very empowering, but at least she knew how to be successful at that. "You lookin' for information?" a woman wearing a pink tutu and silver thigh-high boots asked.

Lennon stopped, hope rising. "Yes. I just have a photo. I was hoping someone would look at it." She started taking out her phone.

"Two hundred fifty bucks," the woman said.

"Two fifty? That's—"

The woman turned and started sashaying away. "Hey, two hundred. It's all the cash I have on me."

The woman turned, looking her up and down. "Two hundred and that phone case."

Lennon glanced at the phone case she'd bought less than a week before on Amazon for almost seventy bucks. It'd been a bit of a splurge, but it was supposed to be military-grade rated, and with her job—

"Fine." She removed her phone from the case and held it out to the woman.

"And that necklace."

Lennon gaped. "No way." Her mother had given her that necklace.

The woman shrugged again, and once more turned away. "Fine," Lennon called after her, and again the woman walked back. Lennon unhooked the necklace and placed it in the woman's open palm.

"Cash?"

"You have to look at the photo first."

"Sis, I ain't gotta do nothin'. *Cash*," she demanded, stressing the word.

Lennon stared at the woman's open palm again. She reached for her small key chain wallet, hanging around her wrist. What the hell was she doing? Was she really about to turn cash over to a woman who was already obviously robbing her? But what other choice did she have? She pulled the two hundred dollars in twenties she'd taken out of the ATM on the way here, intending on doling out twenties for information, and handed the entirety to the woman. Then she opened her phone to the photo of the victim so far only identified as Cherish and showed it to her.

"That's Cherish," she said, her expression going slightly slack when she obviously realized it was a photo of a dead woman.

"Yes," Lennon said. "Do you know her last name or where she lives?"

"No idea." She started to turn away, but Lennon gripped her arm gently, and the woman jerked, pulling her arm away, but turned back toward her.

"This woman was murdered," Lennon said. "Cruelly murdered. She was young, you know that. She looked to be about twenty years old. Not even old enough to drink. But she worked down here, putting herself at risk with men who didn't give a damn about her. One of them might have taken her life. I'm trying to bring her justice. I'm trying to make sure this"—she shook her phone with the picture of Cherish on it—"doesn't happen to another woman who works these streets."

The woman hesitated, glancing up the block and then back the other way before returning her gaze to Lennon. "Please," Lennon said. "Please help me make the person who did this pay."

"I really don't know her last name." She glanced around again as though making sure no one saw her talking to an obvious law enforcement officer. "But she lived over on Ellis Street in the Tills Apartments. I don't know the unit, but her roommate's name is Brandy Wine. Gotta be her workin' name, but that's the only one I know her by."

Brandy Wine. "Thank you," Lennon said as the woman turned and began walking away quickly. "I appreciate it," she said softly.

～

Lennon walked hurriedly to the place where she'd parked her car, her heart giving a hard knock as she approached. "Are you fucking kidding me?" Someone had broken the window of her Subaru. She leaned in tentatively, taking in the ransacked middle console that—less than an hour before—had held her sunglasses, some change, and her car charger. Those things were all gone, and her steering wheel was a mess of broken plastic and hanging wires.

"Airbags," someone said behind her. She whirled around to see a man holding what looked to be a window-washing device, a bucket of soapy water on the ground in front of the window of a laundromat, the light emanating from inside making it easy to see the glass. "They're a hot commodity. Thieves get a pretty penny for them."

"Yes, I know." She groaned. She'd done plenty of reports on stolen airbags when she was a police officer. Car break-ins were so common in the city that in many neighborhoods, people chose to leave their windows down. Thieves might still target your car, but at least you wouldn't have to replace your window.

"Looks like just the one airbag," the man said. "Lucky."

Lucky. Right. Good fortune was really having its way with her. "Did you see who did it?"

The man shook his head. "They're quick. I just came out here. You could knock on some doors, see if anyone else saw something, but I doubt it. People don't blink an eye at it anymore." He gestured up the street, and at first she wasn't sure what he was pointing at until she realized there was broken glass sparkling from the gutter for as far as she could see, making it clear just how common it was.

The man turned back to the laundromat window. "You can't change it," he told her. "Police don't give a shit, so you just have to learn how to minimize the damage. I'd tell you to take the bus, but that's risky too." He dipped his long-handled device into the bucket and then brought a big soapy spongeful of cleaner to the window. Lennon turned back to her vehicle and opened the door to inspect the seat. Thankfully, most of the broken glass had landed on the floor. She picked the few pieces off her seat and dropped them in the empty cup holder of her center console and then climbed inside, hoping no rogue slivers would pierce her ass.

Her career as a lone ranger was already off to a booming start.

She lowered her visor and saw the twenty-dollar bill she kept clipped there for emergencies that the thieves hadn't found. "Ha!" She decided the money was a sign not to let this setback deter her, and so she pulled out her phone and did a Google search for the Tills Apartment complex the woman had mentioned. She was almost surprised that it really did come up and that the woman hadn't lied and bilked her out of two hundred bucks and a couple of personal items. The address was listed, and Lennon whispered it under her breath, committing it to memory before opening the link and glancing over the page.

The building, what had once been a residence, was owned by the Tenderloin Development Company. The tagline read: Serving 25 individuals who currently experience mental health challenges and who were previously unhoused.

There were many such apartment buildings in the Tenderloin, low-income housing that had once been SROs and now catered to underserved populations. She put her car in gear and pulled away from the curb. In her rearview mirror, she saw that the line of cars on Geary had doubled in size since she'd arrived. The johns had gotten off work and decided they deserved some stress relief.

A car was just pulling out in front of the Tills Apartment, and Lennon swooped into the spot and got out. If thieves were going to steal her other airbag, at least now they wouldn't have to break a window.

She set her mouth as she looked up at the structure. There were fire escapes connected by ladders up the front of the building and a metal gate protecting the entrance. Lennon scrolled to the bell that said **BRANDY LOPEZ** and pressed it. A minute later, the intercom buzzed, allowing her entrance, and Lennon pulled the gate open and climbed the stairs to apartment 3A. When the door was pulled open by a young woman with black bushy curls holding a toddler, Lennon said, "Brandy?"

"I thought you were DoorDash. Who are you?"

Lennon flipped open her empty badge and quickly flipped it shut. "I'm Inspector Lennon Gray, and I just have a few questions."

The woman's expression curved into derision. "If this is about that dude who—"

"This is about your roommate, Cherish."

Brandy's mouth gaped slightly. "You know where Cherish is?"

"Unfortunately, yes. Her body was found a little over a week ago. She was murdered."

The woman let out a groan and leaned back against the wall, wrapping her other arm around the little girl and bringing her closer. "Shit. Shit, shit, shit. Where?"

"Shit," the little girl repeated.

Brandy put two fingers to the toddler's lips. "No," she said. "Don't say that."

"I'm sorry to break the news like this," Lennon said. "Cherish wasn't carrying ID, and I only found you through a woman on Geary who recognized Cherish from a photo."

Brandy stared into space for a minute and then pushed herself off the wall, putting the little girl on the floor, taking her hand and turning. "Come on in," she said.

Lennon started to enter when she heard Brandy's buzzer. "There's my food," she murmured. "Hold on."

Lennon followed her into the tiny apartment, which was clean and neat except for an overturned basket of toys. The woman buzzed in the DoorDash driver. She waited at her open door until a young woman appeared, handed her the food, then turned back toward the stairs.

Brandy brought the bags in, and Lennon waited while she set the toddler up in a high chair and cut up a burger and fries into bite-size pieces.

"How long did Cherish live here with you?" Lennon asked after Brandy had washed her hands and turned her way, drying her hands on a dishcloth. She tossed the cloth on the counter and gestured to the two-person table, and Lennon squeezed herself in and sat down.

"Only nine months or so," Brandy said, taking a seat as well and smiling over at her daughter, who was busily shoving fries in her mouth. "She wasn't on the lease, so she wasn't supposed to be living here. But she slept on the couch and shared the rent."

"Where did you think she was when she didn't come home?"

"With a trick. She'd done it before, gone home with some guy who paid her to stay the weekend. Cherish also worked this club where men sometimes would pay her to go home with them." A look passed over her face that told Lennon that Brandy was troubled by the club she'd mentioned—likely the Cellar—and she understood why. "She'd come home all blank-like, sometimes with bruises, and she'd get directly in the shower and stay there so long I knew the water had to be cold."

"Are you in the business, Brandy?"

Her gaze moved to her daughter before she nodded. "I'm trying to get out. Maybe I'll have to, now that Cherish won't be here to watch Nadia. It's tough, though, you know? Especially without a diploma or a GED."

Lennon nodded, even though, really, she *didn't* know. She'd been raised by loving parents who had her back, no matter what. They showered her with affection and praise, and if she ever tried to walk any street anywhere for any reason that put her in danger, her dad would pull up in his car and haul her into the back.

They weren't even thrilled that she was an inspector working in rough areas of the city, even though she was usually armed. "So no idea if she actually went home with a customer?"

"No. I just assumed. Shit," she said again under her breath.

"Is there anything you can tell me that might help us identify the person that did this? Was Cherish dating anyone? Had she gotten into a fight with someone recently?"

Nadia pulled a piece of burger apart and tossed the section of bun on the floor. "No, Nadia," Brandy said halfheartedly, leaving the food on the floor where it lay. "Uh, no, Cherish wasn't dating anyone. If she fought with anyone, I didn't know about it. But Cherish was real chill. She wasn't a fighter, you know?"

Lennon nodded. "Brandy, I don't know if you knew, but Cherish was pregnant. About three months or so."

Brandy seemed to deflate a little. She heaved out a sigh as Nadia launched a piece of burger onto the floor. "Yeah, I know. Stupid chick let 'em go bare. I told her she was gonna get knocked up again, and she did." She met Lennon's eyes. "The thing was, she wanted to keep the baby and get her other kids out of the system. She said she was gonna get herself better, get a legitimate job, something her kids could be proud of."

Lennon held back the cringe at the news that Cherish had other children, and that they were in the system. Now they had no chance of ever knowing their mother.

"Anyway," Brandy said, "Cherish went on and on about it. Some doctor was gonna help her. She was gonna get her boys back too. Blah, blah, blah." She used her hand to gesture a flapping mouth.

"A doctor?" Lennon asked. "Like a therapist?"

Brandy shrugged. "I guess."

"Do you remember his name?"

Her eyes moved to the wall behind Lennon's head. "No. I called him the Candyman."

A chill went down her spine. The name conjured the eighties slasher film, which felt far too close to home in this particular instance. "The Candyman? Why?"

"I don't really remember. Something she said? I don't know. Maybe because she seemed happy when she came back from seeing him, though. Like he was going to solve all her problems. Anyway, I just started thinking of him that way."

Horror flicks aside, the Candyman might also be another name for a pill pusher, right? Lennon pictured those homemade purple pills. Maybe this doctor not only prescribed medication but made his own for reasons unknown. "Did he prescribe medication to her?"

"I don't know. Hold on." Brandy stood, left the room for thirty seconds while Lennon watched Nadia smear greasy pieces of burger on her cheeks. She smiled at the toddler, who gave her a—literally—cheesy grin back. When Brandy reentered the room, she was holding several prescription pill bottles. She put them down on the table in front of Lennon, who looked at them each in turn. They were prescribed to Cherish Olsen. "Dr. Frede," she read the prescribing physician's name aloud.

"That doctor is someone Cherish saw online, so he's not the Candyman. But those are all the meds she was on," Brandy said.

Online. Great. Now doctors were diagnosing and prescribing medications over the internet. *What could possibly go wrong?* Lennon read over the labels again. She'd have to look up a couple of these, but she recognized one for depression and another for anxiety. "Can I take a look at her things?"

"Yeah, sure. Like I said, Cherish had the couch. Her clothes are in the hall closet, makeup in the bathroom. But other than that, it's really all she had." She stood up and gestured to Lennon to follow her. When she opened the hall closet, situated right next to the front door, a whiff of stale perfume hit her nose. Brandy stood back as Lennon riffled through the clothing—a few tiny dresses and shiny pants clipped to a hanger, but also jeans and sweatpants. On the floor sat various pairs of platform heels and a pair each of sneakers and flip-flops. Clearly Cherish had had two very different personas.

None of this would help. "Did she have a purse or a wallet she carried with her? A cell phone?"

"Yeah, but she took it with her. She never left her phone behind."

And yet, no phones had been found at the scene. Lennon nodded as Nadia started yelling for her mom. "Okay. Thank you for your help,

Brandy." She pulled out a business card and handed it to her. "Will you call me if you remember the doctor's name or anything else that might help?"

Brandy took the card, studied it for a moment, and then stuck it in her pocket. "Sure." She worried her lip for a moment, and Lennon waited while she obviously gathered her thoughts. In the other room, Nadia's yells grew more demanding, and she started banging on her high chair. "Cherish seemed different in the last few months . . . I don't know if it was something that doctor gave her or what, but ever since she did that podcast, she had this like, fire inside, to change her life for the better. I don't wanna know how Cherish died. But . . . did she suffer?"

Did she suffer? Almost definitely. But why would she leave this woman with that knowledge? "She died quickly," she said, something occurring to her. "Wait, you just mentioned a podcast? What was that about?"

"Oh, that? That's just a way some people in the TL make a few bucks. It's called *The Fringe*. I never watched it, and Cherish didn't make much of it either. She took the cash and bought her kids some stuff. She seemed happy about that. But that was before she started going to the Candyman. Anyway, I think you can catch that podcast online. Me? I'm not into a buncha sob stories. But I guess some folks are."

The Fringe. Nadia was now using her spoon or cup to bang on the high chair tray. "I'll let you go," Lennon said. "Thanks again."

CHAPTER TWENTY-TWO

"Cruz"
Episode from podcast *The Fringe*
Host of podcast, Jamal Whitaker

"Hello, welcome to *The Fringe*. Cruz. How are you?"

"Been better. Been worse."

Jamal smiles. "Give me an example of each."

The man leans forward and rests his elbows on his knees. He looks to be in his late twenties, his black hair cut short, tattoos peeking from the cuffs of his long-sleeved shirt. Cruz smiles, and a dimple appears in his cheek, making him look suddenly younger. "Better? The day I took my little sister to the pier and we watched the seals for hours. Just laughing, man. It was one of the only times I felt . . . I don't know, free. Yeah, that was a great day." He scratches the back of his neck. "Worse? The day I killed my sister."

Jamal raises his brows. "You killed your sister?"

"Might as well have. I couldn't save her, and she died because of me."

"How did she die?"

"Of an overdose."

"You believe you're responsible for your sister's overdose?"

"Who else? I was the only person she had to look out for her."

"How old were you when she died?"

"I was sixteen, doing time in juvie for some dumb shit. Acting up. If I'd have been out, she'd be alive. I would have made sure of it. I told her I'd always be there to protect her, and I failed. That's it. She was fourteen years old, man. Fourteen. Some motherfucker got her high, and that was it. One time, and that was all it took."

"I'm sorry."

He nods, hangs his head for a minute before looking up.

"What was your home life like, Cruz?"

"Home? I never had a home. Me and Maria got sent to foster care in Arizona, where we're originally from, when I was eight and she was six. Our mom . . . well, I don't talk about her anymore. Anyway, we got put in the system and then moved eleven times before we finally got split up." He looks away for a moment before cursing under his breath. "I told myself I could handle any-thing—any shit those motherfuckers did to me—as long as I was there to keep my sis-ter safe."

"What types of things did you experience in foster care?"

He breathes out and sits back, looking off into the distance again. "What didn't we experience? Some of them starved us. We stayed in this one place that actu-ally put locks on the refrigerator. Been beat up, slapped around, tied up. There was this one . . . this dude with these cigarettes . . ." He zones out, then gives his head a small shake. "Anyway, I always felt like I had a purpose, you know, until Maria died." He's quiet for a minute. "After Maria died, I joined a gang. I'd steered clear, but after her overdose, I just had this rage inside, you know?" He brings his fist up and gives it a slight shake in front of his heart. "Like I just didn't care about anything anymore."

"Are you still in a gang?"

"Nah. That's why I moved here to San Francisco. To get away from all that. But man, it's true what they say—you can't out-run yourself."

"What's your drug, Cruz?"

He hisses out a breath between his teeth. "Heroin, mostly."

"Are you trying to get clean?"

"Sure. I'd like to get clean." He's silent a moment. "I'd like to make Maria proud. If she's looking down on me, I'd like her to say, hey, that's my brother, and he got his shit together. He did good."

Cruz's face contorts, and he puts his head in his hands. "Shut that shit off," he says, waving his hand toward the camera. "I changed my mind. I don't want to do this anymore."

CHAPTER TWENTY-THREE

Ambrose sat at the end of the bar in the only seat where the dim light didn't quite reach. He was faced toward a door that was up a short set of steps. The view and the light from the street ensured that he'd have a visual on anyone who walked in before they could see him. He'd already scoped out the exit door near the back, where he'd slip out if necessary.

Of course you're still putting so much thought into potential escape routes. For one, it'd sort of become second nature. His job presented risk, and he had to be on guard. But also, he had this feeling that Inspector Lennon Gray would be working this case even harder than she had before. It was the gut instinct he'd come to trust over the years, but it was also that he knew he'd upset her with his deception, and she'd want to know why he'd done what he'd done.

Goddamn, he felt guilty about that. He felt even worse that she'd been temporarily put on leave. His source at the SFPD had told him about that. She hadn't deserved being deceived, and he'd taken their relationship further than he'd meant to, even if it wasn't as far as he would have liked. He'd complicated matters and caused her fallout, but he'd caused himself some fallout too.

So yeah, he'd bet anything that, even without police powers, she'd be working this case hard, resentment and anger fueling her need for answers. He had to find those answers first, and he meant to.

As far as this particular lead, she'd have a hard time getting information here. Lennon Gray *exuded* law and order, whether she had the gun to back it up or not. And he doubted she knew how to shrug it off and play a different part.

He didn't like the idea of her in crime-ridden parts of town and seedy bars like this one without protection, and he was to blame for that, so he needed to work even faster than he had been.

It was good that he was already one step ahead of her. Doc had recognized Cherish, and he had her name. Cherish Olsen. She'd gone through some testing but ultimately hadn't been a good candidate for the project. Had she gone somewhere else? Answered another offer? Did this place have something to do with it? Ambrose didn't know but thought it worthwhile to check behind the curtain.

The bartender came over, tipping his chin toward his untouched whiskey. "I'm going to assume since you're not here to drink, you're here for something else?"

"Maybe. What else do you offer here?"

"I just sling the drinks. You'd have to ask Carlo about that. He's in the back office. Red door. I'll give him a call and let him know you're coming. You'll need this." The bartender dropped a key on the bar, and Ambrose eyed it before picking it up and squeezing it in his fist.

"Thanks." Ambrose stood as the bartender took his phone out of his pocket and began dialing. Instead of heading down the hall that had an exit door at the end, and likely the toilets somewhere along the way, he walked the short distance to a door in the corner. He tried the handle, but when he found it locked, he used the key he'd just been given to open it. The hallway he stepped into was dim, a single bulb flickering overhead, giving the whole place an eerie cast. The red door was at the end, and Ambrose walked toward it, his head turning to the other doors along the way, where he heard the muffled sounds of both sex and sobs. It made him grimace, his hands fisting as he walked.

After he knocked on the red door, it was pulled open by a woman in a skimpy white bikini and platform heels. Her expression remained bored as she stepped aside, allowing him entrance. A man sat behind a large desk, facing him. "Carlo?"

"That's right. Have a seat," Carlo said. The woman in the bikini plopped down on a couch on the wall to his right, and Ambrose took a seat in the chair Carlo had indicated in front of his desk. "How can I be of service?"

"I'm here because I have a specific appetite," he said.

Carlo leaned back, looking unimpressed. "Don't we all?" He sat forward, lacing his fingers. "We don't supply kids here, only violence. If you want underage, there's a kiddie stroll over on Polk Street."

Kiddie stroll. He swallowed down the rage those two words caused to rise in his chest. "No, no kids."

"Good. Our girls—and a few boys, if that's your thing—are over eighteen and willing participants."

He tilted his lips, hoping he'd managed what resembled a smile as he thought about how the word *willing* sure could be stretched to fit the needs of the person using it. "That's all I'm looking for. However, I prefer things a little . . . dark."

The man inclined his head. "You go too far, our business is done."

"What's too far?"

"Anything that complicates my life, or brings the authorities here, got it?"

Ambrose gave a single nod.

"We have a doctor willing to make house calls, but he can only repair so much, so don't push it. If one of my girls ends up in the hospital, we're done."

"I understand."

Carlo pushed a binder toward him. Ambrose eyed it and then used his index finger to open the cover, flipping through, anger sizzling through his veins as his eyes hit on one woman after another. Meat. These women were considered meat. Their vitals were listed next to their pictures, photographs of one sensual stare after another that looked so brittle he was surprised there weren't cracks across their lips.

And under that was listed the activities they'd participate in and the cost for each one. *Restraints, choking, flogging, biting, clamps . . .* The next category was called *Edgeplay* and included extremely pricey choices such as electricity, fire, suspension, and knives.

He perused the remaining pages and then pushed it back toward Carlo. "One of your clients, a good friend of mine, mentioned a girl. Name of Cherish. I don't see her in there, but she came highly recommended."

Carlo looked at him suspiciously. "Cherish doesn't work here anymore. She quit. Bitch decided she was too good for the place." His lips stretched into a smile, showing a set of large capped teeth.

"Any way I can reach her?"

"You think I'm going to help you take your business outside my club? Go fuck yourself. You're on your own."

"If I—"

"Out. I don't give second chances around here."

Ambrose sighed, coming to his feet. He might have thought that the guy would attempt to rough him up just for the hell of it or for the fact that Ambrose had wasted his time. But the dude was about a hundred pounds overweight, and the only "sidekick" he had in his office was a petite bikini-clad woman.

This guy sat in a back office and profited off the sale of women's bodies. But the police were past caring about prostitution, because most of the DAs didn't prosecute anyway. Ambrose couldn't help the women in that binder, and likely, most of them would say they didn't need help anyway. The best he could do was his part to help those who wanted to be helped so that another generation of victims didn't wind up in that binder, listed for sale.

What he had gleaned from behind that red door was that Cherish, at least, had decided she wanted something different than what those back rooms offered. Unfortunately, she'd run into something far, far worse.

Ambrose turned and left that seedy office, walking back out through the bar, where no one even looked up from their drink.

~

His next stop was to the address he'd located for Cherish Olsen. She lived in a building called the Tills Apartments and had a roommate named Brandy Lopez that went by the stage name *Brandy Wine*. Of course, there was no actual stage in her "professional" life, from what he could gather, unless you considered what went on at the corner of Geary Street a performance.

He rang the buzzer next to the name Brandy Lopez and waited. When thirty seconds had gone by with no response, he tried again to the same result, before going down the line and pushing one buzzer after another. The gate let out a loud buzz, and he grasped the handle and pulled it open, slipping inside before anyone came out of their apartment and questioned him. He jogged up to the third floor and knocked on the door to apartment 3A. No one answered his knock, but he swore he heard something from behind the door and pressed his ear against it. Was that . . . yes, it sounded like the muffled sound of a baby crying.

He knocked again, this time louder, and from behind him he heard a door open and a woman step into the hallway. "What the hell is all the racket?"

He looked over his shoulder to see an elderly woman in a green bathrobe, holding a spatula in her hands. The smell of something frying met his nose. "It's too late for this kind of noise. Brandy's obviously not home."

"Have you seen her recently?"

The woman lifted her gaze, as though considering. "Not for a couple days, but—"

"I think I hear a baby crying from inside."

The woman frowned, walking to where he was and placing her own ear against the door. "You're right. That's Nadia. I hear her." She looked up at him. "Ah, shit. Brandy left her alone again. I told that girl to bring her over to me if she needed a sitter, but she swore she only left her if it was for less than an hour and she was sleeping. Stupid girl."

"Do you have a key?"

"No. The maintenance man has one, but he'll already have gone home. The owner is an agency or corporation, and they never answer calls. They don't even have an email, just a box on their website where you're supposed to let them know you'd like a call back. Such bull—"

Ambrose stepped back, lifted his leg, and easily kicked in the door as the woman next to him cowered to the side. The door bounced back off its broken hinges, allowing him access. The cry could be heard more clearly now that the door was open, and he drew back at the smell of death. Ambrose moved toward the cry, the sounds of the neighbor woman following behind.

His heart dropped when he stopped in the bedroom doorway and saw the scene inside. A woman, her body purple and bloated, lay dead on the floor, the needle she'd overdosed with still stuck in her arm. And next to her, a toddler girl lay on the floor, hand clutching her lifeless mother's shirt.

"Oh my God. Oh my God," the woman behind him chanted. "Oh, Nadia."

Ambrose swooped up the baby girl, the scent of decay heavy on her clothing, her face red and streaked with tears. She'd soiled her diaper, and the scent of that mixed with the smell of rot almost overwhelmed Ambrose, but he breathed through his nose and held the little girl tightly to him as he left the room.

The little girl, Nadia, started screaming more loudly, twisting in his arms and reaching her arms out for her mother. Jesus Christ, what was this going to do to the child?

"Shh," he cooed. "It's okay. It's going to be okay. You're safe."

He heard the neighbor on the phone with the police, giving them the address of Brandy's apartment. Help would be here soon, and Ambrose couldn't be around when they arrived. The neighbor hung up the phone, and Ambrose handed the sobbing child to her. She laid her head down on the woman's shoulder, obviously exhausted by whatever she'd been through over the past few days while her mother's body bloated with gas and began to decay in front of her. "Take care of her," he told the neighbor, who looked shell shocked, her skin a sickly tint of green, as though she might be sick any moment. But she nodded, managing to hold it down as she stroked the little girl's hair.

Ambrose turned, taking a moment to glance around the living room and into the kitchen on his way out. Nothing looked out of place, but he spotted a single business card stuck to the refrigerator with a magnet. He took the few steps to it, sliding it from beneath the magnet and slipping it into his pocket. *Inspector Lennon Gray.* Just as he'd suspected, Lennon was still on the case, whether she had permission or not. Something about that made him strangely proud, but he also had the urge to swear and topple a table. He did neither, merely leaving through the broken front door, finding some solace in the fact that the baby had stopped crying and the police sirens could be heard drawing closer. She'd been saved. He only prayed she wasn't like the countless children who experienced similar circumstances and were thrown out of the frying pan and into the fire.

CHAPTER TWENTY-FOUR

Courage, dear heart.
—C. S. Lewis

Seventeen Years Ago
Patient Number 0022

Jett followed his guide as she flew down the dirt road that led from the farm, gliding and soaring but never dipping out of sight. And when Jett felt scared or confused, his guide sensed it and immediately came to perch on his shoulder, those feathery wings brushing against his cheek, comforting. *Back, forth, back, forth.*

He followed the dove into the small town where he'd gone to school. Jett walked through the playground, misty images of children running and swinging and climbing the jungle gym, echoes of their laughter a tinny ringing in his ears. He saw strings of light connecting each child to the other, twining and then untangling as they crossed paths, illuminated numbers rising in the air that were slightly off, with odd slants here and double lines there, that he didn't know the meaning of. But somehow he also understood that they weren't really numbers but some language he didn't know that his brain had converted to mostly recognizable digits.

One of the shadows was his childhood self, sitting alone on the bench, trying to be invisible. Jett sat down beside him, and he took his hand. He hurt, and he smelled bad, and the other kids stayed away from him because he was weird and he stank. He pushed others sometimes and yelled when they came up behind him, and the kids thought it was for no reason at all. But there was a reason—not that Jett could ever tell. It was a secret, the one his grandfather had buried him under, and he didn't want it, but there was no way to get out from beneath it now—and the longer he kept it, the heavier it became.

It *fed* off him, and it grew and grew and grew. It crushed him and strangled him, and it was so heavy it trapped the words in his throat. Sometimes Jett pictured that secret like a giant monster wrapped around him, its tentacles invading his body the same way his grandfather did. Except the monster was invisible, and it slithered over his bones and squeezed his organs and penetrated his brain, and he couldn't ever rid himself of the monster . . . because in some way, he'd *become* it. It was bad, and he was bad, and he couldn't differentiate between one and the other. The monster made his body do things he hadn't asked it to do. He yelped and fought when he was startled by the smallest thing. He felt numb, and so he scratched at his skin so he could see if he was still alive. And even then, he didn't know, so he might be dead. Death might be never-ending, forever pain, and that was the most terrifying thing of all. *Shh,* his guide said, brushing feathers across his cheek, quieting his mind. *Back, forth, back, forth. Thud, thud, thud.*

Wiggle your toes.

Feel the dirt beneath your feet.

Jett did, and the ground anchored him. He was in his body, and he was standing on the ground, and he had fingers that could move and a heart that pounded to the same rhythm as the distant beat reverberating in the air. *Thud, thud, thud.*

Are we done here?

Those numbers that weren't exactly numbers mixed and mingled in the air, changing into other numbers and then dripping away like glittery rain. He had this vague flash of understanding that those numbers explained everything. But he couldn't read it, so it didn't matter. The misty images of the children who hadn't understood his pain faded, becoming air that blew away. He clasped the hand of the boy who was him, and the boy turned, laying his head on Jett's chest and falling inside. *Done.*

He followed his guide to the high school and the bowling alley where he'd worked. He saw himself here, there, and everywhere. He watched his happy moments and his sad. He'd hurt people, and they hadn't known why. He watched himself drink his first beer, remembered the way the pain grew fuzzy and the blessed oblivion that had come. He watched himself hurl terrible insults at a girlfriend who had teasingly grabbed his ass while they were making out because he didn't want anyone to touch him there, not ever, but especially not in a moment of weakness, when his guard was down. He liked sex for the same reason he liked beer, for the oblivion it brought. But he had too many triggers, and she'd crossed one. And she'd cried, and he'd apologized, but he'd never spoken to her again after that. He couldn't; the shame was too great. And he set his hand on that boy's shoulder and told him it was okay, and the boy that was him folded inside, and Jett continued on.

To the old mill where he got high every day, to that bus station where he used the last of his money he hadn't spent on drugs to buy a ticket that would take him anywhere but there. Anywhere. *Anywhere* but there. To San Francisco. The city by the bay with the golden bridge that had turned out not to be golden at all.

He started to step onto that bus, to walk to the young man that was him, huddled in the back, trying to make himself small. But a flash of red caught his eye, and he turned, his heart jolting as he saw the little boy step from behind a column. *Shh,* his guide said, her feathers brushing against his cheek. *Back, forth, back, forth.*

Thud, thud, thud.

His heart slowed; he felt the brush of feathers and the earth beneath his feet. He blinked, but the boy remained, gaze hung on him. "Help," the boy croaked. "Help me."

CHAPTER
TWENTY-FIVE

The door to the one-story black building standing between two parking lots was propped wide open. "Hello?" Lennon called, leaning her head inside and looking around. There was a wall directly in front of her, however, and another one to her right. Even with the door open, the hall to the left faded into darkness. Lennon paused, but then stepped inside and walked toward the small glow that came from the other side of the wall. "Hello?"

She'd looked up the podcast that Brandy had mentioned and found that the host was a man named Jamal Whitaker. It appeared he interviewed people—using a video format—who lived or worked on the streets, including prostitutes, pimps, drug addicts, and more.

She'd searched for Cherish on the website but hadn't found anyone with her name, even though a few young women had resembled her. *Close, but no cigar.* She had a feeling she was on the right track, though—thanks to Brandy—and was eager to talk to the host.

She heard footsteps and halted as a man rounded the corner, then drew back slightly. "Hey, sorry about that. I was editing a video. I thought I heard someone, and then—" He gave his head a shake and held out his hand. "Hi. I'm Jamal Whitaker. How can I help you?"

"Hi, Mr. Whitaker. I'm Inspector Lennon Gray with the San Francisco Police Department, and I was wondering if I could ask you a few questions?" *Please don't ask to see my credentials.*

"Inspector? Is there a problem?"

"No. Your name just came up during an investigation."

"Oh. Uh, yeah, sure. Like I said, I was just doing some editing. Come on back. Let me get some light up in here."

Jamal flipped a switch, and light flooded the small space. Directly in front of her was a single velvet couch and a coffee table with a camera off to the side. The entire studio was compact, including the kitchenette to her right. Just one thing in the room was massive—the computer sitting atop a desk nearby, the screen showing the frozen image of a grizzled old man sitting on the velvet couch. Her gaze hung on the still shot for a moment. The old man looked utterly out of place on the somewhat fancy piece of classic furniture, and something about the juxtaposition moved her.

"Can I get you a coffee? A bottle of water?"

"No, I'm good. Thank you."

"Do you want to sit down?" he asked, waving his hand to a plastic chair near his desk. There were papers scattered across the surface, and she recognized the colorful invitation to the award dinner that had also been hanging on the bulletin board at the Gilbert House.

"No, that's okay," she said. "I won't take up much of your time." She looked back at the couch. "I didn't realize podcasts used video."

Jamal perched himself on the edge of his desk and crossed his arms. "Yeah. It's growing in popularity. And with certain topics, visual content is much more engaging. I interview such a variety of people that my audience connects more when they can see the person who's telling their story."

That made sense. You could get even more information about a person just by watching their facial expressions, their body movements, and the like. She was always personally much more engaged by visual input rather than just auditory. Plus, if Jamal interviewed people who lived on the street, listeners experiencing their story would naturally want to see how their lifestyle had affected them physically.

"One of your more recent guests might have been a murder victim."

"Damn." Jamal blew out a breath. "I mean, I can't say I'm too surprised. The people I interview tend to live pretty risky lives."

"I know. And the woman's death almost certainly isn't related to you, and I didn't find her on your website. But I'm hoping you might be able to give me some information."

"Sure. What was her name? Her first name? I don't ask for last names. And often, the name they give me is a nickname or a stage name or a gang name, or whatever."

"Cherish."

He took the side of his lip between his teeth. "Cherish. Cherish." He met Lennon's eyes. "Wait, prostitute? Young?"

"That's her."

"That was, what . . . three or four months ago that I interviewed her?"

"That's what her roommate said, yes."

He pushed himself off his desk, walked around it to his chair, sat down, and started typing on the keyboard. "Yeah, I remember her. I did quite a few interviews that week, and when that happens, I usually stagger the posts. What's your email? I have the interview in a Dropbox folder and can send you a link."

"Great. Thanks, Mr. Whitaker."

"Jamal."

At least the department hadn't confiscated her cards. She handed him one of those so he had her email in front of him, and a few minutes later, he looked up from his computer. "Sent."

"Thank you. Are there any other videos you shot around the time of Cherish's that you haven't posted yet?"

"No. I'm all caught up except for hers, which is why I remembered it. The other most current are on the site. I've been in Los Angeles for the last six weeks on a production job, but I'll resume shooting interviews here in the next couple of days."

"Oh. So this"—she waved her arm around the studio—"isn't the only work you do?"

"I wish. I find a lot of satisfaction in this work, but rent being what it is, this gig doesn't pay all the bills. I take enough side jobs to keep the lights on. And of course, ad revenue helps too. Maybe someday I'll be able to do it full time."

As she nodded, he glanced back to her card. "Lennon," he said. "Imagine all the people living life in peace."

She breathed out a laugh. "That's the one. My mom would love you."

He smiled. "It's a great name. And hey, I hope watching Cherish tell her story helps somehow. I remember her being one that was very lost, with a real messed-up past. Not that that's unusual. I've been doing this for almost two decades, and I'm still not used to it." He gestured to her phone. "Anyway, you'll hear the details."

"While I'm here, can I show you a few other photos and see if you recognize any of them?"

"Yeah, sure."

Lennon pulled up the photos of the other victims she had on her phone and showed them to Jamal. "This one looks familiar," he said when she got to the older woman who had been at the crime scene with Cherish. "But I can't say for sure. I've interviewed thousands of people, and I spend a lot of time in the TL, so faces can run together. Sorry."

"No problem. I'll look through your site again." She wasn't looking forward to it. It'd been tough simply scrolling through once. "Can I ask why you do this? It's gotta be pretty depressing, listening to heartbreaking stories all day of people who are experiencing really terrible lives."

"It is and it isn't. There are some real survivors that walk through my door, whether they're living on the street or not. Whether others would call them crazy or not. And I think I can safely say that many of them would be labeled *severely damaged*. But so many have mustered these incredible survival tactics. These people walked through battles most of us can't even imagine, Inspector. There's a silent war going on in homes across America right this very second. Children are experiencing trauma that adults wouldn't know how to deal with. Those people out there are the walking wounded, and in this studio, I get to find out the *why*. Maybe someday someone will figure out the *what now.*"

What now. What now, indeed. It was the million-dollar question. Not only because children and the adults they'd grow into were suffering. But because damaged people raised more damaged people, and the cycle went on and on, multiplying significantly over time. She'd scrolled through Jamal's website and the lists and lists of videos of people who survived the streets. "Where do they go for help?" she asked. She knew where the police sent them. To the psych ward, or a shelter, or sometimes to a place like the Gilbert House, if it had a bed available. But she also knew that, more often than not, she saw those same people a few days later, right back where they'd started.

"That's not my lane," Jamal said. "I share their stories, and then I can only hope they find the help they need or accept it if the right kind is offered."

She gave a single nod. *The right kind.* But what was that? It seemed to her that nobody knew.

~

Lennon perused the frozen meals in her freezer before pulling out a chicken enchilada and then popping it into the microwave. As it heated, she changed out of her pants and blouse and put on an oversize pair of sweatpants and a T-shirt. She twisted her hair on top of her head and secured it, then washed her makeup off quickly. Her bruise had faded significantly, but the skin around her eye still held a sickly yellow hue under the concealer.

She entered the kitchen just as the microwave was beeping to indicate her less-than-gourmet dinner was ready. She knew she should make a salad or cook a vegetable, or at least put her dinner on a plate. But frankly, she was too tired and hungry to bother. No one was here to judge her, so who cared. She curled up on her couch and set her laptop next to her, booting it up as she ate a few bites out of the box of food.

Box of food. Her mother would be horrified by those three words.

Lennon had already read through Jamal Whitaker's bio when she'd first gone to *The Fringe*'s website, but she clicked on it again so she could read it more slowly now that she'd met the man in person. He'd come across as sincere, a man who genuinely cared about the people he interviewed. She'd asked him why he did what he did, but she hadn't asked what first brought him to do it. Apparently, according to his bio, he'd had substance abuse issues and even lived in his car for several months in his early twenties, during which time he'd become acquainted with the streets and those who lived there. He was able to get his life together and went on to have a career in video production, one in which he obviously still worked, at least part time. But he never could quite get the patchwork people of the Tenderloin out of his mind, and so he returned to tell their stories. "Stories are what connect us," he stated in his bio, making her think of Ambrose the liar, another lover of stories, if even that could be believed. She forced her mind back to Jamal. He wasn't wrong. Stories did connect people. They were, perhaps, one of the few things that did.

Lennon went to her email, clicked on the message from Jamal, and brought up the video. The screen filled with a view of the couch she'd stood in front of earlier today, only this time there was a young woman wearing a pair of shorts curled up in much the same position Lennon was sitting in now.

Lennon hit play and sat eating the rest of her dinner as Jamal asked Cherish questions about her childhood, the food seeming to curdle in her stomach as she listened to the young woman's story.

Lennon set the mostly empty box on the coffee table, stretched her legs, and brought the computer onto her lap so she had an even more up-close view of the screen. Speaking of the walking wounded

Jamal had referred to earlier. Lennon felt a lump forming in her throat, as if that curdled food might not stay down. To be pimped out by your mother? When you were a kindergartener? How did you ever move past something like that? Maybe the answer was you didn't—hence following in the woman's footsteps, creating the same life for yourself you'd been cruelly subjected to before you even knew your ABCs.

Lennon went back to *The Fringe's* website and looked at the lists of categories. There were a seemingly endless number of interviews in each list. Prostitutes. Pimps. Addicts—drugs, sex, gambling. Those suffering from mental illness. She did a search for the name *Anthony Cruz*, and then *Tony Cruz*, and then simply *Cruz*, but there was no hit.

Again she perused the lists and lists of people Jamal had interviewed, overwhelmed in the pit of her gut. She was tempted to slam her computer closed. Did she really need to expose herself to more of this when she already dealt with these people every day she was at work? When she was employed, anyway. Wasn't that enough? She could have an officer or someone else at the station wade through the videos when she got back, cross-checking each one against the photos of the victims from the crime scenes.

Her finger hovered over the X at the top of the screen, but after a moment she blew out a breath and scrolled to the list of videos featuring addicts. She watched a couple of them, hitting pause when she thought she recognized one of the men from the park. A heroin addict named Santiago Garza. She emailed herself the direct link to the video and then scrolled to the next one and watched that. When that one was done, the next one automatically began playing. Lennon sat there watching story after story of trauma and abuse. Ruined lives. Horror spoken of in monotone.

But God, so many of them were also surprisingly funny and sweet and charming. So . . . *human.* Doing the job she did, it was easy to forget that. When she'd started watching the videos, she'd thought it would be more of what she'd been exposed to as an officer and then an inspector, but it was the opposite. It was a glimpse into the humanity behind the drugs and the sex work. And like Jamal had said, it was a glimpse into the *why*, even if the *what now* remained elusive.

Lennon startled and let out a small yelp when her phone rang, bringing her from the harsh world of homelessness and drug abuse back to the safety of her couch. She set her computer aside and reached for her phone, sitting on the coffee table, shocked to see that it was already one in the morning.

It was Tommy's number.

"Hello."

"It's a boy. Nine pounds even. All ten fingers and ten toes, and he looks like his mother, thank God." She could hear the smile in his voice.

"Oh my gosh. A boy. Congratulations. How's Sam?" A tear spilled out of her eye and tracked down her cheek, and she brushed it away, embarrassed, as though he could see her.

"She's amazing. They both are."

"What's his name?"

"Beau Thomas."

"Beau. Oh, I love it. I can't wait to meet him."

"We should be home tomorrow afternoon. No complications, so they're booting us out. Come over anytime."

"Okay. I will. How about this weekend? Tommy, hug Sam for me and kiss that baby. Hold him tight." She pulled in a small sniffle.

"I will. Hey, you okay?"

"Yeah, I'm good. I'm just happy for you. And for him. He's got the best parents."

"Thanks, partner. See you this weekend."

"Bye, Tommy."

She hung up and sat clutching her phone, a tidal wave rising inside. Her phone beeped with a text coming through, and when she looked down at it, she saw a photo of a tired but beaming Sam, a grinning Tommy, and a swaddled infant cradled in his mother's arms. Another one came through right after, a close-up of Beau.

Brand new. Perfect in every way.

The wave of emotion crashed over her, and she dropped her phone, bringing her hands to her face as a sob broke from her mouth.

It'd been so *long* since she'd cried, and now this was the second time in less than two weeks. But she couldn't control it, was helpless against the onslaught of torment that battered her now. Seeing that precious, helpless newborn baby boy after listening to the stories of desolate adults was like a fist squeezing her heart. People didn't naturally end up the way the prostitutes and junkies and mentally ill had ended up. They'd been twisted, most of them from the time they were no bigger than the baby in the photo being cherished by his parents.

Cherish. Cherish Joy. How *dare* her mother give Cherish a name like that and then allow her to be victimized so hideously? And now, after Lennon had looked at little Beau, she wondered—what if Cherish's mother had suffered the same fate as Cherish? What if she'd also been a victim and had known no other way? As the cycle started, it continued. It was the most disgusting irony. Fury mixed with the heartache, and she was glad. Because it made her feel more powerful, like the fire within her might burn something down if she knew where or what or whom to torch. If she knew where to direct the inferno.

But of course, she didn't know, and that was the problem. *What now?* It was the question Jamal Whitaker had asked, and she understood why. If there was only one Cherish, or even only a hundred, the question would be easier to answer. But there were too many Cherishes to count. Maybe there was nothing to be done now.

She looked at the photo of Beau again, her gaze moving over his peaceful features. She had this instinct to hide him away from the harsh world. But of course, his parents were there for that. She had to remind herself that the precious new baby had loving parents who would be his soft place to land. His protectors. An exhale gusted from her mouth. And she couldn't help thinking about all the other babies who might have been born tonight into very different situations.

"Stop," she commanded herself. Because, really, what good was that? There was literally nothing she could do to help those nameless children.

But she also refused to pretend they didn't exist.

CHAPTER
TWENTY-SIX

Ambrose sat down on the side of the bed, running his hands through his hair and then to his shoulders as he tried to loosen the kinks in his neck. He was still shaken by what he'd seen when he'd walked into the apartment where Brandy had overdosed. It hadn't even been the overdose—he'd seen several of those in his lifetime—as much as the sight of that little girl crying over her mother's corpse. How long had she been on her own? And how many times would she revisit those traumatizing days in her nightmares?

He had learned to compartmentalize over the years, a necessary skill when it came to the work he did. If he took the entire world on his shoulders, he'd be rendered useless. And that wouldn't benefit anyone, least of all him.

He stood, walked to the minifridge in his room, and grabbed a bottle of water. Then he removed the case files from his briefcase, laying the photographs of the victims and the crime scenes across the bed.

He gazed over the jumble of files and photos and reports, all of it too close together to even see clearly. With a frustrated breath, he reached for his briefcase again and took out the roll of tape he'd tossed inside, in case he needed to see the papers he'd stolen more clearly.

Ambrose moved the desk aside, and then, one by one, he taped each piece of evidence to the wall, including the online articles he'd printed out before he'd even arrived in San Francisco. He'd heard walls like this called *conspiracy boards* or *crazy walls* or *murder maps*. Investigators gave them all sorts of names, and some even used strings to connect one thing to another. But whatever you called them, they worked. And sometimes you spotted something you would never have spotted because everything you had was directly in front of you at the same time.

It wouldn't necessarily happen immediately after he stood back and studied it, the way he was doing now. But the point was to imprint it on his mind and allow his brain to make connections, if it could find any. And sometimes, something would just niggle at him for reasons he couldn't articulate. And he'd come to count on the fact that 99.9 percent of the time, there was something there, whether he could explain how his brain had made the connection or not. The mind was a pretty miraculous thing.

He stepped forward, reading the report on the light-blue pill that had been at the most recent murder scene. He'd taken it to a lab where someone he trusted worked and had it analyzed. The ingredients were the same as the pale purple pill, only in different doses. And just like the purple pills, this one, too, had a unique LSD coating.

The drug found at the crime scenes had morphed from Doc's original formula to something different. The first question—the one he'd discussed with Finch but still hadn't been answered—was how the person who made it had known the exact formula to begin with. Doc's medication was strictly controlled, and only a very modest number of overages were made in case one was dropped or otherwise tainted. And if that didn't occur, they were immediately destroyed. The second question was, Why was it changing?

His gaze moved from one victim to another, that frozen scream chilling his blood again and making him want to look away. These people, though . . . all their lives they'd been screaming, in one manner or another, and everyone had looked away. He would not.

He'd made a list of the items found at each scene, and he went over them now. A belt. A baseball mitt. Several bottles of strawberry-daiquiri wine coolers that had been found at the first scene. Alcoholic beverages amid a drug-fueled party weren't unexpected. But did people still drink wine coolers? He wouldn't necessarily know, since he'd given up alcohol many years ago. When he'd first seen the empty bottles in an evidence photo, he'd assumed it was because they were cheap and widely available at any corner store in the city. He remembered girls drinking that five-dollar pink wine in his youth—not because it was good, but because it was cheap and tasted like fruit punch.

The names of those victims weren't known, and so he couldn't ask those who had partied with them if that was a standard cocktail choice. But . . . no, something felt off about those to him.

"What is it?" he said aloud, remembering how Lennon had asked him if he minded bouncing ideas off each other. He'd liked it, actually. Or maybe he'd just liked her. He missed it now, though. He missed her, and he wasn't sure how he could miss someone he'd known for such a short time. But the fact was he did. Another one of those connections his brain, or perhaps some unnamed part of him, had made. And he couldn't explain it, but neither did he discount it. She affected him in a way few people had.

He sighed. He'd have to learn to live with that—as he'd learned to live with so many things—because not only did she likely hate his guts, but she would handcuff him and toss him in jail if given the chance.

Strangely, the thought made him smile. Not the picture of him behind bars, but rather, Lennon looking fiery and hell bent.

Okay, but no. Because she was probably hurt, too, and he didn't like that. It was the only regret he had—deceiving Lennon, causing her to trust in him, when he wasn't worthy of her trust.

"Get your head in the fucking game," he murmured to himself. *Focus.*

He looked back at his board, going over the other items found. The baseball mitt was slightly odd, but it'd been found with the victims in the park, so it was possible that it wasn't even part of the crime but instead something dropped by a kid at some point.

His gaze moved to the right, where the photos of items from the second-to-last scene were taped. There were the children's toys, and the sex toys, but there had also been cigarettes on the nightstand. At first, those had seemed innocuous enough, even expected amid a scene like that. But the brand caught his attention now. Parliament Light 100s. He'd never even heard of that brand. He pulled out his phone and looked them up. They were still available for sale, but they were ranked among the least popular brands. And stranger still, they were more expensive than the standard Marlboros or Camels. He tapped his phone lightly against his palm for a moment.

The wine coolers and the cigarette brand, though found at two different scenes, both felt odd to him. They seemed specific, but not necessarily to the victims. What young homeless person chose a cigarette brand that was harder to find and more expensive? Probably not many. And even if they stole them, where would they have stolen them from? Most wouldn't have the means to venture far.

He didn't have the case files for the fourth scene, but he had walked through it and remembered what was there. A rope had been on the floor near the male victim, as had a pair of spark plugs. Again, in the vacant industrial building, where old junker cars had been abandoned in the lot next door, items like that weren't necessarily out of place. But he had a deep feeling they hadn't just been used as weapons when the drugs kicked in. He was becoming more and more sure the items were not random at all.

A message was being sent. The setup was familiar. The results were far from it.

But why? And how? If the props were specific to the victims, how did the killer know such personal information? Was the killer some type of therapist? Someone who'd collected secrets from their pasts and then cruelly used those secrets against them? Or had the victims themselves helped the killer set up each scenario toward a different end? A twisted version of something good?

Who would want to do something so horrific to other human beings?

He sat down on the bed, perusing the board. But nothing else clicked. He wouldn't stop trying, though. He felt responsible for these people now—the ones who had lived and died screaming for help.

CHAPTER TWENTY-SEVEN

Lennon rushed to her bedroom, where her phone was ringing. She wrapped the towel around her as she went, her wet hair slapping on her back. *The station.* Her heart gave a gallop. "Hello?"

"Lennon, it's Adella."

She paused. Adella was the last person she'd expected to hear from. And one of the last people she wanted to talk to. When she remained silent, Adella cleared her throat. "I, ah, I thought you should know that a woman named Brandy Lopez was just discovered dead in her apartment. I called because I heard the inspectors working your case talking, and apparently she was roommates with one of the victims, named Cherish Olsen."

Lennon sank down onto the edge of her bed, gripping her towel between her breasts. Brandy was dead? What about her little girl? Lennon's mind spun. "How?" she finally asked.

"It looks like an overdose. She had an eighteen-month-old girl, and she's okay. Anyway, I thought you might want to be kept up to speed on the case, so when you get back, you can hit the ground running." *Ah.* Adella felt guilty for talking. And this was her way of making amends. Lennon sighed. The truth was, Lennon's circumstances were no one's fault but her own. She'd made the choice to get chummy with Agent Mars or whoever he was, and so she deserved to be investigated. *Is that your new euphemism for amazing sex? "Getting chummy?"* She gave herself an internal eye roll. Sure, why not. It worked.

"Thanks, Adella. I appreciate it a lot. Anything else?"

"Yes, and you'll definitely want to hear this. Apparently, a man heard Brandy's daughter crying from inside, and kicked down the door. The description sounded suspiciously like a certain agent who's not an agent."

Her heart gave another gallop and then started to race. Ambrose. He was still working the case. She *knew* it. "Is he the one that called the police?"

"No. A neighbor did. The man who kicked in the door when they heard a baby crying inside took off before the police got there."

Of course he did. *He kicked in a door to save a baby.* Dammit, she really wanted to keep hating him, but he kept making it hard.

"Okay. Hey, Adella, seriously, I appreciate you calling me." She didn't like what Adella had done, ratting her out, but she could acknowledge Adella's call.

"You're welcome. Take care, Lennon."

"I will. Thanks again." She hung up the phone and spent a few minutes pacing in front of her bed, a renewed vigor to get back to the case making her feel jumpy but energized. Ambrose had gotten close to her—very close—and stolen files, gathered all the official information he could. And now he was working the case on his own, using the leads *she'd* helped him gather.

That energy took on heat, turning to anger. There was no way she'd let him sneak around behind the city's back. Who knew, maybe he was even working on behalf of the killer! Didn't she owe it to the citizens of San Francisco to make sure he wasn't still hindering their investigation of a serial killer and a deadly drug concoction?

She dropped her towel and then pulled on her underwear, a pair of jeans, and a sweater. Then she gathered her wet hair into a bun and secured it on top of her head.

Lennon went to the living room and turned on her laptop, brought it to the kitchen table, and sat down. The news about Brandy had made her think of the doctor she'd mentioned Cherish had seen. *The Candyman.* She'd moved that to the back of her mind as something to perhaps question Brandy about later, when the woman's mind might be clearer and she hadn't just received traumatic news about her roommate. But that was no longer a possibility.

She opened Google and did a search of clinics and doctors' offices in the Tenderloin, going through them one by one.

God, there were a lot of them, not only medical clinics but listings for syringe access and mental health services. For an area that offered so much health care, there sure were a lot of sick people, in numbers that were increasing by the week.

She scrolled through each hit, but nothing jumped out at her about the staff at any of them. There was a large free clinic on Golden Gate Avenue that offered both medical and mental health services under one roof. But again, nothing about the staff caught her attention. With a frustrated sigh, she went back to Google and did a broader search of doctors in the city of San Francisco. When twenty pages of listings came up, she modified her search to psychiatrists. She'd try psychologists and therapists, too, but as she was likely dealing with someone who could prescribe medication, a psychiatrist seemed like a reasonable place to start. She began to scroll, yawning halfway through, feeling a sense of hopelessness about this line of research.

Her eyes caught on a name, and she blinked, then clicked on Dr. Alexander Sweeton. *Sweeton. Candyman.* Just a nickname, based on his real one. People in the TL seemed to like those. But was that a stretch? Maybe. And what made it even more of a long shot that Dr. Alexander Sweeton was this Candyman was the fact that he did business from *an entire floor* of a skyscraper in Union Square, just steps from the Financial District and Nob Hill.

Lennon perused the photos of the building itself, her gaze stopping on the jaw-dropping art deco lobby. *Wow.* She couldn't even begin to guess what price an office space in a building like that might start at, much less an entire floor. She didn't need to attempt to look it up, however, to know that treating drug-addicted prostitutes who lived and worked in the Tenderloin wouldn't help pay it.

Lennon clicked from one link to another, trying to find a picture of Dr. Sweeton, even though she'd basically dismissed him. He was a sixty-eight-year-old board-certified physician who had earned his doctorate in psychiatry from the University of California, San Francisco. And from what it looked like, he serviced the Bay Area elite, who apparently, despite their lofty financial status, had enough *issues* to keep a practicing psychiatrist in a high-priced luxury office in the heart of the city. *Stop being judgmental, Lennon. Problems are problems. Pain is pain.* Yes, and she had to keep reminding herself that just because you weren't a homeless sex worker didn't mean your mental and emotional struggles weren't valid. In fact, if watching the stories on *The Fringe* had been anything, it'd been a reminder that humans were humans, no matter the vast differences in circumstances.

She found information about an upcoming gala, benefiting a private hospital, that he was going to speak at. The event was two months away. And at five thousand dollars a plate, she couldn't have afforded it even if she'd wanted to.

She found a photo of the doctor from a previous event and stopped to study it. His thinning hair was completely white and combed away from his face, his smile slight. And beside him, arm linked, was a glamorous, statuesque brunette who appeared to be half his age and was identified in the tagline below as the doctor's wife, Brittany Sweeton.

Lennon kept scrolling. She paused as something caught her eye, and she clicked on it. It was a journal article published by Dr. Alexander Sweeton titled "The Neurobiology of Trauma."

Trauma. She attempted to read it, but she'd have had to sign up for a subscription to the journal. Instead of taking the time to do that, she picked up her phone and dialed his office number. The pleasant voice of an older woman answered the line.

"Yes, hello. My name is Inspector Lennon Gray with the San Francisco Police Department, and I'd like to speak with Dr. Sweeton, if he's in?"

"Oh. Inspector. Um, no, I'm sorry. The doctor isn't in today."

"Can you tell me when he'll be back? This is quite urgent. It's involving . . . a patient."

"I see. Well, I can ring his cell phone and leave a message, but I'm not sure when he'll return my call. He's giving a presentation to the UC medical school students this afternoon, and it's supposed to begin in about half an hour."

Half an hour.

"If you give me your number, I can have him call you later tonight or tomorrow."

"That's okay. I'll try back. Can you tell me . . . Does the doctor provide psychiatric services anywhere else, by chance?"

"No, not really. He volunteers at a free clinic on Thursday afternoons, specifically helping veterans who live on the street. But that's charitable work."

"Veterans?"

"Mm-hmm. That's why he first went into practice, to help those with PTSD. His practice has grown beyond that, but he still finds satisfaction in giving back to those suffering the most. He's such a good man."

He *sounded* like a good man, and Lennon almost felt bad for even considering looking into him. But her job was not to feel bad. Her job was to investigate every possible lead. "The free clinic you're talking about—is it the one on Golden Gate?"

"Yes, it is. Do you need the address?"

"No, I have it. Thank you again for your help."

Lennon hung up, springing up from the chair and grabbing her jacket and purse before heading out the door.

She pulled into the medical school parking lot exactly thirty minutes later, hurried into the building, and then stopped a woman in the hallway. "Hi. I'm supposed to attend a talk by Dr. Sweeton. Do you know where that's being given?"

"I'm not sure. If it's for all the students, it's probably in the auditorium right around the corner."

"Great, thanks," she called over her shoulder as she sped off in the direction the woman had pointed. There were a couple of men just entering through a double door, and Lennon saw a crowded lecture room filled with people just beyond them and followed close on their heels.

CHAPTER TWENTY-EIGHT

"Trinity"
Episode from podcast *The Fringe*
Host of podcast, Jamal Whitaker

"Hello, welcome to *The Fringe*. Trinity. Beautiful name."

"Thanks. Named for the Holy Trinity. The Father, the Son, and the Holy Ghost. And yet here I am, nothing but a shadow."

Jamal smiles. "How are you?"

The woman with the long dark-blonde curls crosses her legs. She appears to be in her mid- to late twenties, attractive, wearing jeans and a brightly colored peasant top. "Mostly fine," she says. "Thanks for having me."

"Thanks for being here. So, Trinity, you're in the porn industry. You do films?"

"Yeah, I've been doing them since I was seventeen."

"Underage."

"Did I say seventeen? I meant eighteen."

Jamal smiles again. "How'd you get into the business?"

"I met a guy." She adjusts the hoop earring that's caught in her hair. "Every girl's story of woe starts out that way, right?" She laughs. "I met a guy." She raises her hands and wiggles her fingers in a mock-spooky movement. "Dun, dun, dun."

"A boyfriend got you into it?"

She drops her hands and shrugs. "I wouldn't necessarily call him a boyfriend. This guy I used to mess around with. He was a friend of my dealer. Anyway, he introduced me to someone, and I started doing films. Easy as that."

"What was it like growing up?"

"Well. I'm the daughter of a preacher, if you can believe it."

"A preacher's kid. So home was good?"

"No, home was not good. My father preached in the pulpit on Sunday morning and then crawled into bed with me on Sunday night. And Monday, too, if he felt like it. Thursday, as well, if he could get me alone. You can probably understand why I hid a lot. In some way, my father taught me how to be a superhero—because of him, I became invisible."

"I'm sorry."

"I believe you, Jamal, and I appreciate that. What you do, listening to stories, it's a decent thing to do."

"How do you feel about making films?"

"I like it."

"That's not always the case."

Trinity brings her foot up on the edge of the couch and hugs her leg. "I had hands on me growing up, hands I didn't want and didn't give permission to. When I do a film, I'm the one in control. I'm there because I decided to be there. I say yes or no, and then I get paid for it. I'm taking back my own power, you know?"

Jamal nods.

"Plus, it's safe. A lot safer than the girls I see walking the streets."

"That's true. Are you ever asked to do things you don't like to do?"

Trinity hesitates. "Yeah, sure. That's part of the business too. There's always another girl who will do that forbidden something, and they're the ones who get the jobs, so sometimes . . . a lot of times, you end up bending the rules you started out with. But again, Jamal, I know how to become invisible."

"What's your drug, Trinity?"

"Heroin, mostly. Stops the pain, you know? Makes everything quiet. At least for a little while."

"So I hear. Do you see yourself doing anything else besides the pornography?"

Trinity shrugs. "I did pretty well in school. I liked to read." She tugs at her earring again. "And I was always good with clothing. I made this." She points down to the peasant top she's wearing. "When I was a kid, I used to dream about being a fashion designer, going to Paris, seeing my designs on runways." Her lips tilt, even if her expression is slightly sad. "Maybe in another life, you know? Maybe this is just a practice round, and I'll do better next time. Trip the light fantastic, as my granny used to say."

"Trip the light fantastic. What a great saying."

"Isn't it? Brings to mind this beautiful euphoria. But not the kind you achieve from getting high. The joy you get off *life*, you know? The kind kids experience before someone fucks them up."

Jamal nods. "You said you had dreams when you were a kid, but what about now? What are your dreams now?"

Trinity looks off to the side, silent for several long moments. The studio is quiet, only the gentle whir of the camera equipment. "I had a friend in the business. She used to say, 'Trin, dreams are how people get by in a place like this.'" She lets out a small, sad chuff. "Anyway, that friend, she took her life a year ago. Beautiful girl. Legs like a colt. Milk-and-honey skin." She lapses into silence again before her gaze meets the camera. "I regret not telling her that she was wrong about dreams. Dreams are dangerous. Dreams will break the last shards of your heart when you think there's nothing left to shatter."

CHAPTER TWENTY-NINE

Lennon sat down in an auditorium chair near the back, her eyes focusing on the older man at the front of the room. Dr. Sweeton was facing the whiteboard. His name had already been spelled out above what he was currently writing. He finished the last letter with a flourish and turned toward the audience. Lennon's gaze went to the word behind his back: *Trauma.* "What is trauma?" he asked. "And what part of the individual does it affect?"

A young woman in the front row raised her hand, and he pointed at her. "Trauma is an emotional response to a terrible event that the person perceives as inescapable."

"Mostly correct," Dr. Sweeton said. "However, trauma is not simply an emotional response. Trauma affects the body, the mind, and the brain in profound and lasting ways." He joined his hands in front of him. "Posttraumatic stress syndrome is the body continuing to fight back against a threat that's already over. We see this in war veterans and others who've survived a harrowing and highly distressing experience, such as a mugging, being raped, or an automobile accident." He paused as he glanced around. "What happens in our body when we're confronted with trauma?"

A different young woman raised her hand. "The sympathetic nervous system activates, priming your heart and your lungs and your muscles to either fight or flee."

"And if both are impossibilities? If there's no way to escape the threat? No hope in fighting it? What does the body do if the brain ascertains that the person must accept the inevitable incoming horror?" Dr. Sweeton asked. No one answered, and so he went on. "The body experiences a dorsal vagal shutdown. Our metabolism slows so that heart rate plunges very suddenly, our blood pressure drops, our gut and kidney function decrease, as does our immune response. The body 'saves' us"—he lifted his hands and made air quotes—"by dissociating, collapsing, or freezing."

He cocked his head and looked around for a moment. "But what about the child who grew up in a household where they experienced frequent, ongoing trauma? A constant influx of cortisol and adrenaline? What happens to our natural alarm system when it's constantly activated against a threat the individual has no hope of countering? What does the human mind do when its exposure to rage and terror is almost never ending? How does that child cope? What does the body do to save the mind?"

Lennon looked down at the sea of heads below her. Finally a lone hand went up, and Dr. Sweeton nodded to the young man. "Ah, do you mean, like, a child who experiences sex abuse by a family member from the time they're very young?"

"Yes. That scenario is more common than we like to acknowledge. One in five children in this country is sexually molested, according to the CDC. And that number is likely even higher, considering many such instances go unreported and therefore untreated in any manner."

"Damn," she heard a girl in the row in front of her murmur. *Indeed.* Lennon crossed her arms, drawing her shoulders up momentarily. It was a difficult thought to consider, even briefly, that right that minute, untold numbers of children were suffering, their brains twisting as their little systems tried their best to protect them. The very same thought she'd cried over after watching all those videos. Another reminder. As if she needed one. Were those kids all fated to wander the streets someday, in filth and misery? To sell their own bodies? The ones they'd been taught were worthless and did not really belong to them anyway?

"What if someone intervenes and they get help early?" someone asked.

"If early intervention occurs with a mental health professional who understands the intricacies of trauma, especially as it affects the brain, then there is always hope that that individual can heal. Specifically, there are windows where the brain is experiencing rapid periods of growth, such as during the teen years, when such treatments are even more effective. However, often, traumatized individuals are too on guard to submit to normal human relationships where it's necessary to become at least somewhat vulnerable, and this includes a relationship with a clinician. The body doesn't allow this. Even mothers who've experienced extended trauma cannot dial down their natural vigilance long enough to nurture their children. Their mind and body are in a constant state of arousal. Either that or they are too numb to bond with other human beings. They are stuck in fight or flight, or they are permanently shut down. Their circuits need rewiring. Their internal alarm system is very simply broken."

"Are you saying that people who've experienced chronic trauma are brain damaged?" a man in the middle of the theater asked.

"Yes, I am saying that. Individuals who have experienced chronic trauma, especially as children, are brain damaged. The first step in healing must target the brain itself."

A low murmur went up. Lennon agreed that that was a bold statement. But did she disagree? She wasn't sure.

"What I'm saying is not as controversial as it might sound," the doctor went on. "We have scans that record what happens in different sections of the brain when a person is traumatized. It's quite clear. Moreover, traumatized individuals are well aware something is very wrong and suffer because of it. They vacillate between agitation and numbness. They're often suicidal and have extremely low self-worth. They experience chronic mental and emotional pain."

A woman raised her hand. "Thank you, Doctor. Are there medications that can help these people?"

"Mostly no, at least not without getting to the heart of the problem. Diagnoses are thrown at those who suffer with PTSD. Attention deficit disorder. Oppositional defiant disorder. Borderline personality disorder. Intermittent explosive disorder. Reactive attachment disorder. Substance use disorder. And none of these diagnoses are completely off the mark. But none of them address the root of the problem. You can throw all the labels and all the pharmaceuticals in the world at them, and you won't make a dent in the underlying issue. The most these substances will do is temporarily control them. In some instances, a history might be taken and a PTSD diagnosis tossed into the mix. But again, until we have ways of treating these individuals that don't force them to deal with side effects that are worse than the diagnosis, it matters little to the person suffering."

Lennon pulled in a breath and let it out slowly. She was familiar with the list of diagnoses the doctor had just listed. How many times had she arrived at a call for family trouble and met a child who'd been diagnosed with all those things and more? *A child.* In most cases, and in her gut, she believed there was something far deeper going on with a kid who acted out to that degree. And even now, sometimes she saw one of them wandering the streets of San Francisco, still high on something—only now it was of the illegal variety.

"So you believe many of the diagnoses are bullshit?" a man near the back asked.

"To put it bluntly, yes."

The young man let out a short laugh but appeared mildly uncomfortable. "Lots of professionals would disagree with you, Dr. Sweeton."

"Indeed, and they have. But show me one who's helped a previously homeless drug addict with ten mental diagnoses live a full, rich life. Or one who's assisted an incest survivor experience satisfying sexual relationships absent fear or rage. If you can, I will wholeheartedly consider that person's professional opinion and enthusiastically inquire as to their treatment methods."

Shifting and murmurs all around. Was the doctor saying that complete mental health for people like the ones he was describing was an impossibility? If so, why was he in this business?

A woman raised her hand, and the doctor tipped his chin in her direction. "You mentioned mental issues pertaining to a history of trauma. But if the body itself seeks to protect the individual, are there vestiges of that later in life?"

"Absolutely. Victims of prolonged trauma experience many similar physical phenomena. I have seen patients who are numb in many areas of their bodies, specifically where trauma occurred. Some can't see themselves in mirrors. They are far more vulnerable to experiencing long-term health problems. Chronic muscle tension creates migraines, severe back pain, fibromyalgia, rheumatoid arthritis, and other pain conditions. They cannot concentrate and often lash out violently at the simplest of provocations. Speak to any victim of chronic and prolonged trauma, and they will list their physical ailments. But these ailments are only symptoms of their underlying torment. And once again, the drugs they're prescribed may help temporarily, but are ultimately bound to fail, leaving them that much more desperate."

The entire audience seemed to be as rapt by the doctor's passion as Lennon. He looked pained himself, as though the torment of these traumatized patients and the lack of treatment they experienced was a deep personal wound. Maybe it was. Maybe he'd been a victim once too. Or loved someone who was.

"These people are statistics to most professionals. They overwhelm our welfare system, they fill up our prisons, and they flood our medical clinics. What can we do? We must do something. Not only for them, but for the children they will produce—the ones who will almost certainly experience trauma as well, after being raised by emotionally deficient parents who, more often than not, expose their children to the same types of trauma they themselves suffered."

"Other than the traditional protocols, what can be done for people like that?" a girl asked after raising her hand. "People who almost literally need their brains rewired?"

"As of now? We have some promising treatments," Dr. Sweeton answered. "EMDR is one, though it's controversial within the field. I, however, believe it's a worthy area of study and have used it in my practice. It stands for *eye movement desensitization and reprocessing*." All around Lennon, students were jotting in their notebooks. "It's a psychotherapy treatment that involves moving your eyes in a specific way while processing traumatic memories. Holotropic breathwork is similar—though, as the name suggests, it involves breathing techniques to influence your mental and emotional states."

"And those things help?"

Dr. Sweeton paused for a moment. "They can, depending on the depth of trauma." He looked around again. "I realize I have presented a problem that seems to have a lack of solutions. What I would encourage you to do, future doctors, is to think outside the box. An unprecedented problem requires an unprecedented solution, not only for the institutions I mentioned but for the human beings affected by trauma. Push forward with new advances as they arise, and if mental health is the specialty you choose, be dogged in your pursuit of treatments that make a real difference. Don't fall into the trap of medical complacency. And until the problem can be addressed in a meaningful therapeutic way, never stop asking 'What can we do?' We must do something." He looked around the room, almost beseeching. "I leave you with that."

The audience applauded, and Dr. Sweeton gave a small, humble wave before leaving the room. The students began to gather their things, and the chatter grew louder. Lennon scooted out of her seat and made her way down the center aisle, and then through the door where the doctor had gone.

She caught up with him in the lobby near the front door. "Dr. Sweeton?"

He turned, giving her a mild smile. "Yes?"

"Hi. I'm Lennon Gray, and I'm an inspector with the San Francisco Police Department. Do you have a minute?"

"Oh. Yes, of course." He stepped off to the side, and she followed. A stream of students who'd been in the presentation started filing out.

"Thank you." She removed her phone and pulled up the photo of the pills from the crime scene with the "BB" logo and held it up to him. "Have you ever seen this medication?"

He leaned closer, studying it. "'BB'? No. It looks more like a home-made medication than a pharmaceutical-grade product."

"It is. It's related to a crime, and we're trying to trace its origins."

"Ah. I'm sorry to hear that. And sorry I can't be of more help."

She nodded. "I listened to your talk. It was . . . depressing."

He gave her a fleeting smile as the last of the students walked by, the door right in front of them closing, quiet descending in the open two-story entryway where they were standing. "It can be, yes. But there are breakthroughs happening every day in the study of mental health. And human beings can be extremely resilient if given the right tools."

"As a former beat cop, I related to a lot of what you said. I've driven plenty of eight-year-olds to the mental ward who have all the diagnoses you mentioned listed on their forms."

The doctor sighed. "Children. Yes. It's the hardest part, isn't it? Trauma is one thing, but treatment becomes that much more challenging when the child hasn't formed an attachment to their mother, or another caregiver. An understanding of self is formed through such a relationship."

"The mirror thing?"

"Yes. To themselves, they do not exist."

"That's awful."

"It is awful."

"So it's your belief that everyone who is diagnosed with a mental or psychological disorder is really suffering from trauma?"

"Don't be naive, Inspector. There's never an *everyone* in either of our fields. If there was, it'd make our jobs much easier."

He wasn't wrong, but she still wasn't sure how she felt about this man. Now that she was looking directly in his eyes, she felt that he was hiding something. But what or why, she had no clue. "You talked about the lack of options and misdiagnoses of people suffering that way and mentioned the eye movement thing and the breathwork. But what about hallucinogens?"

The doctor paused, the expression on his face enigmatic. "Are you referring to ketamine therapy?"

"I don't know. I'm not familiar with any of these treatments. I do know that ketamine is highly addictive and sold on the streets under the name Special K, or Vitamin K." She'd heard others too . . . Kit Kat, Cat Valium . . . but the ones she'd mentioned were the most common.

"Yes. Ketamine is a dissociative anesthetic medication that is sometimes used off label to treat depression and anxiety disorders. It's not currently approved by the FDA. But perhaps more importantly, patient results are often unsustained—especially without multiple sessions, which become challenging when dealing with certain populations."

"I see. What about other hallucinogens?"

Again, he paused. "As they pertain to therapy? There is evidence that hallucinogens may stimulate nerve cell regrowth in sections of the brain that are responsible for emotion and memory. There are only animal studies thus far, but supporters of psychedelic drugs as a treatment for PTSD believe they can and should be used to decrease anxiety and fear pathways in the brain. Patients become highly suggestible when under the influence of these drugs, which can be used for good."

"Or bad."

"Potentially, in the wrong hands, yes. But that can be true of any drug, Inspector Gray, as I imagine you must know well."

Yes, I do. "You cited studies, but do you have an opinion on the subject of hallucinogen use? Professionally or otherwise?"

"I think that there's potential for hallucinogens as a treatment for PTSD in a medical setting under a doctor's supervision. They can produce extremely intense experiences that are subjectively mystical and accompanied by positive change in insight, motivation, and behavior. I'm hopeful about future studies. But as of now, therapeutic use of psychedelic substances has only been legalized in Oregon and Colorado."

"As a well-known progressive state, California can't be far behind?"

The doctor shrugged. "I don't make the laws."

"And you don't break them."

"No, I don't break them. Look me up. You won't find so much as a speeding ticket on my record." He tilted his head as he studied her. "Have you experienced trauma, Inspector? Do you have any personal experience with it?"

"Haven't most people to some degree or another? Life is often cruel."

He smiled. "Life. Ah, yes. Life *is* often cruel." He paused, his gaze assessing. His phone began to ring, but he didn't break eye contact. "But it's the easier burden to bear. When humans are cruel, specifically the ones who are tasked with caring for you, it is the most unbearable cruelty of all."

~

Lennon had thanked the doctor quickly so he could take his call. She had his information, and she couldn't think of anything else to ask him. Though the talk he'd given was still swirling in her head, making her feel upset and distracted and sort of hopeless overall. *What can we do?* he'd asked in closing. *We must do something.*

What can we do?

She came in contact with the type of people the doctor was referencing all the time, and she had no answer to his question. Most mental health professionals were drowning too. And if they didn't know, if they had no answer—then who did?

No one. No one does.

And so they all just applied Band-Aid after Band-Aid, knowing the underlying wound was growing more and more infected by the day.

She'd been walking slowly through the parking lot, lost in her own thoughts, when the sight of the doctor rushing to his car in the other direction caught her eye. He was still on his phone, talking animatedly. And then he stopped and hung up, seeming to dial again. She held back for a moment, then moved behind him as he resumed walking, the phone held to his ear.

A name caught her attention. *Ambrose.* Her heart sped, a zap of electricity moving down her limbs. The doctor unlocked his car, lights flashing as he stopped near the door, looking around. She ducked behind a minivan, unseen but still close enough to hear. "We can't lay low. We're on day five, and there's no turning back. You know that." Silence for a moment. "Okay. Yes. Be at the offices tonight. I'll determine if we can move through six and seven more rapidly."

She heard the doctor get in his car, and scooted to the other side of the minivan, moving quickly down the aisle of cars as she heard his vehicle start and then pull out of the parking spot, driving in the opposite direction.

She hurried to her car, easy to spot because of the window covered by plastic and duct tape, and answered her ringing phone as she walked. "Hello?"

"Lennon, Lieutenant Byrd. We know who he is. His name is Ambrose DeMarce."

She stopped. "DeMarce?" So *Mars* was an alias, but it hadn't been far off. "Who is he?"

"He's a bounty hunter. Mostly a lone ranger, but he's contracted for the FBI and the US Marshals and who knows what other agencies. He went rogue by infiltrating our investigation, and no one knows why. But they're also blocking any further action against him. For now, anyway."

Her mouth dropped open. *"Why?"*

The lieutenant sighed, and she could see him now, rubbing his left eye the way he did when he was tired and frustrated. Which, honestly, was a hell of a lot of the time—no surprise considering the job he did and where he did it. "Because he's valuable to them and they don't want him in jail or otherwise compromised, I guess. Anyway, it's clear he acted on his own, and you've been reinstated. I'd tell you that you could come back tomorrow, but the chief needs to sign off on it, and he's not returning until Friday."

She huffed out a breath of frustration. Not that being stripped of her police powers had kept her from working, but still. "Promise me you'll call if our killer strikes again or new information comes to light? I want to get right back to it on Friday."

"Sure, Gray. I'll let you know if there's a new development in the case."

She thanked the lieutenant and hung up. She felt that fire again in her gut. Ambrose *DeMarce* was part of this. Some bigger picture that had to do with trauma. Treatment. Hallucinogens. *A miracle treatment.* She needed answers. So she'd be back to work at the end of the week. But first, she knew what she had to do tonight. Because she knew where he'd be.

CHAPTER THIRTY

No legacy is so rich as honesty.
—William Shakespeare

Seventeen Years Ago
Patient Number 0022

The world brightened another shade, and Jett looked around, the bus station shimmering and wavering, like a desert mirage that wasn't really there.

Is he you?

Jett swallowed. He felt the lump move down his throat, felt the breath grow thin in his lungs. Feathers caressed his cheek. *Back, forth, back, forth.* He was him, and the boy was a different boy, and he felt scared and sad and guilt ridden and shameful. He wanted to run, but he wanted to stay, and he knew the boy, but he didn't want to say his name. *No, he's not me. He's someone else. He's my . . . friend.*

Shall we stay? Or shall we board that bus? It's up to you. It's always up to you, his guide said. But now her voice didn't come from a distance. It was right beside him, and it had breath that was minty, and the wings that tickled his cheek and comforted him smelled like flowers and coconuts. The world grew a shade brighter, and he felt something against his back. A chair, or a couch. Soft. It was soft. More scents invaded his nostrils. Something sweet, something bitter. There were sounds outside him, too, but he wasn't sure what they were. Movement, whispers, the whirring of a machine.

"If I stay, it will be bad," he said, and he heard his own voice, he felt it as he pushed it from his mouth. No monster crushed it. He was free to speak if he wanted. He took in a mouthful of air, and his lungs expanded. Full.

There are bad parts of stories, his guide said. *Bad things make up stories too.*

Yes, but it was . . . it was his story, and he could tell it. But he'd also lived it, and it hurt to know that. He felt wetness on his cheeks, and he felt the flowery coconut feathers too. *Back, forth, back, forth.* "I'll have to go back there to tell it," he told her.

"That's okay. I'll be with you. I'll be there to hear your story."

"Will you still like me when you know?" Would anyone like him? How could they?

He felt her release a gust of minty air, and that feathery caress on his cheek never halted, not even for a moment. *Back, forth, back, forth.* "I will love you. No matter what."

He felt his lids fluttering, but he didn't want to open his eyes. They were so heavy, and he was tired, and he could travel without opening his eyes. And so he did, back through town to the road that would bring him to the farm where his story had begun. Back to find the boy. Even though he was scared, and he didn't want to return, he knew he had to.

His story had a beginning, and it had a middle, but it didn't yet have an end.

The sky grew darker as he walked, the low rumble of thunder sounding in the misty air. The rain began to fall in steady streams. It was salty and bitter, and it stung his skin like acid. The little boy peeked out from behind a tree, his red shirt the only color in the dull landscape. He'd been laughter and joy, and he'd been Jett's only friend. The boy gestured with his hand. "Come on." Jett followed, his feet trudging along behind the boy, watching as he darted here and there, hiding, laughing. He was playing a game, a long-ago game with the boy Jett had been, who was now wrapped in the safety of his grown-up body.

He leaned around the tree and tapped the boy on his shoulder, and the boy startled and laughed. "I'm sorry I didn't remember you," Jett said. He was so sad. God, he was so sad. The rain drenched him, falling in sheets.

"You did remember," the boy told him. "You never forgot. And you came back for me."

"Yes, but . . ."

With a burst of laughter, the boy ran off through the rain. The one who'd come from the farm a few miles away to play with him. *Milo.* The name stabbed at his underbelly, wounding him. He saw where Milo was running, alarm ringing through him. "No!"

Jett ran, sprinting through the rain where Milo had disappeared into the fog, running toward that shed that had been his prison and his torture chamber. *Nonono. Oh God, no.* The flutter of white feathers sounded next to him, his guide easily keeping pace.

Breathless, Jett skidded to a stop in front of the shed, going down on his knees as he sobbed. *Nonono.* "Open the door. I'm right here with you."

His shoulders shook, his whole body trembled as he reached his fingers through the rain that now felt thick and sludgy, clutching the door handle and pulling it open, inch by slow inch. And when it was open, the sight stopped his heart, razors ripping down his throat, his muscles seizing. His grandfather was doing what he'd done to Jett. His pants were down around his ankles, and Milo was bent over the bench, facing away. *Agony. Milo's agony ripped through him.* Jett's mouth opened wide, and he yelled, a thousand swarming flies swelling from his lips. He threw himself toward his grandfather, to make him *stop. Oh God, please no, stop.* His grandfather raised his arm and smacked him. Jett's body hit the wood wall of the shed with a sharp thud, ears ringing, those flies continuing to buzz buzz buzz BUZZ BUZZ. Milo had been yelling, but now he stopped. The only sound in Jett's head was the incessant drone. The world spun, and when the hissing black insects cleared, he saw that his grandfather's hands were around Milo's neck and he was squeezing.

"You think you can let someone on my property without my permission, boy?" his grandfather yelled as he shook Milo's body like a rag doll. The child was limp, his face purple.

Jett was frozen with fear, with horror, his head fuzzy, everything spinning and buzzing and swelling and receding. Jett dragged himself to his feet, using his hand to brace himself on the wall, reaching for Milo even though he knew he was already dead. Tar dripped from Jett's eyes and into his mouth, trapping his tongue as it dried and hardened. "Look what you made me do!" his grandfather yelled. "Get out!"

And so Jett did, tripping over the threshold, slamming the door, shutting out the sight, another mass of flies rising in his body, scratching and biting the underside of his flesh.

A gust of wind sprang up, and Jett was whipped around, and he saw the little boy that was him running away, away, away. He couldn't help Milo, not now, and he hadn't then. He hadn't then. Oh God, he hadn't then. And so he ran after the little boy that was him, the one that had been wrapped in the safety of his body but had fled at that long-ago sight burrowed into the recesses of his twisted mind.

He ran and he ran and he ran, the rain coming harder and harder. Soaking. Pounding. *Thud thud thud thud thud thud thud thud thud thud.* His fingers caught on the little boy's shirt, and he grabbed him and pulled, wrapping him in his arms, both of them falling to their knees in the mud and the rain, sobbing and clawing and finally dissolving into one another. He landed on the soft earth, his arms wrapped around nothing, drawing himself into a ball, the soft brush of feathers drying his tears. *Back, forth, back, forth.*

"There you go. There you go. You're okay, now. You're okay. I'm here. I'm here. And so are you. So are you."

Yes, he was here, not there. There was fabric beneath him, and the whisper of voices around him and the whir of a machine, and the scents of flowers and coconut and mint and coffee too. This was now, and that was then, and oh God, that was then. He felt the tears sliding down his cheeks, and he remembered the then. *He remembered Milo.*

He lifted his heavy lids, the watercolor now clearing, the faces around him taking shape. Concerned. Smiling. "Hello, sweetness," the woman said. Her name was Maisie. He'd met her in the before.

A man approached. Dr. Sweeton. He knew Dr. Sweeton. He was the man who'd tested him, and evaluated him, and asked him question after question after question. The doctor smiled and took his hand. "How are you feeling?"

How are you feeling? He took in a breath and let it out slowly. "Tired," he said. His voice cracked. His muscles felt weak, like he'd just run a marathon.

"I imagine you do." The doctor took out a small light and shone it in his eyes. It was bright and caused him to squint and look away. "Do you know what today's date is?"

He thought about that. He'd signed the forms, and he'd sat in the reclining chair where they'd put a sticker on his skin with a wire that led to a machine that monitored his heart. He'd said he was ready even though he didn't know for sure if that was true or not. He couldn't really remember what he'd been thinking then. It seemed blurry and unclear, another life. But it wasn't. It was . . . what had the doctor told him? The therapy would take seven days. So that would make it . . . "April seventeenth," he said.

The doctor smiled. "That's right. And what is your name?"

Jett.

But that wasn't right. That was just a word a prostitute named Maria had called him when he'd rebuffed her advances for what must have been the tenth time and turned away. *Always running off,* she'd insisted. *Jettin' here, jettin' there. Can't stand still enough for a ten-dollar, three-minute blow,* she'd said with a mucous-filled laugh. *I'm gonna call you Jett!*

The thing was, she'd been right. He couldn't sit still. He wished he could. Not that that would have made him take her up on the ten-dollar blow. He'd turned back toward her and tossed her the last of a pack of cigarettes for some reason he couldn't explain, because he usually didn't give things away. Her eyes had lit up like she'd won the lottery, and she'd held that pack of cigarettes in the air and let out a whoop. And when he'd *jetted* out of the hotel, she'd opened the door behind him and shouted to all the drug addicts and pimps and prostitutes milling about the street, "That's Jett right there. I call him Jett cuz he's always jettin' off somewhere. But he's all right! That dude is all right." And someone had remembered that and called him Jett later—or, less often, J.D.—and it'd stuck, and so that's who he'd become. But Jett wasn't his name—not his real one, anyway. "Ambrose," he said. "My name is Ambrose DeMarce."

CHAPTER THIRTY-ONE

Lennon pushed the cabinet door open, peeking out through the small crack. The room beyond was dim and empty, and so she climbed out of the small hiding spot, cringing as she unbent her sore legs. How long had she been in there? An hour? Maybe slightly more? She hadn't dared look at her phone for fear the light would shine from the spaces around the door and give her away. She pulled it from her pocket now and glanced at it quickly. Yes, almost an hour. It was just a few minutes past eight o'clock, and she hoped that any dawdlers had left by now.

This was what she'd been reduced to. Sneaking past receptionists so she could hide in cabinets until the lights went off. But she'd heard noises that indicated people were arriving after the regular staff had left and knew that whatever she'd heard being referenced earlier on Dr. Sweeton's call was, in fact, going on.

She opened the door, swallowing when a small squeak echoed in the outside hall. She waited, but when no sound came in response, she ducked out, leaving the door slightly ajar. She hurried down the hall, looking over her shoulder as she walked. There was something very eerie about a medical building after hours, and she was already freaked out as it was, by the fact that she was walking into a complete unknown.

And now she had to search the place in the near dark. The light from her phone might be seen around a corner, so she put it in her pocket, her hand running over the personal weapon that she'd taken from her home safe and had holstered against her ribs.

It was dark and quiet around the next bend, and Lennon was forced to feel along the wall as she walked. The hairs on her arms stood up, and she wanted badly to turn back. But dammit, she was here for a reason. And dark or no dark, she wasn't going to chicken out.

She had to know.

Her shoes were virtually soundless on the carpet. When she made it to the next wing, there were milky lights along the bottom of the wall, directing her way.

She came to another bend and peered around it slowly, determining that there were no people in sight but a brighter light coming from around a corner up ahead. She pulled her shoulders back, gathering her nerves, stepped into the next hall, and pressed her back against the wall as she listened.

Her heart galloped, but above the noise of her own blood whooshing between her ears, she heard the sounds of voices and . . . maybe the trickle of water? And a drumbeat? Murmurs? All of it was very faint, but she could tell it was coming from the place where the light from around the corner spilled.

Lennon pushed off the wall, and she walked on the balls of her feet, making it to the end of that hall and, again, peeking into the next. Double doors were open, bright light coming from within. The sound of flowing water was louder here, and now she could tell there were several voices—three or four at least.

There was a closed door to her left with a small window, light shining from within. She peeked in from the side and saw a large tank. Was that . . . yes, it was a sensory deprivation chamber. What was this place? Some therapeutic center that Dr. Sweeton ran? And if so, why hadn't she seen any advertisements for it when she'd looked him up?

The other doors in that hallway featured windows, too, but those rooms were dark inside, and Lennon didn't bother to try any of those handles just yet. Instead, she headed toward the brightly lit room at the end of the hall where *something* was obviously going on.

There was a sort of vestibule inside the open double doors, and another door on the opposite wall that was very slightly ajar. That was where the soft noises were emanating from. Lennon pulled in a breath, her heart pounding. She walked soundlessly to the door and, very slowly, peeked in from the side, her mind giving a single bleat of alarm at what appeared in front of her.

People surrounded a woman wearing only underwear and a bra, wires taped to her skin and trailing to various machines surrounding her. That single bleat turned into resounding clangs as Lennon tried desperately to understand what she was looking at. The woman was standing in a plot of grass in the center of the room, and there was a fountain to their right, the peaceful trickle mixing with a soft drumbeat that came from a speaker overhead. Dr. Sweeton was to her left, while another person, a woman, was to her right, speaking softly into her ear. Three others stood behind her, as though she might collapse at any moment and they were there to catch her if she did. One of them was Ambrose. *What the hell?* Her stomach dipped, then rose into her throat. She had no idea what they were doing to the half-naked woman, and it filled her with both confusion and panic. Her heart raced, and her hands shook as she removed the gun from her holster and nosed open the door.

The door gave a soft squeak, which caused the people surrounding the woman to look up, Dr. Sweeton's mouth falling open as the woman who had been whispering in the patient's ear drew back slightly and let out a soft gasp. The mostly nude female with the wires coming off her startled too.

"Back away from her," Lennon told them, moving her gun from one to the next to indicate she was speaking to all of them. "Now!"

The woman let out a high-pitched squeal. Ambrose moved around the patient and then in front of her in one fluid movement, blocking her and holding his hand out, as though to ward Lennon off.

"Lennon, please, back out," Ambrose said, and though his voice was soft, it was also emphatic. She heard the plea, and she heard his distress. Her gaze bounced over the people behind him, wide eyes and stark looks of dread.

"What the fuck is happening here?"

The woman in the bra and underwear with wires taped to her skin moaned behind Ambrose, and Lennon saw her head moving back and forth beyond his shoulders.

"Please, Lennon," Ambrose said. "Her mind is very vulnerable right now. You might break her with an unexpected noise." His voice had lowered further, a mere whisper.

Break her? Lennon's breath came out in one sharp exhale, the gun in her hands shaking as she pointed it directly at Ambrose. The volume of the drumbeat overhead increased, and she realized that at least one person, but perhaps more, were beyond this room, responding to the unfolding situation. The woman's movements slowed, then stilled. She realized that if she shot Ambrose, she'd also shoot the woman, who was obviously drugged or anesthetized or something that made her incapable of controlling her own body.

"Please," Ambrose mouthed, tilting his head to indicate that Lennon should leave the room. Her mouth set, she gestured her own head, demanding that he go with her. The woman in the pale-blue lab coat behind him said something very softly under her breath, and Ambrose's eyes moved to the side as he listened to her, gave a slight nod, and then took a step forward.

He approached Lennon, their eyes meeting, and even in her anger and confusion, she felt the connection between them, some unknown something that flared to life as he drew nearer. She stepped aside, motioning with her gun that he should pass by her and leave the room first. He did so, and she followed, the volume of the drumbeat lowering as she shut the door softly. Ambrose had already moved through the vestibule, and she followed, stepping into the hallway, where he turned to face her.

"I know this must look—"

"It looks like I should call someone to come help that woman," Lennon said, her jaw tight, heart beating swiftly. Why was she even hesitating in calling the SFPD and having them all arrested? What were they *doing* to her?

"She is being helped. She's being cared for. Loved, even. She's going to wake up a new person with her whole life in front of her."

"Who is she?"

Ambrose paused, his mouth forming a thin line for a brief moment. "Her name is confidential. I can't tell you that, Lennon."

"What is she? A prostitute? A drug addict? A victim of abuse?"

"She was those things, yes."

"And Dr. Sweeton is . . . what? Brainwashing her?"

"He's doing nothing of the sort. He's resetting her nervous system and helping her revisit her trauma in a controlled setting. She's being monitored and walked through the process, step by step."

She massaged her forehead. She didn't even know where to begin. "Oh my God. This can't be legal." She turned, pacing one way and then the other. "Of course it's not legal. You're performing this *treatment* after hours in the back corner of a medical facility. You told me I might break her. What if *you* break her? You're using these people as guinea pigs. This is wrong!"

A noise from the room where the treatment was ongoing made Ambrose turn his head before he looked back at her. "I have to go. Please, Lennon. I will explain everything. Go back to your apartment, and I'll meet you there. Please. Listen to your heart and just wait for me to explain."

"Why should I trust you? You've lied to me about everything since the moment I met you."

"Not everything. You know that. Listen to your gut, Lennon. I know I've told you lies, but that was only because I was protecting people."

She was so torn, so confused, and yet . . . no one was trying to stop her from leaving. They were trusting her. Or at least trusting Ambrose.

"Please, Lennon," he said again. "Don't just trust my word. Trust your gut."

She looked at him, and for whatever reason, the story he'd told of that songbird blossomed in her mind. She looked away. "I'm not making any promises other than hearing you out," she said.

"That's all I ask."

"Fine. But Ambrose, if you're not at my apartment in an hour, I'm sending the police here."

"I'll text you so you have my new number. And I'll be there. I promise."

CHAPTER THIRTY-TWO

Hope is the thing with feathers
that perches in the soul.
—Emily Dickinson

Seventeen Years Ago
Patient Number 0022

"Ambrose," Dr. Sweeton said, taking Ambrose's hand in both of his and squeezing. "How are you feeling?"

"I feel pretty good. Sore."

The doctor smiled. "Good sore?"

Ambrose let out a chuckle. He knew what the doctor meant. There was the sore that came from not eating and not sleeping, and filling your body with chemicals. And there was the sore that meant you were moving your muscles in the way they were meant to be moved. "Yeah," he said. "Good sore."

"You like the boxing? That's your thing?"

He smiled. "Very much." He did like boxing. He liked the smack of his fist on the bag, that steady *thump, thump, thump* that almost reminded him of the drumbeat that had been part of his therapy. But he also loved the way it grounded him and made him feel strong and in control of his body, when he'd never, ever had that before. His body had been controlled—abused—by others, and then by the drugs and alcohol. And now it was his. The therapy had given him that, and now boxing added to it and brought it to another level.

And after he'd worked his body to its limits and eaten a good meal, he slept, and he woke up refreshed, with a clarity of mind that he hadn't even known existed. It was like he'd been reborn. And though he'd lived in the world for twenty-one years, everything was new, because he was new and experiencing it with a completely different vision.

"I like the hair too," Dr. Sweeton said. "Much better."

Ambrose chuckled as he ran a hand over his crew cut. It was shorter than he liked, but he'd wanted to get rid of the bleached sections that reminded him of his old self. He'd let that prostitute named Maria who'd first called him Jett bleach his hair because she said she needed to practice if she was going to take her cosmetology exam. He hadn't cared about his hair and hadn't had anything better to do at the time, so he'd let her do what she'd asked. It'd looked awful and kind of freakish, but he hadn't really cared about that, either, because it was a reflection of how he felt.

"You have an appointment for aftercare with Finch tomorrow."

"Finch." He knew that name. "He works at the youth center on Golden Gate? I've met him before."

"Yes, Finch remembers you, even though you were a different person then. He's expecting the new Ambrose."

The new Ambrose. The one he was still becoming acquainted with, even though it'd only been a couple of weeks since he'd completed the therapy that was so much more than therapy. *Therapy.* That word didn't even touch what he'd experienced. A reawakening? A complete reboot? So many times during the day, he found himself expecting that lightning-jolt of electricity that used to shoot through his body in response to any unexpected emotion. And when it didn't come, when there were only manageable bodily sensations, he wanted to weep with relief. A few times he had. "What kind of aftercare are we talking about?"

"The boxing is part of it. Finch suggested that. Not just boxing, but anything physical. Others choose yoga, which can be very helpful too."

Others. He'd forgotten there were others that had gone through this. Twenty-one of them, in fact. He was patient number twenty-two. He'd met a few, of course, but he suddenly had this deep desire to know them all, each one. To hear about their experiences, to bond, especially with those who'd gone through it years earlier than he had. He wanted the confirmation that this would last, that it wasn't just a temporary dream and he'd awaken one morning to find himself thrashing and screaming in some doorway on a trash-strewn street.

"Specific physical activities will assist you in connecting to your body even further, to ensure that you trust it. Finch is the expert on that front, and I leave the aftercare to him. He'll likely take you to Muir Woods."

Ambrose scrunched his brow. "Muir Woods?"

The doctor smiled and shrugged. "Finch swears the redwood trees provide healing. Anyway, he'll get you set up in a room and help you find a job, find a life."

A life. That both scared him and sent a spiral of joy spinning through his system, the first "spiral" of anything physical that produced an enjoyable sensation. It made him feel excited and hopeful. He was capable of living a life, a real one. He felt like a human for the first time, not just a waste of space.

"Ambrose," Dr. Sweeton said, leaning back on the desk and crossing his arms. "I have something else to talk to you about. We looked into the little boy you described and found that a child by the name of Milo Taft went missing almost fourteen years ago, when he was nine years old."

Ambrose's heart lurched, and he sucked in a gulp of air. From the time he himself had been an eight-year-old child, he'd shut the memory from his mind as best as he could, made himself believe that the boy named Milo who had come to play with him was a figment of his imagination. But inside, he'd always known; he'd stored the traumatic memory, wrapped in all the traumatic memories from his childhood. Trauma encasing deeper trauma, combined with guilt and horror and fear. And hatred. Such all-encompassing hatred that had nowhere to go because he was too small to do a damn thing about it. And so he'd turned it on himself.

And the truth was that he deserved some of it because he'd kept quiet. He'd kept his grandfather's secrets, not only the ones that affected him but the ones that had . . . hidden the abuse and killed Milo Taft too. "I have to tell the authorities," Ambrose said.

"Yes," Dr. Sweeton agreed. "You have to tell the authorities what you witnessed. I know your grandfather is dead now, but Milo's body is likely buried somewhere on that farm where your grandmother still lives."

Ambrose nodded. He still felt the echoes of fear when he thought of that farm . . . that shed. But the fear didn't flip a switch in him anymore and send him reeling into some unknown territory where he either wanted to tear down the world or curl up into a ball and disappear. Territory that had him desperately seeking substances to help regulate his damaged nervous system. Of course, he knew this now, but he hadn't before. And even if he had, it wouldn't have done him any good without a way to begin to fix it. Dr. Sweeton had saved his life, and likely his soul. "I already bought a bus ticket," he told the doctor. "In this case, I'm one step ahead of you."

Dr. Sweeton smiled and gripped Ambrose's shoulder. "Are you ready? This is a journey you have to take alone."

"I'm not sure," he said honestly. "But I think so, and I know I'll never fully find peace until I do what I didn't do then—call for help."

CHAPTER THIRTY-THREE

Ambrose raised his hand to knock on Lennon's apartment door, but before he could, it pulled open and she was standing there. He lowered his hand, and she stepped back and waved him inside. "You're late."

"By seven minutes."

"You're lucky I gave you leeway," she grumbled.

She paused in the entryway, not seeming to know where to take him. There weren't many choices in this small apartment. But he understood her hesitancy. The last time he'd been here, they'd made memories in each room. And now she wanted to remain in a neutral location, but there wasn't one that existed here, unless they stood next to the bathroom sink.

After a moment, she turned, obviously deciding the living room was the best choice. But when he followed her the short distance there, she remained standing instead of sitting down on the couch, crossing her arms as she turned to face him.

"It's a form of therapy you're using to treat people with trauma," she said.

He nodded. God, he was tired. It'd been a long day, and then he'd been assisting with Xiomara's treatment for hours, which took an incredible amount of focus. How could it not, when you were basically tiptoeing through someone else's memories? He hadn't played a pivotal role, but he had been part of the revisiting of her story. "Yes," he said. "Dr. Sweeton began working on Project Bluebird twenty-two years ago."

"Why is it called Project Bluebird?"

"Because his daughter, who was his first patient, chose a bluebird as her guide."

"Guide?"

He blew out a breath, raking his fingers through his hair. "You have to keep an open mind when I tell you about this, Lennon. It's difficult to understand before you've been through it. Some of it will sound unbelievable—weird, even, for lack of a better word."

"Go on."

He gestured to the couch. "Please. Can I sit down? I've been on my feet for hours."

She glanced at the couch and then back at him, agreeing with a barely discernible nod. He walked to the couch and sat down, gathering his thoughts. "Nancy was Dr. Sweeton's daughter. She'd been the victim of a crime when she was young. She started acting out, drinking, doing drugs. Eventually she ended up on the streets, experiencing more trauma. Trauma compounding trauma."

Lennon approached the couch and sat down where she had when they'd been here before, but sliding all the way to the very end and then turning toward him. He chose not to face her just yet. It made beginning this story easier. "Nancy spent time in facility after facility. Those places . . . if you're not traumatized before you enter, you probably will be by the time you leave. The doctors and nurses mostly mean well, but they have so few tools other than endless medication. People who are extremely unwell are locked up together and left to interact with each other in ways no therapist would suggest."

"Yes, I went to the doctor's talk."

He did look at her then. "I heard. But you know from experience too. You know because you've met those people. You've peered into their eyes."

She looked away first, but she didn't deny what he'd said. "Nancy attempted suicide multiple times," he went on. "She went to rehabilitation centers. She got clean, then she relapsed. Dr. Sweeton had been having success with veterans suffering from PTSD. He was using some hallucinogens to bring them back to the scene of their trauma in a safe way. But Nancy's trauma had happened when she was very young, before her mind was mature enough to fully parse the event. And so those treatments simply didn't work on her. He needed to go deeper. And so, over the years, he developed the mix of substances and the protocol for what is now known as Project Bluebird."

"What happened to Nancy?"

He paused. He didn't want to start off this way, but it was the beginning of the story, so she had to know. "Nancy died."

"How?"

"In a nutshell, her mind couldn't take the influx of trauma, and she had a heart attack." He'd seen the video of events, because they all had to understand what had happened to Nancy and how to ensure it would never happen again. Her eyes had bulged, and she'd gotten that forever scream on her face as the machines went wild and her body started seizing, and then a massive heart attack killed her where she sat. Long-term drug use had weakened her heart, but it had certainly been the regression back to the moment of trauma that ended her life. "Because of what happened to Nancy, Dr. Sweeton spent a year perfecting the treatment. And then, when it was applied again, it was slowed way, way down. Instead of a single session, it's done over seven days. The patient is kept in a coma in between the delivery of hallucinogens, and in some cases are put in sensory deprivation tanks. It depends on the results of the tests that are run and whether attachment bonds are present in the individual, and a whole battery of other factors."

Lennon let out a small laugh barren of humor and massaged her temples. "This is too crazy to be real. My God." She stood, crossed her arms over her breasts, and paced in front of the coffee table. "You can't mess with people's minds like that! It's deeply unethical. And because of it, someone died. His own daughter!"

Ambrose stood, too, facing her. "These people are already dead. You have to see that. Or if they're not dead, they're dying. A slow, miserable death. Lennon, there are laws about the right to try experimental medication once all your other options have failed. These people are hopelessly sick, too, their brains twisted in ways that can't be untwisted through traditional psychological protocol. They're suffering more immensely than I can communicate, and I'd make the argument that they're suffering far worse than someone with an inoperable tumor or other physical disease. You've grieved, Lennon. You've felt that crushing horror that goes on and on and on."

"Don't. You don't get to use what I shared with you when I thought you could be trusted."

He exhaled a sharp breath. Okay, he deserved that. But it still hurt. "Imagine that pain, but more extreme. Imagine knowing that that pain will never end. What would you do? You'd do anything. You'd do anything at all. Don't others deserve the option?"

She pressed her lips together, turning her face from him. "It's . . . no. I don't know. It's too *risky*."

"These people, Lennon, they're dying on the streets right in front of us. They're scratching and screaming for help, and we walk right by. They're begging for mercy, even though they have no earthly idea what mercy is."

She met his eyes. "Not all of them are looking for mercy. Some of them kill and rape and hunt."

"Yes, and in those cases, it's too late. I respect what you do. You stop those people. You take them out of society. But it's not too late for everyone. Dr. Sweeton helps the ones he can. We keep them safe during their treatment. We treat them with respect."

"I saw it, Ambrose. I walked in."

"I know. And it shocked you. But you weren't looking at it with the right vision."

She gave her head a shake, as though denying his words. And he understood. He did. Because if he'd walked in on the treatment at any phase of it without knowing what was going on, it would seem to him like a drugged-up, unclothed person was being taken advantage of. It looked strange and hard to make sense of. But that was because there was literally nothing like it. The doctor had come up with the protocol, and the plan, and it was something no one else had ever done. "When you do, if you do, you'll see that it's the most loving, beautiful thing you've ever seen. It's how it looks to give someone back their own mind."

"God, you sound like a cult," Lennon said. "This isn't normal."

"Neither is a four-year-old girl being pimped out by her mother. Her small body being ripped apart while the person who is supposed to protect her watches on. You can't know what that type of ongoing trauma, beginning at that young of an age, does to a person's mind and body, the way it damages them, the way it controls them."

She seemed to deflate a little at that, though her posture said she still didn't trust him. "Not everyone who's experienced trauma becomes twisted," she asserted.

"Humans are different, of course. But all people who've suffered that way struggle. Maybe they don't all become drug addicts or prostitutes, but they all carry that trauma with them in some way or another. And for those people, maybe there are other ways. Maybe they can talk it through and breathe it out. But for many, they simply can't. If they could, our streets wouldn't look the way they do."

She chewed at her lip for a moment and then let out a small vacant laugh. "Like insane asylums?"

He felt a breath of relief. She was resisting, but she was also agreeing. He didn't expect her to be on board with the project the moment she learned of it. He expected her to want answers and demand that there was accountability. The woman he'd come to know, even in such a short time, would want nothing less than that. And still, it might not be enough. "Unmonitored insane asylums, yes. No one benefits from that. They're human. They're the walking wounded, and mostly, it's through no fault of their own."

She moved back to the couch and sank down on it, and he followed, sitting down next to her but not too close.

When she met his eyes, he was stunned by the fierceness in her expression. God, he respected her so much. Her mind and her compassion. He wanted nothing more than for her to understand this. Not only because he believed in it to his core, but because it was so intensely personal. And now, so was she. "You can't take on that kind of responsibility," she said. "It's not right, Ambrose. These people can't legitimately consent."

There was some truth in what she said. Many of the people who had gone through the treatment were so deeply wounded, they might have agreed to anything. And so the people who ran the project, in some ways, were their advocates. But they hadn't been chosen by the patients, merely assigned by Dr. Sweeton, and Ambrose understood the ethical concerns. He just believed the good outweighed the bad. No, it was more than that. He knew what it was like to be freed from the prison of self-harm and self-hatred. To finally live a life that had meaning. He knew that firsthand. "There isn't one who isn't deeply grateful. I'll introduce you to all of them."

"Yes, there is. There is one." It only took him a second to realize she was speaking of Nancy.

He ran his tongue over his teeth as he thought about that. "I don't think she'd say that. It's her legacy, Lennon, and it's a hell of a lot better than the one she would have had."

"You don't get to speak for her."

"No, you're right. I don't. But I do get to speak for myself."

She blew out a breath, her empathetic eyes searching his face. He wondered if she realized how much care was emanating from her expression, and he wondered if she'd attempt to hide it if she knew. "You went through it."

"Yes. You didn't know me then, but if you did . . . I'd be the poster child for someone who needed this treatment." He let out a laugh that sounded more like a cough. "I'm thankful every day that Dr. Sweeton gave me what he did. Those with less-ingrained trauma go through a two-day treatment protocol, but I required the maximum seven days. And I came out of it . . . free. That's the best way I can describe it. I took what he gave me, I built on it, and I gained control of my life. I made something of myself."

She studied her hands, fisted in her lap, for a moment before looking up. "You lived on the street?"

"Sometimes. I crashed wherever I could. I lived day to day, hour to hour. I had no plan because I couldn't make plans. I couldn't . . ." He raised his hand and made a grabbing motion in the air. "I couldn't grasp anything. I couldn't hold on to it for longer than a few hours. Then cravings would set in, ones that would be stronger than any ideas I'd come up with to start down a better path." He ran a hand through his hair. "It's difficult to describe if you haven't lived it, and especially if you haven't experienced both a disorganized mind and one that's clear. And I don't mean clear of substances, I mean clear of the knots formed from surviving trauma. Dr. Sweeton would put it in more clinical terms if you spoke with him, but that's the best way I can describe it."

She chewed at her lip again, obviously troubled. But he also saw the glint of curiosity, or maybe understanding, in her expression and also in her silence, and it caused a seed of hope to begin to grow. "He's eloquent and passionate when he speaks about it," she murmured.

He moved just a little closer, and she met his eyes, but she didn't move away. "Lennon, please. Don't put this project in jeopardy. I'm begging you. It's making the world a better place. It's saving lives. It's freeing people. And that freedom—that goodness—doubles and triples and quadruples and on and on, because the people Dr. Sweeton treats go on to help others in so many ways, and to raise children who are emotionally healthy instead of broken, like them."

She sighed. She seemed somewhat depleted all of a sudden, and he didn't know if that was good for his cause or not. "You're not God, Ambrose. Dr. Sweeton isn't God."

"No one's trying to be God. Is a doctor who performs open-heart surgery trying to be God? He or she is simply trying to save a life and repair a broken body."

She shook her head but brought her hand up and massaged her forehead for a moment, as if the conversation was hurting her brain. "That's different and you know it."

"What I know is that ethics laws haven't caught up to the state of mental illness and PTSD in this world."

"That's what the doctors who performed ice pick lobotomies told themselves too."

"The results of that spoke for itself. We're not monsters, Lennon. There are over five hundred people who would happily stand in testimony of what Dr. Sweeton gave to them. Their lives. And he risked his own to do so."

"Maybe he's just planting pleasant memories in your minds. How do you even know what he did to you was real?"

Ambrose let out a soft breath. "Because I know. It's been seventeen years, and I've watched the process hundreds of times now. The goal is not to distort or erase memories. He uses what he can gather from a patient's past to help them remember and process their own stories. Then he lets them guide the journey. What I revisited was far from pleasant. Under any other circumstances, reliving it, mentally or otherwise, would have broken me. But I'll tell you this: even if he had 'implanted' pleasant memories into my head, I'd be grateful. My mind was a war zone. And Dr. Sweeton walked through the battlefield and dragged me out."

She met his eyes then, and again, he saw the empathy there. But he also saw her struggle. And in her expression, he knew that she wouldn't expose them—at least not yet. But she also wasn't ready to allow it to continue. "Dr. Sweeton isn't young. He won't live forever. What happens when he dies?"

"We have plans for that eventuality. He's training others who are now in the medical field. They'll step into his place one day." Dr. Clayton Contiss, who'd gone through the treatment himself only a year before Ambrose, was already in charge of some of the sessions, with Doc only there as backup.

"Well," she said. "Maybe you can go international too. An underground therapy, changing the world one drug addict at a time." When he said nothing, she stared at him for a moment, then murmured, "Oh my God." She set her mouth, but then sighed and used two fingers to squeeze the bridge of her nose. "Tell me why you infiltrated the department. Who are you really, Ambrose?" she asked after a moment.

He lowered his shoulders. "I work as a bounty hunter. I track down fugitives, but I also locate missing people and bring them home or bring them to justice. I work with the government sometimes, but I prefer to work for myself."

"Let me guess. You've done enough shady business for the feds that you banked on them not pursuing legal action against you for infiltrating our department."

She looked away. She obviously didn't need him to confirm her assessment. But he did anyway. "In a nutshell, yes. But any so-called *shady business* I did was for what I considered a noble purpose."

"You seem to like to make your own rules."

"Sometimes I deem it necessary, and justified, yes."

"What if everyone deemed rule breaking necessary and justified? What if everyone thought their purpose was *noble?*"

"Then society would break down."

"Exactly." She massaged her temples again. "How did you hear about the crime I was investigating?"

"Like I said, there are over five hundred people who've successfully gone through Project Bluebird, dating back over twenty years."

Her mouth formed a small O. "You have a mole in the department."

"I wouldn't call the person a mole. They didn't join the department for any nefarious reason, nor did it have to do with the project. They joined because they wanted to work in law enforcement. But when this case became known to them, they saw the links to the project and called Dr. Sweeton, who then contacted me. I learned what I could but needed to get closer. Specifically, I wanted to see those pills."

"And?"

"And originally they were the same, with the addition of the LSD coating. Since then, they've been reformulated into an altered combination of the original, for what reason, I don't know."

"My God," Lennon said. "So someone got hold of this drug that Dr. Sweeton illegally manufactures—"

"There are very strict controls in place. He doesn't manufacture more than needed, and none have ever disappeared or been unaccounted for. Dr. Sweeton has gone through every part of the process and can't come up with how even one pill could have been taken. Plus he trusts the people who work for him."

"Then how? How did our killer come up with the recipe for these drugs, and what's the point? Why is he using it to kill people?"

"That's what we're all trying to figure out."

"If I had this information sooner, the investigation would be further along."

He understood that, and he'd gone back and forth and back and forth on that. "You can understand why I couldn't tell you."

"You wasted time. More people might have died because you waited."

"I couldn't jeopardize the project."

Lennon huffed out a frustrated breath. "This is so fucked up," she murmured. She shook her head. "I need to think. And I can't think right now because I'm too overwhelmed." She was quiet for several moments as he waited. "I won't do anything without giving you advanced warning."

"Thank you." It was all he could ask for, and he trusted her word. "Lennon . . . I want to tell you . . . I'm sorry for lying to you, but I'm not sorry for what happened between us. It had nothing to do with any of this. It was completely separate. For me—"

"How can it be completely separate? It's literally sitting smack-dab in the middle of us."

He felt frustrated and regretful about that, and he was having a hard time explaining himself. Because though she was right, she was also wrong. But before he could say another word, she stood. "Please go."

He stood too. "Thank you for listening to me. Thank you for considering . . . everything. You don't have to turn us in, Lennon. You can help." He left her where she stood, arms crossed, looking like she held the weight of the world on her slender shoulders.

CHAPTER THIRTY-FOUR

The world breaks everyone and
afterward, many are strong at the
broken places.
—Ernest Hemingway

Seventeen Years Ago
Patient Number 0022

Ambrose stepped from the car, shutting the door behind him and watching as the taxi did a three-point turn, the driver giving a salute as he drove by and then out of sight. Ambrose took a deep, sustaining breath and began walking in the direction of the farm, past the leaning mailbox, the empty pasture, and the split rail fence that was falling apart in more sections than it was holding together.

The place where his story had begun.

There was a lump in his throat, and he felt mildly clammy. Ambrose categorized all his body's sensations as he moved toward the place of his nightmares. It looked even more dilapidated than it had in the memories his brain had conjured during Dr. Sweeton's therapy. But of course, his mind hadn't been able to see past what it'd looked like the last time he was here. Back then, the pasture hadn't been overgrown with weeds taller than him.

Back then, his grandfather had been alive. Back then, he'd still been working this land, tending to the animals, making repairs, and performing maintenance. Apparently, his grandmother did none of that, nor did she hire anyone else to do it.

In a way, this slow walk was the culmination of the therapy he'd been through, or maybe the final test. He was here, at the scene of his real-life torment and the place that had haunted his nightmares ever since, and he was . . . okay. He was okay. Sick. Sad. Nervous. Angry. But okay. And Ambrose DeMarce didn't remember a day in his twenty-one years when he would have described himself as feeling okay. Especially standing *here*.

He stepped up on the porch, careful to avoid the sections of rotting wood. Something scurried underneath a hole in the boards, and Ambrose grimaced and stepped over the opening. He brought his fist to the door and banged.

There were the sounds of someone descending the squeaky inside stairs, and a moment later, the door was pulled open. His grandmother stood in front of him, staring blankly.

"Hi, Grandma." Damn, she looked old. Old and slight. What was she now? Seventy-five? She looked like she was a hundred and twenty. Whatever glint of life had once shone from her eyes had been completely extinguished.

The broken old woman looked him up and down, assessing him as well, and then moved back and gave a jerk of her head, inviting him inside.

And honestly? He didn't want to step a foot inside the place. But he did anyway, because he needed to test himself even further, and he wouldn't be sure he'd fully passed until he'd moved beyond the threshold.

It was filthy. Dusty and dirty, with *stuff* everywhere. It'd never been anything but spick and span when his grandfather was alive. What was this? His grandmother's final rebellion? A fuck-you to the tyrant who'd beaten her and then made her clean his floors until they shone?

And if it was, maybe he couldn't blame her.

Even if this was no way to live.

But Ambrose was well acquainted with *no way to live*.

And deep down, he knew his grandmother was no rebel. She was too weak for that. Her body was still alive, but her spirit had curled up and died. He could practically smell the rot emanating through her dry, wrinkled skin. "Surprised to see you," his grandmother said, huffing out a long-suffering sigh as she sank down into a wooden chair at the table in the middle of the room.

"I bet," he said. Was she even more surprised that he was still alive? The cross still hung between the windows over the sink, the piece of dusty reed he remembered still draped over it. He'd read somewhere once that a crown of thorns and a reed had been given to Jesus to mock him before he was strung up on the cross. Ambrose's gaze moved out the window next to that symbol of the rise above human cruelty, where he could see the edge of the shed in which he'd been tortured.

"I'm not here for a visit," he told the old woman. "I'm here to let you know that there will be a lot of people on this farm in about an hour. The sheriff. A few dogs. A coroner."

She showed no surprise, merely stared down at the ancient table, running her finger over a scratch in the wood.

"I doubt you'll be surprised by what they find," he said. A child. He wondered if they'd only find one.

His grandmother still showed no reaction, so Ambrose left the house and walked outside, drawing in a lungful of air and leaning against the porch railing.

Inside, he heard his grandmother climb back up the stairs, her footsteps heavy and slow.

Ambrose stared out at the scenery, and strangely, the first memory that popped into his head was of picking rhubarb and later dipping it in a bowl of white sugar. Even now, his mouth puckered at the recollection of the sweet and the sour.

The steeple of a church could be seen in the valley below, and Ambrose remembered going there on a field trip with his class. He recalled the way the stained glass windows had glittered in the sunshine, tossing rainbows on his skin. He'd expected to be overwhelmed by horrific memories here, and he was shocked that now that he remembered the entirety of his story, he was able to see *all* the threads it'd been woven with.

He leaned his face back and felt the warmth of the April sun, even while a chilly breeze ruffled his hair.

"I'm here, you old bastard," he said. "I'm here, and I'm alive, and everyone is going to know your secret. Your secret will be your legacy, but it won't be mine."

The sheriff arrived forty-five minutes later, the canines a few minutes after that. He'd met the sheriff the day before. He'd sat in his office and told him about the memories of Milo that had just surfaced in his therapy sessions, the memories from when he was a little boy. The man had been kind. Understanding. He'd called Milo's family, and they'd shown up. And miraculously, they'd thanked Ambrose for coming forward.

And now, Ambrose sat there as they worked, walking the property with the dogs, stopping here and there, and finally beginning to dig out near an aspen grove at the edge of the property. Ambrose had asked to help, but the sheriff had kindly told him no. This was a potential crime scene, and they had to make sure they didn't miss or disrupt anything.

As it turned out, there was only one grave. The diggers hit upon a wooden box holding Milo's body a few hours later and carefully transferred it to a white body bag. Ambrose hung his head and closed his eyes as they placed Milo's small bones in an ambulance and rounded the corner, out of sight. "I'm sorry," he whispered. "I'm so, so sorry."

He agreed to meet with the sheriff the next morning, and then he watched all the cars drive in a line down the dirt road, heading back into town, where they'd give Milo's parents the news that their son's body had been found. He didn't imagine it would make it much easier, but at least now they'd have a place where they could visit him.

A mass was gathering in his throat, all the emotion that he hadn't yet expressed for the little boy who had been his friend. *His only friend.* Ambrose pulled the screen door open harshly, and it banged against the side of the house with a loud clatter. He pushed at it again when it bounced back toward him, and he entered the house for the final time.

She was there, sitting at that old table again, a cup of coffee in front of her, her finger trailing over that deep, deep scratch. He vacantly wondered what had made that deep scratch, something sharp and heavy that had dug into the soft wood and left a gaping scar. His grandmother seemed obsessed with it but had paid no mind to the wide-open wounds in the people around her. Or even her own. But he'd been small like Milo too. Completely defenseless.

And suddenly, rage like a tidal wave overtook him, and he grabbed on to the doorframe to keep himself from flying at her, from taking her scrawny neck between his palms and squeezing. A moan escaped his lips, fingers tightening on the jamb. *I'm not like him. I'm not like him.* No, he wasn't like his grandfather, not in any way. And he never would be. "You never did a goddamn thing to help me, you worthless piece of shit," he spat out, his words laced with all the anger and grief and hopelessness he'd carried inside him since he was a tiny boy. "You could have called someone. You could have taken me and left."

"You're right," she whispered. Her voice sounded like unused sandpaper, both abrasive and thin. But her eyes remained glued to the table as she began murmuring under her breath. Prayers. She was whispering prayers.

And he remembered then. "You used to sit outside the door to the shed and say prayers," he said, tears gathering in his eyes. "I heard you. Sometimes I even called to you. But you never came in and rescued me." She'd prayed outside a door when she possessed the key. And maybe Ambrose didn't need to know more than that to understand the woman sitting in front of him.

But it still hurt. The pain inside was agony. It was the pain of the little boy he'd once been, but that little boy was part of Ambrose. And so Ambrose suffered too. He felt small again—unlovable—even though he recognized that his grandmother was only the cracked shell of a woman.

His grandmother began rocking in her seat. Back, forth, back, forth. The last of Ambrose's anger drained, but so did the grief, leaving him with an empty feeling of sadness. But he knew now that he could fill that space with things of his choosing. Not alcohol or drugs, or other types of poison. So, no, this was a sadness that served. A sadness worth holding on to. For now, anyway.

Yes, his grandmother was a husk. He watched her there, rocking herself to and fro, gaze zoned out. Her mother or father had done something terrible to her, and then she'd found a husband who was familiar. She'd checked out long ago. She was an old woman now, and he could only feel sorry for her. There was no Dr. Sweeton to help. But she had this farm, and her abuser was gone. Maybe she could at least let some of the fear go.

"Goodbye, Grandma. I won't be back." And then he turned and walked out of the house he'd never been welcome in, for the final time.

He vowed that the cycle stopped with him. He was going to do his best to heal and to do some good with his life. Because he owed that much to Dr. Sweeton, and he owed that much to Milo Taft too. Because Ambrose had run when he could have . . . what? Attacked? Yelled? *Tried harder.* Even if Milo had already been dead, it might not have killed the final piece of Ambrose's soul if he had *tried harder* in some way. Even now, he didn't know what that was. But how could he forgive himself when Milo was dead and he'd stuffed the memory of his murder so far down in his subconscious that his family had suffered for so many years?

And maybe if he had figured out a way to fight for Milo, his grandfather would have killed him too. But he would never know, because he hadn't . . . and he'd have to live with that now and forever. But living with it was better than trying to stuff it away and cover it up with drugs, frankly, as unexpectedly true as that was. And so he'd live a doubly good life—making up for the void of Milo Taft.

Ambrose walked back along the road, opening his phone and calling for a cab once he'd made it to the leaning mailbox that spelled out his family name.

There would be no more DeMarces—they would die out with him, and that seemed right and the greatest justice he could bring down upon a twisted bloodline. He would never have children, ones that might very well look like his grandfather. What a thing to live with. He couldn't begin to imagine how awful that would be. The small face of his grandfather staring at him for the rest of his days. And perhaps that was irrational—hell, on some level, he knew it was—but it still felt right. Forget the genetics: What kind of father would he be, anyway? The only male figure in his life had savagely abused and tortured him. He wouldn't have any idea what to do with a tender child. He refused to put another ruined person into this already broken world.

Ambrose put his hands in his pockets and waited for his ride. He'd come full circle. This was the beginning of his story, and in a way, it was its end, even though he intended to go on to live a full life. He'd been destroyed here, and he'd come back to stand before it and claim victory. But it wasn't a singular moment of victory. It was a victory that had to be earned, a day at a time. And he intended to do just that.

CHAPTER
THIRTY-FIVE

The call came in bright and early. But this time, Lennon was already home from her run, had showered, and was drinking a cup of coffee as she stared at the wall, trying to sort through all her mixed and confused emotions from the last few days. She'd tumbled into bed the night before and, miraculously, fallen into a heavy sleep. The run had helped clear her mind enough that she felt she had the wherewithal to deal with the information Ambrose had given her, and the choice that lay in front of her.

But apparently, that choice would have to wait, as another "BB" multiple homicide had occurred the night before and was similar to the last—the items used to murder each other were all accounted for at the scene. But . . . there was a survivor.

Lieutenant Byrd called to let her know, and when he did, she didn't ask—she *told* him she was heading to the hospital to find out the victim's status, and attempt to interview her if possible. "I don't need my gun for that," she'd said. "And if they ask for my badge, I'll tell them I left it at home and to call you."

Lieutenant Byrd had paused, as if considering denying her. But in the end, he'd simply said, "Don't push it, Lennon. They moved her from the ICU to the psych ward, because physically she's fine. It's her mental condition that they're worried about. If her doctor says she's unfit to be interviewed, listen. And you're still not allowed to come in to the station until Friday."

"Fine. And I won't push it, I promise." She'd accused Ambrose of enjoying bending the rules the night before. But the truth was, she'd done plenty of rule bending herself, and perhaps she needed to check herself before casting judgment on anyone else.

It took her fifty minutes in rush hour traffic to make it to Zuckerberg San Francisco General, where she parked and took the elevator to the psychiatric ward. She'd been there many times over the years, and it seemed to get more and more overcrowded. There were patients in the hallways, most of them vacant eyed and drooling, but others crying or even wailing. She walked by a young man sitting on a bench, knees drawn up as he visibly shook, face contorted in pain. Her footsteps slowed, her instinct to stop and help. To ask him what was wrong and what she could do. But, of course, there was nothing she could do. He was where he needed to be, in a treatment facility. So why didn't it feel that way? And if he was in the right place, then why was he sitting alone, obviously still suffering? It felt like walking into an emergency room and seeing a man on the lobby floor dying of a heart attack.

These people, Lennon, they're dying on the streets right in front of us. They're scratching and screaming for help, and we walk right by. They're begging for mercy, even though they have no earthly idea what mercy is.

She couldn't bear to hear Ambrose's voice in her head right now, though. She couldn't. And so she shut him out, forcing a polite smile to her face as she stopped at the nurses' station, introduced herself, and asked to see the doctor of the woman who had recently been brought in by the SFPD.

She stood in the waiting room, growing more and more agitated by the sounds of screaming and crying and random crashes from patient rooms. It smelled like the smell of the streets, only not as potent, the underlying stench covered by bleach and pine antiseptic. And something about that almost made it worse. *Good God*, this place made her feel like jumping out of her skin. This was no environment for someone who was traumatized. It made her heart ache to think about being thrown in here during the darkest days when she'd been lost in grief. It was unthinkable.

She turned and gazed, unseeing, out the window, conjuring the picture of those first few days in the private hospital room after Tanner had died and she'd been pulled from that convenience store. Her mother had climbed into the hospital bed with her and refused to budge. And Lennon knew an entire army couldn't have dragged that woman away from her side. She'd needed that strength. She'd needed someone to hold on to. She'd needed the warmth of love pressed directly against her.

Later, at home, her mom had read to her, passages and quotes that had given her hope that she still had a life in front of her. That even though it felt like it, the agony she was in wasn't going to last forever. Her mother had held her as she'd cried, and she'd listened when she was ready to talk. Lennon had even curled up on her mother's lap a time or two, a nineteen-year-old girl who still couldn't have managed without the tenderness of a mother's love.

Her father had been a solid presence, looking on with worried eyes, grief etched into his stoic features. He'd held her, too, but she knew he also held her mother, wiping away his wife's tears so she could be there for their daughter. Her brother had sat on her bed and held her hand, uncharacteristically silent, his fingers laced with hers. Later, he'd stood beside her at the funeral, arms linked. They had cared for her, even while grieving their own loss.

What if she hadn't had all that? What if she'd been left to deal with her grief on her own? Even more unthinkable, what if she'd been forced to hide it away? It would have been unbearable. She didn't think she'd have survived such a thing without losing her mind.

"Inspector Gray?"

She startled, so lost in her own thoughts she'd zoned out for a few minutes. When she turned from the window, there was a middle-aged doctor in a white coat standing near the doorway. "I'm Dr. Sing," she said, giving her a tired smile. "You're here about the woman brought in this morning?"

"Yes. What's her status?"

The doctor sighed. "We had to sedate her. We couldn't get her to stop screaming. The EMTs who brought her in had used restraints, as she seemed to be attempting to scratch her own eyes out." Her expression was disturbed, which was probably saying something, considering where the woman worked and what she likely saw day in and day out. "She was also seizing, and her speech was garbled, indicating brain damage. Basically, Inspector Gray, she's extremely ill. Physically? She has some lacerations, but nothing that won't heal. Her mental condition is the main concern. Unfortunately, we don't currently have a bed for her, so we have her in the hallway while we're attempting to shuffle others around. That usually means sending a few to jail. But that's the system for now."

"Jail?" *For people hospitalized for a mental condition?*

"I wish I had another choice. But it's either that or spitting them back onto the streets. Often they're experiencing suicidal ideation, so that's not an option."

Wow. "Doctor, do you have any guesses about what happened to her?"

"Without knowing more about what she went through, and without her test results back, I'm not willing to make an official diagnosis."

"Unofficially?"

A voice came over the loudspeaker, paging Dr. Sing's name, and the doctor looked behind herself and then back to Lennon. "Unofficially, your victim had a complete mental breakdown. I have to go, but give me your card, and I'll call you if your victim wakes up and is coherent."

Lennon made her way down to the parking lot, walking in a fog to her car, trying desperately to shake off the heaviness of that ward. *Your victim had a complete mental breakdown.* She glanced up at the building behind her, a small shiver going down her spine when she pictured that desolate ward full of society's castoffs. *The fringe.* She understood why Jamal Whitaker had named his podcast as such. And there were so many of them, there weren't enough beds. They spilled out into the halls and onto the streets. She felt so goddamned sad. There was no other way to say it.

She used her key fob to open her door, then got in and sat there for a minute, thinking, her finger smoothing a corner of duct tape that had begun to lift on her window. Her vandalized car seemed so trivial when so many were dealing with catastrophic issues.

She brought her hand to her forehead and attempted to massage away the beginning of a headache. She needed to go into the station and read the case file, get back to work. But suddenly, it all felt so *useless*, and she couldn't let it feel that way. She'd seen the overworked doctors rushing through the halls of the psych ward. She saw frustrated first responders every day at her work, who started out wanting to make a difference but were quickly disabused of that dream by red tape and reality. She saw burned-out inspectors who were stretched so thin they had little time for actual investigation. And often the public worked against you, anyway, so it was easy to ask *Why bother?*

The woman at Dr. Sweeton's office, hooked up to the wires, a team of people surrounding her, had alarmed Lennon. It had disturbed her. It'd looked like nothing she'd ever seen. Because the treatment being given—if she decided to call it that—was completely unorthodox. Illegal. Unethical. *Wasn't it?* There had to be protocols for that type of thing, or people could be hurt. They might regret what they'd agreed to when they were in a vulnerable state of mind.

What else is there?

Not a lot. But that didn't mean it was right.

She thought back to Dr. Sweeton's talk and the man who had asked whether those who've experienced chronic trauma are brain damaged. *Yes,* the doctor had answered. *The first step in healing must target the brain itself.*

But even if that type of treatment were legal, who was going to pay for it? She supposed that right now, San Francisco's elite, who sought out Dr. Sweeton for psychiatry, were funding it. But on a massive scale? Would it even be possible?

You don't have to turn us in, Lennon. You can help.

Surprisingly, her fingers began moving on the steering wheel, tapping out a melody she'd thought she'd long ago forgotten, on invisible piano keys. Her mind had held on to it, and for whatever reason, in a moment of deep confusion and overwhelming upset, it'd sprung from the recesses of her memories.

Lennon remembered when she'd first begun learning to play, and even later, when lessons became more complicated. The way she'd dream about her fingers on the keys, the way her brain would go over and over the movements without her permission. Maybe that's what brains did: learned through intense cerebral repetition. But what if the thing it was learning was a horror being engraved inside? Etched so deep you could never forget. Wouldn't such a thing drive you mad? How could it not?

How could it not?

The decision not to report Project Bluebird could have serious repercussions on her life and her career. It would mean she'd made the conscious choice not to report illegal activity involving victims.

But are they victims? Or are they being saved? That's really what this all boiled down to. And if these traumatized human beings were being saved, as Ambrose said they were, then this was far bigger than her, personal repercussions or not.

She needed to get herself back on track. And God, she was desperate to be sure about something once more. Her whole world had been toppled—again—and she had this vague sense that though she wanted order, it shouldn't be put back the way it was before.

Lennon took out her phone and searched Google for Ambrose DeMarce. The only hits came from seventeen years before. She opened the article from a small-town online newspaper in Kentucky. "Kentucky?" she murmured. He'd told her he was born and raised in San Francisco. Then again, he'd been lying about almost every other personal detail, so why not that one too?

She quickly read through the article and then sat back, tapping that tune again. Ambrose DeMarce had been part of an investigation in Kentucky where he helped solve a cold crime that his grandfather had committed. His grandfather, Waylon DeMarce, had raped and murdered nine-year-old Milo Taft and buried his body on his property. Her fingers faltered. Ambrose had been a child, too, when he witnessed the murder. The traumatic event had been dredged up during a therapy session, and he'd returned to Kentucky to tell authorities what he remembered and give Milo's family the peace they'd been denied for over a decade. Unfortunately, they wouldn't see justice delivered to Milo's killer, as Waylon DeMarce had died years earlier. Ambrose DeMarce had been a twenty-one-year-old young man when Milo's body was exhumed.

Is that what fueled your desire to hunt down criminals who'd gotten away with murder? And others who are lost? She pictured Ambrose's intense expression. He'd spent the last seventeen years tracking down killers and victims, but as what? Amends for the trauma he'd locked away in his brain? Secrets that Dr. Sweeton had exposed?

Who did the treatment ultimately benefit? Dr. Sweeton or the patients?

Was it only those with "brain damage" that could undergo the treatment? She didn't think so. Ambrose had mentioned something about those with less-ingrained trauma going through a shorter protocol. So even if Dr. Sweeton's focus was on those with debilitating PTSD, he'd obviously treated much less severe cases. She certainly didn't consider herself to be traumatized, but she'd lived through a traumatizing event. If she was to truly understand Project Bluebird to decide for herself if she felt it was ethical, shouldn't she . . . *be treated?* Could it actually be of value to society? Help bridge the gap between those tossed back onto the streets and those put in jail?

She had to understand it fully to know.

With one more glance up at the tinted windows of the psych ward, she pulled up the text from Ambrose and used the number he'd sent it from to call him.

"Lennon."

She pulled in a deep breath and then let it out. "I want to experience it."

He was silent for a beat as though he was questioning what she was referring to. "No," he finally said.

"Why? If it's safe, then why? I can't agree not to expose what I know is part of an ongoing multiple-murder investigation involving a serial killer unless I understand what I'm protecting."

"Because, Lennon, with this type of treatment, you have to weigh the risks and rewards. Your mind isn't bent. You don't live with debilitating trauma."

"In small part I do." She didn't pretend to be affected anywhere near the degree others were, but she'd suffered. She'd grieved. But how could she allow others to go through the treatment if she didn't fully understand it? Ambrose had done it. More than five hundred others had done it, and only one, Dr. Sweeton's daughter, had died. According to them. But if she *was* going to trust those numbers, the odds were pretty darn good. "You said Dr. Sweeton had a two-day protocol for people who didn't require the full seven days, like you did."

"Dr. Sweeton rarely treats patients like that. He has far too many who are desperately in need, as opposed to those who struggle mildly but live functional lives. Plus, logistically, it's not possible. He needs weeks to prepare. He requires a full workup, both physical and mental, brain scans—"

"He might not have a choice. And I know exactly what's in the pills. They're hallucinogens. I'll consent to taking them. People have wild weekends in college all the time and come out of it just fine. This is even better because I'll be continually monitored."

"Lennon—"

"Those are my terms, DeMarce. I have to know."

He was quiet for several moments, and she could sense his tension emanating through the phone. "This might take you somewhere you don't want to go."

Somewhere she didn't want to go. *Back there. To that convenience store in the middle of the night.*

"I can handle it," she insisted. "Tell Dr. Sweeton my terms. And Ambrose, it needs to be soon, possibly today. I'm off until Friday, and there was another 'BB' murder last night. We're dealing with a serial killer who's targeting this therapy. And maybe this will help me understand why."

CHAPTER
THIRTY-SIX

December 10
Patient Number 0548

Buzz, crackle, shivery light. Fear. It was up ahead, she sensed it as much as she saw it, the pulse of *light and dark, light and dark*, the way nothing else existed in this black landscape except the pulsing gas station, somehow pulling her toward it. *No, oh no, don't make me go there. Not there.*

That's when she felt the brush of something against her leg, warmth flooding her body as she reached down and petted his head. A Saint Bernard, his fur warm and soft. She continued stroking his head, *back, forth, back, forth*. And when the animal began to walk, toward that pulsing light, she didn't hesitate; she moved with him.

The dog was wearing a thick collar, and Lennon gripped it, finding strength in the canine's sure movements and the fact that she was not alone. She felt the love of the animal radiating through her hand and down her limbs and knew that he would not leave her side, no matter what happened.

The gas station was deserted except for one lone car, the red Mazda that Tanner had been driving since high school. *Oh.* She heard a brittle noise, as though her heart were made of glass and a crack had just zippered down the middle. She'd forgotten that car. Where had it gone?

The dog nudged her thigh, and she kept moving, toward the door to that convenience store where her world had split in two. She was currently in the before, but when she stepped inside, she'd be in the after. She wanted to stay here, in the place where young men with their whole future in front of them didn't die, in the place where life happened just as you'd planned it. Oh, it hurt. It hurt, it hurt, it hurt, and she couldn't bear it. She couldn't bear the feeling of standing in the shoes of the girl she'd been, such hopeful surety in her heart. An ache rose inside so massive that it threatened to sweep her away. *Back, forth, back, forth.* She gripped his collar as the Saint Bernard who loved her rubbed his head on her leg, soothing, comforting. *You can do this. I'm right here.*

But I don't want to. Why must I?

Because you must be able to tell your story. All of it. It has a beginning, a middle, and an end. You've forgotten the middle, haven't you? The middle is the most important part.

The dog nudged her, and so she moved with him, pulling the door open and entering the store. The lights were soft in here, no buzzing. Just a quiet store on a quiet night, the clerk sitting behind the counter, reading a textbook and singing along to the Muzak playing on the speakers overhead. The music became louder, blaring in her head for a moment, about piña coladas and walking in the rain. Then as quickly as it'd blared, it lowered, and that's when she saw him. "Tanner," she whispered, her eyes filling with tears. *Oh.* Her heart squeezed and dipped and expanded. "Tanner." He was laughing, and his hair had fallen over his forehead the way it did. She hadn't remembered so many things about him, and she felt terrible about that. But she could memorize them now because he was here, right in front of her, alive.

Barely visible rays of light moved from her to him and back again, some energy she didn't know how to describe because she'd never experienced it before. Oddly shaped numbers glowed everywhere in that same elusive light, bouncing off each other and changing into other numbers.

She reached for Tanner, but suddenly she was blown back, and she screamed as she flew through the air, the blast of the shotgun so loud that it felt like a bomb had exploded between her ears.

Someone ran past her, the man who'd robbed the store, the one who'd come in behind them while they laughed and sang about piña coladas in the potato chip aisle. The one with the bloodshot eyes who'd shot Tanner. Tanner had dropped the bottle of iced tea he'd been holding, and it'd crashed loudly on the floor. She sat up, watching blearily as a girl in jeans and a white sweater went down on her knees next to him. *Me. That's me.* She watched the horror in her own eyes, and then she watched as that horror increased when her past self looked out the front door.

She knew what the girl who was her was seeing. She was watching the other men who'd been in the car with the robber get out and move back toward the store. *Why? Why? Oh no, oh God.* What did they want? She asked the question then, but she knew the answer now. They were part of a gang, and they'd been taking part in an initiation that went awry. They were supposed to rob the clerk, but they'd accidentally shot a customer. And there'd been a witness. Her. The other members had decided that they had to kill her and the clerk so the murder wouldn't come back to them. And so they'd headed back into the store to clean up the mess. All this knowledge was contained in one short string of numbers that flashed in the air in front of her.

The girl who was her shot to her feet, picking up Tanner under his arms and dragging him toward the back. He moaned. He was still alive. Her breath came out in ragged pants and she could barely feel her limbs, but that small sound gave her the hope and the courage to pull him around the corner and toward the back. She felt the feelings of then mixed with the sorrow of now, and though it was terrible and tragic and hopeless, there was a bright pulse underlying it all, numbers and light smashing and colliding and dancing in a way that was so beautiful her mouth fell open. It was love, love so bright and profound that it made her gasp in wonder. She'd acted in love for Tanner, and she knew through the sight of the light and the numbers that he felt it. Her love was flowing into him despite the fear and the cold and the panic. It was brighter than all those things and more powerful than anything she'd ever felt.

The light lulled her, and for a moment she drifted, but then something sharp poked her ribs and she groaned, moving away from it and opening her eyes.

Come back. The middle is waiting for you. I'm with you. Let's go.

Cold. God, she was suddenly so, so cold. She lifted her head, blinking around. A freezer. She was in a freezer. She'd pulled Tanner inside and his head was cradled in her lap. She shivered, hunching her shoulders against the chill. Next to her, the warmth of the Saint Bernard pressed in, his thick coat giving her comfort and warding off the worst of the cold. He rubbed his head against her shoulder. *Back, forth, back, forth.* Lennon looked down and pulled in a sob. Tanner's lips were curved in a smile, his eyes just beginning to shut. He wouldn't open them again, the her of now knew that. But so did the her of then. "No," she said. "No, no, no."

She heard the robbers in the store, yelling at the clerk. Then she bit down on her tongue so she wouldn't scream when she heard the blast of the shotgun. He'd been killed but only after he'd told them he hadn't called the police. She learned later that his cell phone was dead. He'd been heading for the office to call for help when they returned to kill him. There was no alarm. No one on the way. And Lennon was in the freezer with the dying boy she loved.

"Hey, Picasso." She pulled in a breath, gasping when she looked up to see that Tanner was no longer in her lap but standing, leaned against the wall, one foot crossed over the other. So casually handsome, full of life.

"Picasso? Why do you call me Picasso? I play the piano."

He grinned, completely unfazed by the sounds coming from beyond the door, the sound of something heavy being pushed against it and what she now knew was a broom handle being jammed under the lever. Why make things bloodier when two people had sealed their own doom by locking themselves in a commercial freezer? Or maybe they were sociopaths. Maybe knowing their victims would both suffer, and for longer, excited them. "Are you sure?" Tanner asked with a lift of his brow. "I'm almost positive he's a musician."

"He's an artist." She could visualize his paintings even now. Abstract. Disturbing as far as she was concerned and not at all her style.

"No, I'm pretty sure he plays the piano."

She rolled her eyes. He loved to pretend to be wrong about something and get her nineteen-year-old self riled up. The Lennon of now pulled in a breath of despair. "Your sense of humor would have gotten better," she said. "I was counting on it."

He laughed. "No, it wouldn't have. And no, you weren't. But by the way, I still have a sense of humor."

"You're dead, Tan."

"Whatever you say, Picasso." He smiled again. "But there's a lot you don't know."

"Like what?" She turned toward the sound of another object being shoved in front of the door. She'd known later what they used but she couldn't remember now. It didn't matter, she supposed. She'd finally found the courage to get up, then, and she watched as her panicked, horrified, tearful self moved Tanner gently and then stood, pushing uselessly against the door. She went over to her then-self and took her hand. The girl looked up, startled, eyes blinking as Lennon pulled the girl that was her away from the door. They sat on the floor again, and Lennon put her arm around the girl and pulled her close, the Saint Bernard taking the other side and warming her chilled skin. It'd been so cold. So hopeless and so desolate. So filled with indescribable grief. She could never stand the cold after that. It was the temperature of horror and despair. The mildest chill would send panic dripping through her. She carried blankets and sweaters everywhere she went, refusing to ever be cold again. Trying desperately to ward off the wintry winds of mourning.

The misty numbers split and divided and twirled toward her through the air, disappearing through her skin, marking her, even if she didn't know exactly how.

A second scene rose up in front of her, that moment she'd driven by Ambrose standing in the rain. He'd looked to be shivering, and she couldn't bear it. She couldn't drive by and leave him there in the cold. Not after the story he'd told about the sea lion and the man who'd realized the value of his life in a four-second fall.

In some ways, her freezer had been her four-second fall. But she'd carried such guilt for wanting so badly to live, to come out alive, when Tanner would not. Lines of light and opaque numbers split and jumped and rose and fell, and for the flash of an instant she understood it all. How the universe was made of math and vibrations and everything affected everything each moment of every day. And as soon as that vast knowledge blossomed, it faded away, ungraspable. Gone.

She drew the girl that was her closer, letting her know she was going to be okay. She was going to live, and she was going to heal, and she was going to be pulled from this freezer, almost dead but not quite, her will to live strong and fierce. For herself and for Tanner, who she'd held in her arms that long frigid night, stroking his frozen cheek even after he'd died.

She'd asked him a question a moment ago—*what is it I don't know?* She looked up at him now, and he was watching her, a small smile on his face. "Well, you might not know that classical music very literally lowers blood pressure and reduces anxiety. You should remember that, Picasso. And you should start playing again."

She shook her head. "I can't, Tan. It hurts too much. That was the old me and I can't be her again."

"You can't be me, either, though. So where does that leave you?"

She sighed. He was right, and she had no answer to his question. When she looked back up at Tanner, he still had that gentle smile on his face, and this time, he had a bundle in his arms. He nodded down to what she could now see was a baby. He approached and squatted next to her, holding the baby so carefully. Her heart squeezed tightly in pain. "Is it our baby?" she asked. The one they would have had but now never would?

"No, silly," he said. "It's your baby. He's beautiful. He's going to be a healer." Then Tanner tipped the baby, and Lennon gasped as the baby rolled forward and then disappeared into her. Tanner smiled. He stood and went to the door. "Open it, Lennon."

"I can't. It's locked. It's barred from the outside."

"No, it's not. Not anymore. It hasn't been for a long time. Open it."

She came slowly to her feet, pulling the girl that was her along, the dog following behind. She put her hand on the lever and pushed at the door, opening it easily. *Oh.* Tanner stood outside now, reaching his hand out to her. "I've been waiting for you to leave that freezer," he said. "Come on out. It sucked in there. It's time to leave for good."

She grasped his hand, hot tears leaking down her cheeks. "I don't want to say goodbye to you again," she said.

"I'm not gone for good. But you still have a lot to do here. Use your gifts. Go live, Picasso."

"I love you."

"I know. I love you too."

She stepped forward, through the mist, putting one foot in front of the other, her hand held tight to the Saint Bernard's collar. The mist grew thicker, swirling, the light and numbers dissolving into it as it, too, faded. Outlines formed, and she became aware of soft sounds. Whispered voices drawing closer. She felt something beneath her. A soft chair. She felt so sleepy, but also somehow wide awake. There was this deep feeling of . . . joy flowing through her. Her heart was so *full*. She squeezed her fist. She was no longer holding the collar. That was okay. She wasn't alone.

She felt softness on her cheek, brushing her tears away, and raised her heavy lids. Ambrose. He was right there, peering at her, his expression worried but also hopeful. His gaze went to her lips, and then he smiled, returning what must be her own expression. She swallowed, trying to find her voice. "Hi," he said. His voice was gentle, so gentle.

Those soulful eyes. She'd gotten lost in those eyes the moment she'd met him. Some part of her had recognized them. Perhaps it wasn't only his soul she'd seen, but also her own mirrored there. She lifted her hand and brought it to her stomach, where she knew the tiny flicker of a brand-new heart beat beneath her skin. A son she'd met for an instant, a baby boy who had his father's eyes.

CHAPTER THIRTY-SEVEN

Lennon sipped at her cup of coffee as she gazed out the window of Ambrose's hotel room. It was a plain room even by economy-hotel standards, but to Lennon, even that looked inviting and . . . safe. Yes, it was just a room, but it was comfortable and secure, and she felt gratitude for the fact that Ambrose had invited her here to recover from the experience she'd gone through, the one she was still processing. But though she was still allowing the time she'd spent in the belly of her trauma, so to speak, to settle in, she felt deeply changed by it. It'd been life altering, empowering. And she'd come away with a peace and an . . . understanding that she *felt* but still couldn't quite explain. Maybe she'd never be able to. Or perhaps that would take time.

The most shocking thing was that Lennon had only been in Dr. Sweeton's chair for five hours. Five hours that had seemed like a lifetime. Others completed seven days, or even two. But the doctor had determined that she needed far less than that. It wasn't necessary to bring her to the scene of an event that had lasted months, or years, as was the case with abused children or many soldiers suffering from PTSD. And it definitely hadn't been necessary to take Lennon all the way to her base and build her attachment centers and central nervous system back up again. "You formed bonds," he'd said. "You learned to love and trust. We don't need to rewire you." He'd said it with a smile, but it had caused Lennon's heart to speed, proved by the quickened beeping from the heart monitor connected to her chest.

Ambrose had glanced at it and squeezed her hand, and her heart had slowed, certainty replacing her momentary fear. It said quite a bit about her trust in Ambrose, she knew, who had agreed to be by her side, along with two women she'd met who had also gone through the process. Even so, Lennon had wanted a video recorded on her phone, and once that had been set up, she'd signed consent forms, and then she'd willingly taken the cocktail of hallucinogens and sedatives.

She took in a big cleansing pull of air and then sipped some of the hot coffee, the mug warming the palms of her hands and sending another trickle of gratitude through her body. The rain outside drummed on the pavement, streaking the glass, and everything was just so clear and beautiful. She felt more herself than she ever had, this wondrous, shimmering hope making everything brighter. The only thing she could compare it to was when she'd been a child watching a bubble grow and grow on a wand her mother held. Such wonder had filled her as rainbows appeared in the shifting translucence, her mother laughing as it detached from the wand and floated up into the sky.

Lennon had the mind of an adult now, not a child. But the treatment had brought back that feeling of awe of the world that had been covered over by years and fears and all the other things that life delivered and that she'd taken on. She didn't know if this would last or if it was the residual effects of those drugs still tapping pleasure centers in her mind, but she'd hold on to it while she could. If nothing else, it was a reminder of what she should strive for, even if it could only be achieved for moments at a time.

What must it be like to live with hopelessness and pain every day of your life and then to suddenly feel *this*? *The way Ambrose must have felt.* It made her want to cry.

She suddenly remembered that story of the man jumping off the bridge and the sea lion that saved him. She'd looked that story up in the days after he'd told it. At first, she'd wondered if it might have been

Ambrose's story. But it wasn't. It was true, though, and in the aftermath of the experience, that man went around the country and gave motivational talks. It was inspiring, and she understood now why Ambrose had remembered all the details. Because it was somewhat . . . magical. It was a confirmation about how mysterious the world really was. How many layers there were that people couldn't see.

I think it's important to be able to determine when answers are necessary and when they're not, Ambrose had said to her a few days after she'd met him.

She hadn't known how to interpret that then. But she understood now. She knew exactly what he'd meant. She'd seen beneath the surface. She'd spent five hours there.

Her gaze moved down to the street, where a man and woman laughed as they ran through the rain. She smiled, tilting her head as they splashed out of sight, picturing the block where they'd turned. God, she loved this city. She knew its every nook and cranny, from the wide streets of the avenues where she'd grown up to the narrow neon blocks of Chinatown. This city of her heart was filled with artists and entrepreneurs, rebels and dreamers, and featured every culture under the sun, and had once, very literally, risen from the ashes. You could be anyone in San Francisco and be embraced not despite your differences but because of them. It was eclectic and beautiful and classy and funky. It was *home*, and it would be part of her heart and soul until the moment she took her final breath.

She cared deeply about the people who shared her city, not only as fellow humans but as a sort of extended family too. She wanted them to be well. She wished for them to thrive.

The door opened, and Ambrose came in, holding several to-go bags, his face breaking into a smile when he saw her out of bed and standing by the window. He'd brought her here after the treatment, and she'd slept for—she glanced at the clock—three hours while he'd watched over her. When she'd woken, there was a note on the bedside table that he'd gone to get dinner and would be back.

He held up a bag. "Italian."

"Oh my God, I love you." He grinned, but their eyes met. And she thought maybe she did love him, even though it was far too soon and she really didn't know him. But then again, maybe she did, and God, but life felt so full of possibilities.

"This is going to taste like some of the best food you've ever had," he said. "Some of that is because you haven't eaten in almost twenty-four hours, but you also might still have some of the narcotics in your system."

She let out a breathy laugh. "I'm surprised you're not tempted to take this cocktail on a regular basis."

He gave her a quirk of his lip. "They have their place in treatment, but hallucinogens aren't great for your brain, or your body, on a regular basis. And I value my brain and body. I've been an addict, and I have no desire to live that life again."

"Point taken."

He set the bags down and began opening them and pulling out the fragrant boxes of food, her mouth literally watering as the steamy scents of basil and cheese wafted her way. "Help yourself," he said.

She did, any shyness she might have felt overtaken by her body's craving for food. She picked up a container of spaghetti and a plastic fork and started eating, moaning as the food hit her tongue. She ate in earnest for several minutes, and when she looked up, he was watching her, a smile tipping his lips. "Aren't you hungry?" she asked around a bite of garlic bread.

"I'll eat what you don't want."

She laughed. "I can't possibly eat all that." She nodded down to the six containers, four still filled with food.

"You might be surprised." He shot her a wink, then turned and gathered two water bottles out of the minifridge and set them on the desk.

She looked up at all the clippings and notes he'd taped to the wall, chewing as she considered each piece of evidence from the case. "Real life," she said, the first unpleasant sensation she'd felt since she'd woken up taking hold. "We have to figure out who's using Dr. Sweeton's formula against people." She turned to him. "Tell me what you've learned so far or come up with while we've been apart."

His expression softened as he looked at her. "You're not going to expose the project."

She took another bite, chewing more slowly before swallowing. "I mean . . . I'm still probably just a little bit high, so I'm not making any definitive decisions at the moment."

"Wise," he said, with a cock of his head.

She smiled, but it quickly dwindled. "But I think . . . I think we have to protect the project. It's . . . the most incredible thing I've ever experienced, and I didn't consider myself damaged." She thought for a moment about the stories she'd listened to on *The Fringe*, about the way so many people suffered. And she didn't know how to make something like this available to more people, but the fact that it was being given to any seemed like a small miracle she refused to deny to anyone. "The problem, Ambrose, is that it's been corrupted. We have to figure out how—and why—or it won't be up to us whether it ends. It will have to."

"Agreed."

Lennon opened a container of lasagna and took it over to the bed, where she sat against the propped pillows, eating and considering the wall again. Ambrose was obviously experienced with investigations. "How'd you become a bounty hunter anyway?" she asked. "I read about the crime you helped solve in Kentucky," she said, feeling a moment of apprehension that he'd be angry that she'd looked him up.

But he just nodded, as if he'd already figured out that she'd looked into his past. Of course he had—he'd possessed this uncanny knack for figuring her out from the get-go. Instead of being annoyed by it, like she'd been at first, now it made her want to smile, though currently her mouth was too full of food to do that. "Well, like I told you, I started out as a correctional officer. After going through Dr. Sweeton's treatment, and what happened in Kentucky, I knew I wanted to work in law enforcement. When I returned to San Francisco, the quickest way in was a job at San Quentin."

"Wow, you started in the prison big leagues."

A smile flitted across his lips. "That's one way to put it. Anyway, long story short, I made some solid connections in the law enforcement community, and then I went into business for myself. There was a prison break a year later, and I was called in and ended up apprehending both prisoners within days. After that, a few agencies contacted me to assist on cases, and I proved beneficial on those as well. It snowballed from there. Over the years, I had to turn down more jobs than I could take." He looked at the curtain-covered window for a second. "I seem to have this sixth sense for locating people, especially once I have a profile. Maybe I'm just naturally good at the job, but I think the treatment I went through sort of . . ."

"Honed your instincts?"

"Yes. Others have said similar things. I think you'll find it's true of you as well," he said.

She took another bite, and he watched her for a moment. "Speaking of which, do you want to talk about your experience?" he asked somewhat tentatively.

She thought about that. "Not yet, but I will. I'd like to let it settle for a little while longer. But I'd like to tell you about it, and I'd like to hear about your experience, too, if you're willing to share."

"I'd love that," he said before walking to the bed and sitting down on the edge.

She focused back on the wall, going over the victims and the crime scenes. Her mind felt both slightly foggy and clearer than she could remember it feeling in a long time. She recalled all those illuminated but also translucent lines that had connected one thing to the other while she'd been under the influence of Dr. Sweeton's drug cocktail, and something told her she should take advantage of any connections the residual effects of that might allow her to make. "I think our killer somehow found out about the project and is using it for his own purposes," she said.

"His purposes being terror and death."

"Yes." *Terror and death.* "The exact opposite of what Dr. Sweeton intended."

"Who hates the people who need that therapy enough to turn it around on them? Not to cure them, but to make them suffer further, and suffer horribly?"

She shook her head as she placed the empty container on the bedside table, finally satiated. "Someone very sick. He hates them. He blames them for something."

"Yes. But what?"

"That's the question," she murmured. *One of many.*

She glanced at Ambrose, and she saw that he was looking over the wall, too, his expression deeply troubled. "This is what I've concluded so far. From the evidence, from what I experienced in my treatment, it looks like he or she used Dr. Sweeton's cocktail but tweaked it until they got it 'right.' Let's call him a *he* for ease. He accesses their trauma center, and then he triggers it. He makes them think they're back there and that it's happening again. But this time he makes sure they have the tools to fight back. And they do. All of them at once. It's why he forgoes the sedatives that Dr. Sweeton uses. He wants their body to be active while their mind is submersed in their past."

Her shoulders drew up as a cold shiver blew through her. Who would do that to a fellow human being? Who *hated* that deeply? "If that's the goal," she said, "he seems to have achieved it with the last two killings. I don't have the details on the most recent murder, but Lieutenant Byrd says the murder weapons were all there, which I'm assuming means our killer or . . . whoever's setting these poor souls up, didn't have to be part of it."

Ambrose nodded distractedly. "I think he's using items that trigger their trauma," he said, pointing to the list of seemingly innocuous items at each scene. He mentioned the wine coolers and the cigarette brand and why they felt off.

"I see what you mean," she murmured. "They don't quite fit, do they?" She scratched her head, remembering that she'd had the same gut feeling about the belt but hadn't been able to explain why. "So . . . he's accessing their trauma center with the drugs, then he's triggering them with a physical item that connects to that trauma. It's serving to give the experience texture and weight and maybe sometimes a visual, too, the same way Dr. Sweeton uses dirt under your feet and a drumbeat to ground you."

"Yes. These people are the opposite of grounded, though. They're left to flail, seemingly indefinitely, in the worst moment of their life."

"Hell," she murmured. "It would be like hell. God, no wonder their faces look like that." She pulled in a breath and let it out slowly. It was gruesome.

"It is. We have to stop it."

"How, though? He knows the recipe now, and access to victims who've experienced trauma of that depth is practically limitless." Not only that, but people like the ones they'd found murdered often went unreported. Those who lived transient lives weren't always missed. He might have killed hundreds of them already, and they wouldn't even know. He might have been "experimenting" for years.

Ambrose was quiet for a few moments, and as she watched him, a sweep of affection moved over her. They were a good team after all. He looked over at her as though something had just occurred to him. "He knows their triggers, though. How does he know these particular people's triggers? If we're right and the items listed aren't random, then he knows exactly what to place there to use as triggers—but ones that the police will miss. A belt. A type of drink, a specific cigarette brand."

"The podcast," she said. "That could be how it fits." *At least in one case.*

"What podcast?"

She turned more fully toward him. "I talked to Cherish Olsen's roommate. I know you found her after she overdosed, but . . . I had talked to her a few days before that, and she told me Cherish had done this podcast called *The Fringe*. I watched her interview. It was awful, but . . ." She put her hand on his arm. "Yes. Oh my God, the toys at the crime scene." She stared off into space for a moment, feeling ill as she worked out what had happened. "The killer used those toys to trap her in the hotel room of her mind." The one where her six-year-old self had set her toys up on the edge of the bathtub before the monster in the other room came for her. Oh God, she wanted to weep. She wanted to tear this room apart at the thought of that scene, and it was only a scene in her mind.

"The thing that doesn't fit is that the other victims—Ambrose, why do you look like that?" He looked stupefied.

He gave his head a small shake. "I was on that podcast. *The Fringe*. Years and years ago. Before I underwent treatment."

"You were? But . . . I didn't see you. I scrolled through the thumbnails of all of them."

"My God, I barely remembered," he murmured.

"You must have looked very different—"

"I did, but that's not why you didn't see me. I called later and asked the podcaster not to share it. He honored my request, like he said he would."

"Oh." She thought about that. Could Jamal Whitaker have others, then? Of people that had asked he not post their interview because they'd changed their mind after the fact? If that was the case, she'd certainly have to consider him a more serious suspect. And she would, despite that he had an alibi for at least one of the murders. But . . . his empathy for the people he interviewed seemed so genuine. She'd watched dozens of his interviews, and she could tell by the way he treated them that he cared deeply and was personally affected by their stories. Still, people could be deceptive . . . and she hadn't had reason to check the alibi he'd casually tossed out.

"Unfortunately, it's too late now to contact Jamal," Ambrose said. "I'll take you home, and then I'll meet you bright and early."

She was tempted to request to stay with him here. It wasn't necessarily that she didn't want to be alone, but she desired his presence. She wanted him near her. But she nodded and stood. She was still delicate in any number of ways from what she'd gone through, and some time to herself and a full night's sleep in her own bed were probably a good idea. And then, tomorrow, they'd resume their partnership that had first ended and then begun again under the most unusual of circumstances.

CHAPTER THIRTY-EIGHT

Ambrose had never been at the building he and Lennon pulled up to the next afternoon. He'd *barely* remembered doing the podcast. It'd been in another location then . . . and that'd been an entirely different lifetime. Something he'd merely done for cash, in an endless array of other things he'd done for cash.

They got out of the car and knocked on the door, waiting for a moment as footsteps inside drew closer. Then the door was pulled open by a tall dark-skinned man wearing a ball cap. Ambrose was transported back in time, to a velvet couch, when he'd been called Jett and struggled to sit still for the thirty-minute interview. He swore he could taste the nicotine coating his mouth, even though he hadn't had a cigarette in seventeen years.

"Inspector Gray," Jamal said. "I didn't expect to see you back. Did you find something in one of the interviews?"

"Jamal Whitaker," Ambrose murmured before Lennon could answer. He felt half in a dream, one foot in the life he'd built and one foot in the one that had crumbled.

The man cocked his head and looked at him curiously. "Hi. Do I know you?"

"You did. Once. I did an interview for you a long time ago. I had bleached hair, and I called myself Jett then."

Jamal's forehead bunched, and he rubbed at his lip as he obviously attempted to place Ambrose. "I'm sorry. I do so many interviews, sometimes it's hard to remember faces. And you don't look anything like the people who typically sit on my couch." Jamal opened the door wider. "Come on in."

They followed him to the open space where the studio was, and though the building was different, the furniture Jamal used on his show was the same, or at least very similar. Either he'd kept them in miraculously good condition or replaced them with similar items as they aged over the years. "Recognize that?" Jamal asked.

Ambrose walked over to the sofa, then ran his hand along the plush arm. "Yeah. I do. I remember this."

Jamal watched him, crossing his arms. "I don't get a lot of success stories walking back through my door. You've obviously come a long way from when you were a person I'd be interested in interviewing."

Ambrose smiled, tipping his chin to acknowledge the compliment he knew it was. "Thanks. I'm surprised you're still doing this."

"Yeah. I've thought about hanging it up a time or two, but . . . I don't know. As soon as I start to consider it, I get an email about how watching someone tell their story changed their life for the better, or how a person saw their own story in someone else's. So as long as I keep feeling like it's doing some good, I'll stick around."

Ambrose smiled. "I'm glad to hear that." He joined Lennon where she stood.

"Anyway, you're obviously here for a reason. What did you find?"

"I was able to find one of the women I was attempting to ID in your material," Lennon said. She glanced at Ambrose. "But Ambrose told me that his interview wasn't aired because he called and asked that you not show it. I'm wondering if there are others who might have made the same request."

"Yeah, sure, there have been a handful over the years. They tell me at the end of their interview that they don't want it aired, or they call and say they changed their mind later. I pull it, no questions asked."

"Does anyone besides you have access to the videos?"

"No. I keep them in a password-protected Dropbox and have for many years. No one else has access. That's why I didn't even mention them."

"Okay. I need to see them."

Jamal eyed her. "Do you have a warrant?"

"No," she said. "But I can get one. I'd rather not waste time when there's a killer on the loose who may be targeting those people."

He considered her again, for long minutes, and Ambrose could feel her holding herself still as she waited next to him. "I'll copy them to a thumb drive, but I'd like it back," Jamal finally said.

Lennon let out a gust of breath. "You'll get it, I promise."

～

They went back to Lennon's house to watch the videos, sitting on her couch with the laptop on the coffee table in front of them. The first victim they recognized was the older woman from the very first crime scene. She'd grown up in foster care and been terrorized by a woman in one of the group homes who had been especially vicious after a few strawberry wine coolers. She'd come to associate that scent with torture. And fear. And shame. She'd been in and out of jail or homeless for most of her life.

They were all there. The man who'd been regularly whipped by his father with a belt, the slow loosening of that piece of leather making his guts turn to water as he anticipated the pain to his small body. The humiliation. All the items found at the scene made sense. It was gruesome, knowing they'd been right. They'd been used as tools to dredge up terror, and they'd worked.

It was horrendous and unthinkable. It was deeply evil.

They'd seen enough, at least for now. Lennon's cheeks were streaked with tears, and Ambrose felt the weight of sorrow pressing on his chest, not only for the way these people had died, but also for the way they had lived.

"This is where the killer got his information," she said. "The victims' triggers. This person knew just how to torture them. So it's either Jamal himself, or someone who accessed his Dropbox without his permission."

Ambrose frowned. Jamal had been completely forthcoming, though. And if he had wanted to hide—or destroy—the videos they'd just watched, he easily could have. "What about an outside hacker?" he asked.

"Possibly," she murmured. "Or a different angle entirely that we're not thinking of."

Ambrose nodded, and Lennon let out a frustrated sigh. She went to turn off her computer but accidentally brushed her finger over the play button, and the next video began. Her eyes widened, and his heart gave a sharp knock. It was him. Ambrose. *Jett.* Emaciated, jittery, hunched, his hair bleached. "Oh," she said, the word a breath and a sob. The sight of who he'd been brought him such deep distress and, yes, shame. He'd found peace over the years, and an abundance of gratitude that he'd been healed. He could think about who he'd been and all that he'd experienced without feeling pain. But he'd never expected to sit next to the woman he knew he could fall in love with—if he hadn't fallen already—as she was confronted with the very real vision of his former self.

But she placed her hand gently on top of his and met his eyes. "I want to know you," she said.

"That's not me anymore."

"I know that. But it's who you were, and I want to understand."

And so, with an abiding trust, he drew his hand away and sat back, as she leaned forward to have a better view of who he'd once been but was no longer.

CHAPTER THIRTY-NINE

She watched the interview with Ambrose until the end, her heart swelling so that she thought it might burst. He looked so *different*, but there was no mistaking those sleepy eyes. Seeing him that way—broken, in desperate need of help—brought her such intense sorrow. The man next to her, this kind, loving man, was inside that jumpy shadow on the screen. He was in there somewhere, trapped, and Dr. Sweeton had set him free.

It humbled her. It scared her. It made a pinball of what-ifs ping through her mind.

She closed her eyes and envisioned those ever-changing numbers from her therapy that hadn't *exactly* been numbers, even though they added and subtracted or compiled and diminished or *something*. What were they? Choices, maybe? That felt almost right, but sort of not. What she did know was that they were real, even if she couldn't see them now. They existed, and they were there, all around her. If Ambrose hadn't gone through the therapy, those numbers—or whatever they represented—would be so different. His life would be different, as would so many others'.

Including hers, and the baby they'd created that she hadn't told him about. The baby she knew was inside her, even though she hadn't yet taken a test. Dr. Sweeton had given her a pregnancy test as part of the protocol before she'd been administered the hallucinogens, and it'd come back negative. It was far too early, and yet, still, she knew.

She turned to look at him, tears burning her eyes as she brought her hand to his cheek and ran her thumb over his cheekbone. He looked so uncertain, so intensely vulnerable, and she knew she loved him. Maybe it was too early for that as well. But how could it be, when she felt it in every cell in her body? She knew. And perhaps she'd known far earlier than this.

He closed his eyes, leaning into her palm, nuzzling her. She remembered going to the cemetery a few days after they'd slept together. She'd known, even then, and so she'd gone to Tanner . . . she'd gone to apologize for what she felt inside—a soul that spoke to her own. An acknowledgment—even if deep down—that she'd found the person she was willing to move on with.

But Tanner hadn't needed an apology. She'd been the one seeking forgiveness. Lennon leaned in and kissed Ambrose gently, and he sighed and returned her kiss.

This time they walked together to the bedroom, and when he entered her body, their gazes held, connected in every way two humans could connect.

She accepted him not only into her body but into her heart, fully and without guilt or reservation. She was being given a second chance, and she wanted to weep with gratitude and with the knowledge that there was all kinds of love in the world. Young love, and more experienced love. Love before pain, and love that overcomes heartache.

He moved over her, his beautiful down-turned eyes filling with passion, with love. And if she hadn't been certain before, she was certain now—she would not deny the world more people like Ambrose, people who were trapped inside human shells, begging to be set free.

Afterward, he pulled her against him, running his hand lazily over her arm, and they lay like that for several peaceful moments. She moved back and studied him, struck by his expression. He looked so vulnerable, and she was still knocked sideways by the fact that someone with a past like his could or would allow an emotion like that to show so starkly on his face. As if he didn't know what some people did with such tenderness. But of course he did—and much better than most—and so that made it all the more awe inspiring.

He sighed happily, his eyes—those beautiful soul-searing eyes—moving over her features. "You make me feel like white doves and waffles," he said.

She breathed out a laugh. "White doves and waffles." She considered that. "So peaceful . . . and sweet?"

He turned, lacing his fingers behind his head on the pillow. "My grandfather went away for a week once. It was the best week of my childhood. I don't even remember where he went. But my grandma, she took me into town, and we ate breakfast at Denny's. I ordered waffles. I'd never had waffles. Or syrup. I licked my plate, and my grandma laughed. I'd never seen her laugh." Even from the side, she saw his gaze grow slightly cloudy as his eyes shifted from the wall to the ceiling, obviously picturing those waffles and that unexpected moment of happiness. "I thought if he didn't exist, life might be like that. I understood how other people lived. And it hurt, but . . . it was also the first time I felt hope." He turned toward her, and again, she saw his heart in his eyes. "You feel like that. Like peace, and sweet, and hope."

Oh God. She was moved and honored, and her throat felt full of the emotion that had welled up in her as he described one of the only good memories he had of his boyhood, otherwise filled with so much darkness and despair.

He turned back toward her, leaning in. "And you make me want to lick my plate clean," he said with a grin.

She laughed.

They kissed and cuddled, finding joy in the shared intimacy and solace in the warm safety of her bed. And then they talked for hours, telling each other about the respective journeys they'd taken as they'd undergone Dr. Sweeton's therapy. Lennon, however, didn't yet talk about the baby, as she sensed it wasn't quite time for that. They spoke about the undeniable sense of *love* that had permeated everything, when they'd been given the eyes to see it, and seemed to be . . . an *ingredient*, for lack of a better word, that made up the entire universe. It sounded hippie dippie, and her mother would eat it up. But regardless, she'd experienced it, and knew it was true. Or maybe, she surmised, it was part of *their* makeup—human beings—and it had been accessed with the drugs. It was difficult to explain, and she was grateful she'd gone through it so she could relate. Because otherwise, there would have been no other way. Words . . . mostly failed to describe it, though she knew what he was getting at with his explanations. And she understood even more the white dove, and the terrible, awful guilt and shame and pain Ambrose had lived with for his first twenty-one years. And she also understood that though he'd lied about being born and raised in San Francisco, he'd also told the truth. Or perhaps *reborn* was a better way to say it. *Reraised. Renewed.*

They shared their bodies and their souls late into the night and finally fell into a peaceful sleep. When they woke, the afternoon sun was glowing between the slats in her bedroom shade. Lennon was glad for the extra sleep and could have stayed in bed all day, basking lazily and enjoying her newfound bond with Ambrose. But they had a very clear mission, one they were now facing together.

CHAPTER FORTY

The man in the hoodie walked down the aisle of the church, daylight bouncing off the stained glass windows, the vibrant colors flaring with illumination. *Bloody battles and clashing swords, flayed corpses and weeping mothers.* Who needed to provide triggers when they were etched on every window? And the biggest trigger of all, that larger-than-life Jesus Christ, nails driven through his palms as he hung lifeless from a wooden cross.

Yes, indeed, this would be biblical.

His laughter echoed in the quiet space.

Mercy Cathedral had been built in 1898 and had miraculously survived the 1906 earthquake. Unfortunately, the congregation had eventually been lost to attrition—no surprise in a city that celebrated sin. The empty building had been purchased by a nonprofit group that rented it out for social functions, but in the last six months, it'd been acquired by the city and would be repurposed into housing units for 117 seniors who had experienced homelessness and were now living with health issues.

Or so said the website. The man didn't talk that way. *Experienced homelessness.* Like if something was an *experience*, then you weren't responsible for it. He supposed the disgusting, useless slobs who'd killed his mother had *experienced homicide.*

Well, he was *experiencing homicide*, too, and he was enjoying it immensely. And this, once a place of worship and dignity, now transforming into a smelly hovel for elderly riffraff dependent on tax-payers, seemed like the perfect location to continue what he'd started.

The DJ booth had already been set up, though the tables hadn't been moved in yet. That would all happen later today. He'd perfected the drug. It'd only taken five live experiments and a notebook of formulas. Wouldn't his professors be proud? He'd figured out how to access the trauma centers in the brain where all their nightmares already lived. And with a small trigger—boom! A homicidal maniac was born. The beauty of his improved concoction was that specific triggers were no longer necessary—merely general ones. Screeching sounds. Scary images. A jab or two. Then they'd fight to the death. He'd watched it happen himself just a few days before.

And he'd watch it tonight. And then he'd watch it again and again after that. He looked up to the smaller balcony on his right, even higher than the one once used for a choir or perhaps an organist. No, the place where he'd view this evening's event had once been a lofty box seat reserved for the upper crust. His lips stretched. It seemed an apropos place from which to watch his plans unfold. Not only on video this time but in person as well. He deserved that. Not only to see what played out with his eyes but to hear the screams from below. To smell the tang of sweat and blood. Not only to stand in the aftermath but to *be* there for the slaughter.

It was his final experiment. A mass gathering. Not everyone would take the drug in the manner presented to them, but enough would. Enough to make his point, anyway. That these people were capable of anything, and that eventually, they'd strike. They always did. And hopefully they'd take a few of the activists present with them, especially the ones who used social programs as a way to line their own pockets, ensuring the problem never got fixed. Endless fundraising and, there-fore, endless dregs.

If tonight went well, he'd give his drug to whole neighborhoods. They'd pop it like candy if they thought it'd get them high. Those para-sites would sell their own babies for a hit. He'd clear out tent cities and open-air drug markets. He could see the piles of bodies now. *Beautiful.* The public would pretend to be horrified, but then they'd walk through the clean streets, and in their homes at night, they'd shut the shades and whisper to each other, *Maybe it's for the best.*

The man stood at the altar, staring up at the statue of Mary. The mother. He wondered what his own mother would think about what he was doing and decided she'd probably try to talk him out of it. But that's how she'd been—far too tenderhearted. She'd thought low-IQ scum could be helped. She'd been wrong. And it was why she was now dust in the ground.

CHAPTER FORTY-ONE

Ambrose took a seat on the edge of the bed, his mind returning to that studio where he'd answered questions, fidgeting and suffering, so long ago. Something had crossed through his mind while they'd sat eating sandwiches and brainstorming about the case in Lennon's sunlit kitchen, and he was trying to retrieve it. Lennon exited the bathroom, a towel wrapped around her curves, her hair in a twist on top of her head. She smiled, and time slowed, and he knew he wanted to see this very vision for the rest of his life. It was . . . surreal, and in some ways, it was a full-circle moment for him. He hadn't planned for this; in fact, he'd sworn off it. Love. A relationship. And he'd lived with the belief that he'd never have those things—that he didn't *want* those things—for so long that adjusting the vision of his own future felt like both a small miracle and the riskiest thing he'd ever faced.

She approached him, wrapping her arms around his neck and pressing her body into his. He sighed, embracing her slim body and inhaling her shower-fresh fragrance. He felt the blood move more swiftly, and then more slowly, in his veins, his muscles loosening, even though he'd thought he'd been relaxed a few minutes before.

This. Human touch. It was medicine. His shoulders lowered, his thoughts drifted, as she stroked his hair. "The cameraman," he murmured.

She leaned back. "What?"

"Oh my God, the cameraman. There was a cameraman filming. Jamal sat with me and asked questions. But there was a man behind the camera."

She blinked, stepped back. "Call Jamal," she said, handing him her phone and scrolling to the number.

Ambrose stood and dialed the number as Lennon dropped her towel and began pulling on clothes, late-afternoon light caressing her skin and making it glow. Jamal answered on the second ring, sounding distracted. "This is Ambrose DeMarce. I hope I'm not disturbing you, but we had a few questions based on the videos you gave us yesterday."

"The people who didn't want their interviews aired? Sure. What's up?"

"You told us no one else has or had access to the videos you didn't post, right?"

"Correct. I can't imagine how anyone would have access unless my Dropbox was hacked. But there's never been any evidence of that."

"Not even your cameraman?"

"Franco? No. There's no need."

"Can you tell me a little about him? Franco?"

"Sure. He's a nice guy. Quiet but very dependable. Serious, does his job well. He's generally in and out, not big on small talk. I hired him about five or six years ago, after my original cameraman moved out of town."

Ambrose felt a small tremble move across his nerve endings, the same one he felt when he was hot on the heels of a criminal he'd been sent to hunt down. He knew he was close; he felt it. "What's Franco's last name?"

"Girone." Jamal spelled it for him, and Ambrose nodded to Lennon, who had run into the living room, grabbed her laptop, and now had it open on the dresser.

"Can you tell me anything else about him?"

Jamal paused for a moment. "Let's see. Franco's mom was a big advocate for the homeless. She ran a program . . . I can't think of the name now. Tragically, she was murdered. I don't know all the details. I think I learned about it from someone I interviewed, but I'd already heard her name. To this day, she's often honored at events. When Franco applied to be my cameraman, he said he wanted to carry on in her tradition but he doesn't have her outgoing personality. He prefers to stay in the shadows and help tell the stories of the Tenderloin streets from behind a lens."

Ambrose thanked Jamal and hung up, then joined Lennon where she was bent over the screen of her laptop. "Look at this," she said, pointing to a news article. "Zeta Girone was murdered in her home." She picked up the laptop, turned, and climbed into bed, where she sat against the pillows. She propped the computer on her lap. Ambrose sat down on the edge of the bed and faced her. She took a minute to scan the article, obviously speed-reading. "Zeta Girone was the foster parent of four teens she'd taken in when they were relinquished to the system by clients of her foundation, Rays of Hope, located in the Tenderloin district of San Francisco."

Rays of Hope. Where had he heard that name? Had he passed by it when he was in the Tenderloin? He must have. He waited as Lennon clicked for a few minutes.

"'The goal of Rays of Hope is to abolish family homelessness in San Francisco. Until that time, we offer assistance with housing, financial, and addiction services,'" she said, obviously reading off the website she must have opened in another browser.

"So it's still open?"

Lennon nodded, scanning the screen. "Okay, so Zeta Girone fostered these four teens who then murdered her in her home and were apparently collecting the checks she was getting for housing and caring for them. Before they killed her, however, they kept her confined in her own basement for almost a year." Lennon shook her head. "Holy shit," she muttered, scrolling down the screen. "She'd taken a hiatus from work to put all her effort into helping the teens readjust and catch up on their education, since they were so far behind and still experiencing effects of their diagnosed posttraumatic stress disorder." She glanced up at Ambrose and then back to the screen, pausing as she read for a few moments and then continued to summarize. "Instead, the teens tied her up, tortured, and taunted her for eleven and a half months, according to those familiar with the case. Eventually they stabbed her because the checks stopped coming, a consequence of unfiled necessary paperwork and missed home visits. Her body was found by her son, Franco, who was in college on the East Coast at the time of her captivity and eventual murder." She looked up at Ambrose. "A chemistry major. Franco was a chemistry major."

"Oh Christ." He ran a finger under his lip. "Let me text Doc and see if Franco's name rings a bell with him." He grabbed his phone and shot Doc a quick text and then looked back to Lennon, who was still reading the screen.

"Money was tight, and so Franco worked summer and Christmas breaks to afford tuition," she said. "Correspondence with his mother grew sparse, texts only answered with one or two words. He thought she was angry at him for going so far away. Apparently, they'd argued about it. When he arrived home, he discovered her mutilated corpse."

Sickness swelled inside Ambrose. God, the heinous things humans were capable of.

Lennon turned the screen around, and Ambrose looked at the picture there, of a dark-haired boy and a woman with orangey-red hair. A mother with her arm around her son as they both smiled happily at the camera, a window behind them with a logo that had sunrays fanned out around it. *Rays of Hope.* His eyes moved to Franco. A good-looking kid, his smile close lipped but sincere. Was he the man collecting drug addicts and those living or working on the streets and triggering their trauma in horrific ways, encouraging them to bludgeon and stab each other to death?

"Do you think . . . is he exacting revenge for his mother?" Lennon asked. "Getting even with those he considers irredeemable?" She paused.

"God, she took them into her home, and they tortured and killed her. For a few thousand dollars. It's sick."

"If we're right, so is what he's doing."

"I know. I know. It's all sick." Her shoulders rose and fell as she took in a breath. "I need to update Lieutenant Byrd about all of this." He took the laptop from her and then watched as she called her boss, explaining what she'd found out about the podcast and Franco Girone. To his credit, the man didn't waste time asking her how and when she'd done all the research and footwork that had gone into the discovery when she was supposed to be off duty. Instead, he took the information and said he'd put out an APB immediately.

Lennon hung up and looked at Ambrose. "If Franco knows chemistry, and is the man responsible for these crimes, he probably has some makeshift lab set up in his house. That's the first place the police will go." She looked to the side for a moment, obviously thinking. "So, if it's him, we know how he targets his victims and has so much information about their triggers. But the thing that I don't understand is how he might know about the pills. At the first scenes, the pills were the same recipe as Dr. Sweeton's. Our killer's obviously been experimenting since then, like we said. But initially, he started with those. How? How did he get one of those pills to use to produce more, if any extras are immediately destroyed?"

Ambrose ran his hand over his jaw, something occurring to him. "He doesn't need a pill, though. Just the formula."

"Right," Lennon said, looking away and chewing at her lip. "In fact, that would make it easier than having to reverse engineer. So where might Dr. Sweeton keep that type of information?"

"He has all the files pertaining to Project Bluebird in his home office," he said. "I'm positive that means the formula for the drug he uses too. His office is under lock and key, though. The man doesn't even allow his housekeeper in there. I trust him, Lennon."

"I know," she said. "I do too. But what about his wife?"

"No. She doesn't have a key either. We went over all this with him when the pills first showed up."

"But even if he didn't give a key to her, his wife could find a way into his office, right? If she really wanted to?"

"Why are you asking about Brittany Sweeton?"

"Just spitballing," she said with a smile. He smiled back. The question troubled him, though, and that small tremble he'd come to know as instinct rattled inside. He'd witnessed a few terse phone calls between the doctor and his wife in the last week. He'd sensed some marital trouble but dismissed it as temporary and likely related to the current stress the doctor was under. But murder? Or participating in murder? That didn't sound like the Brittany he'd known for many years. Sure, she was materialistic and somewhat shallow. And she'd made some suggestive comments to Ambrose over the years that were inappropriate, considering she was married. But he'd brushed her off, and she'd let it go. So yeah, personally he wasn't her biggest fan. *But what if?* Lennon's instincts were good—and they weren't muddled by preconceived views because of familiarity.

What if the marital trouble he'd witnessed had been going on for longer than he knew? What if Brittany had done something, either knowingly or not, that had begun this whole cascade of murder and revenge?

He looked back at the laptop, scrolling down the page of photos posted by Rays of Hope, his gaze shifting distractedly over the images. They appeared mostly to be shots from functions either at the foundation or other locations, the outfits and hairstyles of those in the pictures indicating the rewinding years. He froze near the bottom of the page, his heart giving a strong jolt. "Holy shit."

"What?" she asked, leaning forward to get a better view of the screen.

He turned it toward her and brought his index finger to the photo of an obviously younger Franco sitting at a table with Doc and someone he recognized from an old photo he'd seen in Doc's office. "It's Doc and his ex-wife, Gwendolyn."

"Doc and Franco know each other?"

"Either that or they just attended the same event."

She studied the photo for a moment before her eyes met his. "This might be nothing but a coincidence, and that photo is obviously many years old. It wouldn't be surprising if everyone in the TL was connected in some way. But . . . Ambrose, do you think . . ." She looked away, biting at her lip, obviously at a loss for exactly what this meant.

He set the computer aside and then picked up his phone again, this time dialing Doc's number rather than just leaving a text. It went straight to voicemail, and Ambrose hung up with a frustrated huff. "I think we should go talk to Doc," Ambrose said. Lennon nodded, getting up off the bed and putting on her shoes.

He had a deep feeling Franco and Dr. Sweeton being at very least acquainted at some point was anything but a coincidence. He just had no idea what the connection was.

CHAPTER FORTY-TWO

Dr. Alexander Sweeton held the photograph in his hand, gazing down at his daughter, Nancy, and his first wife, Gwendolyn. They'd gone to Disneyland in Los Angeles and spent four days in the park, riding rides, eating snow cones, and buying overpriced mouse memorabilia.

It'd been wonderful.

And the last vacation he'd ever taken.

His first marriage had fallen apart after Nancy's . . . attack. They hadn't survived the grief and the trauma and the guilt of what had happened to their only child. Gwen was remarried now and living close to Disney World in Florida. He wondered if she ever drove past it, or perhaps spent an afternoon there, and thought about those four dream-filled days in another life altogether.

He'd been alone for a long time after Nancy died and Gwen left. He'd devoted himself completely to the project. But then he'd met Brittany at a cocktail party. She was much younger than him, and they had little in common. But she'd made him laugh. She'd made him feel like a man again. She'd helped him remember the true value of a full life and why he'd made it his passion to help others live the one they'd been denied.

He deserved some happiness, too, didn't he? And wouldn't it make him not only a better person but a better doctor for his patients if he enjoyed a more well-rounded life? Those had all been justifications, though. He saw that now. His ego had gotten the best of him, and perhaps it was his fatal flaw.

Their marriage wasn't working. They both knew it. What should have been a quick and pleasant affair had turned into a stale, resentment-filled union. Their relationship had been ill fated from the beginning, but he'd certainly sped their demise along by making her his last priority.

She'd been dressing differently for months now. Sexier. Wearing outfits similar to the ones she'd worn when they'd first started dating, before she'd become a doctor's wife and seemed to change her style to fit the role. And he'd seen her entering a hotel near his office with a man he recognized as a high-priced tax attorney. He'd waited for the anger to come, or even the disappointment. But the only emotion that had washed over him as he'd sat in traffic watching them laughing and disappearing through the front doors was relief. He was responsible for the affair she was obviously having. He'd been absent and distracted, and he'd married her for all the wrong reasons, convincing himself the bounce in his step from her affection was love.

He'd insisted on a prenuptial agreement, perhaps because, deep inside, he was aware that their relationship was unlikely to last, but mostly to protect the money he'd stowed away from his highly lucrative practice and many speaking engagements that he used to fund Project Bluebird. The project he'd dedicated his life to was very expensive. There was equipment, and testing, and lab fees, and aftercare. He had employees to train, and a hundred other expenses, big and small. It was because he'd protected his wealth that the project continued and grew. He could not gamble with it, lest he gamble with Nancy's legacy.

And now he knew that despite Brittany leaving their marriage with no more than she'd arrived with, she'd be just fine.

With a sigh, he set the photograph of Nancy and his first wife back on the bookshelf behind him, facing away from it. He set his elbows on his desk and rested his forehead on the heels of his hands. He'd tried so hard to redeem himself, to leave a legacy that Nancy would be proud of, to make amends for his mistakes with his daughter by helping others who were suffering the same way she had. And he had helped. He had. So many saved souls. He was proud of that. He'd sacrificed for it. But then things had gone so horribly wrong, and he couldn't figure out *how*. Or why.

He'd gone to see the woman in the psychiatric ward who had survived the most recent attempted murder—after all, that's what it was, only not just an attempted murder of the body but of the mind and soul—and it'd almost brought him to his knees. Broken him. Not only had she been dropped into the epicenter of her trauma, but she seemed to be stuck there. Death would have been kinder than that. And so the best the hospital could do was keep her unconscious. The fact that the altered drug had been formulated so that even when the narcotic wore off, the result did not, was a horror he hadn't expected. He'd been working around the clock to create an antidote based on the pill Ambrose had provided him. But so far, the antidote was weak and would likely only work on those who'd absorbed a small amount of the toxin. Not doses like the one taken by the woman in the hospital, who had already dropped in a black hole in her own mind and was too far gone. And he couldn't administer the pill that had been formulated to induce violence just so he could test his antidote. If he did that, he'd turn into the man who'd twisted his project.

Maybe he was no better. He'd thought he was. But because of him, this was happening. The work of his heart had been corrupted. Perhaps everything good eventually was.

Or perhaps if it could be corrupted, it wasn't good at all. He'd convinced himself it was good because he needed it to be. Back to his own ego, once again.

God, he was so tired. He'd come home early to sleep for a few hours. He'd been up for days, and his faculties were failing him. A few hours' rest and he'd feel better, and then he'd persevere.

He began to rise from his desk, picking up his silenced phone and noticing that he'd missed a text from Ambrose, and a call as well. He read the text asking about a Franco Girone.

Franco Girone.

Where did he know that name from? Another text came through from Ambrose.

On the way over.

And there was a link below the message that brought up a photo. He stared, his skin suddenly prickling, mind buzzing. The man in the photo, whom he now recognized as Franco, had been a little older than in this image the last time he'd seen him in person . . . and Franco hadn't been smiling then, like he was in the photo. It all drifted to him in foggy snippets of memory. Franco's mother, the woman who'd run Rays of Hope in the Tenderloin, had just been killed. He'd met the man—how old had Franco been then? Twenty or twenty-one?—at an event, and then later at the free clinic. He'd been deeply traumatized by his mother's murder. Dr. Sweeton had tested him for Project Bluebird but ultimately decided he wasn't a good candidate. The man had exhibited traits that weren't conducive to a successful regression therapy. His psychopathy had been questionable, but the doctor hadn't been able to tell if that was related to his current trauma or something else underlying that was already present.

He slowly lowered his phone as he thought back to the event from the photo. It'd been so long ago, but he wondered . . . Dr. Sweeton stood, going over to his file cabinet and opening the bottom drawer, where he stored flyers and pictures from talks he'd given, and sometimes personal photos he was forwarded from events. Items he didn't necessarily need, but ones he didn't feel right throwing away either. He'd been tossing things here for years.

He picked up the box, carried it to his desk, and dumped it out. It only took a few minutes of sifting before he found what he was looking for. He had a hard copy of the photo that Ambrose had sent him a link to. The man who had organized the Rays of Hope event had put them in the thank-you card he'd sent later.

Dr. Sweeton tossed the card aside and went through the handful of photos, the last one in the stack nearly stealing his breath. The word he whispered as he dropped the pictures scratched over the tender skin of his throat.

Oh God. He was going to be sick. He rushed to the bathroom in his office and barely made it before he lost his lunch. Or breakfast, or whatever last meal he'd eaten. He couldn't remember.

He felt hot and cold, faint. Panicked. Horrified. *No, it can't be. You're wrong.* Dr. Sweeton fell back on the tile floor, slumped against the wall, and cried. *What the hell is happening? This can't be true. You're just tired.*

His mind was so foggy, so saturated with shock. His world was crumbling around him.

He pulled himself slowly to his feet, flushed the toilet, and then used his cupped hand to rinse his mouth before leaving the bathroom.

He stood near his desk for several moments, doing a few deep-breathing exercises before using the search engine on his phone to look up the number for Rays of Hope. He dialed, and a young man answered.

"Yes, hello. My name is Dr. Alexander Sweeton, and I'm trying to get in contact with Franco Girone. His mother was—"

"Zeta Girone." He heard the smile in the man's voice. "Yes, Franco is here a few times a week, but tonight he's at the award dinner."

"Award dinner."

"Yes, you just caught me, actually. We're all heading there in a minute. Franco is accepting one in his mother's honor."

"For Rays of Hope? Posthumously?"

"Yes. She was an amazing advocate for those experiencing drug addiction and homelessness in the Tenderloin. It was tragic, what happened to her."

"Yes. It was. Where is this award dinner being given?"

"Oh. At Mercy Cathedral. Do you—"

Dr. Sweeton hung up. Mercy Cathedral was less than ten minutes away. He had to speak with Franco Girone. He had to be certain he was the one. He had to stop what he himself had unknowingly started.

The doctor left his office, pausing in the hall before turning back and going to the cabinet near the door, where he had a small bar with a minifridge. He grabbed the blue nylon cooler, hooked the strap over his shoulder, and then rushed out of his house, not bothering to set the alarm.

CHAPTER
FORTY-THREE

Dr. Sweeton wasn't answering his cell phone or his front door, and if his car was here at his house, it was locked in the garage. Lennon watched Ambrose lean forward and peer through the glass before ringing the bell again, the chime loud even from outside. "His office door is wide open," he said. "He would never leave it open like that."

She cupped her hands to shield the light from the sunset and pressed her forehead to the glass. "Maybe he's the only one home and just forgot to close it. You said he was exhausted. Maybe he took a sleep aid and is out cold."

"Maybe," Ambrose murmured. "But we don't have time to wait for him to wake up. Lives could be at stake."

Their eyes met, and Ambrose set his mouth before picking up the cement planter and hurling it through the pane as they both leaned away. Lennon winced as the window shattered loudly, and Ambrose reached in and clicked the lock. No alarm sounded. Ambrose pulled the door open, and they moved inside, their feet crunching over the broken glass.

"Doc?" Ambrose called loudly as they both moved toward the open door of his office. The house remained quiet and still. The office looked mostly normal, except for the pile of papers and what looked like photos and brochures littering the top of the desk and the floor surrounding it.

"What the heck was he doing?" Lennon asked as they stepped up to the mess. She picked up an invitation to a talk that the doctor had given. "This is from ten years ago," she said. She looked over at the open drawer of the file cabinet and to the box that was overturned on the floor, as though the doctor had poured out its contents to search for something.

Ambrose picked something up, and she felt him still beside her. "Oh shit."

"What?"

He showed her the same photo of Franco Girone that they'd seen online, and then handed her another that was obviously from the same event. She studied it, realization dawning even if all the puzzle pieces hadn't yet fallen into place. "Is that who I think it is?" she asked, pointing at the young woman standing to Franco's left.

"Yeah," Ambrose said. "It's Nancy."

Nancy Sweeton. Doc's deceased daughter. The one he'd dedicated his project to. The only one of his patients who'd died during treatment. "What does this mean?" she asked.

"I'm not exactly sure." Ambrose took out his phone and dialed and then let out another frustrated breath as she heard Dr. Sweeton's voicemail pick up.

They both exited the house, coming to stand at the top of the driveway, Lennon's gaze on the darkening water of the bay far below this mansion in Pacific Heights. She attempted to organize the information they'd collected over the past hour as Ambrose sent the doctor yet another text.

Her phone rang, and she answered, putting it on speaker and holding it out as Ambrose moved closer. "Franco Girone's not here," Lieutenant Byrd said. "But he's still living in the same house his mother owned. There's a lab in the basement—he must have spent years assembling this. It's completely state of the art. He's definitely our guy, and he intended on doing big things. There are also what look like video recordings of each murder, and lots of product, all with the 'BB' stamp. A hazmat crew is on the way."

Her eyes met Ambrose's. "Is there anything that might tell us where he's gone or what he's doing next?" she asked the lieutenant.

"No specifics found, but there are sketches all over his kitchen table. He plotted out each murder scene in advance. There are notes that must have been done later about ways to improve, some shit I can't even read that's probably drug formulas. He's been very strategic." The sounds of paper rustling came from the background. "There are also what look like plans for a bigger event, but it's not clear what."

"Can you send me a screenshot of that?" Lennon asked.

"Yeah. Take a look. Then we can convene about where to go from here. Of course, we'll have this place staked out in case he returns. Oh, and hey, good work, Gray. We got him, dead to rights."

"Don't thank me too soon," she said. "We still have to apprehend him before he hurts anyone else."

She hung up, and a moment later, Lennon's phone dinged, indicating a text had arrived. She opened it, frowning as she looked the rough sketch over and then turned it so Ambrose could see. "It looks like a dinner . . . or an event," she said. "There are tables inside . . . and . . ." She moved the phone closer to Ambrose. "What is that?"

He studied it for a moment. "A DJ booth, maybe?"

"A DJ booth," she murmured. "Yes, an event. He's targeting an event?" She turned the phone back to her and counted the tables. *Twelve.* "Ambrose, it looks like at least a hundred people are going to be here. Is this what he's been working up to?"

Killing not just one or two or four, but over a hundred at a time? And maybe it wasn't just what he was working up to. Maybe it was only another experiment on his way to more. Just a stop along the route to complete genocide. The evil stunned her, and she hadn't thought she could be stunned by evil anymore. Sickened? Distraught? Yes. But no longer stunned.

"When, though?" Ambrose asked. "And where? If we don't know those answers, we can't do a damn thing."

Lennon looked back down at the sketch. "Ambrose . . . what do you think these are?"

His gaze lingered where she was pointing. "Framed paintings hung on the wall?"

No, not exactly. She chewed at her lip, looking away, her gaze snagging on the shards of shattered glass from the front door. Glass. *Glass.* "Stained glass," she said. "Could these be stained glass windows?"

"You could be right," Ambrose said, his head moving closer to hers. "If so, it's a church. He's targeting a church service."

"One with a DJ booth and tables?"

"Okay, no, you're right. An event at a church." Something was just on the edge of her mind. *Stained glass. Bright colors. An event.* She turned away and then suddenly turned back. "Oh my God, Ambrose. The Heroes for Homelessness . . . there was a DJ advertised. And . . ." Her eyes flared with realization. "Rays of Hope. His mother's organization. Oh my God, he's going to do something horrific there. For her."

She googled the foundation's number and dialed, her heart skittering as she waited, the call finally going to voicemail. She hung up just as Ambrose's head came up from his phone, where he'd obviously been googling the event itself. "It's being held at Mercy Cathedral. Tonight. It's already started."

Lennon called Lieutenant Byrd as they sped toward Mercy Cathedral and told him where they were heading and why. The lieutenant told Lennon he'd send a few backup cars to the church in the hope that Franco Girone was present and that they could halt any potential plan that was underway at the event this evening.

Ambrose reached over and took her hand as he drove and laced his fingers with hers. Their eyes met, and she whispered a silent prayer that they weren't going to be too late.

CHAPTER
FORTY-FOUR

Dr. Sweeton pushed through the people entering the church, his head swiveling as he sought out Franco Girone. He didn't see him in the crowd, but the people present all looked happy to be here, the space filled with the sounds of chatter and laughter. He noticed a woman he'd met at the clinic many months before who he'd asked to come in for testing. She had, and he'd thought she was a good candidate for the project. *Trinity.* Her name was Trinity, and her father had been a preacher who'd molested her for most of her young life. His mind reeled, and for the portion of a second, he wondered if it was difficult for her that this event was being held in a church. She caught his eye, surprise flashing in her expression before he looked away.

God, his mind was everywhere, panic taking over. He wiped the sweat off his forehead. His heart was still beating far too fast, the shock and grief of seeing the photo of Nancy along with what he'd discovered about Franco causing his body to flood with stress hormones.

"Sir, can I take your coat?"

"What? Oh. Yes, thank you." He shrugged off his jacket. The young woman standing in front of a rack of coats took it from him, and he turned away. A DJ was setting up off to the side, and a small stage had been erected at the head of the dozen or so tables, all set for dinner. There were placards in the middle obviously designating which groups were sitting where. One read THE GILBERT HOUSE; another one said OCEANCREST SOBER LIVING. Each place setting had a colorful ribbon tied around the silverware and a plastic-wrapped mint placed just beneath. And in front of each plate was a printed quote. The doctor was too distracted to focus on the one nearest him, but assumed it was something inspirational. "Keep Going!" or "You got this!" It made him want to laugh, and cry. Ridiculous platitudes to people with severe mental illnesses, like the ones suffering lifelong trauma and addiction. And this was what he was going to leave these people with when he went to prison. Another drop of sweat slid down the doctor's cheek, and he worked to calm his breathing.

What was done was done. He had to accept that now and try to stop it from going any further, if he possibly could.

And then he looked up and saw him. Franco Girone, standing on the balcony where a choir had likely once sung odes to a savior. Franco was surveying the space, a small satisfied smile on his lips, as though he were looking out over his kingdom and pleased with the results.

Dr. Sweeton wove through the people in front of him, knocking into someone but not stopping to apologize. He raced to the back of the church and up the narrow set of steps to the higher level. "Franco," he said from the doorway, his chest rising and falling with his quickened breaths, more sweat dripping from his brow.

Franco swiveled toward him, an expression of surprise making him look suddenly younger, the boy Dr. Sweeton had once known, the one who'd discovered his mother's battered corpse.

"The good doctor arrives," Franco said. "Well, this is a plot twist. I certainly didn't expect you to be here."

Dr. Sweeton felt something deflate inside, what he'd feared most confirmed, even if he didn't yet know the details. "It is you," he said.

"What tipped you off?"

His shoulders dropped. Ambrose had come up with Franco Girone as a suspect, and Dr. Sweeton didn't yet know how. All the doctor had were his memories of the boy and the photo that he'd found in his drawer—the photo that made him suspect the horrible possibility that it was the person he'd loved the most in the world who had betrayed him. "Nancy. I have a photo of you and Nancy from a Rays of Hope event," he said.

The two of them had been standing together, heads bent toward one another as they spoke. It'd been obvious they knew each other. That event had taken place right before she died. He could tell because he recognized the pink-and-white-striped sweater she was wearing in the photo. It was the same one she'd worn to the treatment he'd administered that ended her life.

He clenched his eyes shut. He felt like he was in a nightmare and couldn't wake up. He forced himself to look at Franco.

The man smiled. "Ah, Nancy. Strung-out Nancy. She really was a mess, wasn't she?" He smiled again. "Franco," he said, raising his voice an octave as if impersonating her, "You're going to school to be a chemist, right? I'll sell you a drug formula, and you can make it and get rich." Franco laughed. "All those drugs of yours, seemingly right within her reach. She tried and failed to get a hold of your product, but she did manage to lift the recipe and then tried to sell it for some cash. When I didn't bite, she tossed it at me anyway, off to concoct another scheme to buy herself a hit. Crackheads gonna crackhead, you know?"

Oh God, Nancy. This was too much. In the end, it was his daughter, the one who'd been his inspiration for the project, who'd sold him out. "Why did you do it?" He had to know. His work. His life's work had been corrupted, and what Franco had used it for would be Dr. Sweeton's legacy too. And Nancy's, especially since she'd been the one who facilitated this by giving Franco the drug formula. That knowledge was a blade straight to his heart. He was still standing, but he was already dead.

"This? You mean tweaking your brilliant drug concoction to better meet my needs? Because the results have given me joy. Why else?"

But how? How had he managed to get to so many people needing—

The air released from his lungs in a gust. Franco had offered them false hope and healing. And it was all a cruel lie. "You said you could help them," he guessed. "You promised you'd put an end to their torment and then lured them to their personal hell."

Franco smiled, lips tilting, eyes dead. "They tell stories about your magical treatment in the TL," Franco said. "They've all talked about it or heard someone who knows someone who knows someone. It's a fairy tale. A half-baked theory. They speculate on those who've gone through your tests and been deemed a poor candidate and turned away. Turned away from what? A miracle that they weren't quite qualified to receive. No one listens, of course. And more often than not, in the midst of their constant inebriation, all that talk is forgotten or dismissed. Addicts are good for one thing, anyway. Keeping secrets."

Sweeton's heart was pounding in his ears, his vision growing foggy. "You told them you worked for me?"

"No. I told them I was a competitor who offered the same services. Only *I* didn't turn anyone down. *I* didn't require scans and questionnaires. I told them where to show up, and they marched straight to their death."

The doctor clenched his eyes shut, reeling with despair. It was horrendous, what Franco had done to people so desperate they'd believe most anything. The exact opposite of what he'd spent his career working to do. Suddenly his whole life seemed foggy, motivations questionable, when he'd always been so *sure*. "Why did you bother using the 'BB' imprint?" he managed to ask. *Bluebird.* He'd imprinted his own pills that way as a reminder that every treatment session was in honor of his Nancy.

"Because I wanted you to see me," he said. "I wanted you to know what you'd done. And I wanted you to watch me flush your work straight down the sewer, where all your *patients* dwell."

"Why now, though, if you've had the formula for so many years?" Nancy had been dead for two decades now.

Franco eyed him. "It's not the easiest of tasks, saving the money to set up a lab worthy of the scope of my project. You should know that, Doc. And then there's the gathering of the ingredients. Psilocybin from Ecuador? Really? That wasn't specified. It took me many iterations to get that right. Do you even know how many species of mushrooms I had to gather and test? But if you're asking what really sent me down this path? I saw one of *them* eight years ago. One of the parasites who killed my mother. She obviously hadn't served her full sentence. She was passed out in a doorway. I gave her an injection and watched her die. And it wasn't satisfying. I could've done more. Why didn't I? And then later, I remembered what Nancy had given me. All those years, I'd kept it. I'd stuffed it in a book to use as a bookmark, and it was still there, sitting on my shelf. My mind went everywhere. I started thinking bigger. Much bigger."

Behind Franco, Sweeton saw Ambrose and Lennon come in the front door, clearly breathless, heads pivoting in all directions. Franco began to turn, and the doctor said quickly, "I understand the desire for revenge. I do." Franco halted and faced him again. "I don't know if you know what happened to Nancy . . . why she . . . became what she did. But she was savagely victimized. I brought her to the clinic where I did volunteer work when she was only a little girl. She went down the street to get a slice of pizza, and members of a street gang pulled her into an alley. She spent four days tied to a dirty mattress on the floor of a garage, being raped." He pulled in a breath. *Nancy.* Even after all these years, and even with the knowledge of her betrayal, the thought of that garage where her soul had been stolen still caused an internal scream of anguish. He was supposed to protect her, and he'd failed. "But what you did, Franco, it didn't vindicate your mother. It will never bring her back." He didn't dare set his gaze behind Franco again, lest Franco follow it and see help on the way. But the doctor saw Ambrose and Lennon moving forward through the tables.

They know. They're looking for Franco.

Franco tilted his head. There was no compassion at all in his expression, merely derision. "Do you think I have any illusions that this will bring my mother back? I don't. It will, however, make it far less likely that another innocent victim will suffer what my mother did. In any case, this is for *me*, Doctor. It's been great fun. And despite that you're talking in past tense, the fun is only just now beginning."

Just now. What did that mean? Had he been right to bring his bag with him? But if so, how would Franco get all these people to ingest a tablet or pill while they were at a charity event?

Franco put a finger to his lips. "You chose not to help me. You tested and probed me and then turned me away. And I *deserved* to be helped. They do not, you bastard. Maybe this is on your shoulders."

Maybe it was. Maybe so much was. Franco did look behind him then, his gaze obviously falling on Lennon and Ambrose, speaking with a woman near the DJ booth. A man at the table nearby popped something in his mouth before turning to a woman next to him, saying something and shaking her hand.

The mints.

The doctor's stomach cramped, and blood rushed to his head. "The mints," he breathed. *Oh God, the mints.*

Franco turned back toward him, his smile growing.

"Clean clothes," Franco said. "New deodorant. It's been drummed into them. Good hygiene is important. Present yourself well tonight. Our funding depends on it." Franco laughed as the doctor stared in horror. "Like they're toddlers. They'll eat the mints, Doctor. Or at least most of them will. While I've been up here talking with you, enough already have. You don't want to upset them now, do you? The slightest provocation to their nervous system—rushing blood, rapid heart rate—and it will act that much quicker. Specific triggers aren't necessary. Most anything will do. Eventually, they'll attack and trigger each other."

The doctor lurched forward, moaning as he grabbed the rail, overlooking what would almost certainly be a savage melee in mere minutes. He couldn't shout. It would only make the toxin take effect that much sooner if he panicked the crowd. He sucked in a breath as he felt Franco's body heat as the man drew close, and then something sharp sliced into his lower back. "I can't let you report me, Doc," Franco said close to his ear. "But I do want you to last long enough to watch." The doctor sucked in a staggered breath as Franco pulled the blade out of his skin, the agonizing pain where he'd been stabbed making the room below him spin. He felt the warmth of his blood saturating the back of his shirt. Behind him, he heard a door close softly and latch. He was locked on the balcony, losing blood quickly. He couldn't yell for help, and in moments, he would be forced to watch a violent mass murder. If the police had been alerted, they'd ensure it was that much bloodier if they came in guns blazing. There was little hope of stopping this. Franco was right: it was just beginning. The doctor leaned over the ledge and waved his arm, trying desperately to get Ambrose's attention.

CHAPTER
FORTY-FIVE

Ambrose spotted the doctor from above just as Lennon approached the DJ to ask if she could use his microphone to address the crowd. The doctor's face was bright red, and even from a distance, Ambrose could see he was sweating profusely. As he met Ambrose's eye, he mouthed "No" and pointed to Lennon.

Ambrose didn't understand what was happening, but he reached for Lennon's hand anyway, pulling her back and directing her gaze to the doctor. Their attention was diverted momentarily by the sight of a man appearing on a higher platform to their right and peering from the edge. Franco Girone. He stood gazing down, as though waiting for a show to begin.

"What the hell is going on?" Lennon asked. The doctor was gesturing now to his pocket and then pointing at the coatrack.

"There's something in his jacket pocket?" Ambrose murmured.

The DJ raised his microphone and smiled over at a woman standing next to him who appeared to be about to say some welcoming words. The microphone let out a high screech, and several people at the table next to her shrieked in response, covering their heads as if under attack. Eyes widened, and a low murmur took up. A woman next to one of the cowering people put her hand on the other's back in comfort. The hunched woman lifted her head and punched her would-be comforter in the face. Several gasps of shock sounded around the room.

"What's going on?" Lennon asked, her head moving left and right.

"I don't know," he said. "Something's wrong with them."

Another man let out a bellow, wrapping his arms around his waist, his face scrunching as if in pain. Were they sick? "Oh my God, Ambrose. Do you think Girone has spiked their drinks? Or put a pill in their food or something? Would that be possible?" Lennon asked.

"Maybe." Ambrose's gaze hit on another woman, who was whimpering and rocking to and fro. They looked both pained and . . . drugged. And not just one or two, but many. How, though? And so suddenly? But then he noticed several uneaten mints sitting at place settings in front of people at a table that identified them as Rays of Hope staff. *The mints.*

He whipped his head to look at another table, this one with a placard for Oceancrest Sober Living. His heart sank when he saw only empty wrappers. The mints were laced with the mix of hallucinogens; he was certain of it.

His gaze flew back to the doctor, who had his finger to his lips. "I think he's put his drug in the mints. We have to keep them calm," he whispered. His heart was racing, and a cold sweat broke out over his back. "Go," he said to Lennon. "Turn the microphone off."

Lennon darted forward, and Ambrose turned, heading to the coatrack and beginning to tear through the coats. Moans had started up, and voices rose in volume, attempting to calm the confusingly distressed people and asking questions. *Shut up, shut up, shut up,* he chanted in his head as he ripped a jacket he thought he'd seen the doctor wearing off the rack. He searched the pockets, but they were empty. He threw it aside and continued the hunt.

CHAPTER FORTY-SIX

Trinity's feet were encased in mist, fog swirling in slow circles as she tried desperately to figure out where she was. She took one hesitant step forward, then another, and then a crack sounded behind her, the outside world where she'd just been falling away into nothing. She screamed, leaping forward and landing on her belly on the floor of her father's church. She knew it—oh God, she knew it. The smell. The feel. *No. Oh no. How?*

She gasped, her head whipping back and forth, her fingers gripping the tile floor beneath her as her body slid forward. She was flipped sideways, and then back on her belly, a scream caught in her throat, and she was pulled, her shirt riding up as the cold travertine met her ribs.

You're a whore, aren't you? Little whore who likes that.

Some unknown force was pulling her like a magnet. She took one hand off the floor and used it to grip a leg of one of the pews and sit up, her hair flipping in the direction of that unknown force as she turned to see what it was.

A gaping hole. Black and somehow undulating. It swirled and pulsed, and Trinity turned her head away, tears streaking down her cheeks. It was horror. It was grief and pain and shame and loneliness and all the things her father had made her feel. It had a name, and she heard it whispered, and she didn't know the language. But she knew what it meant: *unloved.*

Trinity leaned over and vomited on the floor, the puddle of sickness moving and swarming and hatching and then becoming insects that burst into her face and screamed, "*Whore!*" She twisted away, the magnetic horror whipping her onto her stomach and dragging her again. The thing that was the opposite of all goodness had come to life and was trying to suck her inside it.

Shh, shh, shh. The soft sound somehow rose above the others. Soothing. A lifeline in the mist. It gave her the strength to resist that incessant pull, to turn her eyes away from the black hole from which she could hear shrieks emanating. She grunted with effort, her body being dragged . . . dragged ever forward. Those shrieks, they curdled her blood and made the slow tears turn to breathless sobs.

Her father appeared suddenly, standing at the front of that sunless chasm leading to the lowest depths of despair. His hand was raised to the heavens, and he was ranting, speaking of judgment he proclaimed came from the Lord, his voice drowned out by the sucking, swirling void. The screams and shrieks emanating from the blackness became louder, a merciless howl that beckoned Trinity ever closer. And though she tried, she was helpless to resist.

CHAPTER
FORTY-SEVEN

Lennon grabbed the microphone from the DJ just as he was raising it to his mouth. Less than thirty seconds had elapsed since the woman had punched her tablemate and Ambrose had realized the mints were laced. "Hey!" the DJ said, causing another chorus of pained yells to sound behind him. Lennon shook her head dramatically, her eyes widening as she put her finger to her lips. She turned to all the startled people looking around in alarm, some beginning to stand, and Lennon put her arms out at her sides, pushing her palms down in a plea to keep quiet, keep calm.

Ambrose approached slowly, opening his hand to show three nasal inhalers. "Doc was working on an antidote," he whispered so softly she could barely hear. "But his last batch was weak. It won't work once they've descended too far." He looked around. The moans were rising, and it was obvious those who'd initially thought a food poisoning situation or something similar was unfolding had realized it was far more worrisome and were backing their chairs away from the tables, creating distance between themselves and the moaning, squirming people around them. "Panic makes the toxins absorb faster," he said, talking rapidly. "Keep them calm. I'd estimate we have less than ten minutes."

Her limbs began shaking. She remembered the woman from the psychiatric ward, the one who'd "survived" the crime scene, and knew that once the drug had fully taken hold, the people around her would become savages who had to be kept in permanent comas. But before that . . . before that . . . ready-made weapons. *Knives. Forks. Glass. Chairs.* So many potential weapons. And Franco had ensured they'd use anything and everything they could, even if that only meant their hands and teeth. "The police are on the way," she said, the words soft and breathy, filled with panic. "I have to warn them not to bust in here." These people would attack—viciously—and the cops would have to open fire, which would result in more panic and so much death.

"Go," he said, pointing to the front of the church, where there was a quiet corner. Then he turned to a woman attempting to soothe one of the sobbing, howling men, speaking to her and handing her one of the inhalers. *Myrna Watts.* Lennon recognized her as Myrna Watts from the Gilbert House.

Lennon ran as silently as possible to the corner of the church and dialed the lieutenant. "Call off the officers dispatched here. Immediately," she said. "Or you'll kill them all. We have to keep these people calm, to distribute an antidote to those we can save. Trust me, please." Then she hung up before the lieutenant could even respond, praying that he would do as she asked and trust her without explanation.

She met Ambrose where he was, cradling the head of a woman who was staring, her head bent back as tears slid down her face. He brought the inhaler to her nose and sprayed it, her features evening out as she sank back into her chair.

"Give me one," Lennon said, and after he did, she moved to another table. The sobbing moans and punctuated shrieks were getting louder. In a few minutes, it wouldn't matter if they all kept calm or not. The ones who hadn't been already would be quickly hurled into the pit of their own mind.

Lennon sprayed the nasal spray into an old man's nose and then moved on to another. She, Ambrose, and Myrna split up and began traveling around the tables. It was clear now who was under the influence. "Keep them calm," she whispered to the others, their expressions full of wide-eyed panic. "No sudden movements. Help them. Please don't flee. It will start a stampede."

But when a man let out a loud bellow, coming to his feet and snatching a fork, whirling around and stabbing at the air, the people around him rose from their chairs, gasping with terror and grabbing for weapons to defend themselves.

The sounds of panic caused others to rise from their seats, twisting and punching and kicking as they fought invisible monsters that were deep inside their minds.

Lennon was driven back, ducking away from a man who swiped at her with a broken piece of glass from a bottle he'd smashed on the table. He lunged after her, and she tripped but righted herself quickly, her heart beating so harshly she could barely breathe.

They had so little time, and the sounds were increasing in volume, those who'd already descended growing in number—four, five, now six. Off to her side, a wide-eyed older man had his hands clamped over the ears of the young man next to him, who was shaking with sobs, his eyes clasped shut, trapped in his trauma. But not too far gone, not yet.

Suddenly, from above her came one monstrous, resounding howl, and she looked up to see Franco on a smaller balcony, head tipped back as he let out a demonic shriek. He'd seen that the people who had taken his poison were being helped, and he was attempting to offset that help. Lennon's adrenaline surged, fear and panic making her lightheaded.

What do I do? What do I do?

Classical music very literally lowers blood pressure and reduces anxiety. You should remember that, Picasso.

The words streamed through her mind as though Tanner had leaned in and repeated them, and she let out a gasp of breath as she brought the inhaler to the young man's nose and released a spray. He whimpered, his head going to the table, eyes opening as he blinked around. She handed the inhaler to the older man who'd been helping him hold on. "Help them," she said. "One squirt in a nostril. Quickly."

"I will." He stood immediately and moved toward the table next to him.

The fighting near the front grew louder, and Lennon jerked her head so the petrified DJ would step aside. She turned the volume all the way down. "A slow drumbeat," she whispered to the DJ, eyes beseeching. *Hurry. Hurry.* He wasted no time, pressing a button that began the slow percussion, and then Lennon put her fingers on the keyboard and began to play one of Chopin's nocturnes. For a brief moment, she was almost shocked that the piece came back so easily, and especially under the circumstances. But it did, moving through her fingers as though the notes had been waiting there all along, trapped, but now joyful to finally be set free.

Franco howled and pounded and shrieked from above while Lennon's fingers moved over the keys from below, the slow drumbeat keeping time.

The fighting continued, a woman launching herself halfway across the table as those who'd run began streaming out through a side door. What did they have? Three minutes? Maybe less, before so many of these souls were trapped in an eternal nightmare.

Tears streamed down Lennon's face. She knew the people in front of her, twisting and writhing and sobbing, were fighting unthinkable battles. Alone.

But the physical fight was spreading, and soon even those who'd remained still and calm, protecting the people silently suffering, would have no choice but to abandon them to save themselves. And then they would plunge to their own internal death, too, and it would all spread like wildfire until the police had no choice but to come in and kill them all.

There were still several tables of victims clawing at the tabletop, barely holding on, as Ambrose, Myrna, and the older man Lennon had given the inhaler to made their way over. A fight had broken out in front of them, however, and a man who'd submitted to the drug was swinging a broken chair leg around, his grunts of pain causing two women who'd been on the floor to rise and join the melee.

Oh God. Ambrose. Hurry. Hurry.

They had to save as many as possible. But not at the expense of more innocent lives. Once the antidote was out, she'd be forced to shoot the ones who were intent on fighting to the death. They were victims, too, though, and it was going to kill her to have to do it.

From the corner of her eye, she saw the doctor appear at the bottom of the stairs. He'd dropped down from the choir balcony, leaving his vaulted place of protection and deciding instead to enter the fray.

CHAPTER
FORTY-EIGHT

Pounding down the door that led from the choir balcony to the stairs wasn't an option—he wouldn't risk even one tender psyche with the loud sound of splintering wood—and so in the end, Dr. Sweeton had jumped to the floor below. His leg was likely broken; useless, anyway. And he was bleeding out. The room tilted, but he managed to pull himself upright. Ambrose and the other two people were hurrying among the tables, administering the antidote. There was no more time left, though, and the man had turned, holding up the tiny bottle to Ambrose, gesturing that his was empty.

There were only two more tables to go, and the people there appeared to be on the brink of total mental collapse as Ambrose and the woman rushed toward them, in the direction where the doctor now stood. Next to each of them was a brave, kind soul who was taking a great personal risk to calm and soothe. *Hold on. Hold on.* Tears gathered in his eyes, and he felt a sob building inside. Humans could be terrible, and beautiful too. It was the only certainty he had left.

Two more tables, and Ambrose and the others would have reached all those who could be helped.

Maniacal laughter echoed from above, but Lennon's music floated in the air. He saw a few expressions smoothing, shoulders lowering. They were caught in that beautiful song, their minds so suggestive. She was offsetting the horror, and he didn't know how she'd known to do that, but she had. The music, the beautiful music, had interrupted their nightmare. *Good thinking, Lennon.* She played effortlessly, not a single harsh note. Not one forgotten melody. And that unceasing drumbeat, the one that mimicked a heartbeat, the first thing that grounded and comforted all humans, even before sight or touch. Lennon seemed to know exactly when to pick up the tempo of her accompanying music and when to slow it down, responding to the hellish sounds Franco was bent on making from above. He was banking on a violent free-for-all, the only thing that would allow him to escape now.

A man wielding a chair leg swung it at Ambrose, and he ducked as others rushed forward, seeking the threat, fighting the monsters in their minds.

Ambrose and the others weren't going to make it here, and the antidote must be mostly gone. These people were already on borrowed time, the music likely the only thing keeping them from sliding into their personal torment.

He knew Lennon could only play so long. She'd have to begin shooting them, if it came to that. And if they didn't die . . . they'd live submersed in that torment forever. Or if the police came in, as they must be about to do, they'd capture and restrain them, and unknowingly sentence them to eternal hell.

He couldn't allow that.

Another man joined in the fight, and then a woman. It was spreading, growing, and now Ambrose and the woman helping him distribute the antidote would have to retreat from the fray and be forced to abandon the victims still hanging on. Only moments ago, maybe half an hour, these people had considered themselves colleagues, if not friends. Certainly not enemies. *And now? They are intent on destroying each other.* It was nearly over, but there were still lives to be saved. And he could still do something to help with that.

With the last of his effort, he picked up a chair and raised it over his head, threatening those closest to him with it, hating every moment of contributing to their agony. Their fear. Their terror. And as expected, several of the people swiveled toward him, rushing, lunging at him as he toppled backward. His heart broke. Shattered. But he used his quickly dwindling strength to punch and kick and engage. Fists connected, and something sharp pierced his neck, blood spurting as that man then turned on another. He lay back and allowed them to brutalize him. It was too late to save their minds, but he could save their souls.

He could ensure they'd die fighting. Like warriors.

CHAPTER FORTY-NINE

Trinity watched as her father screamed and ranted, his face purple with rage, arms raised, that pit at his feet swirling faster, oily bubbles rising, the face of the little girl she'd once been reflected in the ebony emptiness. The screams and wails and dead laughter that rose were hers. She was already in there—parts of her, at least—and so was every horror she'd forgotten. The terrible aching loneliness. The fear. *Why, God? Why did you send me to him?*

Shh, shh, shh.

She clutched the leg of the final pew, pulling herself to a sitting position again, the wooden leg bending and moaning and beginning to snap. *Thud, thud, thud, thud.*

A misty glow appeared in front of her, the light shimmering and taking shape. An angel. And she was . . . singing. The music made her turn away from her bellowing father, away from that magnetic hellhole, transfixed by the notes that drifted from the angel's mouth and bobbed in the air, their round bottoms moving slowly past. The wooden pew leg snapped, and she gasped, propelling herself upward as she grasped one of those notes and held on for dear life.

You nasty little slut. You deserve this.

The pull intensified, a vacuum lifting her from the floor and spinning her around, her legs hanging over the pit. But still she held on to that note, bobbing gently above her, the feel of it warm and soft, yet weighty too. The sour wind whipped, and the screeches rose, but the angel song continued on. The celestial being remained next to her, her gaze steady, orangey-red hair a bright contrast to the pulsating darkness all around. *So beautiful.* How could such beauty exist at a time such as this? The black, hellish ugliness thrashed and moaned. It hated the beauty.

Shh, shh, shh.

Her fingers were slipping; sobs ripped from her throat as she used every vestige of strength she'd been told she didn't have to grasp the beauty tightly and turn from the pain. The angel's hand came over hers, helping her to hold on. *Hold on.*

Thud, thud, thud, thud.

A puff of vapor hit Trinity's nose, and she inhaled, drawing in a massive pull of air as her father fell into the chasm and it closed around him, sucking itself up into nothing.

The angel smiled, and the last note dissolved under Trinity's fingers. She dropped to the floor, the air knocked from her lungs.

She opened her eyes, and they darted around in fearful confusion as she gripped empty space. A handsome man with down-turned eyes was peering at her with deep concern, and he caught her hand and squeezed it. "You're okay," he said. "You're okay."

Next to her, the music ended, the final note lost to the swarm of police rushing through the door.

CHAPTER FIFTY

Ambrose pushed through the crowd outside, head swiveling as he scanned the people around him, his breath releasing in a rush of relief when his gaze fell on the singular face he'd been desperately seeking. Lennon spotted him a heartbeat later, her face mirroring the emotion he knew must be on his own. "Ambrose." He saw her mouth move as she said his name but couldn't hear it over the cacophony of sirens and shouted commands. The police had control of the situation, and he'd watched as Franco Girone was captured and handcuffed and dragged from the building, still yelling incoherently. But the injured—and the dead—were just now being wheeled out, and he'd lost Lennon in the chaos.

"Excuse me," he said, pushing past someone, the myriad red strobes from the dozens of police cruisers blocking the street giving the evening an otherworldly, pulsing glow. For a moment he could believe that he had awoken in the middle of a treatment session and none of what he'd witnessed had really happened. None of his surroundings were real.

But then he reached her, pulling her body against his own, and she was warm and solid. And she gripped him back, repeating his name again and again, saying it like a prayer.

"You did good, Lennon. You saved so many of those people." He knew there were ones who had not been saved, and they'd grieve those poor souls later. But now, he needed to let her know how proud of her he was. How in awe.

"You did, too, Ambrose. We did everything we could. I think it was all we could do."

He nodded, running his hands over her hair, bringing his lips to her temple.

"I have to find my lieutenant," she said after a moment. "I have to get to work."

"I know," he said. He felt her tremble. "Hey, everything is going to be okay." He didn't know how or when, but he knew it would be, knew they'd both land on their feet, and believed that something good— somehow, someway—would result from this terrible day, where innocents had lost their lives and he'd watched the doctor he loved and revered sacrifice himself. But right now, he couldn't even begin to articulate the complexities of that, and so he hoped she heard it in his voice and felt it in his embrace.

She looked up at him, her eyes so trusting, and he vowed right then and there that he would do everything in his power—for the rest of his life—to prove himself worthy of that expression.

She pulled him close again as though she needed the contact for another moment more, and he felt her heart beating against his, *thud, thud, thud,* a breath of calm descending even amid the noise and disbelief and heartache. *My anchor. My soft place to land. My peacemaker.*

After a moment, she let go, kissing him quickly on his lips before she turned away and headed toward the bevy of unmarked cars arriving at the scene. Ambrose turned, too, his gaze falling on the quiet city beyond, far away from the bedlam surrounding him, ignorant of the horror that had occurred so close to home. The moon shone against the dark sky, and stars blinked to life, and everything looked so peaceful out there. He remembered how he and Lennon had once talked about all the small pockets of darkness. Those existed; he knew that well. But even now—*especially* now—he would never forget that small pockets of light existed, too, and they were worth searching for.

EPILOGUE

Twenty-seven years later

The sheer curtains fluttered in the breeze from the open window at the end of the hall, the scents of rosemary and basil growing in the garden outside tickling Kaison DeMarce's nose. He glanced back at the piano, the only piece of furniture left in the room. It was scheduled to be moved in the morning. He smiled as he turned toward the window again, swearing he could hear the notes of his mother's favorite concerto echoing in the air.

Kaison turned and began a slow walk through the rooms of the empty Pacific Heights mansion, which had once belonged to Dr. Alexander Sweeton but had been left to Kaison's father and Jermain Finchem, the pioneer of the Project Bluebird aftercare-treatment plan, in the wake of the doctor's death.

Kaison had spent so much of his childhood here, after his parents and the rest of the team had turned the grand house into a respite for those who had recently come through treatment, and he wanted to walk its halls one last time. A sort of closure that made his heart squeeze with nostalgia, and also swell with pride.

He entered the room that he might have called his father's office if his father had ever sat at a desk long enough to designate it as such. The mahogany desk was still there but would also be moved in the morning, along with the few boxes that held the items that his dad had kept in its drawers.

Kaison used his index finger to lift one of the flaps on a cardboard box sitting atop two others. Inside was a file folder that he recognized, and he pulled it out, setting it on the desk and opening it and then leafing through the newspaper articles and printouts inside. In the wake of Franco Girone's arrest, his dad had gathered all the publicly available information and kept it here. Kaison had read all this long ago, but he had the inside scoop as well.

Six months after the horrific crime committed by Franco Girone at the church—the one Kaison had only been told about but swore he could picture—his mother had resigned from the SFPD. Kaison could only imagine how the stress of covering up the scope of Dr. Sweeton's project had weighed heavily, especially since Franco Girone was all too willing to describe where he'd come up with his own evil plot.

All evidence, however, pointed to Franco's statement being the ravings of a madman who'd attended one of Dr. Sweeton's talks and hatched wild ideas based on his own sick fantasies.

Yes, Dr. Sweeton had dabbled in the use of hallucinogens in treatment of his patients suffering from PTSD, and perhaps, had he survived, the medical board would have reviewed his license. But the doctor was gone, and his patients had nothing but praise for him, and so that door had been shut. If Dr. Sweeton had been performing an experimental—not to mention illegal and unethical—treatment on vulnerable victims of abuse for almost two decades, certainly one of them would have come forward to verify such an implausible claim. But no one had, not a single soul.

Kaison flipped one page and then another, his gaze moving over the dated articles, musing about how much of this story was missing. But he'd lived it. He knew.

His mother had begun managing an in-house art program within these very walls while she was pregnant with him. And in what his father described as a beautiful twist, when Lennon had told his grandparents and his uncle Peter about Project Bluebird, they'd clamored to be involved.

The fact that they'd had the courage to move forward with Project Bluebird, even after the vicious way Franco Girone had used for evil what Dr. Sweeton had meant for good, was a testament to the team's belief in the work. And they'd been right. So many thousands of lives saved since then, so many cycles broken.

He'd heard Franco Girone had died in prison a few years before. Kaison didn't exactly feel glad about it, but . . . when he envisioned the way Girone had attempted to summon evil but failed to inspire the mass violence and pandemonium he'd counted on, a chill still engulfed him. And so no, he didn't feel glad, but he didn't feel sympathy for the man either. Because of him, eighteen innocent people had died. Dr. Sweeton had ensured twelve of them died fighting, and the other six had been shot by police when they'd gone to attack.

The other thirty-two people who had eaten the mints had been saved by three miniature bottles of antidote and the three people administering it, with dozens more souls remaining beside those who were suffering, even though it would have been far easier and less terrifying to run. And by the beautiful music that had found them in their nightmare and helped them hold on.

Kaison was well acquainted with every aspect of the crime, both the lead-up and the aftermath. It was imperative that they all understood what had happened, and how to ensure it never did again.

After Dr. Sweeton's death, when the team had restarted the project with Dr. Clayton Contiss at the helm, they'd had to be supremely careful. No one knew better than they did that the project was vulnerable and that the smallest mistake or impropriety could risk not only the treatment they performed but real human lives. Kaison's uncle, Peter, had been instrumental in helping them set up a protected system where they could store necessary data, analyze gaps in security, both technical and otherwise, and create an incident plan in which they could act immediately to an outside—or inside—threat. It was a simple reality that they took the strictest precautions possible while their operation was still outside the bounds of the law. If any positive at all had come from what Girone had achieved, it was that they'd identified the areas susceptible to a breach.

But it'd also helped them realize that, despite the very serious risks, they were all still committed.

Kaison shut the folder and stuffed it back in the box. All that was ancient history.

So much had changed since then. Laws had been passed. Breakthroughs had been made. Their protocol had been updated with the times. They were now able to operate within the bounds of the law.

Mostly.

$\sim$

He left the office, smiling as he caught a glimpse of the back drive, flanked on both sides by privacy hedges. Originally, the team had brought people in covertly through the hidden drive so as not to alert neighbors. And though the location required using extra vigilance, the beautiful, serene mansion on the hill was too perfect not to use to help people who had once been victims begin to heal.

When he reached the back of the house, he opened the french doors to the backyard, where the garden still flourished. He pictured his grandma puttering through the rows, teaching horticulture and herbal remedies to once-traumatized people. He had a specific memory from when he was about sixteen of her kneeling next to a young woman who'd been walking the streets only weeks before, the teenager—not much older than him at the time—up to her elbows in the dirt, with this look of stark childlike wonder on her face.

God, they'd changed so many lives for the better.

Kaison pulled the doors closed and turned toward the kitchen, walking through the massive room where he and his sister had nabbed chocolate chip cookies fresh from the oven when they could barely reach the counter and, later, where they'd helped prepare meals for those who had just arrived from treatment.

There was joy in these rooms.

Purpose.

Healing.

Love. Not only for the work they did but for the individuals they served. The ones who then went on to serve others. A network of healed people that multiplied and expanded in ways they couldn't even begin to measure. The thousands of individuals who had been released from the tethers of their trauma now worked in positions all over the city and the world. Initially, those who had completed the treatment helped ensure the project continued and operated successfully under the radar. Then they'd worked to lobby for changes in laws. And now they helped advocate for the treatment by raising awareness and training others. Since Dr. Sweeton's death, whole areas of study had been added to universities and medical schools. There were opportunities for grants and other fundraising programs. Studies were being published in medical journals, and clinics were now using the same methods Dr. Sweeton had employed.

Kaison had graduated from just such a medical school that afternoon. He still had many years of study in front of him . . . a residency, his licensing exam . . . but he was so proud and excited to be one step closer to being an integral part of a trauma-treatment team that was based on the work of what had once been known as Project Bluebird.

He heard the front door open down the hall and footsteps heading toward where he now stood, at the large kitchen window. He turned and smiled when his father entered the room.

"I thought I'd find you here."

Kaison wasn't surprised to see his dad. His parents had a knack for knowing what he and his sister were going to do before they'd even decided themselves. It made him feel known—loved—but it'd also made it frustratingly difficult to get away with anything when he was younger. "I wanted to say goodbye to these rooms."

His father smiled, coming to stand next to him. "Me too. I'm going to miss this place. But . . . the new location is pretty darn sweet."

"Yes, it is." They'd recently secured a facility forty minutes outside the city that was on an acre of land. This home had served its purpose beautifully, but it was time to expand. The new property would have walking paths and benches and plenty of space to park the vehicles used to transport newly recovered patients to the beach, or the woods, or any of the places Jermain Finchem had believed were healing to the soul. Jermain, sadly, had passed away ten years before, but his son still worked with the aftercare team and created a safe place for youth in the TL. The new facility would have a whole wing devoted to the arts and a garden three times the size of the one here at the house. It was going to be wonderful, but Kaison knew a part of his heart would remain here, where he'd first witnessed so many miracles.

"Your mom told me she was pregnant with you right here at this window," his dad said.

Kaison smiled. "And you freaked." His dad had told him that he'd intended to stop the DeMarce genes from continuing on. The story didn't bother him, not only because his dad had clearly been unsuccessful in his mission but because he'd felt his father's unconditional love all his life. Not a day had gone by where he didn't feel wanted. He had not a doubt in his mind that his father cherished him and his sister beyond words.

"Freaked." His dad chuckled. "In a word, yes. It knocked me sideways." He paused, a small smile on his face as though the memory was a sweet one now. "I ran out of here and got in my car and—probably unadvisedly—started driving."

Kaison looked over at him. "I didn't know that part. You left Mom just . . . standing here?"

He clenched one eye closed in a mock grimace. "I did."

"Where'd you go?"

"I ended up in Muir Woods."

"Ah." Of course he had. His father loved that area. So did he. He'd gone there a few times over the years as well, when he needed the solace of those sentient trees, their unseen energy infusing his cells with a certain harmony that he had no clear way to define but knew was as real as the rough bark on their massive trunks he could see with his eyes and touch with his fingers. Maybe it was in the genes. Or maybe it was that his parents had taught him where to look for magic.

His dad set his hand on his shoulder. "I stood there, staring up at those trees, and then I just started to laugh."

Kaison raised a brow. "So you lost it?"

"I laughed with *awe*." He shook his head even as his smile grew. "I'd vowed I'd never be a father. I'd promised not to allow the DeMarce name to continue, or to let my grandfather's blood flow through a new generation. I'd vowed and promised and planned."

"And yet . . . here I am," Kaison said.

His dad grinned, squeezed his shoulder, and then dropped his hand. "Yes, here you are. You and your sister. Both a reminder that something greater than me is at work. A reminder that it's okay to surrender. That's what I felt that day, standing there in the mist with the knowledge that all my fearful plans had crumbled and you were on your way, despite me."

He took in his dad's profile. God, he was so lucky to have parents like the ones he had. He loved them, but even more, he admired the hell out of them. He wanted to live his life as they had—risking and fighting for others who had no way to fight for themselves. What else was life about, if not that?

"And I thought, why *can't* I father someone? Why can't I teach a small person how to trust the world—not later, after damage had been done, but right from the get-go? And it was like a miracle had descended over me. Here I was, unworthy me, being tasked with presenting the beauty of the world to a brand-new soul. To teach my own child what it felt like to be loved and protected and valued so that he or she could spread that love far and wide. And all I could say was 'Thank you.'"

Kaison felt a lump forming in his throat, and so he cleared it. "Thanks, Dad. Did, uh, Mom forgive you for running out on her?"

His dad grinned again. "She was calmly folding laundry when I came home. She just looked up and smiled as though she'd known exactly how I would return and expected me just as I was—breathless and hopeful."

"Sounds like Mom." His beautiful, gentle mother, who played the piano like an angel sent to earth to mend hearts with her music. A look came over his father's face, the same one Kaison had seen all his life whenever his mom was mentioned—love and awe and just a small amount of surprise, as if, even after all these years, she was still unexpected.

"Speaking of your mom, we should go. Reservations are at six."

His graduation dinner. His whole family would be there. His parents and grandparents and his uncle, his sister and her boyfriend, who they were all looking forward to giving as hard a time as possible. If the guy could handle it, and was deemed good enough for his sister, he'd be welcomed with open arms.

"Let's go," Kaison said. A new chapter with a new facility, and a new phase of his education. As they approached the front door, his father turned back and stood there for a moment, eyes closed, as though he needed this short pause the same way he'd needed to gaze at those old trees, to ground himself before stepping into yet another new beginning.

ACKNOWLEDGMENTS

Stories always begin with an idea, and I knew even before I began this book that it was an odd one, and that it might be difficult to weave. I take the credit—and the blame—for the idea and the execution. But it is the people who helped me make it the best it could be who deserve the bulk of the praise, because it arrived to them as a tangled web of loose strings and gaping plot holes. Sorry about that.

Thank you to my tireless agent, Kimberly Brower—literally, I don't think you sleep. How could you and still do the million and one things you do?

I'm so grateful to Marion Archer for being both my safe place and my critic in such perfect percentages.

To Charlotte Herscher, who is smart and articulate and sensitive and insightful. It's such a gift to have an editor who I trust so much. And a world of appreciation for Maria Gomez and the entire Amazon team, who are true professionals and such lovely people.

To you, my reader, thank you for spending your precious time on this journey, and for showing up for all the different sides of me, even the odd ones. I love each and every one of you.

To all the book bloggers, Instagrammers, and BookTokers who are so passionate about books: I am in awe of you and so very thankful for the work you do. Shining light on novels you love and bringing stories to others are not small things. In fact, they're often life changing.

To my husband, you are that singular face I will always search for in every crowd. I love you.

ABOUT THE AUTHOR

Mia Sheridan is a *New York Times*, *USA Today*, and *Wall Street Journal* bestselling author. She has written several romantic suspense novels, including *All the Little Raindrops*, *Bad Mother*, *Where the Blame Lies*, and *Where the Truth Lives*. She lives in Cincinnati, Ohio, with her husband. They have four children here on earth and one in heaven.

 You can find Mia online at https://miasheridan.com or follow her on X (@MSheridanAuthor), Instagram (@MiaSheridanAuthor), and Facebook (www.facebook.com/miasheridanauthor).